THE AUTHOR AND THE SHORT STORY

"The real short-story writer is a jeweler. He stays in his shop, he polishes those jewels, he collects craft, lore, confirms gossip, assays jeweler's rouge, looks to steal the tricks of the arcane. . . .

"Now consider the hearty protagonist who has collected his short fiction for your pleasure, entertainment and approval; here is a big, brawny nineteenth-century version of Renaissance man—a prospector, son. He's not looking for jewels, no, he's digging up buckets of ore, he's panning by all various vigors and methods. The trust is that he is seduced more by method than by gold or gem. . . ."

— **Norman Mailer,** from the Introduction

THE SHORT FICTION
OF
NORMAN MAILER

A DELL BOOK / An Original Volume

Published by

DELL PUBLISHING CO., INC.

750 Third Avenue

New York, N.Y. 10017

Copyright © 1967 by Norman Mailer

Dell ® TM 681510, Dell Publishing Co., Inc.

First Dell Printing—May, 1967

Printed in U.S.A.

CONTENTS

PART SEVEN *Mutants*

PART EIGHT *Clues to Love*

THE SHORT FICTION
OF
NORMAN MAILER

INTRODUCTION

It has been remarked that the short fiction of this author is neither splendid, unforgettable, nor distinguished, and I hasten hereby to join such consensus. A man may go his way, look for his education, grow cultivated, even become superb, yet he need never come in contact with a short story of mine. He will still seem almost perfect. Nay, he will be almost perfect. Of course one would not want to chance this of a man ignorant of *An American Dream, The Deer Park, Barbary Shore,* or *The Naked and The Dead*—no, they should not be avoided. Why, others in fact might go on so far as to insist this highly cultivated fellow was directly hurting his appreciation of American rackets and letters by not catching up on the journalism, politics, essays, and general nonfiction of the author under examination. But, one place, there is agreement. The friends of the author, and his detractors, may argue over his position as novelist, philosopher, essayist, journalist, personality, cathartic, spark, or demiurge, but they hold hands on the short fiction. He's a journeyman there. And he agrees. The author agrees now twice. He does not have the gift to write great short stories, or perhaps even very good ones. In fact, he will confess he does not have the interest, the respect, or the proper awe. The short story bores him a little. He will admit he rarely reads them. He is, in secret, not fond of writers who work at short stories. Nor are they often, he suspects, fond of him. He has a private sneer for the reputations they have amassed. There is a terrible confession to make: he thinks the short story is relatively easy to write. You have only to be good for a day or a week—there is none of that arduous collaboration between character and passion, inspiration and asceticism, which goes into keeping one's balance on the teeter-totter of a novel where work goes on day after day through many a season into the years. Anyone can be good for a week, but who can be good for a year, or two, or three? So, while there may be admiration or affection for a few writers of the short story, for Chekhov, for Hemingway, for Isaac Bashevis Singer, for James T. Farrell—the list is really not that long. One does not really want to include de Maupassant, Steinbeck, or Katherine Anne Porter, or Katherine Mansfield. If Maugham always gave pleasure, and A. Conan Doyle and Edgar Allan Poe, Hawthorne seemed unreadable. While Joyce was admittedly a master in *Dubliners,* no one cared less, Katherine Anne Porter was an avatar of the art but dependably left you flat. Mary McCarthy—yes, that lady wrote very good short stories, and there was Truman Capote, and one story by Paul Bowles, but: Eudora Welty—couldn't read her, Flannery O'Connor—somehow never did read her, John Cheever and John Updike—old Prince and young Prince of good old maggie, *The New Yorker*—why push on with the list? It is evident we are confronting the tastè of a mucker. He obviously doesn't care about the short story. The man is telling the truth. His short stories show it. They have little in common. They do not give us a great many different facets and situations and glimpses of people in a very specific milieu as Isaac Babel's stories about the Red Cossacks did, nor do they have that private vision of the whole you can find in the short fiction of Hemingway, Singer, Farrell, Sholem Aleichem, or Scott Fitzgerald—another favorite, Fitzgerald. When one thinks of the charm which resides in even the worst of his quick commercial stories, it is painful to push one's own plain efforts so far forward. Yet we do it. Yes, for the bucks first, paperback reader! For the good wives and good kids; for the ego—that snake who won't die no matter how we beat it on the head—that ego is a *muscle.* Finally, it is done for a legitimate motive—to keep Renaissance man alive. Yes. You see every one of these stories is different from every other one. They are all excursions and experiments. We might just as well be in at the birth of science— Renaissance man is looking for his experimental method, which he encounters, let us suspect, by dramatic contrast.

Should we explain? Then shift the metaphor this round. The real short story writer is a jeweler. Like most such craftsmen, he does not—unless knighted by genius, as Hemingway or Faulkner—do much else. No, he stays in his shop, he polishes those jewels, he collects craft, lore, confirms gossip, assays jeweler's rouge, looks to steal the tricks of the arcane, and generally disports like a medieval alchemist who's got a little furnace, a small retort, a cave, a handful of fool's gold, and a mad monk's will. With such qualifications, one in a hundred becomes an extraordinary writer, but on the other hand, the worst of this guild makes a life from kissing spiders.

Now consider the hearty protagonist who has collected his short fiction for your pleasure, entertainment and approval; here is a big, brawny nineteenth-century version of Renaissance man—a prospector, son. He's not looking for jewels, no, he's digging up buckets of ore, he's panning by all various vigors and methods. The truth is that he is seduced more by method than by gold or gem. He is, you see, possessed of extraordinary greed. He is a modern man like all nihilists. So he does not wish to pick up a nugget or two and reduce it to its proper wealth, its full sheen; rather he's impatient, ambitious, and obsessed with one idea—move on fast. Keep looking for the biggest mine of them all. He doesn't want to get caught in the refining and polishing. So he sticks in a shovel here, sets off dynamite there, diverts a fast stream, builds up a dam, slap dash, bang and boom, move on fast. Look to learn a little about everything. That is the instinct of the Renaissance— it speaks not only of the energies and techniques of that twentieth century which will eventually issue out of it, but gives a hint as well of the wastes which are also to follow.

Yes, these short stories are imperfect artifacts—various drillings, diggings, tests, and explosions on the way to finding a certain giant mine, well-advertised over the years by the prospector. If some show too little evidence of the craftsman, others are even overpolished. There is in fact a spectrum, nay, a panoply of fictional techniques: we can go all the way over from the total solid conventionality of the three war stories to the experiments in style of *Truth and Being, Nothing and Time;* or *Advertisements for Myself on the Way Out.* We can travel on the scale of literary merit from the precisions of *Ministers of Taste* down to the casual, even slovenly, prose which mars the narrative tension of *The Last Night.* The point to this collection is found in its contrast. It is therefore not without value to the young college writer of the short story, for an exploration

to a given fictional point is often done more than once, but
by opposite means. So, for example, *Truth and Being,
Nothing and Time,* and *The Killer* are both about the slow
deadening of the self, and that is their last resemblance,
for *The Killer* is vastly impersonal—one could not determine the author from the style—while the other could
have been written by no one but the servant of letters here
in the stocks. Yet both stories were done within a month
of each other.

Look further: *A Calculus at Heaven* and *Advertisements
for Myself on the Way Out* are about the deaths of two
men, both murdered—it is just that the deaths are very
different, for one is killed in war, and the other is slain
criminally, although we do not know how. Also—they are
written sixteen years apart.

Continue: *The Greatest Thing in the World* and *Maybe
Next Year* are stories composed in college, so predictably
are about people in trouble because they have no money.
But the styles are searching for their object in opposite
directions.

See here: three war stories, *The Paper House, The
Language of Men,* and *The Dead Gook,* all complete with
sturdy construction of atmosphere are presented alternately
with three humorous stories—one dry, *The Notebook*—one
episodic, *The Patron Saint of Macdougal Alley*—one arch,
Great in the Hay. The first five of these six stories were
written in the same few weeks.

Now consider that *Great in the Hay* is followed by *The
Last Night,* a treatment for a projected movie which bears
no relation to *Great in the Hay.* No relation but the most
umbilical one—guys like Bert are the guys who make
movies like *The Last Night,* that is if you are lucky. From
what I hear, guys like Bert are getting rare. Next, two
extraordinarily short stories, *It* and *The Shortest Novel of
Them All,* are set side by side for instant examination.
(One dare not say more or the comment will be longer than
the stories.) They are followed by two ventures in mixed
genre. Short stories full of resonance, evocation, style,
mood, horror, outrage, etc., which began nonetheless as
something else—*Ministers of Taste* as a letter, then two
letters; *The Locust Cry* as a commentary on *The Early
Masters* by Martin Buber.

Finally, we have *The Time of Her Time* and *The Man*

Who Studied Yoga—two subtle ways are here presented by which love may be made to women. Since, however, no bad taste is so seductive as to write about oneself with iron objectivity—we will not go on to talk of what is very good or even—now it is confessed—superior in *The Time of Her Time* and *The Man Who Studied Yoga*. It is enough to say they are superior to most good short fiction. (But then these last two are also short novels and were written with the idea that they were the beginnings of real, full-length novels, so the dedication was deeper. Which proves a previous point. But, at this stage, resolutely we turn the book over to the reader. May he consider the introduction modest, too modest by far.

—NORMAN MAILER

PART ONE

The Disappearance of the Ego

THE KILLER: A Story

"Now," he said to me, "do you think you're going to bear up under the discipline of parole?"

"Yessir," I said.

He had white hair even though he was not more than fifty-two. His face was red. He had blue eyes. He was red, white, and blue. It was a fact I noticed before. They had this coloring. Maybe that was why they identified with the nation.

"In effect you're swearing that you won't take a drink for eight months."

"I know, sir, but I haven't had a drink inside for four years." Which was a lie. Three times I had come in with my cellmate on part of a bottle. The first time I was sick. The second time we had a fight, a quiet fight which I lost. He banged my head on the floor. Without noise. The third time we had sex. Democratic sex. We did each other.

"You understand that parole is not freedom."

"Yessir."

They asked these questions. They always asked the same questions, and they always got the same answers. It had nothing to do with what you said. It had nothing to do with how you shaved or how you combed your hair because you combed your hair the way everybody else did, and the day you went up to Board you shaved twice. Maybe, it had to do with how many shaving cuts you had, but I didn't have any. I had taken care, wow. Suppose it had to do with the way you moved. If two of the three men on the parole board liked the way you moved, you were all right, provided they didn't like the way you moved too much. Sex. No matter who I'm with, man or woman, always get a feeling off them. At least I used to. I always could tell if they were moving inside or moving away, and I could tell if anything was going on inside. If we ever touched, I could tell better.

17

Once I was in a streetcar and a girl sat down next to me. She was a full barrel. A very fat girl. Pretty face. I don't like fat. Very fat people have no quick. They can always stop. They can stop from doing a lot of things.

This girl and me had a future however. Her hip touched. I could feel what I did to her. From side of my leg, through my pants, and her dress, through some kind of corset, cheap plastic corset, something bad, through that, through her panties, right into her, some current went out of me, and I could feel it in her, opening up future. She didn't do a thing, didn't move. Fixed.

Well, five minutes, before I got off at my stop. In those minutes I was occupied by a project with that girl where we projected five years. I knew what I could do to her. I say without exaggeration I could take her weight down from one hundred eighty to one-eighteen in a year and it would have been a pleasure because all that fat was stored-up sugar· she was saving. For somebody. She was stingy, congealed like lard, but I had the current to melt that. I knew it would not be hard to pick her up. If I did, the rest would happen. I would spend a year with her. It is difficult to pick up a fat girl, but I would have used shock treatment. For example, I would have coughed, and dropped an oyster on her skirt. I think it is revolting to do something like that, but it would have worked with this fat girl because disgust would have woke her up. That's the kind of dirt sex is, in the mind of somebody fat and soft and clammy. Sex to them is spit and mucus. It would have given me the opportunity to wipe it off. I could trust my fingers to give a touch of something. The point to the entire operation (people watching in the streetcar, me standing with my handkerchief, apologizing) would be that my fingers would be doing two things at once, proper and respectful in the part of my hand everybody else could see, flame through the handkerchief on her lap. I would have begun right there. For the least I would get her name. At the end of the five minutes I turned to take a look at her, and under that fat face, in the pretty face which could be very attractive, I could see there was a dumb look in her eyes that nothing was going to improve. That stopped me. Putting in a year on a girl like that would be bad unless she was all for me at the end. Stupidity is for nothing, not even itself. I detest stupidity in women—it sets me off. So I got off the car.

Didn't even look at the girl. After she gets married to somebody fat and stupid like herself she will hate any man who looks like me because of that five minutes. Her plastic corset must have had a drug-store smell after I got off the trolley car. Think of plastic trying to smell.

I tell this as an example. On the outside it used to be that I never sat down next to anybody that I didn't feel them even when we didn't touch and two or three times a week, or even a day, I would be close to the possibilities of somebody like the fat girl. I know about certain things. I know with all policemen, detectives, correction officers, turnkeys, hacks, parole-board officials, that sex is the problem with them. Smartest cellmate I had said one time like a philosopher, "Why, man, a judge will forgive any crime he is incapable of committing himself." My friend put it right. Sex is a bitch. With police. They can't keep their hands off. They do, but then it builds tension. For some it's bad. They can get ready to kill. That's why you comb your hair. Why you must look neat. You have to be clean. Above sex. Then a cop can like you. They ask you those questions knowing how you will answer. Often they know you are lying. For example they know that you will take a drink in the next six months. What is important is not that you are lying, but the kind of lie they hear in your voice. Are you afraid of them? Are you afraid they will see down into your lying throat? Then you are okay. They will pass you. If you are afraid of them, you're a good risk. But if you think they are stupid, faintest trace of such a thought in yourself, it comes through. Always one of them will be sensitive to condescension. It gets them ready to kill. A policeman never forgives you when you get him ready to kill. Obviously he can't do it, especially in a room performing official duty with a stenographer at the side. But the adrenalin goes through him. It is bad to take a flush of adrenalin for nothing. All that murder and nowhere to go. For example when you're standing up talking to a parole board it's important the way you stand, how tight your pants are. Good to be slim, trim, shipshape, built the way I am, provided you are modest. Do not project your groin forward or your hips back. It is best if your pants are not tight-fit. Younger juvenile delinquents actually make this sort of mistake. It is not that they are crazy so much as egotistical. They think older men will like them so much they will give them parole in order to look them up. A mistake. Once read in the newspapers about a Russian soldier who picked up a German baby and said, "It's beautiful," but then he got angry because he remembered the baby's father had been shooting his children, so he killed the baby. That's a cop. If you strut, even in good taste and subtle, they will start to get a glow where it is verboten, and they will like you, they will get a little rosy until they sense it goes nowhere, and wow the sex turns. Gets ready to kill you. If cops have an adrenalin wash for their trouble, you are remembered badly. It is much better to be slim, trim, shipshape, and a little peaked-looking, so they can see you as a thrifty son, which is the way they must have seen me because they gave parole that day, and I was out of there in a week. Out of prison. Out of the can. I think I would have died another year. Liver sickness or go berserk.

Now you may ask can police be so dumb as to let me go on an armed-robbery sentence, six years unserved out of ten. Well, they saw me as thrifty. I was careful that day with voice and posture. But how can police be so stupid as to think in categories like thrifty? That's easy, I can answer. Police are pent up, they're apes, they're bulls. Bulls think in categories.

2

Well, I've been feeling small for four years now. Prison is a bitch for people like me. It cuts your—I don't want to use doubtful language. It's a habit you build up inside. Some do use language that way. Some lifers. Spades. People who don't give a damn. They're playing prison as if it is their life, the only one they are going to have. But I am conservative in temperament. I comb my hair every morning, I comb it the same way. Minor matter you may say, but it isn't for me. I like to comb my hair when I feel like it. Animal of the woods. I have the suspicion—some would call it superstition—that combing my hair can spoil some good ideas. I would never say this to a hack but why is it not possible that some ideas live in your hair, the way the hair curls. I have very wavy hair when it is left to itself. Whenever I get a haircut, I have the feeling I'm losing possibilities I never got around to taking care of. Put it this way: when I comb my hair, it changes my mood. So naturally I prefer to comb it when I want to. In prison forget that. Comb your hair the same time same way every day. Look the same. If you're smart, keep your mood the same way. No ups. Nor downs. Don't be friendly. Don't be sullen. Don't offer company. Don't keep too quiet. If you stay safe, in the middle, and are the same thing every day you get a good report. The reason I get parole first time out, six years off a ten-year sentence is that I was a model prisoner which means just this: you are the same thing every day. Authorities like you if you are dependable. Be almost boring. I think what it may be about is that any man in authority finds his sleep important to him. People in authority can't stand the night. If you wear a uniform and you go to bed to sleep and a certain prisoner never bothers your dreams, you'll say a good word for him when it comes time to making out reports.

Of course you are not popular. Necessarily. My bunky shakes my hand when I get this good news, but I can see he is not happy in every way. So I complain about details. I am not to possess liquor at home, nor am I to frequent any bar even once, even at Christmas. Moreover, I am not to eat in any restaurant which serves liquor.

"What if you don't drink? But just eat there?"

"I'm not to go into any premises having a liquor license."

"A restaurant that don't serve liquor is a tearoom or a hash house."

"Crazy," I say. I don't like such expressions, but this is perfect to express my sentiments.

"Well, good luck."

It is possible we are thinking of the same things, which is the three times he got a bottle into the cell and we drank it together. The first time sick, second time we had a fight, third time sex. I remember I almost yelled in pain when my rocks got off, because they wouldn't stop. I was afraid I'd hurt myself. It had been so long. It seemed each time I took liquor something started in me that was different from my normal personality. By normal I mean normal in prison, no more. You wouldn't want a personality like that on the outside any more than you would want to smell like a laundry bag. But so far as inside personality went, I couldn't take liquor and keep the same. So if I started drinking on the secret when outside, I was in trouble. Because my style of personality would try to go back to what it was before, and too many eyes would be on me. My parole officer, people in the neighborhood. The parole board was getting me a job. They just about picked out the room where you lived. They would hear about it even if I didn't get into a rumble when I was drunk. If I kept a bottle in my room, I would have to hide it good. The parole officer has been known to come around and pay a friendly visit which is to say a sneak visit. Who could enjoy the idea of him sniffing the air in my room to see was there liquor on the breeze? If they caught me drinking in the eight months, back I would be sent to here. A gamble, this parole. But I was glad to take it, I needed out. Very much. Because there was a monotony in me. It had been coming in day after day. I didn't have the feeling of a current in me any more, of anything going. I had the feeling if I sat down next to a girl like the fat girl now, and our legs touched, she would move away cause there was a blank in me which would pass into her. Something repulsive. There was something bad in me, something very dull. It wasn't in my body, it wasn't even in my mind, it was somewhere. I'm not religious, but it was somewhere. I mean I didn't know if I could keep control or not. Still, I couldn't have done it the other way. Eight more months. I might have flipped. Talking back to a hack, a fight. I'd have lost good time. There is only one nightmare in prison. It's that you don't get out, that you never get out because each time you come close the tension has built up in you so that you have to let it break out, and then your bad time is increased. So it's like being on the wrong escalator.

"Take it slow, take it easy," said my bunky. "Eight months goes by if you get yourself some sun."

"Yeah, I'm going to sleep in the sun," I said. "I'm going to drink it."

"Get a good burn your first day out, ha-ha. Burn the prison crap out of your pores."

Maybe the sun would burn the dullness away. That's what I was thinking.

December 1960

TRUTH AND BEING:
NOTHING AND TIME

A BROKEN FRAGMENT FROM A LONG NOVEL

Now that there is no doubt I am going to die, and my death
will be by that worst of diseases (for it is other than disease), I think the time may be here to tell the story of the
revolution which came to New York in the second half of
the Twentieth Century, of its outrageous internal history,
of my part in it, and the style of my mind. If I do not
offer my name, it is because I am one of the actors in the
mystery, a principal of the revolution, and I would not like
to detract from any excitement attached to my actions by
linking all of my person in this first breath with the four
consonants and two vowels of cancer. For it is indeed just
that rebellion of the cells from which I am dying . . . at the
rate . . . it is curious that I do not know the rate. Might
it not tell us something of the impulse within the disease if
we were to measure this rate of growth from day to day of
the malignancy of the cells? I am certain the formula would
belong to one of those exquisite curves of increase or de-
terioration which lit my adolescent comprehension of mathe-
matics, as for example some equation to determine an ex-
ponential expansion, or the curve of the logarithm. (Even
the terms are no longer secure to my memory; but as meaning dissipates, sound presents its attractions.) Since I
mention these curves, however, best it is for me to admit
that there is only one curve I expect to be found in the
graph of the rate of growth of my mutinous cells—it would
have, I suspect, some relation to the formula for the rate of
increase in the decomposition of radium to lead. For this
is not merely a scientific image to me, but the precise metaphor to describe the possessions and dissipations of my
Self over these years, it is exactly the measure—this transit
from radium to lead—of certain beauties of love, sex, flesh,

and other sweetmeats of Being, which were transmuted by
the intensity of my ambition into purposeful and more or
less lost radiations of consciousness. Radium emits that
which it will radiate and in giving of itself to whatever matter surrounds it, or is brought before it, radium diminishes
to lead. One can feel little pity for it: radium has never
learned to receive. So its history among the elements must
present an irony or two: among themselves (that is to say,
among the elements) do they speak of radium as the royal
fool, the King Lear of the atoms? They do not dare, I
think. Radium is too dangerous. It alters wherever it reaches.
But in fact I am close to indulging an unwise vice because
metaphors live for me with the power of mechanical laws.
It is an evil philosopher who cannot mourn his own passing,
and if that art work—a tear of pure compassion for oneself
—were to emerge in my eye, it would be for the loss of my
sensitivity to the dialect, a sensitivity which was perhaps as
exquisite in me at my best as any mind in this century.
There were others who possessed the dialectic with greater
power; the Frenchman Jean-Paul . . . Sartre I remember
now was his last name had a dialectical mind good as a
machine for cybernetics, immense in its way, he could peel
a nuance like an onion, but he had no sense of evil, the
anguish of God, and the possible existence of Satan. That
was left for me, to return the rootless disordered mind of
our Twentieth Century to the kiss *sub cauda* and the Wel-
tanschauung of the Medieval witch. The kiss *sub cauda:*
if I had not come to recognize over the years of my career
that nobility of form and aristocracy of manner are the last
hope of man, I would not explain that *sub cauda* means
beneath the tail, the hole in the highness of the cat, the place
the witch would kiss when out she voyaged to visit the
Demon (or is it in?), cats being classified by Medieval logic
as the trinity of the Devil shaped into One. Naturally. But
to give a taste of what I offer, to prove that there are
dreams, essays, baths of flesh I never found behind each
word and curious phrase, let me hold for a moment all dis-
quisition on the character of my compassion for myself and
offer instead a nugget of new ore. The hole, the royal hole
(forgive my gentility, but I do not wish to jar the ghosts of
the Time whose style I inhabit for this writing), the hole,
the brown one, rich as purple in some, withered to
dun-green for others, flower, weed, perfume, ill-fumed,

cathedral and shanty, pleasure, pustule, muscle, orifice, avatar, pile and grave, is the final executor of that will within us to assign value to all which passes through. Do we bite into an apple? It is not perfect, not often. Good cells and poor, tastes, monotonies, and taints mill in the vaults of our digestion; the needs, desires, snobberies, and fashions of our will devil one's sense of selection, twist our taste: good cells of the apple, tart let us say, brave in the way the cell of an apple can be brave—I think such a bravery might exist, might it not? (the tart cell could maintain its taste against a bland environment for the years of its life) and yet brave or bland could be ignored, could be flushed away, good mistaken for bad, nourishment lost, because the form of *our* character was too insensitive to absorb the most particular character of my brave cell in the apple. So out it goes, pushed into the Styx by the body, buried with the foulest hoodlums and lowest slime, the dullest scum and deadest skin of those fecal molecules, ejected already into the journey to the end of the hole. What rich possibilities and poor wastes are shit into the vast bare lands of sanitation by the middle-class mind. So it is that some of the best and some of the worst of us are drawn to worship at the congregation of the lost cells. (Why is their color brown?— I have pondered this question for years.)

Yes, there are those of us who worship our own, there are all too many who prostrate themselves before another, and there were even a few like our revolutionary leader who was drawn toward his own and rarely repelled by others. It is characteristic of revolutionaries, passionate lovers, the very ambitious, the greedy, the stingy, and dogs, to fix on what is excreted by others; it is typical of Narcissists, children, nuns, spinsters, misers, bankers, conservative statesmen, dictators, compulsive talkers, bores, and World War I generals accomplished at trench warfare, to be forever sniffing their own. But the intelligent and conservative among you are annoyed already for there is a tendency to my remarks which you detect with unease, you fear I lead the argument into the alp of the high immoral. I do; but perhaps my aim is to rescue morality. To be conservative does not mean to be cowardly: follow my argument, for you quit it at a loss—I am not necessarily archbishop of the New Royal Scatological in our society.

Good. We are drawn to shit because we are imperfect in

our uses of the good. If all we eliminated was noxious, hopeless, used up or never-intended, it would be a pervert or a maniac who found the subject attractive. But not all of what we give away is useless. There is a spirit to nourishment, an élan to food, a dash of the existence of an Other —who among you would presume to argue that the flesh of a brave animal is the same in flavor, substance, or final effect upon us as the meat of a contented cow? Each cell in each existence labors like all of life to make the most of what it is or can be, each cell is different, perhaps even so different as one of us from another. So perhaps we do not digest all that is good for us. Indeed, some is lost because it is too good for us, we do not deserve it, the guilt in the enzymes of our stomach prevents the process. (Who among you? scientists? chemists? doctors of organism? can prove that guilt is *in*capable of entering an enzyme?) Yet other riches elude the peristalsis—the best of us cannot absorb a nutrient which is beyond the possibility of our style: particles of food which urge us to be generous are disagreeable to the stingy; spices which gratify our sense of the precise are lost and refused by thicket-witted minds. The dung of the brave is filled with riches for the fearful: precisely those subtleties, reservations, and cautions the courageous dislike are grace and wit for the coward; the offal of the fool has sweets to accelerate a genius—a dull mind must reject those goods for fear the head would hemorrhage from unexpected and indisposable enthusiasms. All the mineral riches of stone, the essences of earth, the spirits of the Wind, creativities of the Sun, omens and intimations of the moon, scalding and compassionate courses of rain, pass upward into the aristocracies of nature, into the nutrient offered us by plant and animal. The wealth of our ground enters us—we digest a million insinuations a day, and fail to digest perhaps a million more, for all of us are too narrow for the wealth we devour, and expel the exquisite in time with the despised.

But if excrement is the enforced marriage of Tragic Beauty and Filth, why then did God desert it, and leave our hole to the Devil, unless it is because God has hegemony over us only as we create each other. God owns the creation, but the Devil has power over all we waste—how natural for him to lay siege where the body ends and weak tragic air begins. Out of the asshole pour the riches of Satan— these souls of nutrient, these lost cells spurned by the uni-

verse of the body they traversed, their being about to be
cast into the lower existence of Chance. For you see, and
do not be altogether nervous (since the explanation, if given
in haste, will be amplified at leisure), there are three possibilities of Being. There is Culture when one exists in a
milieu, when one's life is obedient to a style—the peasant
in his village lives in Culture like bacteria in a petri dish.
There is History, the highest form of life; it has the turns
and starts, the surprises, the speed of change and the fires of
courage an animal knows on a long trip to search for food.
And there is Chance. That is the life of an organism which
has been deprived of the possibility to organize itself—it is
the lowest form of active life, it is entropy. (A word to remember.) With Chance we can depend no longer upon ourselves (which is the grace that History offers) nor can we
even depend on growth in obedience to the shape of the
culture which conceived us, no, we are cast loose, we are
blown, we are transported, we are shifted, pushed, we are
carried by forces larger than ourselves toward fates of
elimination which inspire terror. Those freight trains dense
with the bodies of victims moving from a camp of concentration to a camp of extermination (small intestine and
colon of German Idealism), these souls so soon to die by
gas in a room as bleak as the lavatory of a men's peniten-
tiary, they were souls ripped from Culture or defeated in
History, and so linked into the purposeful streamings of
Chance as she went toward the abyss. Yes, it was I who first
demonstrated to the world by the rigor of philosophical
argument (a Herculean labor) that the state of Being in
the Twentieth Century was close to the extinction of itself
because of the diseases and disasters of soul over the centuries, the victories of the Devil. Being was now warped.
History, Culture, and Chance—that choice offered to Being
from the beginning of our existence was turning into the
contrary of itself. History was now made by cowards who
gave no shape to History even as they blurred the shape of
what we saw (those modern buildings without faces). Culture was untimely ripped—the foods of Being and the main-
tenance of Being grown thick, anomalous, and bland with
hybrid growths from the field, antibiotics, and a technologi-
cal jargon for the cure of the body. Only Chance prospered
in the Twentieth Century. The circuits of the circuitless
turned to purpose. One had only to rip one's root free from

Culture, relinquish one's dreams of authority, one's sense of self, one's love of adventure, one's desire to make a History, relinquish oneself to Chance, and all was planned. One's life, emptied of novelty, organized, cleansed, plotted, secure, unpursued, could then proceed in the monotonies of welfare from the cradle to the tomb. Chance was a purposeful stream moving the bodies of all millions of us away from roots, below history, out of grace. The progression was from man to *merde,* the Twentieth Century was the rush of all souls to search out shit, to kiss the Devil, to rescue a molecule of the brown from its extinction. For think: we began all this (and disturb yourself not unduly if you have comprehended but little, for we return again and again) but we began with the kiss *sub cauda,* the kiss to the hole of the cat. The cat—that marriage of grace and cruelty, self-centered, alien, alone, what can the cat use in its food of tender cells, compassionate meats, philosophical greens? It cannot— the drop of the cat is rich in royal and generous affections; one has only to absorb, and one will love with grace. Yes, such waste has all the darting odors of fish-meat and love. The witches knew it; they were burned for no less than the addition of this dung to their cakes-for-the-encouragement- of-love and more than one saint was present, the rack of hagflesh burning in his nose, his legs twisted with the ache of a witch's soul being returned finally to her separate masters. St. Exquisitas of Odometamo, that unpredictable and much despised saint of the Twelfth Century, almost excommunicated three times for heresy (that rare and only saint admired to my knowledge by the Marquis de Sade), was the first I know to suggest that the witch was the finest jewel of the Devil because she was a woman originally of noble soul much beloved by God, who had been rifled by Satan in the womb, which is to say that witches generally are born of evil mothers, God investing the cruel placenta with the spirit of a rare soul, as if God wished to steal—if one may speak this way (for St. Exquisitas of course could not)—one human of evil back from the Devil. What the Devil owns, he generally cares for, although he is not perfect as a custodian any more than God is all foreseeing as a lover, but as a rule of thumb (since one is hardly so divine oneself as to speak with authority of the Divine Economy) God must raid upon evil to recover it, even as the Devil lusts to capture love. So St. Exquisitas gave his formula for the creation of a witch: God anoints the womb of an evil creature in the moment of her conception and in turn is tricked of his effort by the Devil who is so alert that this particular one of his creatures might be lost (for God being wealthy and a snob never chooses any ordinary lady of evil) that Satan follows behind God and poisons the anointment with his tongue.

Thus, at last, a hint of my style and the character of my mind.

December 1960

PART TWO

The Air of the Dying

A CALCULUS AT HEAVEN

FATHER MEARY, APRIL 1942, THIRD DAY

He will not be a part-time thing.

Sometimes they all were running, sometimes walking running crawling. All of them, Rice the Indian, Father Meary, the captain, cursing and stumbling; thirty men, gouging, elbowing, crawling through their narrow increment in space. "Come on," the captain shouted, "Come on, come on," and Father Meary looking back at him, stumbled and fell. In the distance, he could hear the guns debating still, fiercely as if they were intolerant of each other, and the sounds were breaking and bursting in his head. He rolled over on the ground, feeling the captain tugging at his shoulder, swearing at him. "Come on, we got to get to the house." He saw men passing him, running isolated from each other, and although the panic was in him too, he felt separated from them. Not understanding, he stumbled to his feet. Jogging after the retreating men, feeling the captain by him, motivating him through space by his presence, he told himself that the man should not have sworn at him, he was an officer of God.

He did not understand, everything had suddenly mixed inside him, burbled like the running mass of men, and what had happened back in the second trench line he did not know. For two days they had been holding back the Japanese, and then suddenly the trench line had broken, had gone, and he was running with the men. "Oh, Heavenly Father," automatically he began, and then the harshness of the machine gun, the mechanical signpost to death, had sounded behind him, and feeling a hand against his back, he had prostrated himself before the earth only to hear the enemy's cry of victory, pulsing behind him, working its way up from

33

the beach. Then they were up again, running all the time now, dropping whenever a gun sounded, stumbling up the leisurely pitted street of Tinde. His prayers lost their logical sequence, became jumbled. "Hail Mary, Pax est. . . ."

Then himself, once more a part of the struggling ill-formed matrix of men running hoarse-breathed to . . . to where? He needed assurance, his plump hands wavering uncertainly away from his body as he tripped, and caught up and tripped, trying desperately not to fall behind the men running . . . running to where? The captain was leading them, the captain must know, he thought. The captain was a military man.

Under him, he felt his thin legs bend together once more, felt himself breathing in the dirt, the city of Tinde flowing into his material self as the sounds from the arena—the Roman arena, he thought—as the sounds came closer and closer, became embodied in the intolerance of the machine gun. He didn't have to fall, he thought, he was already on the ground. But the gun had stopped, and then he felt the earth careening away from him. After a moment he realized that someone had picked him up, carrying him with his head down, his face near the man's back. He watched the cross on his shoulder, swaying from his uniform, jerkily in an unholy rhythm, and when it fell off, he found himself gazing after it, as if it were a bird disappearing in the sky. When he could see it no more, he still kept his eyes focused for it, seeing the ground twist and recede under him. He was terrified; his head upside down felt heavy and uncomfortable, the back carrying him was not broad—he felt an augment of his fear. The men running beside him, was there terror at their faces too? The lines had broken, he kept telling himself, but how, but when; he felt his absolute sense of time leaving him. He didn't understand such affairs, he was a godly man, he did not know of such matters, but the Japanese had come through, their faces yellow with lust. The pagan men, they would not understand, they would not respect a man of God. He had lost his cross, they would shoot him with the rest. The smoke of death was over the city.

The gun came back, hovered about him; the man carrying him made a sound, lurched and fell. Father Meary fell with him, the two tangled in the dirt. He felt blood on his face, and turning his head on the ground, realized that none of the men were running any more, that they all lay in random prostration on the ground, while the gun and then another gun spoke angrily over them. Hearing screams, he could no longer feel that men were dying, but their souls . . . it meant . . . he thought of Conditional Absolution for them. There was blood on his face but he felt no pain. . . .

Once in San Francisco an unhappiness had come to him and had remained for many months. One evening in the winter, he had been traveling through the city and, feeling hunger, had entered unthinking the first restaurant he passed. The food was not expensive, and feeling his unhappiness more pointedly, he had ordered the highest priced dinner. The meal had been excellent, the waitress attractive. She had seemed to him a little bit like a Madonna from the school of Florence, and after the meal had been over, he had given her the dollar for the meal, and happy with her face, had added half of it again for the tip. He had noted the surprise on her face, and feeling happy he had said, "If there is anything I like, it is a well-prepared meal, well served, by a pretty young waitress like yourself." Embarrassed by the effort he had made to keep his voice deep, he left before she could thank him. Outside, he had suddenly felt more unhappy than before.

. . . The machine gun came back, licking at the bodies of the men about him. Overhead, a few planes distorted the sky. "It's a death trap, it's a death trap," he heard someone muttering beside him. The terror had worked its way into his finger tips; every muscle seemed to have sprung free, quivering loosely. The fact of his probable death came to him, and it loosed a new type of fear. Already, in the road, the *tap-tap-tap* of men's souls changing existences had begun. He was afraid, he had lived his life for the moment of meeting his death, and he was afraid. He did not understand—but why? And then all thought in his mind trailed out along the ground, and he could only feel his fear. After that, only the sun, warm on his back. The machine gun, indecent, angry again; God taking His inscrutable will.

Were they all to die here, lying in a road, while a machine gun worked from body to body, seemingly never satisfying itself that the body it was striking was dead? He saw a man beside him waver to his feet, throw a hand grenade at the machine gun. Somewhere he heard a shout, and then the grenade fulfilling itself. The machine gun did not sound any more. Then the men about him, on their feet again, running. On hands and knees he saw himself counting them, guessing they were ten or twelve, until abruptly he realized that in their run down the road he was being left behind. On his feet, laboring after them, shouting, "Captain Hilliard, Captain, Captain," shouting, and then he fell. Someone had run back, was dragging him; he felt dirt forcing against his face, abrading his plump white flesh. He was trying to hold back his groan, but then the pain ceased, the rough dirt changing to mud, becoming actually wet. He remembered. They were going into the stone house by the edge of the swamp. The sounds about him seemed to be changing, perhaps he heard a cheer. The man let him go, he saw it was the Indian, Thomas Rice; he must thank him. Another machine gun ripped at them from a hill, men falling about him again. Dirt was in his eyes, he could not see; in the terrible moment, he felt a hand pulling him; half crouching, he felt himself led to the cellar window, felt its rough stone sides scraping against his flanks as he crawled through, fell suddenly for two or three feet onto a pile of sandbags. Men kept coming over him, he crawled away. Still dazed, he was able to see a little out of his eyes. Someone had kicked him angrily. Looking up, he saw it had been DaLucci, but he could feel no anger. Was the man Catholic and godless? . . . Ahh . . . these Italians.

His situation came back more clearly. He remembered now that the house had been prepared as a defense three days before. On the edge of the swamp . . . it was cool here, if only it didn't become too wet. He felt himself drifting away again . . . the cellar walls seemed sandbagged . . . that meant less splinters, he imagined, it was functional, he was certain. . . . If only his wrist weren't so painful. He must have sprained it when he fell through the window. Were they safe from a cannonading, he wondered, and then abruptly, he sat up, panic catching at him. How many men left? He counted four, counted again, there were only four besides himself—Captain Hilliard, DaLucci, Rice and a blond soldier he did not know. Did it mean he was to die after all? He could see the Indian firing the gun, the blond soldier feeding. He heard him say, "That's it, Sergeant, give it back to 'em, Sergeant, give it to those bastards."

The priest noted it numbly, long conditioning having accustomed him to the sound of the profanity. He wondered how safe they were, could the brick house really shut out the Japanese? Fascinated, he watched the sunlight glancing through the window, leaving the cellar almost completely dark. . . .

For months, Sister Vittoria had been treating him with especial attention, complimenting him on his lessons when he had prepared them well; looking sad and unhappy rather than angry, when he had played ball out on the street too long the day before. He noticed, even, that he spoke of him to Sister Josette and pointed to him often, as the best student in the class. He liked it; the kids used to call him "teacher's pet," but it didn't bother him as much as it had used to, because somehow, he had always liked studying a little better than fighting the kids on the block. So that when she called him over one day and pinched his cheek, and gave him a letter to his mother, he was not surprised.

His mother had read it slowly several times; he feeling shame for her at the unease with which she read. He kept thinking of how his mother didn't smell as cool and starchy as Sister Vittoria. But then his mother had looked up at him, from her chair, and smiled at him very happily. They talked a long while. "Be a priest, be a priest, Timothy," she kept saying, "and God will always be with you." He kept feeling how uncomfortable she was with the words. "It's an honor, do you know, it's an honor." Then later . . . "God will not be a part-time thing to be shared with a woman, and sure with a paycheck, but He will stay." And he, the boy, after a long while, "But I do not want to be a priest, Mother, I do not feel a vocation." She had sighed. "You will be the most important man of all your friends, you will be more important than any rich man; do you know what that means for a poor man?" He had shook his head, unhappy. "Think of it," she had said.

Then two weeks later, Sister Vittoria had called him into her private little study room. She had talked to him in her beautiful soft voice, and he had been unsure beneath it. At last when she asked, "Do you not feel a vocation stirring within you?" he had tried, contracting his stomach forcibly to feel some inner tenseness or emotion, as he was to squeeze it in later years when he looked at religious paintings. "I

*think, Sister, I think I do feel a small vocation within
me." She had smiled. "You are fortunate, Timothy, you
will feel it grow and grow, there are very few men who are
godly enough to feel even the beginnings of one." As he
had been about to go out the door, he had turned to her
and said, "Sister Vittoria, I feel, I think I feel it growing
a little more already."*

Light red dust was filtering across the column of sunlight
in the cellar. He saw the Indian firing every now and then,
saw the captain speaking beside him. "We're going to save
the mortar until they bring one up; just keep firing the gun.
We're protected here, we'll be able to knock their mortar
out first. Now look, we've got to hold the road out there,
there's only one other way to the coastal road, and that's
being defended by a house like this one . . . only with more
men probably."

Father Meary forced himself into devotion. Oh, my God,
I am ready to meet you, he thought desperately. But a piece
of plaster broke from the ceiling, its fragments landing on
his chest, and he felt death with it. Once, he had said, in
speaking to the men, "There are no atheists in foxholes.
All of you do not have the same faith I do, but all of you
believe in the supremacy of God." "But, Father Meary,"
someone had interrupted him. He had stared back coldly.
"When you meet your Maker, you believe. . . . You must
believe. . . ." Then why this persistent fear? His tired mind
fought against relaxing, fought against the temptings of
Hell. But the words sounded ornate to him for a moment.
Almost crying, he demanded all the resolution within him.
The men must not see him crying, they would have their
faith weakened if they did. And they would have need of
him in the house when the Japanese threatened even more.
He got to his feet; he would comfort them.

In the semi-gloom of the cellar, they were crouched
against the wall or under the window, firing the machine
gun irregularly, being answered irregularly. They did not
seem to know he was with them. He slumped, feeling his
resolution ebb. Three days before, in preparing the house
they had dug a slit trench against one of the side walls. It
would be better if he were to remain in it, where a chance
bullet could not reach him. After all, he could not do the
men any good if he were dead. And then mockingly, he felt

his fear disappearing, as he dropped into the greater safety
of the trench. He shut his eyes. Why, why had he been
afraid; it disturbed the order of things, the certainties were
not so . . . well, not so certain. But he believed, he was
certain he believed more than ever. For with the horrors he
had seen, well of necessity God existed, for men could not
bear up under the horrors they saw, if it were not for God.
He kept thinking of this, trying to strengthen it in his mind.

The silence disturbed him; he realized that the guns had
stopped for a moment. Crouching in the darkness, he wished
for them to start again, so that he could think about it and
reinforce it even more in his mind. . . .

THE CAPTAIN, 1926–1930.

Two tight kids on a red silk coverlet. . . .

He spent his college life with the creative clique; sur-
realist poetry was in vogue. He drank a lot, he would be
very happy for a while, and then very unhappy, but in back
of it all, he felt a certain integrity within him, a certain
feeling which made him know that he would paint, that he
would slap the lie of America across a thousand canvases,
that he would shove beauty into a million people who had
never felt it before, that he would shake people up, stamp
on them, blast their smugness away, and say, "Here, here
is your graft, here is your marriage morality (a picture of
a businessman sleeping with a prostitute, with a little locket
on the canvas entitled 'Sister') here is your democracy (a
portrait of a syphilitic Negro), and finally, here is your
life (which was a triptych of a motion picture, a clerk, and
a plain woman to represent the clerk's wife)." Only . . . in
hating all this, he was reaffirming himself, for like all college
men who stop believing, he was at the particular point
where he was the only person who had ever realized a slum
or recognized the lie in a politician's voice.

He had come to this endowed university, wondering,
already beginning to disbelieve, but he was young and enthusiastic. (Later he was to say, "You stop believing in God
at seventeen, in communism at twenty-seven.") Breaking
from his family, he was to paint (it was not a new situation,
he had read it in several books), but his father was an army
colonel, and he had been allowed to go to this university

only on the agreement with his father that he, Bowen Hilliard, was to join the R.O.T.C. and to remain in it until after graduation when he would have attained a reserve commission. So that in 1926, when of the class of '30, he was one of the forty-one freshmen out of eight hundred to sport the khaki uniform with the blue lapels, it was to be to him a sign of disparity as painful and unique as the soda jerker who from some outside compulsion had been forced to grow a beard.

Bowen Hilliard, not believing, made the university's literary magazine; Bowen Hilliard, not believing, was known as the best artist in college. Bowen Hilliard went up to Boston and picketed the streets before Sacco and Vanzetti were killed, and came back to write an editorial in the magazine which was to suspend it for a half-year, "Listen, America, listen to your shame. . . ."

He defended nothing intellectually, almost everything emotionally. He said, "The only thing infinite about man is his vanity," but he liked to walk in the streets, to feel people about him. He painted a great deal, read a great many books of art criticism, so that his painting was always conscious, articulate; he was one of the few artists who could explain his work clearly, and what it made him feel. He said he believed in nothing, and he enjoyed it, for he found that believing in nothing meant believing in himself, and at that time he was capable of it. Certainly, he was growing as an artist, his line (always his weak point) was becoming more certain; he had always had an acute sense of texture, but beyond that his canvases had a measure of structural feeling, unusual for a college painter. During this time he painted a discordant abstraction in which the color did not coincide with the line area, very much like a badly printed comic in a newspaper—and he had termed this his masterpiece and called it "Society Out of Whack." . . .

He was to believe in someone else by his senior year. . . . At a party, he met a girl named Cova—there was to be a lot of drinking—and somehow at the end, he was to sleep the night with her. Eventually they were to know each other very well, but in the darkness only the crudest attempts were to be made. "What color are your eyes?" she had asked, and when he had told her brown, she sighed. "I thought they were blue, somehow," she said. Then she laughed. "Of course it doesn't matter. . . ."

The intellectual's passion is ramified by its implications; the artist's is augmented. Cova became an absolute to him, and, in many ways, since she was beautiful and intense and clever, and therefore was like his image of himself (the image of the artist), he was to become an absolute for her. In the last year of college, they had their unhappinesses, but they felt them more healthy, for they came from acute realizations rather than from a doubting of themselves.

They came to a certain understanding early, for she had other lovers besides Bowen Hilliard. "I can't paint," she had said, "and I can't write music, and I don't write nearly so well as I should like to. You must see it; when I take a man, and I may take him for a lot of reasons, in back of it all is the feeling that that is when I'm making something, and that that is something I can do better than any other woman. I don't envy you your paintings, Bowen, you can't envy mine. Some women are born to have a lot of men."

In a measure he understood, and by the time they were out of college and married, it even made sense to him. For he had found that she might take a man for a variety of reasons, because (although this was not often), he attracted her, or because the situation warranted it, or because she was sorry for him. (He once said, "You like any man who is under five feet four and has acne,") or in many cases because it was necessary in the evolution of the friendship, but always she had come back to him, loving him more, taking him more fiercely, reaffirming and even re-evaluating their absolute. She said to him once after a long silence, "We're like two tight kids on a red silk coverlet," and that was what they went by. That was what they believed in. . . .

THE MEN, APRIL 1924, FIRST DAY

There was a dame once. . . .

Heavy with morning and the tenseness of the night before, the men lay encrusted in their double line of trenches, gazing out to sea. Tight and uncomfortable with a fear of butterflies and leadenness in their bellies, gazing nervously out to sea, out between the two arms of the harbor of Tinde. All through the night, polishing the weapons, preparing themselves, cleansing themselves with furtive finalities in every motion. Anxiously, eyes at sea, waiting, who will see the first boat? Looking with dry eyes and throat, tongues licking at the backs of dry and sticky teeth. What will it be like, what will it be like, Jesus Christ . . . Jesus Christ. . . .

The major in command of the three companies at Tinde had written a dispatch for his men that morning. It read:—

THE JAPANESE ATTACKED AT OTEI 0623. THE FORCE CONSISTED OF A FLEET OF ARMORED BARGES. WE HAVE RECEIVED A REPORT THAT HALF OF THE BARGES HAVE CONTINUED ON TOWARD TINDE. ANALOW ISLAND IS SURROUNDED BY IMPASSABLE CLIFFS ON THIS SIDE. THE ONLY POSSIBLE LANDING PLACES ARE AT HANSON BEACH, OTEI, AND TINDE. SINCE THEY HAVE ALREADY ATTACKED THE OTHER TWO POINTS IT IS A CERTAINTY THAT THEY WILL PROCEED ON TO HERE.

I knew this dame once, it was back in Albany. She was saying to me I know your kind, bud, they come twenty to the dozen, so I say to her, you count a funny dozen sister, why don't you come here and play dozen with me? Funny, she says, aren't you. I wasn't going to take that from any dame, I tell her, listen, after they made me, they threw the mold away, it was cracked from laughing so hard at my line. Well, she took it a little easier after that, but . . . I dunno, it was still no deal. . . . When the hell are they gonna come? . . .

WE ARE DEFENDING ONE ISLAND IN A CHAIN OF ISLANDS. THE JAPANESE DO NOT CONSIDER THIS ISLAND IMPORTANT ENOUGH TO SEND ANY NAVAL UNITS ALONG. WE ARE GOING TO SHOW THEM THEY HAVE MADE A MISTAKE. THEIR MOTORBOAT FLEETS ARE PROGRESSING FROM ISLAND TO ISLAND. IF WE HOLD THEM HERE, THEY WILL HAVE TO REVISE THEIR PLAN OF ATTACK. CONTROL OF THE CHAIN DEPENDS ON THE CONTROL OF ANY SINGLE ISLAND. CONTROL OF THIS ISLAND DEPENDS ON CONTROL OF THE COASTAL ROAD WHICH RUNS ALONG THE NORTHERN SIDE OF THE ISLAND, FROM HANSON BEACH TO OTEI TO TINDE. OUR MAIN FORCE IS AT HANSON BEACH AND WILL HOLD THE JAPANESE UNLESS THEY ARE ABLE TO SEND REINFORCEMENTS FROM OTEI OR TINDE. WE MUST HOLD THE CITY, BUT MORE IMPORTANT, WE MUST MAINTAIN CONTROL OF THE COASTAL ROAD.

There was this movie, Jimmie Cagney, I think. Did you see it when it played in town? 'Cause I saw it you know at the Strand in New York. They had a band there . . . I can't remember the name, only the vocalist with them was all right, I can still remember her. But anyway, the movie was all about war, only it was in France; there was no little island fighting in the last one ya know, and this guy Jimmie Cagney is yellow, it gave me quite a jump 'cause you know Cagney, but then I figured that it's anybody's turn to be yella maybe when it all starts happening. Have you got any idea of the time? . . . That picture gave me quite a smack, I ain't forgetting it in a hurry. . . .

IF OUR LINES SHOULD CRACK, WE MUST STILL KEEP THEM FROM TAKING THE COASTAL ROAD WHICH IS ABOUT TWO MILES INLAND FROM THE CITY AT THIS POINT. THERE ARE TWO STREETS LEADING OUT TO IT, AND WE HAVE CONSTRUCTED FORTRESSES IN A SEPARATE HOUSE COMMANDING EACH ROAD. FOR THE RIGHT FLANK WINDOWS COMMAND EVERY DIRECTION. THE HOUSE ON THE LEFT FLANK IS THE OLD BANKERS STONE HOUSE, SITUATED IN THE SWAMP WITH ONLY ONE SIDE ON SOLID GROUND. ALL WINDOWS HAVE BEEN SEALED WITH THE EXCEPTION OF ONE CELLAR WINDOW WHICH COMMANDS THE ROAD. IF BY ANY CHANCE YOUR LINES CRACK, YOU MUST TRY TO REACH ONE OF THE HOUSES, THAT IS ESSENTIAL.

Tamping rifle butts slowly on the ground, snapping cigarettes nervously against thumbnails, waiting, waiting for the attack, I dunno, I never saw action before. The end of his heel delicately clicking against the other, waiting for the fall of a little clod of mud. It kinda gets ya waitin', doesn't it? I wish there was somethin' to do sort of. Fingering at a button, moving the hat back and forth. These cigarettes taste kinda good, I mean, you know, you smoke 'em all, and they taste the same, and then maybe ya find one ya like . . . I dunno, you know what I mean.

IT IS NOW APRIL, FOUR MONTHS AFTER WAR HAS STARTED, YOU ALL KNOW THAT WE ARE UNEQUIPPED, WITHOUT TANKS AND AIRCRAFT. INSTALLATIONS ARE NOT EVEN A WEEK OLD ON THE ISLAND. HOWEVER, THE JAPANESE HAVE TO MAKE A LANDING, AND THAT ADVANTAGE RESTS WITH US. YOU WILL FIGHT FOR YOUR COUNTRY, THE GREATEST IN THE WORLD. GOOD LUCK.

Just where do ya think ya're shovin' that rifle? Get it out of my face.

Take it easy bud, take it easy.

Well, I like my face, see, I don't like it ruined, there're girls back home, got to go for this face.

I said I was sorry, what the hell were ya blockin' the path?

Listen, bud, you ain't talkin' to Joe Crap, see; you watch what you say with me.

Aaaaah, save it for the Japs.

Well where are they, well when the hell are they comin'? The goddam yellow bastards, what are they, afraid to fight? . . .

THE CAPTAIN: 1931–1936

Something soothing, yet jolly. . . .

The year Bowen Hilliard married Cova Reynolds was the year of the unemployment march on Washington. They were not to do very well. His art was still improving, still powerful, still better than competent in execution, but it was not the year to sell paintings. Their friends bought a few, but their friends had no money either, and Bowen, hating the talk of price, had valued his paintings low, so that when his friends bought them, they said, "I'm sorry as hell, Bowen," and he took to snarling back, "It's all right, goddam you, it's all right." Cova had a small income from her family, which she increased with her earnings as a twelve-dollar-a-week shop girl, but he hadn't seen his family since college, and there was no money in them anyway.

After a while, when the country didn't come to see his work, and he knocked no people down with it, he began to get a little tighter. Occasionally he compromised with some mantlepiece art, but even that wasn't selling very well. The galleries were closing down everywhere. Once, in one of the back galleries in the fifties, a dealer had agreed to put on a two-week exhibition of his work. . . .

For three days they sat around, Cova by him (she had lost her job), and they would not speak very much until a friend came in. Then they all started chattering very violently, becoming satirical or enthusiastic in turn over painters, screaming platitudes on Munch and Beckman and Marin, and then abruptly going quiet. The dealer, Mr. Loestler, was taking three hours for lunch by this time. They all knew it was a mistake. Hilliard looked at his fourteen canvases, at the gray carpeting of the dealer's office, and then muttered something about the light being bad. "It's killing them," he said slowly. "It's killing them, I tell you." Cova was pacing around. She turned to his friends, who were polite, sympathetic and enthusiastic to the best degree of taste, and said, "I still can't learn anything about when they're good or not, but they are good, they are good, aren't they?"

"Cova!" he said.

He watched her coming toward him, making the most of her red dress. It fitted with the carpet he thought. "I'm sorry, Bowen," she said. He gained control of himself. "It's all right, I'm sorry, too," he said.

Their friends left. Another batch would be coming in soon, he knew. The dealer's shop was dry smelling. "They *are* good," he whispered desperately to himself. He thought of their two-room flat. If only they would let him do something for the walls he thought. A mural perhaps, "The Artist Out of Whack."

Then the terrible event occurred. A woman came in to buy something. She was forty, had dark hair, and was growing fat. She wanted a picture for her children's room. "Something soothing, yet happy-looking. In good taste, of course." How many jokes had he heard like that. How many long tedious artist's jokes. She looked about for a while. "I'd like that," she said. It was an experiment with a Barbizon Landscape. Something about the composition of the field he had been in reminded him of a bad Corot, but beyond that, the entire view had been a little too rich, a little too green, a little too much foliage, almost as if any brown cow that had strayed into the field would have had its flanks of a deep purple to maintain the color order. "What is it called?" she asked. "Whore in a Green Negligee," he said. Cova looked at him in horror, a protest of poverty in her eyes. The woman recovered, "Well, I don't have to call it that, I suppose," she said. He held his anger, "No, of course not." Afterward, she bargained with him for the painting, making the final bit of bad taste in the artist-patron breach of etiquette, he decided. She got it for thirty-five dollars. He had spent two weeks on it. After that, when he could not sell a painting right away, he gave it to somebody, be it a boy roller skating, or a shopkeeper, or a laborer in a ditch. (He once said, "I have more paintings in delicatessens than any other representative artist in America.")

For four years he held on, working with the WPA for a while, but Cova and he were losing something. People no longer thought them clever and talented; men were not so interested in making love to Cova any more. As for him, she became the last outpost. Over and over through the bad years, he took her with a terrible kind of fury, performing almost every time, it seemed, a lover's last entrance. But they were depending on each other too much, trying to draw everything, able to believe in nothing else.

Once, when his depression had lasted for months, he started to write his autobiography. As a book, it was amorphous, but since he added to it from time to time, the brunt of his thought began to fill it. He would write; "Malraux says that all that men are willing to die for tends to justify their fate by giving it a foundation in dignity. Perhaps, everywhere, this is felt. But in America, men live, work and die without even the rudest conception of a dignity. At their death . . . well then they wonder what the odds are on a heaven, and perhaps they make futile desperate bets on it, adding up their crude moral calculus, so that if the big team, heaven, comes through, and wins and therefore exists, they will be able to collect their bets that evening. . . ." And much more like that, but he felt himself weakening.

He was to surrender at last. Cova's family had been architects for several generations, and in 1936 he gave up, accepting a job with them as a draftsman. After a year, by studying on the side, he was an architect of sorts. They were living much better (they could afford to live in the Village now), but he found very little desire to paint. . . . To make up for it, he worked on his book quite steadily. . . .

DALUCCI, APRIL 1942, FIRST, SECOND, THIRD DAYS

it's cheap . . . it's cheap. . . .

After the boats had come into sight around the end of the harbor, DaLucci hadn't known what he was doing for two days. Every now and then, though, he could remember them coming nearer, coming nearer, he wishing there was a cannon around somewhere, any lousy bit of fieldpiece to keep them away, but they just kept coming. A coupla Jap planes had started fighting with an American one and they had whipped all around the sky, going out to sea and then coming back. When they started to strafe the beach and the trenches he just sort of ducked automatically, going up and down with the rest like he was a goddam jack-in-the-box, or something, but he didn't know, Jesus, they kept actin' like they was out to get him first. He wished he could shoot something, but the Jap boats were too far away, although he could see them keep coming and coming.

His sergeant, the Indian, kept bending over the machine gun, waiting for them, whistling something, lining it up this way and that, firing it short, just a little *ta-ta-ta*, to see how it was working, but all DaLucci knew was that he felt just like puking.

Holding on to his Garand, he didn't know what to do with it. After a while, with them moving in all the time, he had picked it up, and started shooting, until someone pushed him down. Then the Jap boats started beaching, and the machine guns on each side of him started going, there was more noise than he'd ever heard in his life before, he didn't know, he just kept emptying and loading his rifle, shooting at them but not taking aim. When he looked up, he could see that with all their boats coming in at once, they'd been able to sneak one up on the shore. First thing, before their men tried to come out, they started lobbing with a field mortar from the boat, but then the machine guns on each side of him and all over the place had started cutting that boat to pieces, and even a coupla of their own mortars started cracking down. It mighta been Fourth of July if it wasn't for all that black smoke.

Only during all this, the Japs got a coupla of other boats on the shore, and they were shooting for all hell from the guns they had mounted in the front part of the barge. He ducked down for a second, scared, and when he looked up again, and started shooting, he could see that there was four boats on the beach now, with their guns all going, and mortars—he heard a whistle, someone shoved him down, and then there was a guy screaming his yap off next to him, falling down, holding his face. For a second, he thought the guy's blood was his own, 'cause it was all over him, but then he knew he was standing, and there was nothing hurting him. The guy was grabbing at his feet and looking up at him. He couldn't look at the guy's face, there was so much blood, so goddam much noise. "What the hell," he said, "what the hell, whatthehell," and then another mortar came, and he had to duck again. . . .

In Terre Haute where he lived in the poor part of town, the people used to have their coalbins under the sidewalk, with big metal plates, like sewer covers, over them. When the coal trucks came along, they would unscrew a plate, and dump as much coal in as they ordered. The metal covers were to keep the coal from getting wet.

When they first moved in, there was no cover for their bin. A few years before, a cover had broken, and after that, whenever a family moved out, the house without the cover would take the one that was left.

He was too young to know this when they started living there, but the first thing in his whole life that he did remember was when the family next to him moved out, and they had gotten a coal cover for their house at last. Everybody in the family was very happy, and they kept showing it to him, saying, "Here, Tony, look, look, see the cover," but he was too young and hadn't understood. Not knowing why, he had struck at the cover, and started crying. When they laughed at him for this, he had a temper fit, and Mama DaLucci had to give him a little wine.

For two days the whole thing kept up. The Japs kept losing men, and coming in, and where they had gotten four boats in at one point, they caused a lot of trouble. Everybody was working on them (and it was hard to hit them because only the machine gunner showed, and the Japs crouched behind the steel front of the barge), and while they were trying to take care of the four boats, another two had landed on the other side of his flank, and had gone over the barbed wire with mattresses, piling into a front trench and going like mad there. They couldn't fire any mortars into the trench, because the men were fighting too close together there, and then when another part of the front trenches half emptied to send men over to where the Japs had gotten in, the first Japs, waiting in the four boats, had emptied out, and captured almost a hundred yards of front trenches. From there they set up a fire so hot that DaLucci didn't even stick his head up for five minutes. But while this was going on, all the other Jap boats, or most of them, were able to land behind the part of trench that the Japs held. All the rest of the afternoon, the Japs kept fighting in the front trenches, and along toward night, he heard a guy say that they had control of the front trenches down the whole line. After that, it got so he couldn't stick his head up without going to lose it too, and the two trenches, not seventy yards apart, had kept firing up and down at each other. For two days, he had been ducking into the dugout, catching a bit of sleep that kept being interrupted, choking down a chocolate bar, and standing around under a trench, not knowing what to do, afraid to stand up and aim that gun of his, but even more afraid of the sergeant who kept yelling at him to get up and shoot. So every now and then, he just had to close his eyes almost, stand up, just fire his gun, three or four times as fast as he could, and then drop back in the trench. He never saw anyone long enough to take aim on him like they taught him at target school. The three planes that had been fighting the day it all started, had crashed, he thought, but every now and then an American or a Jap plane would come out and take shots until another plane came to fight it, and then the two of them would lace it up all over the sky, sometimes twisting all the way out to sea, or maybe getting lost on the jungle side of the island. Once, he heard that a Jap plane had crashed in the swamp, but he didn't know about that.

After two days though, it seemed as if both sides were all finished, and everything let up on the morning of the third day. The lieutenant came along, and told them that half of them could get sleep. The sergeant had picked him out as one of them, saying it looked like he wasn't any use anyway, and he might as well sleep so the sergeant could have him off his mind. He didn't like that at all, but he figured it would be awful good to get out of that goddam noise and heat.

But after he got down to the dugout, he found that he just lay on his bed going tense all over. After a while, he turned over, and that seemed to loosen him a little bit, but all the while he could feel this anger growing in him, and not knowing why, he kept murmuring, "It's cheap, it's cheap." He kept thinking of his house and his job back in Terre Haute, and somehow that made him get angrier. He kept seeing the porch with the railing in the place where it had come off, and how through the years each of the vertical sticks that held it up were pulled off to fight with, or had worked off in the rain and wind. Even when the guns sounded every now and then, he was so excited he couldn't listen to them, but kept thinking of his old man, the fat . . . and here he started cursing him, sobbing a little between the words, which he pulled out one at a time from his stomach. He remembered the old man sitting on the porch of the house that was coming apart in Terre Haute, not even a drinking Italian, goddam him, sitting there all pooped out after work . . . after working twelve hours a day, breaking a length of railroad track in, making sixteen a week, sitting on the porch in his shirt sleeves, reading a newspaper . . . turning to the sports page, and reading it slowly, talking to his friends, telling old riddles to the kids, pinching Mama's bottom, with a huh, haw, huh, not even playing cards with his friends, just sitting there on the porch, all pooped out, just a fat hunk of flesh, talking about Italy. Frig him, frig him, frig the old man, he kept saying to himself.

A shell from a mortar cracked apart ten or fifteen yards away. Some dirt came flying down the dugout steps, and all through it he heard a guy give out a bunch of yelps that died slowly, like a dog he had once heard after a car ran over it. He kept thinking that maybe some of the guy was mixed up with the earth that was blowing in the dugout, and his stomach felt like it was trying to move around.

He sat up on the bunk sweating, and for a couple of minutes he couldn't get to relax at all. He lit a cigarette, and then after the first couple of inhales, he felt the anger coming back in him, only he started crying. A guy across from him in the next bunk sat up too. "Take it easy, bud," he heard him say, "let's have a cigarette."

"Shut up, you goddam bastard," he yelled. He tossed over the pack. He felt all funny inside, he kept thinking of the lousy jobs he'd had, first blacking shoes, smelling the stink of people's feet, smelling the stink of shoe polish, he could still smell it, it made him sick even now, being laughed at in school because he had the smell on him. (His fingers came up to his nose, he sniffed at them automatically.) Then, older, another job after another; washing dishes, balancing them on his finger tips when they came out of the machine and were too hot to grab hold of, picking up two-foot piles of plates and lugging them to hell and gone, working at a gas station, best pay to start thirteen a week, he'd worked there for two years, they gave him fifteen, Mary wet against him in the park, "Why don't we get married, Tony?" he getting angry and tight, "Aaaah, go frig yourself, I play it the lone way. Whata you got that I can't get for a buck fifty?" the guys hanging out on the corner, not enough money to go to a whorehouse, sometimes enough to play pool, what I say, you bastards, is get yourselves a trade, that's the way to make dough, stay off the railroads, they bleed ya dry, looka your old man, what I say is, "Tony, for crise-sakes, whena you gonn' fix that porch railing . . . ?" He sat up again, his head was whirling. "What the hell's it all about?" he kept saying to himself softly. "What the hell . . . ?" Only very softly now.

A soldier stuck his head in. "Come on, they're starting again. Get up here." Numbly he reached for his helmet, slung the pack up, grabbed his gun, and lurched out into the sky that was like the Fourth of July only blacker. The Japs were coming over, he kept hearing, and then he began to see it a little. They were doing it the way they had with the boats, charging first at one stretch of trench, and then while all the guns were working there, setting off at another, until there weren't enough guns to cover them all. Then finally, when they did get into a trench, and waited for the reinforcements to come at them, the Japs in the second trenches really charged over with all they had wherever the reinforcements had left.

An order passed down to his platoon to march on to another section, but before they were halfway over, the Japs started racing for the part of trench he was in. Just before this, his head still whirling, he had asked of himself furiously, "What the hell am I in it for, what for, what for?" and then while the Japs came over, he kept screaming, it's cheap, it's cheap, and something musta changed in him, because when the Japs started pouring into the trench not more than forty yards away, he hadn't given a damn about the sergeant or anything, he'd just hurdled out of the trench, and started running for the city. And pretty soon it seemed to him as if the whole goddam army was running with him. . . .

THE CAPTAIN, 1936–1941

> *"I don't know, Bowen; we're rotten."*

To believe in nothing was no longer a source of comfort to him. At the architect's office, the days passed slowly. He who used to argue that to analyze the relation of line to line without considering texture was an artistic affectation, now placed line on line, inserted textures where they were necessary, only now instead of painting cement-rubble, or reinforced concrete, he sketched in the cross-sectional symbols for them. In the drafting office, the men worked with their sleeves held up by little bicep garters, bending over the long stools, their heads lower than their shoulders. Several of the draftsmen sported spats. He considered this worth a generalization, and said, "Draftsmen are not happy unless they wear spats," but since the people he told it to had never been in a drafting office, they did not consider this particularly profound.

On most mornings when he woke up, he made a grimace. For in a short while he was to spend the rest of his working day transcribing one symbol into another, but he had not invented the symbols. A day at the introverts convention, he used to say to Cova in the mornings, but she rarely smiled at it. He realized that Cova held it against him, considered that he had sold out, and for a while remembering that she had wanted him to take the job, had talked her family into it, he was angry and hurt; but later, he realized that she had felt they were at an impasse, that more money was necessary, and that the opportunity had to be made so that they could refuse it, and reaffirm each other. She had told him to take the job because that was part of the balancing factor; he was to make his decision with the scales even. He knew now that she had wanted him to say, "We'll stick it, we'll keep the WPA job, I will not sell out," which was not to say that she was not tired of living without money, for she was, but the art, he realized too late, was what kept the two tight kids on the red silk coverlet.

One evening, they were out drinking in a bar with a friend, Henry, who had several parallels with Bowen Hilliard. They had all gotten quietly drunk on sidecars, until Henry had broken the silence by chanting over and over,

"We are the people of the death-urge, we are the people of the death-urge." "Shut up," Cova had said, but he kept talking. "We are the people of the death-urge. . . . Sounds like Eliot, doesn't it, Bowen?" Then Cova had done something unexpected, reaching over and slapping Henry's face.

"No don't, Cova, don't hit him," he had shouted, and then all three had become conscious of the place they were in. Cova looked at him for just a moment, and then she was crying. "Come on, let's go," he said. "I'll be late at the office tomorrow, I'll be late. I gotta put in fifteen johns on the third floor of the apartment house we're planning." Henry had started laughing. "Sounds like Eliot, doesn't it, Cova? The artist putting fifteen johns on a blueprint." He had gotten up then. "All right, Cova, let's go. . . . I'm not an artist any more, Henry. You can't paint when you're dead, can you?" He sucked in his breath. Henry looked up. "I'm sorry," Henry said.

"Forget it."

"No, I said I'm sorry. . . . *Don't* forget it."

After that, when Cova Hilliard slept with a man it was not because it was her act of creation, but because her husband had nothing left to give her. And he, knowing that, had worked harder at the plans for the tan brick apartment house, or had found a passing woman, or even had tried to paint, feeling the rage growing in him as the paint built up on the canvas, until the moment when what he had wanted to do would not superimpose over what he had done, and he had destroyed the painting.

They were reaching a point where they would give the last hard veer away from each other. Already they had broken up several times, but every time, frightened of the step from sensualism to irrevocable cynicism, they had stopped and come together. In one of these rightings, one of the unexplainables happened, and something of the old certainty had come back. It could not remain, however. There was nothing to hold it any longer. One night, very embarrassingly, he had come home too early. Even in the pain it reminded him of the triteness of the dark-haired woman in the art gallery. When they were alone, he had tried to talk.

"What's the matter, Cova?"

"Oh, go to hell, Bowen, I don't want any sharing of our mutual troubles."

He lit a cigarette. It was very necessary to maintain

whatever existed of the situation. "You're not feeling very good, Cova, are you?"

"I don't know, Bowen, we're rotten."

How many times had he asked himself that? "People like us can't afford to go in for labels."

"Listen, Bowen, I'm not afraid of them, I don't mind the words. All right I'm not creative, I'm a bitch. That's still perfectly all right. So I'm a bitch."

He let some ash drop on his pants. Abstractedly, his finger rubbed it in. "I didn't mean that, Cova. I still don't think we're rotten. Maybe we had just a little too much to buck. Maybe two people do suck each other dry."

She had worked one of her shoes off irritably. "Look, Bowen, that's been on the wall for a long time."

He stood up slowly. "And after I leave?"

"I'm sure we'll be even more pointless than ever. . . ."

He did a lot at once after that; he left his job, he moved in with Henry (feeling the symbolism of it, but he didn't have to pay Henry any rent), and he finished his book, which in one of his recurring moments of anger, he entitled *The Artist in Transit Inglorious*. It was an angry book. Published by a wildcat liberal firm, it made him very little money, but it served as meat for more than a few of the family-newspaper critics. He thought of painting some more, but it seemed a little like a dirty joke to start all over again. He spent a year working from job to job.

A good deal of his time now, he tried to re-evaluate his life. He felt that somewhere along the line he had missed not a turn so much as perhaps a flubbed traffic signal, stopping when he should have moved forward. It seemed to him that in college he had been talented, clever, and even sincere within the limits of his life that he had defined. And it seemed to him that Cova had been that, too. They had not been mismated, and yet they had broken up, because in not believing they had had to expect too much of each other. If they had believed in something outside themselves, it would have been all right, but everything they had been told for the first twenty years of their lives had become on examination a piece of disjunctivity. The form and the matter had not coincided. So that having no end for their life, they had tried to get by on style.

It seemed to him that his life could be compared to the friendly quarrel over an after-dinner check; that when for some reason two people wanted to pay a check, the battle was always fought out by jockeying, so that very rarely would two people both reach at the same time and tear the check. It was like two trucks entering a one-lane junction at the same time. Inch by inch they might try to ride the other out, but unless the stakes were very high, there was never a collision.

Since in his life he had believed in nothing external, he had never found the stakes high enough to collide. By the time he had broken with Cova this had been so ingrained in them that even then, no great wreckage had occurred. It seemed to him that he had gotten quite far away from anything direct, and that the lack of meaning in his life might be explained by that.

In early 1941 he wrote to his father that he would like to take advantage of his reserve commission to enter the army. A half-year later, he was made (after reinduction school) a captain, by virtue of his age. He thought that the United States would be at war within a short time, indeed, that was why he had entered. He told himself that he had no illusions about the war to come, that his stake was personal.

He had entered the army, because at the end of his recapitulation of himself, he had come to the conclusion that to justify his life, to find some meaning in it would be possible only when he faced death. He remembered Malraux's foundation in dignity. It might be necessary for him to die to find that dignity. Certainly, he thought, life and death and violent action were the fundamentals, and he would find no lie there. He had decided that it was time for him to clutch at the check, even if it were to tear apart in his hands. He had traveled the bridge from sensualism to mysticism, but he preferred it to cynicism. And in the meantime, he wondered like the rest what the feel and sound of actual bullets was like. . . .

WEXLER, APRIL 1942, THIRD NIGHT

He could just see it in the Freehold papers. . . .

Jewboy, blond Jewboy Wexler perched by the cellar window, tackling Japs with machine-gun bullets, tackling them dead, for the University of Minnesota. Swearing to himself, blond Jewboy Wexler, the farmer from Freehold,

New Jersey, the big blond tackle for the Golden Gophers firing machine-gun bullets, blocking tackling the dirty yellow team from across the tracks in Trenton, doing it for the big football team. The gun bucked away from his hand. Tearing after it, he caught the elusive runner, ran his sights on the incoming interference, hit them low with machine-gun bullets for hands, and got the ball carrier. They were a little team holding off the big team he said to himself, they were a little team, and the big team couldn't get to score.

"Take it easy," Rice, the sergeant, said to him. "You're wastin' your shots."

"Listen, Sergeant, I'm firing this gun."

A grenade splattered unsuccessfully against the outside wall. He started firing again. No half-Indian sergeant was going to tell him how to fight, he was born fighting, playing football for the University of—but he had to correct himself —for the Freehold High football team.

Outside, it had become dark, and the Japs looked like bushes, or like tackling dummies in the evening when practice was over. They were the little team, they were Brooklyn College standing off the University of Minnesota, they were Minnesota standing off the world. "Come on, you Japs, come on, you yellow-shirted bastards," he muttered. "Stop holdin', come on, start tryin' to nail me."

Every now and then he could get to see them, especially when they tried to cross the flat football field in front of the house; that was when the moon coming over the house's shoulder guard played him okay, that was when he could see the faces, that was when he could see death slapping them. It was just a spray, he was holding the garden hose on them, giving feed to the hens on the farm, making butter of the Japs. The Indian next to him, feeding, fighting quiet, not talking, he didn't like the Indian, dark, whistling, doing it like it was his business. It wasn't a business, it was a game, the most it was a business was a professional football team. Come on, you Chicago Bears, this is the Philadelphia Eagles, this is the Pittsburgh Steelers, and they're holdin' you on the three-yard line. A gun behind the other goal post tried to put its fingers in his eye. He ducked down, feeling the bullets pouring through the window, smacking against the opposite wall back of him. In the distance, he could hear guns going off, this was big, this was being fought all over the island. The machine gun kept chopping at the back wall.

"I tell you not to fire so much," the Indian said. "You spot them the window."

"Don't fire, Wexler, unless they come within a hundred yards, we can't have them hitting the gun." The captain came out of the trench, wiggled over to the window. "DaLucci, you relieve at the gun in five minutes." A sound of consent came from the dugout. "I don't like the way DaLucci's actin', Captain," the Indian said, "he's too quiet." "You're quiet yourself, Sergeant," Wexler let himself say. "Me?" Rice grunted, "I'm an Indian." The captain smiled slowly. "How many do you think are out there?" he asked. "There ain't many, Cap'n, there's just a coupla platoons." "There's more, Captain," Wexler said. He must have killed thirty of them already.

The captain looked worried. "They need this road, there ought to be more." "Yessir," the Indian said. The guns outside had become quiet, the moon making divots on the field wherever a body lay. Wexler felt caught. At home he had his field, he had the hens and the butter and eggs, he had the place outside Freehold where they played football on Sunday afternoon, the biggest toughest blond Jewboy ever to play football for Freehold High. The cellar was too small, he didn't like bein' caught here. "Yessir, it's a tough war," he said to himself. The captain took out a chocolate bar, broke it in three. They chewed slowly on it. "DaLucci," the captain said, "come up here." The Italian came up slowly, bellied over. The guns of the Japs were still quiet. They were scared quiet, Wexler thought. He focused on a few broken trees at the end of the moonlit plain. He said to himself that they looked like tackling dummies too, but they didn't. He thought they were too ragged to get away with that.

"I'm afraid the other house may be taken, men," the captain said. He separated a piece of silver foil from his teeth, and dropped it to the ground. "I need the sergeant," he said. "Father Meary obviously cannot be considered. I want one of you men to make a reconnaissance over to it. If you can get in, which I doubt, tell them we need more men. If you can't, come back, and tell me how they're making out. The most important thing is that you get back.

The radio here is shot out. Does one of you want to go?"

DaLucci scowled in the darkness. "Naw," he said. Wexler spat softly on his hands, "Why not?" he asked. "I'll make it, Captain." "But get back." He grinned: "You bet, Captain, that's one thing I'm gonna do." The Jewboy running broken-field, the Freehold papers carrying the story.

He was starting out the window, when the Indian held his arm. "Wait," he said. "They're quiet now, they're look-ing. Stay back yet." Rice fired a few random bursts. The other gun answered, crawling along the outside wall, becom-ing quiet after awhile. "All right, now," Rice said. "Keep to the shadow of the wall as long as you can. When you come to the end, I'll start firing, then run." Jewboy inched his way through the window. The air felt looser outside, and the field seemed enormous as he crawled near the wall, his face close to the ground. He felt excited, this was tough stuff. The air of Tinde was cold suddenly, he could see the trees shivering a little. He shivered too. Hell, he didn't want to be in the papers dead.

Creeping along in the shadow, the wall seemed to go for fifty yards. It was so damn light outside, why couldn't the Japs see him, he could see them. He glanced back at the house. From his angle the window was foreshortened so that he couldn't see inside. It felt very lonely out here, no interference, no tacklers, just the Japs. "This is no damn football game," he muttered to himself.

Coming to the end of the shadow, he paused, crouched into a halfback's position, waiting for the ball. If that Jap machine gunner ever saw him now, by Jesus. Jewboy Wex-ler alone in the dark, playing games for keeps. The machine gun sounded abruptly from the house, cutting white lines into the darkness. The Jap gun answered, both of them throwing blocks; he started running, there was forty yards in the clear, if they ever saw him, it would be like stepping on stunned bugs. He ran. The darkness of the bushes forty yards to the side of the house's shadow came toward him, whipped into his face. He sprawled in them, resting, feeling scared. To be putting eggs in crates now, that was all he asked.

The other house was a mile away, he had to keep off the road. What if all the men, including the captain, were killed back there while he was away, what then? He would be killed with them if he hadn't gone away, he thought. Was

Vera making out the invoices for the eggs now, he wondered, was Vera worried about the butter?

On the other side of the bushes, the gound rose and fell in gentle slopes, with enough trees sticking out of it to make it okay for him. He had to cut in back of the town somehow, he'd be caught going through it. Running quickly, from tree to tree, he headed inland. A patrol was coming by, and he stiffened behind a branch. After they passed, he felt the tightness pulsing through his legs. He had to relax; you broke a leg taking back a kick unless you were loose. If he coulda gotten to the University of Minnesota like he'd wanted, then he'd be a captain too, sittin' on his tail sendin' out the privates to see this and to see that. He crawled through some bushes. When he poked his head out the other end, it seemed like a tree was standing with its back to him, only it was no tree, it was a sentry. He lay there waiting for the man to move, but he didn't. Slowly the Jap turned around, then showed his back again. Jewboy Wexler caught in a trap. He waited there, wondering if he should make a sudden tackle. Could he get the guy before he yelled? But he couldn't get himself to do it, the legs gave out first, every good athlete got it in the legs first. Slowly, holding his body an inch from the ground, he began to edge away on hands and toes, one foot back, one hand back, the other foot back. When he was thirty yards away, he stood up in a crouch, and backed into the shadow of a tree. He wanted a cigarette. How the hell was he expected to go over a mile like this and back? In the hills, away from the ocean, a couple of machine guns were going like all hell. That must be the jungle already, he thought. The coastal road was at his right, but he'd never make it that way, that was where the Japs were fighting.

After a while he started going again, running, crawling at times, gliding from tree to tree. He felt better; this was the longest damn run any man ever made. No Minnesota back ever did this. If only they woulda given him that football scholarship, he'd be back in the cellar now, and DaLucci would be sweatin' here. The hell with the Freehold newspaper, what the hell good would that do Vera and him? They could use that Freehold newspaper for toilet paper. And he almost started giggling. It was soft paper.

He came to the top of a hill, worked his way through the tall grass, afraid to stick his head up. From the next

hill, maybe, he could see the other house. It had oughta be
away from the town, like the cellar was. He heard Japs
laughing, slid on his belly away from them. Something,
maybe it was a snake slicked across his face. He almost
yelled. When the sound of the Japs came too near, he
stopped, wondering how he was to breathe. He didn't have
a big Jewish nose, that was one help, and he blew his nose
that was another. Minnesota hadn't given him the scholarship 'cause he was Jewish, but for crise-sakes what was in a
name? He had blond hair, didn't he? He was five feet eleven,
fast, and weighed one-ninety before a shower. Jewish, hell,
in Freehold they said he played like a big Swede. Swede
Wexler, he thought, holding his breath. The Japs were passing. Swede Wexler waited, and then ran, duckwaddling
through the tall grass. At the bottom of the hill he had to
cross a stream, and his shoes started squishing. After a
while, he took them off, and held them in his hand, while
he worked his way up the hill. A butter-and-egg farmer,
what the hell kind of a life was that for Swede Wexler, he
woulda been a pro footballer by now. They'd heard of him
all around Freehold, Asbury, Long Branch, he bet Point
Pleasant even.

When he came near the top of the other hill, he got excited, he was gonna make it after all. The road and the
house oughta be on the other side, but it worried him 'cause
there was no shooting. At the top, he felt his way around
some rocks, looked down. The Japs were marching along
the road, the house seemed broken in two, he could see a
little fire in places from it.

Jewboy Wexler put his shoes on, turned around, and
started back. There wouldn't be anything for the papers
now, they paid off on touchdowns. There wouldn't be any
ads to sign and get money so the mortgage could be paid
off in ten years instead of the twenty it was amortized at.
It was easier going back, somehow. He kept telling himself
not to get sloppy, to keep blocking, or his head'd be off,
and they'd be fryin' the fat from it. He wondered what it
meant now that the other house was gone. The captain'd
know, he guessed, although the captain didn't look on the
ball either, but he supposed it was important. He kept tellin'
himself to think of Vera 'cause he might as well think of the
best friend a man had which was no dog, you could bet

your life on that, but he felt all free and easy now, not scared of being killed, and he didn't need to think of her.

Before he knew it, he was sticking his head out of the bushes, and looking at the house with its windows all filled in, and the cellar under it, where the gun still was firing. He didn't know how to get back in there, he'd have to cross the part where the moon was, and he couldn't signal them to keep the Japs' minds off him. He guessed he'd just have to wait. The guns stopped tangling with each other, and then started again. He remembered that the Japs would be busy firing. There might be a coupla them stickin' out away from the guns, and they might spot him, but he'd have to chance it. He darted across the field in the moonlight. A couple of rifles started banging at him, and then just as he hit the shadow, the machine gun changed over toward him. He scrabbled for the wall, burrowed into the right angle it made with the ground, hunching his body up, hoping they couldn't see him. He didn't have time to be scared. The damned gun kept spraying around him. They didn't know where he was. The cellar machine gun wasn't going now. They wouldn't know where the window was. He ran along the wall, dived through the window, almost knocking the gun over, and landed on the ground. The gun started going again, and he crawled up against the wall, breathing as noisy as he felt now, sort of snug against the sandbags.

"Nice goin', kid," Rice said to him. DaLucci was firing now, the captain feeding. The captain made a sign, and Rice took over the feeding. "I wonder they haven't gotten a trench mortar up yet," the captain said. Rice grunted. "They ain't many of them, they just seem to be wantin' to hold us here."

The captain kneeled beside him. "Can you talk yet?"

"Yeah," he said, trying to get control of his heaves, feeling kind of weak and tired all over.

"What happened, what's at the other house?"

"They took it, there's Japs all around, they're marchin' along the road." The captain nodded, whistling tunelessly. "That's the answer, Cap'n," Sergeant Rice said. The captain nodded again. He bent down beside him. "Oh, and say . . . Wexler, ahh . . . what was it like?"

"What?"

"Out there."

"Oh," he shrugged. "All right, I guess. Kinda tough, maybe."

It looked like the captain was going to ask him something else, but he stopped. After a while he asked, "You're sure about the house?" "Yessir," he said. He was getting control of his breath.

All of a sudden he realized that the captain had bellied over to the dugout in the middle of the floor. He was coming back with Father Meary, the two of them crawling up to the wall near the gun. "Keep firing as usual," the captain said, "there's something we have to talk over." They were all huddling around the gun emplacement. "The other house fell, and the Japs are going through on the road. They don't need this house any more. Do you all understand me?" The priest stirred a little. "Do you mean, Captain, that this is no longer an important objective?" The captain seemed to be smiling. "Yes, that's right . . . Now, they're not going to let us stay here. They don't want any little pockets left. So sooner or later they're going to bring up some small fieldpieces and blast us out of here. There's really no point in staying. We might be fighting them on the other road, but I doubt it."

"They didn't look like they was fighting," Wexler said.

"All right. Now I . . . for personal reasons," he halted. "I'm going to stay here. But since I have no right to ask your lives, any of you that wish may surrender. There's no point in heroics in all this. I will not consider it cowardice. Now which of you wants to surrender?"

The priest spoke a little nervously. "You say there's absolutely no point in remaining."

"Too doubtful a one to demand it of any of you."

Rice made a sound of impatience. "I been in tougher spots than this." The priest made a soft sound of indecision. "There will be a lot of captured men, no doubt?"

"Yes," the captain said.

"The hell with it," DaLucci said suddenly, standing up, "I'm going. You can frig this goddam war."

"You, Wexler?" the captain asked.

He didn't want to be out in the open again. If they held, maybe he'd be in the papers, maybe. . . . He didn't know what the hell to do. "I'll stay," he said slowly, before he knew it.

"All right, and you, Chaplain?"

Meary got to his feet. "The captured men will have need of me. Captured men need God perhaps . . . more." His lips were trembling. "Are any of you Catholic?" he asked. . . . "Well, God be with you anyway." DaLucci and Meary knelt by the window. "Go out with your hands up," the captain said. "Don't yell, because they won't understand you, and they may think it's a charge." The priest crossed himself. Slipping the gun to the side, Rice put his back to the wall. "So long, you bastard, DaLucci," he said. "Frig yourself," DaLucci said, his short squat form heavy with anger. They went out.

All of them watched from the window. Wexler didn't know how to figure it. He saw them pass into the light, start walking to the Japs. The moon kept catching a piece of their hands. For a moment the priest stumbled, and then went on. They had separated from each other, and walked about ten yards apart. There wasn't any sound from the Japs. They had walked across the entire field almost when the Jap gun started. DaLucci went down first, then the priest. The gun kept playing over them for a few moments.

The first thing Wexler heard was the captain saying slowly, "I never thought of that, I just didn't think of it." A yell of derision came from the Japs. Wexler grabbed the gun. "Let me at those goddam bastards, let me at them, I'll cut their goddam hides off." Rice pushed him away. "Shut up, they had it comin' to them."

"Why, you goddam Indian," Wexler said.

"Shut up, both of you!" It was the captain.

Wexler stopped. The funny thing he kept telling himself was that he didn't really feel sore, he didn't feel much at all.

A Jap soldier came crawling forward cautiously to see if any men were left. Rice bent over the gun, sighting it carefully. He pulled the trigger for just a few bursts, then ran it back and forth on the fallen soldier. He catcalled across to the Japs. "Jeez, they haven't got anything, not even flares. This ain't so bad."

The captain was silent for a few minutes. After a long while he said, "What did DaLucci do before he joined the army?"

"He was a gas-station attendant, I think," Wexler said. "I didn't get to know him very well."

"Yes, I see," the captain said.

"Huh, why sure, sir?"

"All right, start feeding the gun," the captain said to him.

The Japs were holding back now. There just wasn't anything doing. He wondered how long they had been there, maybe three hours, that was pretty long for a little team to hold off a big one. But as he thought it, there kept running something else, and he couldn't keep it back. He didn't know why it was, but he kept thinking that it was more like they were the big team and they were gettin' pushed around by the little one. He didn't know if he believed it or not, but he wasn't sure of anything. He didn't know what to think. . . .

THE CAPTAIN, APRIL 1942, FOURTH DAY 4 A.M.

. . . like men standing in line, naked, waiting to be examined. . . .

He had seen death in many forms during those three days and nights. And to the captain, waiting in the cellar now beside Wexler and the Indian, waiting for the final irrevocable attack, it seemed to him that all his life he had been waiting for his death, and now that it was approaching, there might not be any meaning extracted from it. All day and night, for three days and nights he had been seeing men fighting and dying, and perhaps it had all happened too quickly, but all he knew was that it had no emotion or meaning to him. He remembered the burnt body of a man that he had looked at for quite a time. It had seemed a terrible degradation, as if the man in burning to death had reverted to a prehistoric type. He had been blackened all over, his flesh in shriveling had given the appearance of black fur, and his features, almost burnt off, had been snubbed and shrunken, so that the man's face in death had only registered a black circle of mouth with the teeth grimacing whitely and out of place in the blackness of the ape.

It was not inconceivable to him that his own death could produce a similar violation of his flesh, and yet he felt no emotion from it. It seemed as if for the past three days, he had been numb, numb, not so much from fear, as from a voidity of sensation. Lying in the cellar, his back against a wall, he wondered how long it would be until morning when the Japanese would be able to see the window, and could release a fire through it that would kill any of them trying to answer it. Under that morning fire, he knew, would come Japanese, bellying forward across the plain outside. He wished for a cigarette, knowing he could not smoke one till morning when its light would no longer be dangerous. About him, the Indian and Wexler crouched on either side of the gun, only a small part of their helmets turning the angle of the window. "Stop moving around so much," he heard the sergeant say, then Wexler answering, "I feel itchy."

Now that the forces of his life were approaching this final result, he tried to imagine what his death would feel like, and whether at the very end there would be some all-encompassing sensation. Feeling the night throbbing about him in the dampness of the cellar he was trying to find some resonating quality, some bit of beauty that would have meaning before the final result enacted itself. In this darkness, he was trying, as desperately as his mind would allow, to plumb the content of it, and throw it up against the form of his life. His hand reached out tensely in the night. To achieve the ultimate in his death, to reach out and catch it and pin it up against himself in death—his arm relaxed. It would not be that way. Nor would it be, he thought, in terms of a common denominator, it would be no more and no less of one than a group of men standing in line naked, waiting to be examined.

Wexler stood up and walked away from the machine gun. In the darkness, the captain could only hear him, but it seemed as if he had felt his confinement, and wanted some sudden release. "Listen," Wexler said, "Sergeant! Did I ever tellya how I got to throw a pass in the Red Bank game one year?" A grunt came from the window. "You know I played guard, you don't even get to handle a football that way, but we had this play see? . . ." The sergeant flexed his feet, "Get away from the window. You never can tell when I can fire this gun."

The captain counted three cigarettes in his pocket. In two hours it might be light enough outside to smoke. Wexler was ranging the blackness with his large feet. He stumbled over something and swore indistinctly. "You see the thing was I could pass. They ain't many guards can do anything with a ball, but ya see I got these big hands. . . ." He reached the other end of the cellar, and headed back for the window, talking slowly. The captain felt a desire to make him stop. "Well, they had this play built around me, where I shift into the backfield"—he moved a few steps sideward in the dark—"making me eligible to hold the ball, see, only it don't go to me, it looks just like I'm protection for the ball carrier, like I pulled out of the line for it, so they ain't worryin' about me." His body moved tensely now—"and then after I miss a block purposely, the ball's whipped over to me, I'm eligible, see? . . ." The machine gun started suddenly from the window. "Got him," the Indian said.

"So then I pull back, hold the ball up," his arm cocked, "set to throw and . . ." The Japanese gun answered through the window. Wexler folded slowly, his arm reared back almost to the last.

The captain stood up and, then, knowing the man was dead, sat down more slowly. "I told him, the dumb bastard," the Indian muttered.

"Do you want me to feed the gun for you?" the captain asked.

"It's okay, I can handle it myself. It's kinda quiet now."

They sat there silently. By turning his head and leaning forward a little, the captain could see out the window, and he suddenly understood, now that Wexler had died, a little more what his own death would be like. He doubted if he would feel anything. It would be as casual as Wexler's, with no emotion for him. Too late, it seemed to him ridiculously clear that emotion could only come from the connotations of experience, and not from the experience itself. Things like first sex experience, if it were unexpected, violent action, death that did not come after a slow sickness, would all give no emotion when they happened. The captain, having experienced the first two, remembered that they had left him numb; the emotion was to come later in tiny quanta until a week or a year later, the remembrance of the experience would arouse a surcharge of feeling in him; at the origin, however, was only the numbness. So that his death, he knew at that moment, would come in casual form without the death orgasm, the instinct for ultimate ecstasy never to be gratified. And to anyone else, his death would be meaningless. To Cova it would be a shock, to his friends, a jar that would merely titillate them because it was expected, perhaps would mean an extra drink at some late hour. To his nation it would be a line in some newspaper, far less interesting than the line about a murdered prostitute. To anyone else . . . he couldn't think of anyone else. Perhaps someone would discover his paintings. He smiled wryly. . . .

He kept coming back to Cova. Little by little a scene was building up for him. And because he could see so much of his own shadow in it, so much of what he might have been if the war hadn't come, he let himself amplify it, not paying any attention to the scattering sounds of battle outside. . . .

He didn't know how she would find out; he supposed, he preferred to have his father called because his father would be ill-equipped for it, and because Cova listening to his stumbling would feel compelled to exhibit some emotion while listening. After she would have cradled the phone, she would go upstairs to her room and lie down to think. She would be living, he thought, in a private house, perhaps a suburb by now, sharing the rent and fornications with a woman perhaps three years older than herself.

Lying in her room, her bed would begin to feel lumpy, and in shifting her position she would begin to cry. There was so much of herself in Bowen; she would feel a little bit as if she had died too. And crying, she would begin to whisper to herself, "I feel rocky as hell, I feel rocky as hell. . . ."

There would be a ring downstairs, and she would remember that she had an appointment that night. The first impulse would be not to answer, but she didn't want to be alone; the second would be to call the date off, but that would be just too damned ostentatious. After a while, she would run downstairs, and catch the man just as he was about to go away.

"I'm sorry," she would say, "I . . . I was just sleeping a little. . . . Come in."

He would be a man of medium height with a dark sen-

sitive face. This would be—let this be his first date with her. He would be very interested in sleeping with her. They had met at a party.

"You've . . ." but he would not say, "You've been crying." He would smile sympathetically, leaving the admission or rejection to her.

She would throw her head back as if to balance the tears on her eyeballs, preparatory to absorbing them. "Oh . . . it's too stupid," she would say. "I just found out that a man I was married to died on some damn island. I used to love him."

He would say, "You must be very unhappy." His voice would be low, in good taste, calculated to serve for emergencies such as this one. Also, he would not have declared himself by the question. He would be finding out more about this woman, and if she held her husband's death in war against his civilian's bed-courtship, he would be turning her thoughts away from himself.

She would smile a little. "Oh, I've got a bad case of nostalgics" (she had coined the word once), "but they always dissolve in cointreau."

"It's difficult to get cointreau, nowadays," he would say. "Perhaps you would prefer to remain at home; our evening can wait for a week or two." He would be thinking that for this evening she would be loving her husband again.

"Oh, no, we must go out," she would say, but the false gaiety in her voice would be misunderstood by him to mean that she wanted to be alone with her rewarmed love, whereas she had made the gaiety false so that he would be indebted to her, and if during the evening she felt a letdown, no compulsion to be witty and entertaining would exist.

The man would make his fatal error here. He would say, "I know how you feel, we would hate each other. After all, while it may be a convention to mourn and stay at home, it is also one to keep one's engagements, and since you must be conventional tonight, it would be better to do what you want, which is, I think, to stay home." He would be thinking that she would remember the kindness, but even more, the insight, so that he could enact his seduction a week later when it would have a certain logical sequence, whereas on this night it would smack too much of a perversion.

She would recognize then that all protestations would only convince him the more, and so she would acquiesce, chat for a few minutes, and then close the door to go back to the empty house. Only now, wanting perhaps a little more to cry, she would not be able to, for the moment had passed, and the situation no longer would warrant it. . . .

He swallowed slowly. There was a painful saltiness in his nose, and he felt a sudden hatred for himself. It was occurring to him that he was emotionally convinced of his death, and he wondered at how far he had come to feel like this, amazed that he felt no fear for it seemed to him that the fear of death must be stronger than anything else in a man's life, and that few were the men who surmounted it. Perhaps, he thought, a few that were really religious or that believed in something hard enough to clamp down on all the other feelings, but he did not know. Perhaps to die for your country, but here the captain felt a rebellion in himself. For a long time, in his moments of reaction against his fate, he had postulated, rather than believed in, he had postulated a something to rail against. And that "something" had most often been the word America; he would feel sometimes, America has cheated me, but the phrase was uncomfortable; it sounded alien to him, made up perhaps of a self-pity he was not wise enough to realize. For although it might have been true, it was too large a word to attack; it sounded awkward, and perhaps a little cheap in the language of his logic. And yet now, he hated the word America for a moment; he felt that the wreck of his life had come out of himself to a great extent, but he felt also that America had cheated him, had taught him all the wrong things, and had offered him nothing in return. He felt that it had not been strong enough to admit its faults, that when it had made a mistake or was ashamed of something, it had yelled a little louder, and had waved the flag about a little too hard. He did not know, he wanted to believe in her, but he knew that was impossible in the hour or two that remained to him. But for some little part of him, he hoped idly that others would find something there in the next few years . . . that something would come out of the country, and that it wouldn't go hard and selfish as it always had before. But he was very doubtful of this, for he had never learned anything from America to make him feel that anything worth while would come after him. He had been told to love God, but to love God beyond the mechanical emotion of the religious ritual was for very few people; he had been told of an equality, but it was only a frame; he had been told of a morality, but finally it was not of the context of its people. . . .

When his book had come out, years before, all the critics had attacked it; they had called it cynical, and cheap, filled with an undue proportion of self-pity and glory, and he, months later, had had to agree with them that in most ways it was.

But one review hurt him terribly. There had been one part in the book that he had written honestly and sincerely; centering about one sentence that had been a summation to him of the futility about him. He was thinking of the war to come when he wrote it, and he had wondered that everybody had not seen it.

Only this review noticed it. He remembered holding it in his hand for a long time. It had read:

> There have been cynics, I suppose, less witty, bitterer and less unepigrammatically epigrammatic than Bowen Hilliard. It would be very easy to dismiss Hilliard as another misanthrope, if it were not that the man advertises himself as a sage. After deciphering his key sentence . . . which is . . . "To die in terms of a subsequent humanity is a form of emotional sophistication that may be achieved only by the people of that nation which puts its philosophy in action" . . . I have been compelled to believe that Bowen Hilliard's book would have been more accurately entitled, *The Artist in Belly-Ache Inglorious.* We have had enough rot these days. . . .

Soon he could smoke a cigarette, a last futile cigarette of distaste. And yet, amused with himself, there was a hope remaining that it would taste a little better than all the thousands preceding it. He was waiting for the dawn, wanting to see a last day, hoping too that he would feel this dawn more intensely than any that had come before. He heard the Japanese outside, firing, then the Indian answering, then silence once more. The Indian with his neat efficient motions at the gun aroused his interest. For a short while he thought of the Indian and himself in terms of "they" but he could not feel it. At last he compromised by bellying over to the window, and relieving him of the gun. . . .

THE INDIAN, APRIL 1942, FOURTH DAY 5:30 A.M.

Some guys are born to go to whorehouses. . . .

The trouble with Rice started when he was adding up his accounts. Perched by the window, his knees bent, feeling the tight roll of his bottom against the backs of his heels, he had just picked off a Jap who was trying to sneak down the side bushes, and in relaxing had thought to himself that that made fourteen he had bagged. Rice knew what he knew, he always used to think that. He knew when he had to hit a guy, and when talking would get him out of it; he knew how to tell when a whore was tired, and if you felt like talking (which wasn't often with Rice) how to pick out the right tired whore. He also knew not to think when thinking made you crazy, which is what made his thinking now so unusual.

He'd been trading bursts with the Japs every ten minutes or so, feeling it was the slack season. Naturally, he'd been fighting so long in so many places, he had gotten to the point where if he wanted to think he could do it while he fired a gun. And he had been telling himself with pride that of the Japs that had been killed, he had knocked off thirteen out of fifteen as near as he could tell. He had to admit that he'd been firing the gun more than Wexler or DaLucci, but then they'd gotten killed which'd meant no one spelled him at the gun. And he knew that your accuracy went down when you were tired. So it all balanced out, except that he couldn't figure what percentage thirteen out of fifteen was. He tried for a while to work that out, but he quit school too early at the Indian reservation in Oklahoma ("Where whores were born," he used to say sometimes), and he didn't have much luck. He was also thinking that they'd held out for pretty long, although the Japs only had one machine gun and no flares. The thing was they hadn't gotten any more guns because the main body was probably halfway to Tinde by now, he guessed.

He was estimating about how, for an afternoon and a night, they had killed off fifteen Japs to only three of theirs, and how at the very worst the last profit-and-loss would be fifteen to five. This was where the trouble came in. He stopped. He realized he'd been figuring himself in the five. That meant they got him, the Indian. It hit him that way, he hadn't figured on being killed since . . . since, Jesus, since the first World War. He'd been eighteen, and it had been in Belleau, or wasn't it? . . . All he remembered was that he'd been sick and scared, and now although there was something in his stomach, it wasn't anything like that. He felt kinda surprised almost, he just never figured it that way. With the things he'd done, the Marines in Nicaragua, Bolivia on his own, rumrunning in New Orleans, somehow he'd kinda forgotten that you stood a chance of dying too. . . . He kept wondering what it would be like.

He had felt like talking; it had been a tired whore that night. Except that when he'd been in the room with her, sitting on the soiled blanket, batting his eyes against the glare from the bulb naked-looking in that room, he hadn't been able to say much at all.

They smoked a couple of cigarettes. It wasn't that she was pretty, he hadn't found many pretty whores, but there was something about her that moved him back three years, or up ahead to what he would do if they gave him a grand out of nowhere one day, no strings attached.

Finally she said: "You're a funny guy" (one thing was she didn't use "dearie"), "you never talk much."

He blew his smoke out. "I'll tell ya somethin'." He paused. She nodded at him to go on. He felt queer. "I had a lot of girls in my day, for a long time, but none of them was amatures. I paid on the line every time."

She still nodded, still receptive. "I tried to think it out once. I ain't a good-lookin' guy, but I'm awright. I finally figured it out that I started too late. The first time was at twenty-two, New Orleans, I think."

She lay back on the bed. "That could be it, of course," she said, "but I dunno, darling, the way I see it is just that some guys are born to go to whorehouses."

He felt dumb for talkin'. "Yeah, that's it," he said, and left soon after.

For a while he was busy shooting the gun off, and that took his mind off his troubles, as shooting a gun always did, but there was something uncomfortable in the back of his head all this while, and the first lull there was, it popped back again to him that he was going to get his, come two three four hours. That was all right, of course, you didn't live forever, but at the same time, he had the damn craziest feeling thinking about death, because he just couldn't guess what it was like. He knew you didn't think any more, that was obvious, but, you . . . you just didn't do anything after that. It was just the end. He fired his gun viciously, ducking down as the return came back. That meant . . . no more. It was like wrestling trying to figure that out, only with your head.

He wanted suddenly to know why the hell he was gonna get his. He just wanted to know what it was all about. They called him Creepy Joe around the army camps, and said he knew all the answers 'cause he never asked questions. But he had to ask questions now, because he was buying something that cost a lot. He'd never asked what the fightin' was about; fightin' was his business, and you didn't ask questions if business was good, but now he kinda liked to know. The papers said Freedom, and he guessed maybe they were right because that was something they knew about, just like he knew about whores, but Freedom . . . ? Did it figure with a slug in the belly . . . he didn't know . . . and by now, he was damn sure he wanted to know. He wanted it put in words. He wasn't scared of dying, but he wanted it down on paper, some of the reasons anyway. Anyway, he wanted, that in the fifteen-to-five ledger, there would be a remark after his name. He'd never thought that way before, but he could see it now, a business ledger, all written in, like the mess sergeant used, with something after his name, THOMAS RICE, THE INDIAN.

He felt a hand tugging at his shoulder. It was the captain: "I'll take over the gun now." He crawled away, propping his back against the wall. For about ten minutes, he just sat there thinking. He shoulda known enough not to think when thinking didn't do any good, but he couldn't keep from it this time. After a while he crawled back to the machine gun. The captain hadn't fired in a long time. He fingered a couple of bullets in their jackets before he spoke to him. "It's getting light out, Captain." He felt funny, he was talking just for the talking. The captain turned toward him. "They've brought another machine gun up. They're not moving, so I haven't fired." He felt himself nodding, feeling more like talking than he had in a long time. The captain said, "I think they'll wait till it's light out, they only have twenty minutes, and they can take it safe." He saw the captain slap his breast pocket. "We'll be able to have a cigarette soon," he was saying. The Indian felt uncomfortable. "Of course, there's a chance," he said, "we might have knocked them back; maybe we got a patrol coming up or something." "Yeah, there's always a chance," the captain said to him. They were silent. He felt himself having to speak, and he couldn't understand it.

"Think they'll win this island?" he asked.

"I never thought we had a chance to keep them from winning here. They had more time to get ready."

He nodded. He could have answered that himself . . . but . . . "Do ya think we'll win the war?" he muttered suddenly.

The captain took so long in answering, he wished he hadn't asked it. "I think so," he said finally. "We're taking a licking now, but we've only been fighting four months." He went silent again. "Yes, I think so," he repeated. "We have more men and materials, and you know, our allies are pretty good."

"Yeah," Rice said. He felt balked somehow. Not knowing what to do he took out his pistol. "Well, what are we . . ." but the question was too damn lousy. "We *gotta* win, don't we?" he asked. "Yes, that's the thing," the captain said, "we're fighting because we can't lose."

He felt at his buckle. "That's all?" he asked. "Just because we can't lose? Isn't there anything else?" He felt just too damn dumb, but the questions hurt him until he got them out.

"I don't know; it's too early in the war yet," the captain said.

"Well, what about us, we're goin' to have to die, because we can't lose. . . . I don't know, I want more than that."

"That's all there is," the captain shouted, his voice going hard. "Now shut up!"

It didn't matter any more whether he talked. He saw the captain's face pulsing, and he didn't want to hear him speak. The captain got control of himself. "We're dying alone, Sergeant, that's all."

"I'm sorry, sir," he said.

They could see each other's faces by now. Across from them the bushes were beginning to change from black to green. "They'll be over very soon, Captain," he said. He just felt tired, that was all. "The trouble with you, Sergeant," the captain said, his voice drawn out thin, "is that you think it is one of man's inalienable rights to have a little idealism with his death. You wouldn't mind that, would you, Sergeant?"

"No, I don't know what. I'd like a cigarette, sir."

They lit them away from the window, cupping their hands. The captain came back and felt at the gun. "The sun's starting to show," he said. "We really ought to get the trench mortar out." As he spoke, the Jap gun fired at them again, and they both ducked. The captain peered around the side of the window. "It's going to be one hell of a sun," he said.

"Yes," the Indian answered slowly, "sometimes you want to look pretty carefully at it."

October 1942

ADVERTISEMENTS FOR MYSELF
ON THE WAY OUT

Prologue to a Long Novel

1

To be forced to admire what one instinctively hates, and to hate all which one would naturally love is the condition of our lives in these bad years, and so is the cause beneath other causes for our sickness and our death. If some of you will understand immediately what I mean, I still must think of the others who are to take the trip with me: that mob of readers whose experience of life is as narrow as it is poor, and worse if the truth be told—they are picking up this book because they have heard it is good for the bathroom and so may palliate their depression; this book! my tale of heroes and villains, murderers and suicides, orgy-masters, perverts, and passionate lovers, my lust to capture Time.

For those readers courage is required. My passion is to destroy innocence, and any of you who wish to hold to some part of that warm, almost fleshly tissue of lies, sentimentality, affectation and ignorance which the innocent consider love must be prepared instead for a dissection of the extreme, the obscene and the unsayable.

The mark of a philosopher is that he puts his name to his work, he wants his ideas to carry the connotation of the syllables (those primitive sounds) which make up the armature of his character. So, properly, I should introduce myself here, and indeed I would, if I were able, but my name eludes me and at present would slip by without meaning to you—I am virtually married to Time unless she has already divorced me (of which indigestible statement, more explanation later) and so my name alters as Time turns away from me, and it is not all that natural to explain who I am. Let it go. Only a dreary mind cannot bear mystery.

Yet I do not know if I should evade your questions. The most murderous emotions are aroused when we cannot find the word to fit the particle, and murder (in favor of which I will find some arguments) still has the disadvantage of distracting the attention. Since I wish the various intelligences who take the trip with me to finish with stimulation to their brains and sweet for their bodies, I must necessarily take into account that the duller minds among you cannot support the luxury of listening to a voice without a face unless you are handed some first approximation to my state. I will therefore suggest it is possible I am a kind of ghost, the ghost of exhausted passion—but I prefer to believe this is completely untrue. How much less disagreeable to be some breath in the caverns of the unconscious of one of the figures in this unnatural mystery, or indeed to be the consciousness brought into being by the relations and mutilations of the exceptional characters I will introduce.

Only to say this is to deny it, for if I am the creature of relationship, I must be not so much consciousness as corporeal, containing a blastopore whose nucleic proteins limn a signature, the given first half of my destiny. Yes, I must be the breath of the present-present, a point of size swimming in my unglimpsed mother's first freshets of amniotic fluid, an embryonic two-cell, me, engaging no less than the fluid consciousness of a God, His comprehension still in mine, as I believe is true of all beings not yet born but budding in the belly. So I could be an embryo eight instants old, a work of gestation away from light and noise and pain, and yet knowing more than I will ever know again because I am part of Him. (Or is it Her?)

But to step without benefit of clergy onto the moot worms of theology is to lose our ground. The dock of our embarkation is the mystery of my eye and to whom or what it belongs: am I ghost, embryo, intellect, wind of the unconscious, or some part of Him or Her or Hem or Hir?—but there it is—Hem or Hir—a bona fide clue; only the Devil would ever boast of being thus intimate with the Divinity. So, through this work, at the best of times between us, when we are even laughing together, there should remain a reservation, a polite terror that the illumination is furnished by the Prince of Darkness, and the color of my light is satanic.

Of course, I could be as easily the old house in which the

end of this story takes place (what resonances are contained in the studs, the joists, and the bowed floor planks of an old house). I could be a tree—there is a tree outside this house, an unusual maple whose bole divides into four trunks only a few hands from the ground, and whose branches in the leafless winter articulate the noble forms of the nerve paths of a brain as one might see them in the surgically drafted plates of one of those sturdy grisly nineteenth-century handbooks on medical practice. There is even a garden, a most delicate garden—we are near the sea—and the flowers in summer have that rare electric vivaciousness which comes from salt air, sandy soil, and fertilizer laced up overrich with artificial nectar and mead. Flowers have always been sinister to me when they are lovely—they seem to share the elusive promise of a woman who is beautiful and whose voice is too perfect —one never knows if she is the avatar of a dream or some masterwork of treachery, she is so different from ourselves.

If I make such a comparison, it is obviously quite unnatural to me that I should share my existence with a flower, yet I advance the hypothesis in the interest of being comprehensive, and because the possibility is perversely appealing: where better could a demon hide himself than in the vulva of a garden bloom—if some pleasure-snatcher plucks the stem (have you ever heard *that* cry of pain?) the ex-flower can poison the house before it withers away. Yes, one does well to fear plants—once, out of an ill-timed overabundance of energy and boredom I kicked over a giant mushroom. It was five inches across the head, and I could have sworn it gave a venomous cry of rage as death came to it—"You bastard," I heard it say; such a vile fate for that exceptional mushroom, skull-like in its proportions and bold in size. I was sorry. Not every mushroom grows with such lust, and I had violated a process perhaps centuries in the chain. So from fear I mention the flower as well as the tree, and while whispering that vegetative life repels me more than not, I would add my bow to nature—I could be of the ocean and the sand dunes, that primal marriage of the little stones and the vast water—I could be of them, but I hope not; certain embraces are too monumental and so become dull. To say that the oceans of the world are but one tear of God's compassion is a metaphor so excruciatingly empty that the flatulence of a celibate must have been its first wind. But to believe that God like man can suffer occasionally from diarrhea is an infectious thought which stimulates all but the churchly and the vicious.

I will leave the oceans then, I will leave the flowers and the bees and the trees, reminding you that the extraordinary can hide in the meanest maggot, and will reduce myself as an interesting speculation to the dimensions of a dog. There is a hound in this book, brought to a climactic party we are soon to talk about, a poodle dog, Standard, pedigree, A.K.C., descended by his dam from a line of Westchester champions, his sire merely certified, and like all large poodles who have gained the attention due a rich pervert, he is an incredible dog. I know him so well that I cannot evade the last hypothesis—I could be that dog, for the vision of our life which is soon to disrupt your brain is in part a dog's view: a dog has no more than to meet another dog on the street, smell the hindquarters, and know whether friendship is possible, which well may be why dogs are invariably gloomy.

Enough. It would be unseductive to boast of how I will probably travel from the consciousness of one being to the emotions of another—a house, a tree, a dog, a cop, a cannibal, all equal to my hunter's eye and promiscuous ear.

2

There is a master pimp in our presence who is a candidate for the role of hero (his rivals for your vote, a television celebrity and a psychoanalyst) and for a time some years ago, this pimp, whose name is Marion Faye, dabbled at the edges of painting (giving for excuse the observation that such study might enrich his conception of the pornographic photography by which he then was making his living). Faye was a poor painter, but he had a love affair which went on for several weeks with the form of the spiral, and it was a matter of no mean significance to him that the valve of a snail shell as seen through his microscope (Zeiss, 2,000 Deutschmarks, oil immersion, binocular eyepiece) was a spiral galaxy of horny cells whose pigmentation had the deep orange of a twilight sun. Staring into the eye of the snail valve, he would wonder what heats of emotion had breathed into its red—he was of course on

drugs at the time—and afterwards, giving his marijuana-
refreshed eyes to the whorls on the ball of his thumb and
the tips of his fingers, he found the spiral again, and he
had that thrill of fright so common to medieval alche-
mists, psychics, drug addicts, and perhaps available to a few
of you: that exquisite terror of sensing oneself at the edge
of secrets no other being has been brave enough to invade.
For there it was: the tips of the fingers were for touch,
as indeed was the snail valve (obliged to close at the lick
of danger) and so for touch were all the other natural
spirals he knew—he was by profession an accomplished
familiar to the intricate double helix in the vaginal expansion, and the other holes of women, and for that matter,
men; so he accepted the logic of his intuition: the natural
spiral, wherever it appeared, was the mark for a complex
of feeling, and if parts of the night sky disported in a
spiral, there was sensation behind them, light years of
space vibrating with sensuality and anguish, desiring . . . ?
But this was another question, too vast. Temporarily he
gave up the investigation—in truth the form of his
thought was also spiral: he would have to make that all
but circular voyage through experience before he would
come back to contemplate the spiral again.

Which perhaps is why I have chosen this way to introduce so active a man as a master pimp. If one is interested
to begin to understand one's own life, the first of the useful
axioms is that genius appears in all occupations, and as a
pimp, Marion Faye was a genius. The proof is that he made
a million dollars in a few years. Just how is a matter of such
interest that it will later concern us in great detail, for one
can explore such minutiae only by discovering the psychic
anatomy of our republic.

Good. He was a millionaire, and still young, and he
owned several houses in different parts of the country and
one in Acapulco, and he had his private plane which he
flew himself, and various cars, accouterments, servants,
jewelries, larders, and investments. Not to mention several
going businesses and the two endowed lovers who attended
him, man and woman. He had done this all in a few years,
after coming out of prison without a penny, and he was of
course not nearly satisfied, at least not at the moment I describe. Like all men who are Napoleonic in their ambitions
and wide as the Renaissance in their talents, he had instincts

about the nature of growth, a lover's sense of the moment of crisis, and he knew, perhaps as well as anyone alive, how costly is defeat when it is not soothed by greater consciousness, and how wasteful is the profit of victory when there is not the courage to employ it. So he knew the danger of inertia (if one does not grow, one must pay more for remaining the same), and for months there had been a decision he was unable to make: as had happened before, he felt his powers leaving him. His strength came from decision and action, he was religious (in a most special way to be sure), he was superstitious with the most sophisticated of superstitions, but as a practical matter he believed in the reality of Hell, and he had come to the point in his life, as he had foreseen in terror many a time, when the flux of his development, the discovery of the new beauties of his self-expression, depended on murdering a man, a particular man, perhaps as exceptional as he, a man who could hardly fail to be aware that his own development, as opposed to Marion's was also at an impasse which could be breached equally, if in the opposite direction, by the murder of Marion Faye who once had been his friend.

It was a problem, then, and one of no mean proportions. The tension to murder is as excruciating as the temptations to confess when on a torture rack. So long as one holds one's tongue the destruction of the body continues, the limbs and organs under question may be passing the last answer by which they can still recover, and if one is going to confess eventually it is wiser to do it soon, do it now, before the damage is irrevocable. So with the desire to murder. Each day we contain it a little of that murder is visited upon our bodies, the ulcers seat themselves more firmly, the liver sickens, the lungs wither, the brain bursts the most artful of our mental circuits, the heart is sapped of stamina and the testicles of juice—who knows? this may be indeed the day when the first of the exploited cells takes that independent and mysterious flip from one life into another—from the social, purposive, impoverished, and unspeakably depressing daily life of an obedient cell, to the other life, wild-life, the life of the weed or hired gun, rebel cell growing by its own laws, highwayman upon the senses, in seige to the organs, rife with orgiastic speed, the call of the beat drumming its appeal to the millions of cells, for if other-life is short, it is wild as well, and without work. Yes, to

hold murder too long is to lose the body, hasten that ir-
reversible instant when the first cell leaps upon the habit
of stale intelligence and gives itself as volunteer to the un-
formed cadres in the future legions of barbarian and bohemian.

Of course, murder is never simple for old thieves. Old
thieves have tired balls, and if Marion Faye often thought
with distant pride that he was one of the few to have
climbed beyond the killing precipice of manners, morals,
the sense of sin and the fear of germs, he knew how much
he had paid—yes, he had lost a part of his gift, he had
drained the more extraordinary pleasures of his balls, dulled
the finer knives of his brain, and left himself prey to such
inertias of exhaustion as he was experiencing in these
weeks before he sent out the invitation to the party in the
old house at Provincetown, the party which was properly
to come off in calculated murder.

3

It is time now to say a little about this house and where
it is situated. The peninsula of Cape Cod is perhaps eighty
miles long, and bent in its middle like the knotty, no longer
agreeable arm of an old man who once was strong. To the
forearm and hand of this coast is given the name of The
Upper Cape, and it is pleasant land if one's humor is
mournful—wind-swept, with barren moors, lonely dunes,
deserted ponds and stunted trees; its colors are gray and
dun and the foliage is a dull green. Off the arterial highway
with its savage excremental architecture of gas stations,
chromium-paneled diners, souvenir traps, fruit stands,
motels, blinker lights, salt-eroded billboards, all in cruel
vision-blunting pigments, in contrast to this arterial highway garish in its petrifactions of the overextended American will, the side roads are quiet, hardly more than lanes,
with small mouse-gray salt-box houses inhabited for the
most part by retired Protestants, decent, lean, spare and
stingy, gray themselves for the most part with a mouse
gray.

There is no excess of life in the fall and winter, and it
is country which can be recommended for the solitary—
the lonely walks on sandy trails pass by cranberry bogs
whose thorny undergrowth is violet in color against the

lavender hues of the dunes when the sky is gray. Near Provincetown there are a few miles of empty sand between the bay and the ocean which have the sweep of the desert—the dunes rise into small hills and fall away to valleys where one could believe oneself lost in the Sahara—I have heard of people who wandered about in circles over one dune and down another, never reaching the ocean and never finding the bay, at least not for hours. There are few places on the eastern seaboard where one could bury a man as easily and leave one's chances so to nature, for the wind could leave the corpse under twenty feet of fill, or as easily could discover the cadaver before the cells were cold.

Beyond this desert, at the tip of the Cape, in the palm of the almost closed hand, is one of the last great fishing villages of the world, the place called Provincetown, in winter 3,000 population I suppose, its situation one of the most easterly promontories of the Atlantic coast. Three miles long and two streets wide, the town curls around the bay on the skin of the palm, a gaudy run with Mediterranean slashes of color, crowded steep-pitched roofs, fishing piers and fishing boats whose stench of mackerel and gasoline is as aphrodisiac to the sensuous nose as the clean bar-whisky smell of a nightclub where call girls congregate.

It was in Provincetown the Puritans landed and held to a starving bivouac for three months before they broke the encampment and moved on to Plymouth Rock. They were without food and besides there was the spiral to wear them down: the Cape from the wrist to the fingers curls like a snail shell, the harbor an eye of water in the center, and one's sense of direction is forever confused. Without looking at the sun one could not point across the bay in the proper direction to Boston, Portugal, or the shores of Barbary. It is a place which defies one's nose for longitude and latitude, a cartographer's despair and a Puritan's as well. (The character of narrow intense faith is rectilinear in conception, which is why the clitorine cove in the façade of most New England churches is triangular or ice-pick steeple in its form rather than obeying the feminine Catholic arch of almost equally narrow Gothic faiths.)

The house Marion purchased was on a sand dune behind the last hill overlooking the town, and it was isolated, especially in fall and winter, reached by a sandy road

which dipped down one dune and up another to give a
view of rolling furze, rain water ponds, and the ocean and
beach of the back shore. In bad weather the wind was a
phenomenon, a New England wind of the lost narrow faiths
which slashed through open doors, tempted shutters loose
from their catch and banged them through the night,
vibrated every small pane in every Cape Cod window and
came soughing out of the sky with the cries of storm water
in its vaults—on such nights the hundred years of the
house were alive with every murderous sleep it had ever
suffered: it was the kind of house in which the dogs
barked insanely in bad weather, and the nurse could not
rest, and the baby awoke in hysterical terror at one in the
morning while the mother would feel dread at the hundred
rages of her husband restless beside her in marriage sleep,
and the house shifted and swayed to the wind like a ship
in North Atlantic seas, yes it seemed to contain every
emotion which had died a frustrated death in its rooms
and walls through a hundred New England winters, each
ghost of emotion waiting to seize the storm feelings of
the present; it was a house which had the capacity to set
free, one upon the other, dank sore-rotted assassins in the
dungeons of a family's character. A storm at the wrong
time came on with the horror that this was the night—
and indeed there had been one killing there, an unex-
plained nineteenth-century crime, an old ship captain's
widow who had worn a rectangular trough in the planks
in the widow's walk at the ridgepole center of the steep
roof. She was found dead on a late February night after
three days of rain, the wind howling like a wounded shrew.

Now I know it is not in the mode of our pompous
obliteration-haunted years to encourage such pathetic fal-
lacies as the animism of the wind and an old house, but
since (be I ghost, *geist*, demiurge, dog, bud, flower, tree,
house, or some lost way-station of the divine, looking for
my mooring in the labial tortures and languors of words)
be I whatever, it must be evident that I am existentialist
and would propose that when the wind carries a cry which
is meaningful to human ears, it is simpler to believe the
wind shares with us some part of the emotion of Being
than that the mysteries of a hurricane's rising murmur
reduce to no more than the random collision of insensate
molecules. Yes, if I were to meet that saint with the body

of an ox, St. Thomas Aquinas, a gentleman with whom I agree about very little, I would still be obliged to nod in obligation to his exceptional phrase, "the authority of the senses," exactly because I now feel the frustration of a wind which knows so much and can tell your ears so little. As our century moves toward its death, and the death of all of us, so our senses die first, and who has ears to hear the wind when the smoke of mutual hatred is thick on commuter trains, and the subway rails of an evening's television batter into stupidity the sense of the sensual, leaving us null and dumb to the almost ineffable sounds which touch beyond the vanity, the will, the force and the imprisonment of the ego, grim and God-murdering ego, champion of the practical, peasant divinity of the Reformation, that Faustian burgher who built our mills of steel on the stern, the palpable, and the self-evident notion that through a point only one line can be drawn parallel to a given line, when already we are traveling through the non-Euclidean present of space-time. Sooner than we think, lo, the line parallel to the given line will prove to be nothing other than the same line once around the route in the expanding spiral of Being.

And as yet I have said hardly a word about Time.

4

But if through a given point, a line is drawn parallel to a given line, and proves to be nothing other than the same line, why then we have abstracted a first theorem on the nature of Time: that lines in parallel represent a function of the natural unwinding of Time (its onanistic tracings) when Time left to its own resources is excited into action neither by murder nor love, and so remains in step to the twitching of a clock. Such is passive Time, Time on its way to death; but Time as growth, Time as the excitations and chilling stimulations of murder, Time as the tropical envelopments of love (even if murder is lusty in the chest and love a cold sweat on the hip), Time is then the hard of a hoodlum or the bitch on her back looking for the lover whose rhythm will move her to the future.

But this conjunction is too soon complex and blurs the attention—let us leave it, let us fall away again to the

cold palpable house of Marion Faye in the back sands of
Provincetown, this sea-salted building which first gave me
the thesis that houses are polar in their nature, tending to
be boudoirs or churches. This purchase, if we are to agree
in what we see, was a church of a house with an enormous
two-story cathedral of a living room in dark overstained
walnut, the dining room, kitchen, pantry and servant quar-
ters built into what had been the cellar, and the bedrooms,
studies, studios, and sun rooms clustered like white-
guanoed barnacles, cubicles of rooms all over the top
sides of this two-story chapel with its Gothic arched
windows and sombre light. Marion Faye bought it in the
hour he saw it—it was a bargain—so big, so chill, so impractical—one had to go down to the cellar to make a
sandwich—so gloomy, so sonorous, so sepulchral that it
was church for him, and all his other houses (with the
exception of the town house, a complex affair) were no
more than boudoirs for his pleasure, doll houses in liege
to the attractive childhood he had never spent except for
some rare bitch-perfumed hours with his mother.

Yes, this was a house for rare occasions, and he visited it
seldom, and never in summer when Provincetown was a
whore's trunk of frying hot dogs, boat excursionists from
Boston, battalions of the gay and regiments of the hip—
he saved it for rare weekends in fall and winter, and so far
as most people knew, it was not even his house—he had
given it on virtually permanent loan to the most extraordinary of his former call girls, a tall dignified Negress with
a velvet sensuality who had made her fortune in company
with Marion, and now—her various investments concealed
—was a rich hostess of no small reputation in many parts
of New York, her parties indeed so well run that her net of
fine jazz captured the best of intellectual stimulation—what
little there was in that dying electric city. This Negress,
who had through her career a series of names (the last, by
which people now knew her, being Cara Beauchamp) had
found in herself a set of exquisitely parallel personalities
like hand-worked nesting tables, and so had avoided the
hermetic fate of many call girls and almost all prostitutes—
she had dissolved that cyst of character, that prison of
nonperceptive muscles which maroons even a high-grade
whore in self-pity, hysteria, and loathing for her material.
No, this one was fluid, she had a touch of accomodation

for all perverse duties, blown into a not uncool flame by
her fortune in studying with a master. So she was capable
of using her encyclopedic knowledge of the colliding con-
gesting rhythms in the bodies of the strangers she met;
and the shyest poor parcel of a man, distinguished physicist
let us say, ashy, halfway to the grave, with a dull gray
suit and black scuffed shoes dulled to gray, and a pallor of
face whose equivocal good health was yellow, and whose
oncoming death was gray, was capable still of appealing
to her: somewhere in his habit-haunted body and far-
departed mind, somewhere in his racked frame which had
all the animal magnetism of a catatonic worm (chill and
bitter-smelling in its parts) there was a piston of will which
would (all whore-patience and art properly applied) give
her a memorable night even if the poor will-driven gentleman were half into the grave afterward with the outrage
to his sedantary heart. So here was a man who could give
her a furious pleasure, for an evening at least, and therefore meeting him at the door to her party, accepting the introduction from her good friend and favorite psychoanalyst
(who will become for us a figure of obsessive interest later
on) (he had introduced the physicist as an old college
friend), she dipped into her enormous reserves of relaxed
sensuous attention, took an immediate plot of the physicist's
clang-riddled nerves, and came back with a tight formal
smile and the suggestion of a feminine will-driven tic at
the corner of her own eye (if she thus momentarily de-
based her beauty, she was seizing the opportunity to relax
the muscles of her eye and make a friend—on the whole
a profit for our hostess). Indeed she succeeded; the
physicist liked her—he liked her even more when late in
the evening and pleasantly if quietly—in his way—hysterically drunk with the blending of the tongues, the reentrate
cool jazz of the combination for the night—four homo-
sexual Negroes in horn-rimmed glasses—and the murderous
ambiguities of such varied honey-wild pussy as paraded at
that party, the physicist had the fair opportunity to discuss
physics with the remarkable knife-eyed intelligence of the
face in *café au lait* who had greeted him at the door. I
choose their conversation to repeat because it is essential
to our mystery, and if you find it bizarre you must recognize that we hover at the edge of an orgy of language, the
nihilism of meaning fair upon us.

"Isn't modern physics to the square side?" she asked of him.

A true language of indeterminate functions, he was thinking, an expression of the off-phase waves of the Negro masses. "Oh, no not at all, not really," he said. "After all, Einstein was no square."

"I could die that he is dead—so hoped to meet that man," Cara Beauchamp said, "he was hip—a funny man." She sighed for the dead. "But, like I mean, *procedurally*— aren't you physicists nowhere with Time?"

"Nowhere—the philosophical groundwork is lacking I suppose."

"Yes, you don't make the scene." She restrained her force and added softly, "Like Time is when you connect."

"It doesn't exist in between?" He had answered easily, pleased at how well he had picked up this contextual field, but then he repeated it, "Time does not exist when it makes no . . . connections?" Perhaps he was too drunk, but there was an old physicist's terror in the beauty of the thought. My God, maybe she's on to something, he was thinking.

"Well, it don't exist, and yet it does."

"Time rests as potential?" he asked, excitement in his dry sad voice, "rests there until the gap is jumped to Time dynamic."

"Yeah—potential and dynamic—that's Time. It dies if it don't connect," and for an instant she was as fond of him as a mother learning from her child. For the rest of her life she had two new words, and what words they were. Through all her unconscious were flexings of cellular pleasure—so much of her experience was rushing to the higher plateau of more precise language.

Actually she had been not altogether inspired in this conversation. She still had the masculine mind of a whore or a hostess—she was a businessman—she searched for synthesis, the big view, and her ideas on Time had come from Marion. Finally she was a salesman—she cannibalized the salvageable from the junk of old conversations to put together some speed for the pitch of her conversation.

She could hardly have done otherwise. She came from a poor Harlem family, late-migrated to New York from the North Georgia line, and her mother had run a cheap Georgia brothel (three girls) and sold heroin in New York until the arithmetic of cutting the ounces wore her down.

Cara was the first child in the family to be able to read and write with less difficulty than it took to load a trailer truck. Yet she now had the pride that they all came to her parties, the hothouse haul from Madison Avenue, advertising men and television people laughing at homey house jokes about the sick, curling themselves around a Martini or a model like ivy which slides over ubiquitously from vertical support to vertical support; there was the subtle cream of Negro entertainers from certain particular bistros at the moment not out of favor with Cara Beauchamp, there was a sprinkling from the theatre (those flamboyant timid people), there was a gossip columnist who exercised the discipline not to print a word of what he saw, one or two of the most overrated and/or berated young writers in America would be there, and one fashion photographer, not to mention the pads of Harlem and the cellars of the Village, painters (a growing collection of Abstract Expressionists on her walls), pimps and pushers (those who had proved the most talented of her childhood companions), musicians, a labor leader (yes, there was one) and a banker. It had taken her months but a lawyer who was a friend had induced him to come, and Cara found enough in common to draw him back—her ideas about the personality of those investors with some credit rating whom an exurban bank, proud of its personal touch, might allow to kite a check for twenty-four hours so intrigued the banker as a merger of psychological nuance with fiduciary practice that he returned once or twice. Yes, there was a horde: movie stars who left early, promoters, producers, occasional professional athletes, surgeons, psychiatrists, councillors, pot-heads (discreet to be sure), hoodlums (who could contain themselves), college girls, poetesses . . . the apocryphal story was of her middle-aged Irish elevator operator who became so used to her odd visitors that even a plump Episcopalian prep school instructor, wearing his go-to-New-York homburg, hand in hand with a sloe-eyed Arab boy who looked like an untamed pet on the prowl from the Casbah gave the elevator man no pause: only a brace of bull-dykers ever did him in—a famous actress in a sailor's peajacket and a gargantuan blonde in pink mink went up together sipping away from long platinum cigarette holders at sticks of Turkish hashish until the smell of sugar and death made the elevator operator so high with the smoke of contact that he was as stone on the return down, and for the first time in thirteen years he dug into the hanging of his cage and floated it on loverly skill to the lobby with the awesome anticipatory joy of the first lunar explorer to kiss the tail of his rocket onto the acned skin of the moon.

So, there it was, the home of Cara Beauchamp, a ten-room co-operative apartment and circus overlooking the East River of the fifties, with a collection of guests almost every Saturday night whose intellectual and physical connections were accelerating Time, and weighting the charge of future acceleration. No wonder that Cara gave it up for a month each year and disappeared into Provincetown where she had nothing more than a few close friends and entertainers to visit out the nights in Marion Faye's private church. Yes, she needed her *schule* as she called it, and she liked the surf-soothing hurdy-gurdy of this fishing town so poorly considered for even her social purposes that hardly anyone she knew was found there.

But I must interrupt, for one pretense I can maintain no longer. I notice that I wander back and forth, speak of the pages which follow, and yet, even as I have the illusion that I put words together at a desk, and the little actions I describe have already happened to me, or to others, still I do not know who I am nor where I am, nor even if literally I write. Yet, just so soon as I suggest that I am without particular embodiment I feel bubbles of laughter at the peculiar present tense of my consciousness which sees into the past, is recovering the future, and yet does neither, for perhaps I scramble the order of Time in order to retrieve the order of form from what is formless and yet over-real. Like the easily distractible feather of attention in the gales of infancy, I move from dread to light amusement to metaphysical certainty, and yet away again as if no one is so real to me as the consciousness which leads me now, but for a moment probably, to the breath of my narrative, and I feel certain—I know not exactly why—that it was after this party, after the conversation between Cara Beauchamp and the physicist, that Marion called for the proper tuition to his instruction and made his demand: Cara was to give a weekend party in Provincetown for a select two dozen from their acquaintance, the guests to be flown up and back by chartered plane, and this in the middle of November when the New York season was on, and the weather in Provincetown was bound to be bad.

"Marion," she had answered, "explain what you're doing."

His extraordinary face (one of the handsomest cleanest most sensual faces ever cut from a block of boyish ice) smiled back in arch thought at her. "I feel in the mood for a party that will go on for a while." Then he yawned, and his groin in remonstrance for this thespian's triumph of the casual, gave him a cruel pinch of a grip. He was empty again, the charge was down, he was moving into the late middle-age of some men's middle-thirties, a Dorian Gray whose secret portrait was fleshed within, painted by the outrages he had exacted of a hundred thousand nerves. He knew the prescription to reverse the process on the portrait, it was the last of the nostrums and it had worked once before; it was murder. Brave murder. Brave murder gave the charge of the man one killed. Time potential and Time dynamic—it was the grand connection, and the dead man's Time became one's own Time, his energies regenerated the dead circuits of one's own empty-balled Time, and one moved away with greater strength, new nerves and a heavier burden. For the balance (that natural grasp of moral justice which the old murder-tempted God still retained—should one hope so?) would be laden even more on the side of Hell, and Marion knew what would await him in Hell, the onanisms of connectionless Time, the misery of the lone chance in one out of the billion of billions to be born again. Hell, where his nerves (those advance intimations of a flesh-terrifying fire, electric in its cold) would unwind their unspeakable tension with the infinite slowness of nerves become Time in its death, the spiral spinning a blind spider's path, the dreams collapsed, the empire lost, and the fate of the world as well. That was the worst; that was his vanity; that he alone held the vision to save the world—if he failed, his agony would be all the greater for what a rage would be the rage of God. "Am I ready to die?" he asked, listening to the answer the portrait might give him, and the portrait said *no* with a murmur of dread. The balance of his deeds was dark to Marion, and from the God-like eye with which he contemplated himself he knew he was still not Godly enough—it was beyond his vision whether the force of his life upon others had accelerated new love into the agonized fatigues of Time, or had worn Time closer to her hag-ridden dreams of the destiny that failed because it arrived too late, of the new conception which never reached the womb.

5

The invitations went out, were accepted by almost every-one, the plane was chartered—two flights proved necessary —and the party took place. It is with some hesitation, and the awareness I have betrayed certain premises of your interest, that I must now confess I will not be able to describe this party in rousing detail until we have taken a wide and still unforeseeable circuit of the past. Indeed, it would probably be a disservice of the first order to insert ourselves too brusquely into the dance of deceptions, seductions, perversions and passions which the party whipped into being, the riot of new relationship an un-lashed acceleration of the Time of the ladies and gentlemen present. To be successful a party must become more than was intended for it, and I can give you the mean content-ment that by my measurement the party was not boring: it had an artist's assortment of those contradictory and varied categories of people who made up the obdurate materials of new sociological alloy in the heat-forge of a ball at Cara Beauchamp's. What gave this party an added attraction, an unconscious verve, was that there were guests who were not altogether what they appeared to be, a Russian spy for one, avid to snap up the friendship of our physicist, a spy of such importance that an agent of the FBI was also present, each of these gentlemen carefully furnished with a false life which was not his own. To com-plicate matters, there were two other operators with port-folio from the police: one, a narcotics agent, unfortunately addicted himself; another from the vice squad of New York City—what completed the circle was that the detec-tive from the vice squad believed himself close on the proof that Marion Faye had murdered another detective from the vice squad some years before, which in fact was true, but what was unknown to any of these policemen (although the agent from the FBI smelled hints of the possibility) was that the Russian spy, suffering from the mitotic tension latent in the psyche of all spies, had not been content with a double life, but indeed had divided a part of himself again; certain of his more desperate and unprofessional activities in this country had spilled him into the broth of blackmail which nourished the vice squad detective who had been killed; Marion, in taking care of this precise act, had discovered the profession of the spy and so was able to use him for purposes which were by now related to his program for the party—if all of this seems complicated, I can only say that it is but a super-ficial counterfeit of the real complexities which involved a dozen other guests as well, including Shawn Sergius (born perhaps as Sergius O'Shaugnessy), the only creative personality ever to dominate television, and Dr. Joyce, the psychoanalyst, who had become so overextended beyond his humane means, and had so compromised his career, his profession, and his intimate honor that he was contemplating suicide long before he came to the party.

Indeed a suicide did take place (I do not yet know whether it was the doctor), it was followed by murder, a murder inflamed into fury by exactly that suicide, the suicide preceded by an orgy, the orgy by a series of communions in the act of coitus, both natural and illegal, by sodomists who dictated their characters upon weaker flesh, and copulations which failed as well as fornications which captured pure smell of the fact and left the lovers fluxed with the rhythms and reflexes of one another. It was a ball. There were two dead bodies when all was done, and on one of them the town police found a notebook which contained a list, a peculiar list, for it included everyone, and yet there were more items on the list than people present, and titles applicable to more than one, as if some of the guests contained several categories within themselves. I give it as it was scribbled down, a most appetizing menu:

a queer
a cop
a crook

a Negro

a war hero
a movie star

an athlete
a dope addict
a socialite

a fisherman
an analyst
a call girl

a whore
a businessman
a mother
a father

a child
a sibling
a television entertainer
a politician

a writer
a painter
a jazzman
a rapist

a Timeless wonder (originally a man but altered to a
        facsimile of woman)

(There was a line drawn here)

a physicist
a doctor

a taxicab driver
an assembly-line worker
a poodle

a police dog
a boxer
servants

(and another line drawn here)

a ghost (God?) (from the hole—he?)
a house
a tree
a pact
a cemetery

a bug
a flower
a rat
a cow
a horse

an insane man

a storm
a plane
an executioner

a bullfighter

One could do worse than to read this list again. I wonder if in the history of our republic there has been a party equal in montage: a movie star and a rat, a rapist and a war hero, a psychoanalyst and a call girl, poodle and assembly-line worker, child and sibling, an executioner and a ghost, a cemetery and a television entertainer; yes, it is like one of those new games which trap psychology and sociology in a three-dollar cardboard box—"Theatre" it could be called, for one chooses one's role: be a whore, a physicist, a jazz musician, a queer—how dreary is our republic that so few people would buy the game.

A bloody aye! What is to be said of the dead body? How extraordinary a man—if it was a man—to compile such a schedule of personality when he must have known how close he was himself to being taken to the cleaners'—that quick phrase which contains the notion that death purifies.

But death does not purify says my Reason, death dissipates: our consciousness radiates away from ourselves as the cellves deteriorate (forgive the pun, but we speak of death), we slip away—wastefully, unheard but for the night air, our emotions, sneaks, smells, terrors, titillations, thoughts, projects, plans, and—if we have died too late— the dull blanketing gas of our boredom all enter the air, are breathed by others and exhaled away again—perhaps we have influenced the million light years of their imagination by a millimeter. The fats, the blood, the muscles and the bone sink into the earth again (if we are so fortunate as not to stifle in a deluxe hermetic crypt) yes, with the pores of a pinewood box, we give of our poor soured flesh to the wistful cemetery grass—in a century or two perhaps they will let the cows enter there to eat and make the milk and give the meat which will permit one distant relative of a molecule, ten hundred dynasties of family removed, to slip into a human body again. A few of our cells may make the transmigration from our body, which is gone, to the body of another—all that was us reduced to a molecule whose minor deviations from the classical form of the giant protein chain recapture (as do all deviations from classical form) some wry shrunken ion's head of the contradictions and possibilities which were once a man, general of the armies of his cells, Deus to his body-universe.

And is that all? a sacred cow ("I dig the Hindu bit," said Marion once) our best poor bridge to make it back, no matter how cruelly reduced, to the life of those beings who have the power—all too unconsciously—to shift the changing beat of Time? Or is there more?

And if I say I think there is, I turn the key into the category of my own secret, for as some of you may have sensed by now, the list I offered up to your amusement is from me, and I am, oh yes, now I know who I am or was, I am the dead man on the floor, for so I am, yes (what a pure moment of grief at all that has not been done), I am in the endless deliberate instant of the vision given by death, the million dying spasms of the radiating consciousness of words, this last of me, wailing within, turbulent with the terror that I no longer know where I am, nor if there are voices to hear me and answer back. I am off finally, departed on the demented journey whose first echoes I knew in those overpromiscuous moments of malice, license, promise and horror at the heart of a cocktail party when, too drunk with the knowledge of what courage was de-

manded of me, and what little I had, I used to close my
eyes, sitting in the saviorship of a chair, and I would give
up the ghost of ego-erect will, and let the vertigo of the
liquors suck me away, a far long way in those few instances
when I was spinning out with a rapidity to match the salac-
ious pace of our revolving earth, and I was one with something other until the wife or the mistress or whichever
latest embodiment of the royal bitch was at my elbow,
nudging me back, feminine fingers of fury at spineless
disappearing man wrenching me with procreative determination clean up to the living so I would hear:

"Are you all right?"

"I was thinking of something," I would say, "and I like
to think with my eyes closed," but that was the lie of ap-
pearances to share between us, a bread of false flour,
forcibly refreshing me back to my determinations, back to
the party after the long swoon away.

But now I go, the vortex does not stop, the winds of the
whirlpool—God's gyre again?—are heavy with consequence, and I sink or do I fly? all vectors gone, while in
my center, clear as the icy eye of cocaine, I race toward a
point of judgment, my courage and cowardice (my masculine thrust and retreat from the avaricious energy-plucking
hairy old grotto of Time) trailing behind me in that comet
of connotations which is the past topologically reversed by
the vision of *now,* as if in recovering the past I am chas-
ing after the future, so that the past, the net of the name-
giving surface-perceiving past, is my future again, and I
go out into the past, into the trail of the cold eye of past
relationship, the eye of my I at home in the object-filled
chaos of any ego I choose, at least for this short while between the stirrup and the ground, for in an instant—will
it be eternally long? like some cell at the crisis of its cellvish
destiny, I race into the midnight mind, the dream-haunted
determinations of that God of whom I was a part, and will
He choose me to be born again? have I proven one of his
best? am I embryo in some belly of the divisible feminine
Time, or is the journey yet to make? Or worst of all am I?
—and the cry which is without sound shrieks in my ears—
am I already on the way out? a fetor of God's brown
sausage in His time of diarrhea, oozing and sucking and
bleating like a fecal puppy about to pass away past the
last pinch of the divine sphincter with only the toilet of

Time, oldest hag of them all, to spin me away into the spiral of star-lit empty waters.

So I approach Him, if I have not already lost Him, God, in His destiny, in which He may succeed, or tragically fail, for God like Us suffers the ambition to make a destiny more extraordinary than was conceived for Him, yes God is like Me, only more so.

Unless—spinning instead through the dark of some inner Space—the winds are icy here—I do no more than delude myself, fall back into that hopeless odyssey where libido never lingers, and my nature is nothing other than to search for the Devil while I carry with me the minds of some of you.

PART THREE

Poor Kids

THE GREATEST THING
IN THE WORLD

Inside, out of the rain, the lunch wagon was hot and sticky. Al Groot stopped in front of the doorway, wiped his hands and wrung his hat out, and scuffed his shoes against the dirt-brown mat. He stood there, a small, old, wrinkled boy of eighteen or nineteen, with round beady eyes that seemed incapable of looking at you unless you were in back of him. He stopped at the door and waited, not sure of his reception, examining the place carefully, as if he might have need of this knowledge soon after. It was a little fancier than the ordinary lunchroom, having dark, old wood booths at the left that fronted the sharp, glittering stools and counter of well-polished chromium. A clock on the wall showed that it was after ten, which might have explained why the place was almost empty. There was no one at the counter and the few truck drivers, sprawled out on two adjoining booths to catch a late dinner, were tired, and very quiet, engrossed only in their sandwiches and hamburgers. Only one man was left behind the counter, and he was carefully cleaning the grease from the frank-furter griddle, with the slow motions of a man who has a great deal of time on his hands and is desperately afraid of finishing his work, to face the prospect of empty tables and silent people. He looked at Al, uncertain for a moment how to take him, and then he turned back to the griddle and gave it a last studious wipe. He spoke, without looking up, but his tone was friendly.

"Hi," he said.

Al said hello, watching the man scrape some crumblings off.

"It's a hell of a night, ain't it?" the counterman asked.

"Lousy."

"It sure is. Guess we needed it," he said. "The crops are hit bad when it don't rain enough."

"Sure," said Al. "Look, what does coffee and doughnuts cost?"

"Ten."

"Two doughnuts?"

"That's it."

"Uh-huh," said Al. "Could you let me have one doughnut and half a cup of coffee for five cents? I ain't got but a
nickel."

"I don't know," he said. "I could, but why should I?"

"I ain't had nothing to eat today," Al pleaded. "Come
on."

The man looked up. Al sucked expertly on his cheeks,
just pulling them in enough to make it look good.

"I guess you could stand it. Only, pay me now."

Al reached into his pocket, and tenderly extracted a
nickel from two halves of a dollar bill. He finished over
one-third of the doughnut in the first bite, and realizing
how extravagant he had been, he took a small begrudging
sip of the coffee.

"Nice place," he said.

"I like it," the man said.

"You own it?"

"You're damn right, buddy. I worked to get this place.
It's all mine. You don't find me giving anything away on it.
Every cup of coffee a guy drinks feeds me too."

"Top of the world," Al said.

"Nyahr," he answered bitterly. "Lot of good it does me.
You see anybody in here? You see me clicking the cash
register? The hell you do."

Al was thinking of how tough his luck was that the
truck drivers should be uniformed, which was as good as
a NO RIDER sign. He grinned sympathetically at the owner,
trying to look as wet as he could.

"Boy," he said. "I sure am stuck."

"Been hitching, huh?"

"Yeah, walked the last three miles, ever since it started
to rain."

"Must be kind of tough."

"Sure, I figure I won't be able to sleep if it don't stop
raining. That was my last nickel. Say, look, you wouldn't
have a job for me?" he said stupidly.

"What'll I do, watch you work?"

"Then let me sleep here tonight. It won't cost you nothing."

"I don't run a flophouse."

"Skip it, forget it," Al said. "Only let me stay here a while to dry off. When somebody comes in, maybe they'll give me a ride."

"Stay," he said. "I have such a fancy trade. New chromium, brass fixtures. Ahhhhr."

Al slipped off the stool and sat down at a table in the rear, out of sight of the counterman. He slouched down against the side of the booth and picked up a menu, supported between the salt and pepper shakers, looking at it interestedly, but past all craving or desire. He thought that it had been almost a year since he had had a steak. He tried to remember what it tasted like, but his memory failed, and to distract him from that tantalizing picture he started examining the spelling on the sheet, guessing at a word first, then seeing how close he had been. Another company truck driver had come in, and Al shot a quick look back to see where the owner was. Finding him up front, almost out of sight, he quickly picked up the ketchup bottle and shook large gobs of it into his mouth as fast as he could get it out. It burned and stung inside his stomach, and he kept blowing, trying to cool his mouth. Noticing a few drops on the table, he took a paper napkin, and squeezed them over to the edge, where they hung, ready to fall. He ran his little finger along underneath, gathering them up, and catching the drops in his mouth as they dripped off.

He felt for the split dollar bill, and fingered it. This time, he thought, it was really his last. Once, three months ago, he had five dollars. He thought back and tried to remember how he had gotten it. It was very vague, and he wondered whether he had stolen it or not. The image of five separate bills, and all that he could do with them, hit him then with all its beauty and impossibility. He thought of cigarettes, and a meal, and a clean woman in a good place, and new soles to his shoes, but most of all he thought of the soft leathery feel of money, and the tight wad it made in his pants. "By God," he said thickly, "there's nothing like it. You can't beat it. If I just had five dollars again."

He withdrew his hand, taking the two pieces out, smoothing them lovingly on the table. He considered breaking the bill for another doughnut, but he knew he couldn't. It was the last thing between him and . . . He stopped, realizing that he had passed the last thing—there was no "and." Still, he did not think any more of spending this last bill. Tomorrow or tonight he would be in Chicago, and he could find something to eat for a day or two. He might even pick up half a buck by mooching. In the meantime he felt hungry. He stayed in the booth, staring at the end wall, and dreaming of his one-time hoard.

Three men came in to eat. Al saw them hesitate at the door, wondering whether to eat in a booth or at the counter.

"Take a booth," one said.

Al looked at them. This might be a ride, he thought. He waited until they had started eating, and then he went over to them, hitching at his faded grey-blue dungarees.

"Hi, sports," he said.

"Hello, sweet-face," one of them said.

"They call me Al Groot."

"His father's name was Groot," said one of them turning to the others.

"I ain't asking for any dough."

They eased up a little. "Boy, you sure ain't, sweet-face," one of them said. "Sit down, sit down," he said. "My name's Cataract, account of my eye, it's no good, and this here is Pickles, and this is Cousin."

They all looked alike.

"I guess you know what I want," Al said.

"Ride?"

"Yeah, where you going?"

"Chicago."

"Start warming the seat up for me," Al said.

They grinned, and continued eating. Al watched Cataract go to work on a hamburger. He held it between thick, greased-stained fingers that dug into it, much as they might have sunk into a woman. He swallowed a large piece, slobbering a little, and slapping his tongue noisily against the roof of his mouth as he ate. Al watched him, fascinated. Wild thoughts of seizing the hamburger, and fighting the man for it, devilled him. He moved his head, in time to Cataract's jaws, and he felt madly frustrated as Cataract dropped the last bit into his mouth. Cataract lit a cigarette, and exhaled noisily, with a little belch of content.

"Jesus Christ," Al whispered.

He turned his attention to the other two, and watched them eat each piece down to the very bitter end. He hated them, and felt sick.

"Let's go," shouted Pickles. "Come on, sweet-face."

The car was an old Auburn sedan, with a short, humped-up body. Al sat in back with Cataract; Cousin was driving. Cataract took out a pack of Luckies, and passed them around. Al took the pack, and fumbled with it, acting as if he were having trouble extracting a cigarette. When he handed it back, he had a bonus of two more cuddled next to his dollar bill.

"Where you from?" Pickles asked.

"Easton," Al said. "It's in Pennsy."

Cataract rolled his tongue around. "Good town," he said, .extending his arm, fist closed, twisting it in little circles at the wrist.

"Yeh," Al said. "One of the best. I ain't been there in four, no three, years. Been on the road since."

"Hitching?"

"Hell, no," Al exploded with contempt. "It's a sucker's game hitching. I work the trains; you know, 'Ride the rails in comfort with Pullman'."

"Yeahr. How're the hobo camps?" Cousin asked.

It was Al's turn to extend his arm.

They all started laughing with wise, knowing, lewd laughs.

"What do you boys do?" Al asked.

They laughed again.

"We're partners in business," Cataract said.

Al looked at them, discarding one thing after another, trying to narrow down the possibilities. He decided they were sucker players of some sort.

"You guys know of any jobs in Chicago?" Al asked.

"How much you want?"

"About twenty a week. I'm in now. Got thirty-four bucks." ,

Pickles whistled. "What're you mooching meals for, then?"

"Who's mooching?" Al demanded. "Did I ask you guys for anything besides a ride?"

"Noooo."

"Awright, then don't go around being a wise guy."

Pickles looked out the window, grinning. "Sorry, bud."

"Well, awright then," Al said, acting sore.

"Well, awright then, dig, dig, dig, well awright," Cousin mimicked.

Cataract laughed, trying to be friendly. "They're funny boys, you know, just smart. They wish they had your thirty-four, that's all."

It worked, Al thought. He let himself grin. "It's okay," he said.

He looked out the window. They weren't in Chicago yet, but the lights shining from the houses on the side of the road were more frequent, making a steady yellow glare against the wet windows, and he knew that they must be almost at the outskirts by now. Just then, he saw a CITY LIMITS and WELCOME sign flash past. Cousin turned off the highway, and went along for a way on a dirt road that in time turned onto an old oil-stained asphalt street. They passed a few factories, and Al thought of dropping off, but he wondered if it might not pay him to stay with the men a while.

Cataract yawned. "What about a game of pool now, boys?" he asked.

So that's what they are, Al thought.

"Say," he said, "I'd like to play too. I ain't very good, but I like the game." He had played exactly three times in his life. Pickles assured him. "We're no good either, that is, I'm no good. You and me can play."

"Yeah," Al said, "it ought to be fun."

Cousin was driving up Milwaukee Avenue now. He turned left, slowing down very carefully as he did so, although there were no cars in sight.

"That Cousin drives like an old woman," Pickles commented. "I could drive faster going backwards."

Cousin jeered at him. "You couldn't drive my aunt's wheelbarrow. I'm the only guy left who hasn't lost his license," he said speaking to Al. "It's because I take it easy when I drive a car."

Al said he didn't know much about cars, but he guessed maybe Cousin was right.

The car pulled up in front of a dark grey building on the corner of a long row of old brownstone homes. It was a dark street, and the only evidence that people lived on it were the overflowing garbage and ash cans spaced at irregular intervals in front of the houses. The poolroom itself was down in the cellar, underneath a beauty parlor and a secretarial school. On the steps going down, Al could see pencilled scribblings on the walls: some hasty calculation of odds, a woman's telephone number with a comment underneath it, a few bits of profanity, and one very well-drawn nude woman.

The foot of the stairs opened right on to the tables, which were strung out in one long narrow line of five. The place was almost dark, only the first table being used, and no lights were on in the back. Pickles stepped over to the counter and started talking to the boss, calling him familiarly, and for some reason annoyingly, by the name Nick. Nick was a short, very broad and sweaty Italian. He and Pickles looked up at Al at the same time, and Pickles motioned to him.

"Nick, this is a pal of mine. I want you to treat him nice if he ever comes in again. Tell thick Nick your name, sweet-face."

"Call me sweet-face," Al said.

"H'lo," Nick said. "Pleased to meet you."

"Where we play?" Al asked. He noticed that Cataract and Cousin had not come down yet.

"Take number four."

"Sweet-face and me on number four," Pickles said. "Got it."

He walked down turning on a few lights. He stopped at the cue rack, and picked one at random. Al followed him, selected one carefully, sighting along it to see if there was any warp, and sprinkling some talc over it. "Should we play a rack for table?" he asked.

"Sure," said Pickles. "You mind if we play straight? I don't know any fancy stuff."

"Me neither."

They tossed a coin, and Al had to break. He shot poorly, hit the wrong ball and scratched. Pickles overshot and splattered balls all over the table. Al sunk two, shooting as well as he could, knowing that Pickles would notice any attempts at faking. They both played sloppily and it took fifteen minutes to clear the table. Al won, eight balls to seven.

"We're pretty close," Pickles said. "What about playing for a couple of bucks this next table?"

He watched Cataract and Cousin, who had just come in and were starting to play.

Al could feel the sweat starting up in the small of his back and on his thighs. I can still get out of it, he thought. At least I'll have my buck. The thought of another five dollars, however, was too strong for him. He tried to think of what would happen to him if he didn't get away with it, but he kept remembering how it felt to have money in his hands. He heard himself speaking, feeling that it was not he but someone right in back, or on top of him.

"Make it a buck," he said.

Pickles broke, again shooting too hard. Al watched him flub balls all over the table, slightly overdoing it this time. They finished the rack, Al getting a run of three at the end, to win, ten to five. Pickles handed him a dollar, and placed another on the side of the table. Al covered it with the one he had won. I wonder when he starts winning, Al thought. If I can only quit then. They played for a dollar twice more, Al winning both times. A first drop of perspiration drew together, and raced down his back. He saw Cataract watching them play, juggling two balls in his hand. They played for three dollars, Al winning, after being behind, five to two.

He straightened up, making an almost visible effort to relax.

"That makes six bucks," he said.

"Sure," said Pickles. "Let's make it five this time. I want to win my dough back."

This time Pickles won. Al handed him five dollars, separating the bills with difficulty, and handing them over painfully.

"Another one for five," Pickles said.

Al looked around him desperately, wondering if he could get out. "Five," he croaked. Cataract was still juggling the balls.

It was the longest game he ever played. After every shot he stopped to wipe his hands. In the middle, he realized that this game was going to be given to him. He couldn't relax, however, because he knew the showdown would merely be delayed for another game or so.

He won, as he knew he would, but immediately the pres-

sure was on again. They played once more for five, and he
won. After it was over, he didn't trust himself to stand,
and he leaned against the cue rack, trying to draw satisfaction from the money in his pocket. He dreamed of getting
out, and having it all to do as he pleased, until he saw
Pickles and Cataract looking at each other. Cataract threw
a ball up, and closed his fingers too soon, missing it. It
came down with a loud shattering crack that made Nick
look up from his counter. That's the signal, Al thought.

They were the only ones in the place now.

Pickles stroked his cue, grinning. "Your luck's been too
good, sweet-face. I think this is going to be my game. I
got twenty bucks left. I'm laying it down."

"No," said Al. "I don't want to."

"Listen, I been losing dough. You're playing."

They all looked at him menacingly.

"I want to quit," Al said.

"I wouldn't try it," Cousin said.

Al looked about him, trapped, thoughts of fighting them
mixing with mad ideas of flight.

Cataract stepped toward him, holding a cue in his hand.

"All right," Al said, "I'll play."

Pickles broke, making a very beautiful "safe," leaving
Al helpless. He bent over his stick to shoot. The balls
wavered in front of him, and he could see the tip of the
cue shaking up and down. He wiped his face and looked
around to loosen his muscles. When he tried again, it was
useless. He laid his cue on the table and walked to the
back.

"Where you going?" asked Pickles.

"To the can. Want to come along?" He forced a laugh
from the very bottom of his throat.

He passed through a small littered room, where old soda
boxes were stored. The bathroom was small and filthy; the
ceiling higher than the distance from wall to wall. Once
inside he bolted the door, and sank down on the floor,
whimpering softly.

After a while he quieted and looked around. The only
other possible exit was a window, high up on the wall
facing the door. He looked at it, not realizing its significance, until a chance sound from outside made him realize
where he was and what was happening to him. He got up,
and looked at the wall, examining its surface for some

possible boost. He saw there was none, crouched down, and jumped. His hands just grasped the edge, clung for a fraction of a second, and then scraped off. He knelt again, as close to the wall as he could possibly get, flexed himself, and leaped up. This time his palms grasped hold. He pressed his finger tips against the stone surface and chinned up enough to work his elbows over. He rested a moment, and then squeezed his stomach in and hung there on the ledge against the window, his legs dangling behind. He inched the window open noiselessly and, forgetting he was in the cellar, looked down into blackness. For a moment he was panic-stricken, until he remembered he was in the cellar, and had to look up. He shifted his position, and raised his head. There was a grating at right angles to the window, fixed above a dump heap, much like the one beneath a subway grille. It was very dark outside, but he could make out that it opened into an alley. Overjoyed, he took his money out, almost falling off in the act, kissed it, put it back, and tried to open the grating. He placed his hands under it and pushed up as hard as he could in his cramped position. The grille didn't move. He struck one foot through the open window, and straddled the ledge, one foot in, one foot out. Bracing himself, he pushed calmly against the grating, trying to dislodge it from the grime imbedded in it. Finding his efforts useless, he pushed harder and harder until his arms were almost pushed into his chest and his back and crotch felt as if they would crack. Breathing heavily, he stopped and stared up past the grating. Suddenly, with a cry of desperation, he flung himself up, beating against it with his hands and arms, until the blood ran down them. Half crazy, he gripped the bars and shook, with impassioned groans. His fingers slipped against a little obstruction on one of the end bars. His hand felt it, caressed it, hoping to find some lever point, and discovered it to be a rivet between the foundation and the grille. He sat there, huge sobs torn from him, his eyes gazing hungrily at the sky above. After a bit, he withdrew his leg, wormed his body in again, closed the window, and dropped heavily to the floor, lying in a heap, as he had fallen, his face to the wall. I'll just wait till they come for me, he thought. He could hear someone coming toward the door. Pickles knocked. "Hey kid," he yelled from the other side of the partition, "hurry up."

Al stood up, a mad flare of hope running through him as he thought of the money he still had. He held his hand to his throat, and struggled to control his voice. "Be right out," he said, managing to hold it through to the end. He heard Pickles walk away, and felt a little stronger. He started to wash himself, to get the blood off. His hands were still bleeding dully, the blood oozing out thickly and sluggishly, but he was able to stop the flow somewhat. He backed away, glanced out the window once more, and took his money out. He held it in his hands, and let the bills slip through his fingers. Gathering them up, he kissed them feverishly, rubbing the paper against his face and arms. He folded them tenderly, let down his pants and slipped the cash into a little secret pocket, just under the crotch. He flattened out the bump it made, and unlocked the door to go out. His heart was still pounding, but he felt calmer, and more determined.

They were waiting for him impatiently, smoking nervously.

Al took out one of Cataract's cigarettes and asked for a match. He lit it, sucking deeply and gratefully from it. They glared at him, their nerves almost as tight as his.

"Come on," said Pickles, "it's your turn to shoot."

Al picked up his cue, gripping it hard to make his hand bleed faster. He bent over, made a pretence of sighting, and then laid his cue down, exposing the place where his hand had stained it.

"What's the matter?" Cousin snapped.

"I can't hold a cue," Al said. "I cut my hand in there."

"What do you mean you can't play?" Pickles shouted. "My money's up. You got to play."

"You can't force me. I'm not going to play. It's my money, it's mine see, and you can't make me. You guys can't pull this on me; you're just trying to work a sucker game."

It was the wrong thing to say. Cataract caught him by the shirt, and shook him. "Grab ahold of that stick," he said.

Al wrenched loose. "Go to hell," he said. "I'm quitting."

He picked up his hat, and started walking down past

the tables to go out. He had to pass three tables and the counter to get to the stairs. He walked slowly, hoping to bluff his way out. He knew he had no chance if he ran. He could feel the sweat starting up much faster this time. His shoulders were twitching, and he was very conscious of the effort of forming each step, expecting something to hit him at every second. His face was wet, and he fought down an agonizing desire to turn and look at them. Behind him, they were silent. He could see Nick at the entrance, watching him walk towards him, his face expressionless. Fascinated, he hung on to Nick's eyes, pleading silently with him. A slight smile grew on Nick's face. It broke into a high unnatural laugh, squeaking off abruptly. Terrified, Al threw a quick glance back, and promptly threw himself on his face. A cue whizzed by, shattering on the far wall with a terrific smash. Before he could get up, they were on him. Cataract turned him on his back, and knelt over him. He brought the heel of his hand down hard on Al's face, knocking his head on the floor. He saw them swirl around him, the pool tables mixed in somewhere, and he shook his head furiously, to keep from going out. Cataract hit him again.

Al struck out with his foot, and hit him in the shin.

"You dirty little bastard," Cataract said. "I'll teach you."

He slammed his knee down into Al's stomach. Al choked and writhed, the fight out of him for a moment. They turned him over, and stripped his pockets, looking for his money. They shook him. "Where is it, sweet-face?" Pickles asked.

Al choked for breath.

"I lost it," he said mockingly.

"It's in his pants somewhere," Cousin said. "These rats always got a secret pocket." They tried to open his pants. He fought crazily, kicking, biting, screaming, using his elbows and knees.

"Come on," Cataract commanded, "get it off him."

Al yelled as loud as he could. Nick came over. "Get him out," he said. "The cops'll be dropping in soon. I don't want trouble."

"What'll we do with him?"

"Take him out on the road where no one will hear you.

After that, its your imagination." He squealed with laughter again.

They picked him up, and forced him out. He went with them peacefully, too dazed to care. They shoved him in the car, and Cousin turned it around. Al was in front, Cataract in the back seat, holding his wrist so he couldn't break loose before they started.

Al sat there silently, his head clearing, remembering how slowly Cousin drove. He looked out, watching the ground shoot by, and thought of jumping out. Hopelessly, he looked at the speedometer. They were going around a turn, and Cousin had slowed down to less than twenty miles an hour. He had jumped off freight trains going faster than that, but there had been no door in the way, and no one had been holding him. Discouraged, he gave up the idea.

Cousin taunted him. "See that white sign, sweet-face? We turn left there, just around it, and after that it won't be long."

Anger and rebellion surged through him. They were taking away something that he had earned dangerously, and they were going to beat him up, because they had not been as smart as he. It was not fair. He wanted the money more than they did. In a fury, he decided to jump at the turn. The sign was about a hundred yards away; it would be his last chance. He figured it would take seven seconds to reach it.

He turned around to face Cataract, his left elbow resting loosely against the door handle. He had turned the way his wrist was twisted, holding it steady, so that Cataract would not realize the pressure was slackened. One, he counted to himself, "Look," he begged Cataract, "let me off. I ain't got the money, let me off." Maybe thirty yards gone by. Cataract was talking. "Oh, you're a funny boy, sweet-face. I like you sweet-face." Another twenty. "Yeh, sure I'm funny, I'm a scream," he said. "Oh, I'm so funny." The sign, where is it? We should have reached it. Oh please God, show me the sign, you got to, it's my money, not theirs, oh please. "Goddam you, please," he shouted. "What?" Cataract yelled. Cousin slowed down. The sign slipped by. They started to turn. Al spat full in Cataract's face, and lashed out with his wrist against the thumb. His

elbow kicked the door open, and he yanked his hand
loose, whirled about, and leaped out, the door just missing
him in its swing back.

His feet were pumping wildly as he hit the ground. He
staggered in a broken run for a few steps, before his knees
crumpled under him, he went sprawling in the dust. His
face went grinding into it, the dirt mashing up into his
cheeks and hands. He lay there stunned for a very long
second, and then he pushed hard with his hands against
the ground, forcing himself up. The car had continued
around the turn, and in the confusion had gone at least a
hundred feet before it stopped. Al threw a stone at the
men scrambling out, and plunged off into a field. It had
stopped raining, but the sky was black, and he knew they
would never catch him. He heard them in the distance,
yelling to each other, and he kept running, his legs dead,
his head lolling sideways, his breath coming in long ripping
bursts. He stumbled over a weed and fell, his body spread-
ing out on soft wet grass. Exhausted, he lay there, his ear
close to the ground, but no longer hearing them, he sat up,
plucking weakly at bits of grass, saying over and over
again, "Oh, those suckers, those big, dumb, suckers. Oh,
those dopes, those suckers. . . ."

At two-thirty, Al Groot, his stomach full, swung off a
streetcar near Madison Street, and went into a flophouse.
He gave the night man a new dollar bill, and tied the
eighty-five cents change in a rag that he fastened to his
wrist. He stood over his bed, and lit some matches, moving them slowly over the surface of his mattress. A few
bedbugs started out of their burrows, and crept across
the bed. He picked them up, and squashed them method-
ically. The last one he held in his hand, watching it
squirm. He felt uneasy for a moment, and impulsively let
it escape, whirling his hand in a circle to throw it away
from the bed. He stretched himself out, and looked off in
the distance for a while, thinking of women, and hamburgers, and billiard balls, and ketchup bottles, and shoes
and, most of all, of the thrill of breaking a five-dollar bill.
Lighting the last of Cataract's cigarettes, he thought of how
different things had been, when he had first palmed them.
He smoked openly, not caring if someone should see
him, for it was his last. Al smoked happily, tremendously
excited, letting each little ache and pain well into the bed.

When the cigarette was finished he tried to fall asleep. He felt wide awake, though, and after some time he propped himself on an elbow, and thought of what he would do the next day. First he would buy a pack of cigarettes, and then he would have a breakfast, and then a clean woman; he would pay a buck if he had to, and then a dinner and another woman. He stopped suddenly, unable to continue, so great was his ecstasy. He lay over his pillow and addressed it.

"By God," Al Groot said, about to say something he had never uttered before, "by God, this is the happiest moment of my life."

1940

MAYBE NEXT YEAR

The trains used to go by, used to go by very fast in the field past the road on the other side of my house. I used to go down there and walk and walk through the fields whenever Mom and Pop were fighting, fighting about money like they always were, and after I'd listen awhile, I'd blow air into my ears so I couldn't hear them, then I'd go out in the field, across the road from my house and slide down the steep part of the grass where it was slippery like dogs had been dirty there, and then I used to climb up the other side, up the big hill on the other side, and walk and walk through the fat high grass until I would come to the railroad tracks where I'd just keep going and going and going.

Why don't we have any money, we never have any money, what kind of man did I marry, what good is he, what good is he, look at him, look at his boy there, look at your boy there, look at him, he takes after you, look at him walk away like he never hears us, look at him, no good like you, why don't you ever get any money?

The grass sticks would be rough and sharp sort of, like sharp pages in a book, and I had to walk with my hands in my pockets so I wouldn't cut my fingers. They were tall, the grasses, and sometimes they would hit me in the face, but I would hit them back, only that used to cut my fingers, and I'd start crying, but I stopped soon, because there was nobody around, and I knew that when there was nobody to hear me, I always stopped soon, although I never could figure it out, because I always could cry for a long time, and say I was going to run away and die if people were around.

I can't help it if I'm not making money, my God there's limits to what a man can do, nag, nag, nag, all the time. My God I can't help it, there's limits, there's a depression,

116

*everybody's losing money, just worry about keeping the
house, and don't compare the child to me, the God-damn
child is splitting us up the middle, I can't help it if he's a
stupid kid, he's only mine, maybe he'll get smarter yet, I
can't help it if he's dumb, there's a depression going on
I tell you, everybody's losing money, there just isn't any
money around.*

The railroad tracks made a funny kind of a mirror. I
could see myself in them, one of me on each side, I was
so tall in them, but I was awfully short, as short as my
arm, but I was awful tall, I looked as tall as Pop, except
as tall as if I was to see Pop all the way in the distance
coming up the hill to our house, when he looked as tall
as my arm, but I knew anyway that he was oh ten times
bigger than me.

*Why is the boy always disappearing, why don't you find
him, you haven't a job, you just sit around, you might keep
him near you, you might teach him to be like you, and
sit around all day, and make it easier for me so at least I
wouldn't have to look for him, but you can't even teach
him that, I never saw such a man like you, they didn't
make my father out of men like you.*

If I walked and walked along the tracks, there was a
spot where I could get to a place where all the big slow
trains came into town. If I was careful I could sneak up in
the grass near to where the men who jumped off the big
trains camped in the fields.

They were dirty old men, they just sat around, and
smoked pipes and washed their dirty old shirts in the yellow water spot where I used to go swimming before Mom
started yell yell yell about the dirty old men and wouldn't
let me swim there.

*They're filthy old things, you'll get sick and die, they're
diseased, they're diseased, why did the town let them
camp and flop in a meadow like that, right on the town
limits, what's the good of living out of town when our only
neighbors are bums, what's the good, what's the town
mean, why aren't they put in the coop where they belong,
why should they be flopping so near our house in a
meadow?*

I didn't like the men, they used to talk and laugh to
themselves all the time, sometimes they would sing songs.
I knew they were dirty men 'cause Mom said they would

give me diseases, but one time I came up and talked to them, when I went out Mom and Pop were shouting, and the men looked at me, one of the old ones who was sitting on his old stork bundle bag sort of, got up and looked at me, he made fun of me, he said sonny got a dime for a poor old man to have some coffee, and then all the men started laughing, haw haw haw kind of laughing. The other men came around me, one of them said he was going to take my shirt and use it for a snot-rag, and they all laughed again, the big man in the middle of them making believe he was going to throw dirt at me only I didn't know he was going to fool me until I started crying, and he laughed too, and dropped the dirt.

That boy is going to get in trouble, why don't you take care of him, keep him around you, he goes off into the meadow, and God knows what those bums are going to do to him, they're all vile, they don't live like men, they're not men I heard, they're no more men than you are, both of you are, why don't you take care of him, he'll turn out weak in everything like you, those bums will get him in trouble.

Pop came over, grab-me picked me up, and carried me upstairs, and licked me, and locked the door on me, and then he went downstairs, and he and Mom yelled and yelled right through my crying. I waited and waited for them to hear me, but I must have fallen asleep because the next thing it was morning, and I didn't remember stopping and rubbing my hands on my nose to wipe off the crying. They unlocked the door before I sneaked downstairs, the front door was open and Mom and Pop were sitting around front, not saying anything, I hated them, I ran out the door between them, and hid around the side of the house. Pop and Mom came running out, they ran the wrong way calling to me, they were looking for me, and they weren't smiling, but they were talking nice the way they did when they didn't mean it, just like when they wanted to catch our dog, and that made me feel sad, and oh I felt just terrible, and then when they started coming back I didn't want to get another licking so I ran away without their seeing me, and sneaked across the road further down, into the field, and up the slippery hill, run run running away off until I got to the railroad tracks. I sneaked along them to where the dirty men with the disease were, and I hid down in the grass, and hid behind some to look at them, but they were all gone, there weren't any of them, but the old man who had made fun of me the day before, and he was lying on the ground crying and yowling like he was hurt or dead.

I walked over to him, he looked at me, he started crawling to me. I could see it was his foot that was hurt 'cause it was all bloody like, and bleeding near the knee. Help me kid, help me kid, he kept yelling.

Go ahead, hit the child, hit it, hit it, it deserves it, playing with dirty old men, hit it, it's a terrible child, it never listens to us, there's something wrong with it.

The old man looked like a snake, and I stepped back to run away from him, but he kept crawling after me, yelling don't go away kid, I won't hurt you, please don't go way kid, but he looked like a snake, only bleeding. I yelled at him, I said go away, you're a dirty old man, but he wouldn't stop, and I picked up a rock, and threw it at him, it missed him, but I threw another rock, and it hit him in the head, he stopped moving to me, he was crying something terrible, there was a lot of blood all over his face.

Why kid, why kid, why kid, why hit me?

You're a dirty old man, leave me alone, I don't like you, you're a dirty old man.

Kid for God's sakes help me, I'm going crazy kid, don't leave me here, it's hot here kid, it's hot here kid.

Then I picked up a stone, and threw it at him again, only I didn't see if it hit him because I was running away. I heard him crying, screaming, and I was scared, but I kept running and then I said I hate them, I hate them, the grass kept cutting at me, I couldn't run with my hands in my pockets, kept cutting at me and cutting at me, I fell down, and then I got up and kept running home.

I walked down the last part of the hill, and across the road, and when I got back Mom and Pop were sitting around again, and I started crying. I cried and cried, they asked me what's the matter, what's the matter with you, why are you crying, but I just kept saying the dirty old man, the dirty old man.

And Mom said I thought they all were kicked out of town, I don't know how any of them were left, you're not lying?

I'm not lying, I'm not lying.

And Pop got up, and said to Mom I told you not to do it, you get an idea in your head, and you can't stop, those men were beaten, I don't know how any were left in the dark, we had flashlights, but there might have been, it's the boy's own fault, he had no business going around there today, and anyway he wasn't hurt, he didn't start crying until he saw us, I saw him before he saw me.

And Mom said, if you were a man you'd go over there now, and finish them off, you wouldn't even go last night without any help, if I were a man I'd thrash the man that touched my boy, but you just sit there and talk talk talk that it's the boy's fault.

Pop got up, and walked around and around, and he said it isn't the boy's fault, but it isn't the man's either, and then he stood up, and said I'm not going to do anything about it, what with the boy between us, and the job ruined, and everything God-damned else, I might be one of them myself, maybe next year, and then Pop stood up and walked off down the road only farther out of town, not the way the old man was. I could see that Pop's shoulders were screwed up around his neck, and then I was happy, because all I could think of was that I'd seen two big men cry that day, and maybe that meant I was getting bigger too, and that was an awful good feeling.

1941

PART FOUR

Sobrieties, Impieties

THE PAPER HOUSE

Friendship in the army is so often an accident. If Hayes and I were friends, it was due above all else to the fact that we were cooks on the same shift, and so saw more of one another than of anyone else. I suppose if I really consider it seriously, I did not even like him, but for months we went along on the tacit assumption that we were buddies, and we did a great many things together. We got drunk together, we visited the local geisha house together, and we even told each other some of our troubles.

It was not a bad time. The war was over, and we were stationed with the understrength company of men in a small Japanese city. We were the only American troops for perhaps fifty miles around, and therefore discipline was easy, and everyone could do pretty much what he wished. The kitchen was staffed by four cooks and a mess sergeant, and we had as many Japanese K.P.s to assist us. The work was seldom heavy, and duty hours passed quickly. I never liked the army so much as I did during those months.

Hayes saw to it that we had our recreation. He was more aggressive than me, older and stronger, much more certain of his ideas. I had no illusions that I was anything other than the tail to his kite. He was one of those big gregarious men who need company and an uncritical ear, and I could furnish both. It also pleased him that I had finished two years of college before I entered the army, and yet he knew so much more than me, at least so far as the army was concerned. He would ride me often about that. "You're the one who'se cracked the books," he would say as he slammed a pot around, "but it seems none of those books ever taught you how to boil water. What a cook!" His humor was heavy, small doubt about it. "Nicholson," he would yell at me, "I hear there's a correspondence course in short-arms inspections. Why don't you advance yourself? You too can earn seventy-eight bucks a month."

He was often in a savage mood. He had troubles at home, and he was bitter about them. It seems his wife had begun to live with another man a few months after he entered the army. He had now divorced her, but there were money settlements still to be arranged, and his vanity hurt him. He professed to hate women. "They're tramps, every one of them," he would announce. "They're tramps and I can tell you it's a goddam tramp's world, and don't forget that, sonny." He would shift a boiler from one stove to another with a quick jerk-and-lift of his powerful shoulders, and would call back to me, "The only honest ones are the honest-to-God pros."

I would argue with him, or at least attempt to. I used to write a letter every day to a girl I liked in my home town, and the more time went by and the more letters I wrote, the more I liked her. He used to scoff at me. "That's the kind I really go for," he would jeer. "The literary ones. How they love to keep a guy on the string by writing letters. That's the kind that always has ten men right in her own back yard."

"I know she dates other fellows," I would say, "but what is she supposed to do? And look at us, we're over at the geisha house almost every night."

"Yeah, that's a fine comparison. We're spending our money at this end, and she's coining it at the other. Is that what you're trying to say?"

I would swear at him, and he would laugh. At such moments I disliked him intensely.

There was, however, quite another side to him. Many evenings after finishing work he would spend an hour washing and dressing, trimming his black moustache, and inspecting critically the press in his best uniform. We would have a drink or two, and then walk along the narrow muddy streets to the geisha house. He would usually be in a fine mood. As we turned in the lane which led to the house, and sat in the vestibule taking off our boots, or more exactly, waiting luxuriously while a geisha or a maid removed them for us, he would begin to hum. The moment we entered the clean pretty little room where the geishas greeted the soldiers, his good mood would begin to flood him. I heard him be even poetic once as he looked at the girls in their dress kimonos, all pretty, all petite, all chirping beneath the soft lights, all treading in dress slippers upon the bright woven straw mats. "I tell you, Nicholson," he said, "it looks like a goddam Christmas tree." He loved to sing at the geisha house, and since he had a pleasant baritone voice, the geishas would crowd about him, and clap their hands. Once or twice he would attempt to sing a Japanese song, and the errors he made in pitch and in language would be so amusing that the geishas would giggle with delight. He made, altogether, an attractive picture at such times, his blue eyes and healthy red face contrasting vigorously with his black moustache and his well-set body in its clean uniform. He seemed full of strength and merriment. He would clap two geishas to him, and call across the room with loud good cheer to another soldier. "Hey, Brown," he would shout, "ain't this a rug-cutter?" And to the answer, "You never had it so good," he would chuckle. "Say that again, Jack," he might roar. He was always charming the geishas. He spoke a burlesque Japanese to their great amusement, he fondled them, his admiration for them seemed to twinkle in his eyes. He was always hearty. Like many men who hate women, he knew how to give the impression that he adored them.

After several months he settled upon a particular girl. Her name was Yuriko, and she was easily the best of the geishas in that house. She was quite appealing with her tiny cat-face, and she carried herself with considerable charm, discernible even among the collective charm all geishas seemed to possess. She was clever, she was witty, and by the use of a few English words and the dramatic facility to express complex thoughts in pantomime, she was quite capable of carrying on extended conversations. It was hardly surprising that the other girls deferred to her, and she acted as their leader.

Since I always seemed to follow in Hayes's shadow, I also had a steady girl, and I suspect that Mimiko, whom I chose, had actually been selected for me by the artifice of Yuriko. Mimiko was Yuriko's best friend, and since Hayes and I were always together, it made things cosy. Those alternate Sundays when we were not on duty in the kitchen

we would pay for the girls' time, and Hayes would use his
influence, established by the judicious bribes of cans of
food and pounds of butter to the motor pool sergeant, to
borrow a jeep. We would take the girls out into the country, drive our jeep through back roads or mountain trails,
and then descend to the sea where we would wander along
the beach. The terrain was beautiful. Everything seemed
to be manicured, and we would pass from a small pine
forest into a tiny valley, go through little villages or little
fishing towns nestled on the rocks, would picnic, would
talk, and then towards evening would return the girls to the
house. It was very pleasant.

They had other clients besides us, but they refused to
spend the night with any other soldier if they knew we were
coming, and the moment we entered the place, word was
sent to Yuriko or Mimiko if they were occupied. Without a
long wait, they would come to join us. Mimiko would slip
her hand into mine and smile politely and sweetly, and
Yuriko would throw her arms about Hayes and kiss him
upon the mouth in the American style of greeting. We
would all go together to one of the upper rooms and talk
for an hour or two while sake was drunk. Then we would
separate for the night, Yuriko with Hayes, and Mimiko
with me.

Mimiko was not particularly attractive, and she had the
placid disposition of a draught animal. I liked her mildly,
but I would hardly have continued with her if it had not
been for Yuriko. I really liked Yuriko. She seemed more
bright and charming with every day, and I envied Hayes
for his possession of her.

I used to love to listen to her speak. Yuriko would tell
long stories about her childhood and her parents, and although the subject was hardly calculated to interest Hayes,
he would listen to her with his mouth open, and hug her
when she was done. "This baby ought to be on the stage,"
he would say to me. Once, I remember, I asked her how
she had become a geisha, and she told about it in detail.
"Papa-san, sick sick," she began, and with her hands,
created her father for us, an old Japanese peasant whose
back was bent and whose labor was long. "Mama-san
sad." Her mother wept for us, wept prettily, like a Japanese
geisha girl, with hands together in prayer and her nose

touching the tip of her fingers. There was money owed on the land, the crops were bad, and Papa-san and Mama-san had talked together, and cried, and had known that they must sell Yuriko, now fourteen, as geisha. So she had been sold and she had been trained, and in a few moments by the aid of a montage which came instinctively to her, she showed us herself in transition from a crude fourteen-year-old peasant to a charming geisha of sixteen trained in the tea ceremony, her diction improved, her limbs taught to dance, her voice to sing. "I, first-class geisha," she told us, and went on to convey the prestige of being a geisha of the first class. She had entertained only the wealthy men of the town, she had had no lovers unless she had felt the flutterings of weakness in her heart, her hands busy fluttering at her breast, her arms going out to an imaginary lover, her eyes darting from one of us to the other to see if we comprehended. In ten years she would have saved money enough to buy her freedom and to make an impressive marriage.

But, boom-boom, the war had ended, the Americans had come, and only they had money enough for geisha girls. And they did not want geisha girls. They wanted a *joro,* a common whore. And so first-class geishas became second-class geishas and third-class geishas, and here was Yuriko, a third-class geisha, humiliated and unhappy, or at least she would be if she did not love Hayes-san and he did not love her.

She was moody when she finished. "Hayes-san love Yuriko?" she asked, her legs folded beneath her, her small firm buttocks perched upon the straw mat while she handed him a sake cup, and extended her hand to the charcoal brazier.

"Sure, I love you, baby," Hayes said.

"I, first-class geisha," she repeated a little fiercely.

"Don't I know it," Hayes boomed.

Early the next morning as we walked back to the dormitory where the company was installed, Hayes was talking about it. "She jabbered at me all night," he said. "I got a hangover. That Jap sake."

"The story Yuriko told was sad," I murmured.

He stopped in the middle of the street, and put his hands on his hips. "Listen, Nicholson, wise up," he said angrily. "It's crap, it's all crap. They'd have you bleed your eyes out for them with those stories. Poor papa-san. They're all whores, you understand? A whore's a whore, and they're whores cause they want to be whores and don't know nothing better."

"It's not true," I protested. I felt sorry for the geishas. They seemed so unlike the few prostitutes I had known in the United States. There was one girl at the house who had been sold when she was thirteen, and had entered service a virgin. After her first night of work, she had wept for three days, and even now many of the soldiers selected her shame-facedly. "What about Susiko?" I said.

"I don't believe it, it's a gag," Hayes shouted. He gripped me by the shoulder and made a speech. "I'll wise you up. I don't say I'm Superman, but I know the score. Do you understand that? I know the score. I don't say I'm any better than anybody else, but I don't kid myself that I am. And it drives me nuts when people want to make me swallow bull." He released my shoulder as suddenly as he had gripped it. His red face was very red, and I sensed what rage he had felt.

"All right," I muttered.

"All right."

In time he came to treat Yuriko the way he treated anyone with whom he was familiar. He indulged his moods. If he were surly, he did not bother to hide it; if he were aggressive, he would swear at her; if he were happy, he would sing for her or become roisteringly drunk or kiss her many times before Mimiko and myself, telling her that he loved her in a loud voice which often seemed close to choler. Once he abused her drunkenly, and I had to pull him away. The next day he brought Yuriko a present, a model of a wooden shrine which he had purchased from a Japanese cabinet maker. All the while it was evident to me that Yuriko was in love with him.

I used to think of the rooms upstairs as paper rooms. They were made of straw and light wood and parchment glued to wooden frames, and when one lay on the pallet in the centre of the floor, it seemed as if all the sounds in all the adjoining rooms flowed without hindrance through the sliding doors. Mimiko and I could often hear them talking in the next cubicle, and long after Mimiko would be asleep, I would lie beside her and listen to Yuriko's voice as it floated, breathlike and soft, through the frail partitions. She would be telling him about her day and the events which had passed in the house. She had had a fight with Mama-san, the wrinkled old lady who was her madame, and Tasawa had heard from her brother whose wife had just given him a child. There was a new girl coming in two days, and Katai who had left the day before had proven to be sick. Mama-san was limiting the charcoal for the braziers, she was stingy without a doubt. So it went, a pageant of domesticity. She had resewn the buttons on his battle jacket, he looked good, he was gaining weight, she would have to buy a new kimono for the number two kimono had become shabby, and the number three was hopeless. She was worried about Henderson-san who had become drunk two nights in a row and had struck Kukoma. What should she do about him?

And Hayes listened to her, his head in her lap no doubt, and mumbled gentle answers, relaxed and tender as she caressed the bitterness from his face, drawing it out with her finger tips while her childlike laugh echoed softly through the rooms. There were other sounds of men snoring, girls giggling, two soldiers in a quarrel, and the soft muted whisper of a geisha crying somewhere in some one of the rooms. So it washed over me in this little house with its thirty paper cells in the middle of a small Japanese city while the Japanese night cast an artist's moon over the rice paddies and the pine forests where the trees grew in aisles. I envied Hayes, envied him with the touch of Mimiko's inert body against mine, envied him Yuriko's tenderness which she gave him so warmly.

He told her one night that he loved her. He loved her so much that he would re-enlist and remain in this Japanese city for at least another year. I overheard him through the parchment walls, and I would have asked him about it next morning if he had not mentioned it himself. "I told her that, and I was lying," he said.

"Well, why did you tell her?"

"You lie to a dame. That's my advice to you. You get them in closer and closer, you feed them whatever you want, and the only trick is never to believe it yourself. Do you understand, Nicholson?"

"No, I don't."

"It's the only way to handle them, I've got Yuriko around my finger." And he insisted on giving me a detailed account of how they made love until by the sheer energy of his account, I realized what he wished to destroy. He had been sincere when he spoke to Yuriko. With her hands on his face, and the night drifting in fog against the windows, he had wanted to re-enlist for another year, had wanted to suspend her fingers upon his face, and freeze time so it could be retained. It must have all seemed possible the night before, he must have believed it and wanted it, seen himself signing the papers in the morning. Instead, he had seen me, had seen the olive-drab color of my uniform, and had known it was not possible, was not at all possible within the gamut of his nature.

He was drunk the following night when he went to see her, moody and silent, and Yuriko was without diversion to him. I think she sensed that something was wrong. She sighed frequently, she chatted in Japanese with Mimiko, and threw quick looks at him to see whether his mood was changing. Then—it must have meant so much to her—she inquired timidly, "You re-enlist one year?"

He stared back at her, was about to nod, and then laughed shortly. "I'm going home, Yuriko. I'm due to go home in one month."

"You repeat, please?"

"I'm getting out of here. In one month. I'm not re-enlisting."

She turned away and looked at the wall. When she turned around, it was to pinch his arm.

"Hayes-san, you marry me, yes?" she said in a voice sharp with its hurt.

He shoved her away. "I don't marry you. Get away. You skibby with too many men."

She drew in her breath and her eyes were bright for a moment. "Yes. You marry skibby-girl." Yuriko threw her arms about his neck. "American soldier marry skibby-girl."

This time he pushed her away forcefully enought to hurt

her. "You just go blow," he shouted at her.

She was quite angry. "American soldier marry skibby-girl," she taunted.

I had never seen him quite as furious. What frightened me was that he contained it all and did not raise his voice. "Marry you?" he asked. I have an idea what engaged him was that the thought had already occurred to him, and it seemed outrageous to hear it repeated in what was, after all, the mouth of a prostitute. Hayes picked up his bottle and drank from it. "You and me are going to skibby, that's what," he said to Yuriko.

She held her ground. "No skibby tonight."

"What do you mean, 'no skibby tonight'? You'll skibby tonight. You're nothing but a *joro*."

Yuriko turned her back. Her little head was bent forward. "I, first-class geisha," she whispered in so low a voice we almost did not hear her.

He struck her. I tried to intervene, and with a blow he knocked me away. Yuriko fled the room. Like a bull, Hayes was after her. He caught her once, just long enough to rip away half her kimono, caught her again to rip away most of what was left. The poor girl was finally trapped, screaming, and more naked than not, in the room where the geishas met the soldiers. There must have been a dozen girls and at least as many soldiers for an audience. Hayes gripped her hairdress, he ripped it down, he threw her up in the air, he dropped her on the floor, he laughed drunkenly, and among the screams of the girls and the startled laughter of the soldiers, I got him out to the street. I could hear Yuriko wailing hysterically behind us.

I guided him home to his cot, and he dropped into a drunken sleep. In the morning, he was contrite. Through the dull headache of awakening, he certainly did not love her, and so he regretted his brutality. "She's a good girl, Nicholson," he said to me, "she's a good girl, and I shouldn't have treated her that way."

"You ripped her kimono," I told him.

"Yeah, I got to buy her another."

It turned out to be a bad day. At breakfast, everybody who passed on the chow line seemed to have heard what had happened, and Hayes was kidded endlessly. It developed that Yuriko had been put to bed with fever after we left, and all the girls were shocked. Almost everything had halted for the night at the geisha house.

"You dishonored her in public," said one of Hayes's buddies wih a grin. "Man, how they carried on."

Hayes turned to me. "I'm going to buy her a good kimono." He spent the morning selecting articles of food to sell on the black market. He had to make enough to amass the price of a good kimono, and it worried him that the supplies might be too depleted. The afternoon was taken up with selling his goods, and at dinner we were two weary cooks.

Hayes changed in a hurry. "Come on, let's get over there." He hustled me along, did not even stop to buy a bottle. We were the first clients of the evening to appear at the geisha house. "Mama-san," he roared at the old madame, "where's Yuriko?"

Mama-san pointed upstairs. Her expression was wary. Hayes, however, did not bother to study it. He bounded up the stairs, knocked on Yuriko's door, and entered.

Yuriko was sweet and demure. She accepted his present with a deep bow, touching her forehead to the floor. She was friendly, she was polite, and she was quite distant. She poured us sake with even more ceremony than was her custom. Mimiko entered after a few minutes, and her face was troubled. Yet it was she who talked to us. Yuriko was quiet for a long time. It was only when Mimiko lapsed into silence that Yuriko began to speak.

She informed us in her mixture of English, Japanese and pantomime that in two weeks she was going to take a trip. She was very formal about it.

"A trip?" Hayes asked.

It was to be a long trip. Yuriko smiled sadly.

Hayes fingered his hat. She was leaving the geisha house?

Yes, she was leaving it forever.

She was going perhaps to get married?

No, she was not getting married. She was dishonored and no one would have her.

Hayes began to twist the hat. She had a *musume*? She was going away with a *musume*?

No, there was no *musume*. Hayes was the only *musume* in her life.

Well, where was she going?

Yuriko sighed. She could not tell him. She hoped, however, since she would be leaving before Hayes, that he would come to see her often in the next few weeks.

"Goddammit, where are you going?" Hayes shouted.

At this point, Mimiko began to weep. She wept loudly, her hand upon her face, her head averted. Yuriko leaped up to comfort her. Yuriko patted her head, and sighed in unison with Mimiko.

"Where are you going?" Hayes asked her again.

Yuriko shrugged her shoulders.

It continued like this for an hour. Hayes badgered her, and Yuriko smiled. Hayes pleaded and Yuriko looked sad. Finally, as we were about to leave, Yuriko told us. In two weeks, at two o'clock on Sunday afternoon, she was going to her little room, and there she would commit hari-kari. She was dishonored, and there was nothing else to be done about it. Hayes-san was very kind to apologize, and the jewels of her tears were the only fit present for his kindness, but apologies could never erase dishonor and so she would be obliged to commit hari-kari.

Mimiko began to weep again.

"You mean in two weeks you're going to kill yourself?" Hayes blurted.

"Yes, Hayes-san."

He threw up his arms. "It's crap, it's all crap, you understand?"

"Yes, Crap-crap," Yuriko said.

"You're throwing the bull, Yuriko."

"Yes. Hayes-san. Crap-crap."

"Let's get out of here, Nicholson." He turned in the doorway and laughed. "You almost had me for a minute, Yuriko."

She bowed her head.

Hayes went to see her three times in the week which followed. Yuriko remained the same. She was quiet, she was friendly, she was quite removed. And Mimiko wept every night on my pallet. Hayes forbore as long as was possible, and then at the end of the week, he spoke about it again. "You were kidding me, weren't you, Yuriko?"

Yuriko begged Hayes-san not to speak of it again. It was rude on her part. She did not wish to cause him unnecessary pain. If she had spoken, it was only because the dearer sentiments of her heart were in liege to him, and she wished to see him often in the week which remained.

He snorted with frustration. "Now, look you . . . cut . . . this . . . out. Do you understand?"

"Yes, Hayes-san. No more talk-talk." She would not mention it again, she told us. She realized how it offended him. Death was an unpleasant topic of conversation in a geisha house. She would attempt to be entertaining, and she begged us to forgive her if the knowledge of her own fate might cause her to be sad at certain moments.

That morning, on the walk back to the schoolhouse, Hayes was quiet. He worked all day with great rapidity, and bawled me out several times for not following his cooking directions more accurately. That night we slept in our barrack, and in the early hours of the morning, he woke me up.

"Look, Nicholson, I can't sleep. Do you think that crazy honey is really serious?"

I was wide awake. I had not been sleeping well myself. "I don't know," I said. "I don't think she means it."

"I know she doesn't mean it." He swore.

"Yeah." I started to light a cigarette, and then I put it out. "Hayes, I was just thinking though. You know the Oriental mind is different."

"The Oriental mind! Goddammit, Nicholson, a whore is a whore. They're all the same I tell you. She's kidding."

"If you say so."

"I'm not even going to mention it to her."

All through the second week, Hayes kept his promise. More than once, he would be about to ask her again, and would force himself into silence. It was very difficult. As the days passed, Mimiko wept more and more openly, and Yuriko's eyes would fill with tears as she looked at Hayes. She would kiss him tenderly, sigh, and then by an effort of will, or so it seemed, would force herself to be gay. Once she surprised us with some flowers she had found, and wove them in our hair. The week passed day by day. I kept waiting for the other men in the company to hear the news, but Hayes said not a word and the geishas did not either. Still, one could sense that the atmosphere in the house was different. The geishas were extremely re-respectful to Yuriko, and quite frequently would touch her garments as she passed.

By Saturday Hayes could stand it no longer. He insisted that we leave the geisha house for the night, and he made Yuriko accompany us to the boot vestibule. While she was lacing our shoes, he raised her head and said to her, "I work tomorrow. I'll see you Monday."

She smiled vaguely, and continued tying the laces.

"Yuriko, I said I'd see you Monday."

"No, Hayes-san. Better tomorrow. No here, Monday. Gone, bye-bye. You come tomorrow before two o'clock."

"Yuriko, I'm on duty tomorrow. I said I'll see you Monday."

"Say good-bye now. Never see me again." She kissed us on the cheek. "Good-bye, Nick-san. Good-bye, Hayes-san." A single tear rolled down each cheek. She fingered Hayes's jacket and fled.

That night Hayes and I did not sleep at all. He came over to my cot, and sat there in silence. "What do you think?" he asked after a long while.

"I don't know."

"I don't know either." He began to swear. He kept drinking from a bottle, but it had no effect. He was quite sober. "I'm damned if I'm going over there tomorrow," he said.

"Do what you think is best."

He swore loudly.

The morning went on and on. Hayes worked rapidly and was left with nothing to do. The meal was ready fifteen minutes early. He called chow at eleven-thirty. By one o'clock the K.P.s were almost finished with the pots.

"Hey, Koto," Hayes asked one of the K.P.s, a middle-aged man who had been an exporter and spoke English, "hey, Koto, what do you know about hari-kari?"

Koto grinned. He was always very polite and very colorless. "Oh, hari-kari. Japanese national custom," he said.

"Come on," Hayes said to me, "we've got till three

o'clock before we put supper on." He was changing into his dress clothes by the time I followed him to the dormitory. He had neglected to hang them up the night before, and for once they were bedraggled. "What time is it?" he asked me.

"A quarter past one."

"Come on, hurry up."

He ran almost all the way to the geisha house, and I ran with him. As we approached, the house seemed quiet. There was nobody in the vestibule, and there was nobody in the receiving room. Hayes and I stood there in empty silence.

"*Yuriko!*" he bawled.

We heard her feet patter on the stairs. She was dressed in a white kimono, without ornament, and without make-up. "You do come," she whispered. She kissed him. "Bye-bye, Hayes-san. I go upstairs now."

He caught her arm. "Yuriko, you can't do it."

She attempted to free herself, and he held her with frenzy. "I won't let you go," he shouted. "Yuriko, you got to stop this. It's crap."

"Crap-crap," she said, and suddenly she began to giggle.

"Crap-crap," we heard all around. "Crap-crap, crap-crap, crap-crap."

Squealing with laughter, every geisha in the house entered the room. They encircled us, their voices going "crap-crap" like a flock of geese.

Yuriko was laughing at us, Mimiko was laughing at us, they were all laughing. Hayes shouldered his way to the door. "Let's get out of here." We pushed on to the street, but the geishas followed. As we retreated across the town, they flowed out from the geisha house and marched behind us, their kimonos brilliant with color, their black hair shining in the sunlight. While the townspeople looked and giggled, we walked home, and the geishas followed us, shouting insults in English, Japanese and pantomime. Beneath their individual voices, with the regularity of marching feet, I could hear their cadence, "Crap-crap, crap-crap."

After a week, Hayes and I went back to the house for a last visit before we sailed for home. We were received politely, but neither Yuriko nor Mimiko would sleep with us. They suggested that we hire Susiko, the thirteen-year-old ex-virgin.

1951

THE NOTEBOOK

The writer was having a fight with his young lady. They were walking toward her home, and as the argument continued, they walked with their bodies farther and farther apart.

The young lady was obviously providing the energy for the quarrel. Her voice would rise a little bit, her head and shoulders would move toward him as though to add weight to her words, and then she would turn away in disgust, her heels tapping the pavement in an even precise rhythm which was quite furious.

The writer was suffering with some dignity. He placed one leg in front of the other, he looked straight ahead, his face was sad, he would smile sadly from time to time and nod his head to every word she uttered.

"I'm sick and tired of you," the young lady exclaimed. "I'm sick and tired of you being so superior. What do you have to be superior about?"

"Nothing," the writer said in so quiet a voice, so gentle a tone that his answer might as well have been, "I have my saintliness to be superior about."

"Do you ever give me anything?" the young lady asked, and provided the response herself. "You don't even give me the time of day. You're the coldest man I've ever known."

"Oh, that's not true," the writer suggested softly.

"Isn't it? Everybody thinks you're so nice and friendly, everybody except anybody who knows you at all. Anybody who knows you, knows better."

The writer was actually not unmoved. He liked this young lady very much, and he did not want to see her unhappy. If with another part of his mind he was noticing the way she constructed her sentences, the last word of one phrase seeming to provide the impetus for the next, he was nonetheless paying attention to everything she said.

"Are you being completely fair?" he asked.

"I've finally come to understand you," she said angrily. "You don't want to be in love. You just want to say the things you're supposed to say and watch the things you're supposed to feel."

"I love you. I know you don't believe me," the writer said.

"You're a mummy. You're nothing but a . . . an Egyptian mummy."

The writer was thinking that when the young lady became angry, her imagery was at best somewhat uninspired. "All right, I'm a mummy," he said softly.

They waited for a traffic light to change. He stood at the curb, smiling sadly, and the sadness on his face was so complete, so patient and so perfect, that the young lady with a little cry darted out into the street and trotted across on her high heels. The writer was obliged to run a step or two to catch up with her.

"Your attitude is different now," she continued. "You don't care about me. Maybe you used to, but you don't care any more. When you look at me, you're not really looking at all. I don't exist for you."

"You know you do."

"You wish you were somewhere else right now. You don't like me when I'm nasty. You think I'm vulgar. Very well, then, I'm vulgar. I'm too vulgar for your refined senses. Isn't that a pity? Do you think the world begins and ends with you?"

"No."

"No, what?" she cried.

"Why are you angry? Is it because you feel I didn't pay enough attention to you tonight? I'm sorry if I didn't. I didn't realize I didn't. I do love you."

"Oh, you love me; oh, you certainly do," the young lady said in a voice so heavy with sarcasm that she was almost weeping. "Perhaps I'd like to think so, but I know better." Her figure leaned towards his as they walked. "There's one thing I will tell you," she went on bitterly. "You hurt people more than the cruellest person in the world could. And why? I'll tell you why. It's because you never feel anything and you make believe that you do." She could see he was not listening, and she asked in exasperation, "What are you thinking about now?"

"Nothing. I'm listening to you, and I wish you weren't so upset."

Actually the writer had become quite uneasy. He had just thought of an idea to put into his notebook, and it made him anxious to think that if he did not remove his notebook from his vest pocket and jot down the thought, he was likely to forget it. He tried repeating the idea to himself several times to fix it in his memory, but this procedure was never certain.

"I'm upset," the young lady said. "Of course, I'm upset. Only a mummy isn't upset, only a mummy can always be reasonable and polite because they don't feel anything." If they had not been walking so quickly she would have stamped her foot. "What are you thinking about?"

"It's not important," he said. He was thinking that if he removed the notebook from his pocket, and held it in the palm of his hand, he might be able to scribble in it while they walked. Perhaps she would not notice.

It turned out to be too difficult. He was obliged to come to a halt beneath a street light. His pencil worked rapidly in nervous elliptic script while he felt beside him the pressure of her presence. *Emotional situation deepened by notebook,* he wrote. *Young writer, girl friend. Writer accused of being observer, not participant in life by girl. Gets idea he must put in notebook. Does so, and brings the quarrel to a head. Girl breaks relationship over this.*

"You have an idea now," the young lady murmured.

"Mmm," he answered.

"That notebook. I knew you'd pull out that notebook." She began to cry. "Why, you're nothing but a notebook," she shrieked, and ran away from him down the street, her high heels mocking her misery in their bright tattoo upon the sidewalk.

"No, wait," he called after her. "Wait, I'll explain."

It occurred to the writer that if he were to do such a vignette, the nuances could be altered. Perhaps the point of the piece should be that the young man takes out his notebook because he senses that this would be the best way to destroy what was left of the relationship. It was a nice idea.

Abruptly, it also occurred to him that maybe this was what he had done. Had he wished to end his own relationship with his own young lady? He considered this, priding himself on the fact that he would conceal no motive from himself, no matter how unpleasant.

Somehow, this did not seem to be true. He did like the young lady, he liked her very much, and he did not wish the relationship to end yet. With some surprise, he realized that she was almost a block away. Therefore, he began to run after her. "No, wait," he called out. "I'll explain it to you, I promise I will." And as he ran the notebook jiggled warmly against his side, a puppy of a playmate, always faithful, always affectionate.

1951

THE LANGUAGE OF MEN

In the beginning, Sanford Carter was ashamed of becoming an army cook. This was not from snobbery, at least not from snobbery of the most direct sort. During the two and a half years Carter had been in the army he had come to hate cooks more and more. They existed for him as a symbol of all that was corrupt, overbearing, stupid, and privileged in army life. The image which came to mind was a fat cook with an enormous sandwich in one hand, and a bottle of beer in the other, sweat pouring down a porcine face, foot on a flour barrel, shouting at the K.P.s, "Hurry up, you men, I ain't got all day." More than once in those two and a half years, driven to exasperation, Carter had been on the verge of throwing his food into a cook's face as he passed on the serving line. His anger often derived from nothing: the set of a pair of fat lips, the casual heavy thump of the serving spoon into his plate, or the resentful conviction that the cook was not serving him enough. Since life in the army was in most aspects a marriage, this rage over apparently harmless details was not a sign of unbalance. Every soldier found some particular habit of the army spouse impossible to support.

Yet Sanford Carter became a cook and, to elaborate the irony, did better as a cook than he had done as anything else. In a few months he rose from a private to a first cook with the rank of Sergeant, Technician. After the fact, it was easy to understand. He had suffered through all his army career from an excess of eagerness. He had cared too much, he had wanted to do well, and so he had often been tense at moments when he would better have been relaxed. He was very young, twenty-one, had lived the comparatively gentle life of a middle-class boy, and needed some success in the army to prove to himself that he was not completely worthless.

142

In succession, he had failed as a surveyor in field artillery, a clerk in an infantry headquarters, a telephone wireman, and finally a rifleman. When the war ended, and his regiment went to Japan, Carter was still a rifleman; he had been a rifleman for eight months. What was more to the point, he had been in the platoon as long as any of its members; the skilled hard-bitten nucleus of veterans who had run his squad had gone home one by one, and it seemed to him that through seniority he was entitled to at least a corporal's rating. Through seniority he was so entitled, but on no other ground. Whenever responsibility had been handed to him, he had dischaged it miserably, tensely, overconscientiously. He had always asked too many questions, he had worried the task too severely, he had conveyed his nervousness to the men he was supposed to lead. Since he was also sensitive enough and proud enough never to curry favor with the noncoms in the platoons, he was in no position to sit in on their occasional discussions about who was to succeed them. In a vacuum of ignorance, he had allowed himself to dream that he would be given a squad to lead, and his hurt was sharp when the squad was given to a replacement who had joined the platoon months after him.

The war was over, Carter had a bride in the States (he had lived with her for only two months), he was lonely, he was obsessed with going home. As one week dragged into the next, and the regiment, the company, and his own platoon continued the same sort of training which they had been doing ever since he had entered the army, he thought he would snap. There were months to wait until he would be discharged and meanwhile it was intolerable to him to be taught for the fifth time the nomenclature of the machine gun, to stand a retreat parade three evenings a week. He wanted some niche where he could lick his wounds, some army job with so many hours of work and so many hours of complete freedom, where he could be alone by himself. He hated the army, the huge army which had proved to him that he was good at no work, and incapable of succeeding at anything. He wrote long, aching letters to his wife, he talked less and less to the men around him, and he was close to violent attacks of anger during the most casual phases of training—during close-order drill or cleaning his rifle for inspection. He knew that if he did not find his niche it was possible that he would crack.

So he took an opening in the kitchen. It promised him nothing except a day of work, and a day of leisure which would be completely at his disposal. He found that he liked it. He was given at first the job of baking the bread for the company, and every other night he worked till early in the morning, kneading and shaping his fifty-pound mix of dough. At two or three he would be done, and for his work there would be the tangible reward of fifty loaves of bread, all fresh from the oven, all clean and smelling of fertile accomplished creativity. He had the rare and therefore intensely satisfying emotion of seeing at the end of an army chore the product of his labor.

A month after he became a cook the regiment was disbanded, and those men who did not have enough points to go home were sent to other outfits. Carter ended at an ordnance company in another Japanese city. He had by now given up all thought of getting a noncom's rating before he was discharged, and was merely content to work each alternate day. He took his work for granted and so he succeeded at it. He had begun as a baker in the new company kitchen; before long he was the first cook. It all happened quickly. One cook went home on points, another caught a skin disease, a third was transferred from the kitchen after contracting a venereal infection. On the shift which Carter worked there were left only himself and a man who was illiterate. Carter was put nominally in charge, and was soon actively in charge. He looked up each menu in an army recipe book, collected the items, combined them in the order indicated, and after the proper time had elapsed, took them from the stove. His product tasted neither better nor worse than the product of all other army cooks. But the mess sergeant was impressed. Carter had filled a gap. The next time ratings were given out Carter jumped at a bound from Private to Sergeant T/4.

On the surface he was happy; beneath the surface he was overjoyed. It took him several weeks to realize how grateful and delighted he felt. The promotion coincided with his assignment to a detachment working in a small seaport up the coast. Carter arrived there to discover that he was in charge of cooking for thirty men, and would act as mess sergeant. There was another cook, and there were four permanent Japanese K.P.s, all of them good workers. He still cooked every other day, but there was always time between meals to take a break of at least an hour and often two; he shared a room with the other cook and lived in comparative privacy for the first time in several years; the seaport was beautiful; there was only one officer, and he left the men alone; supplies were plentiful due to a clerical error which assigned rations for forty men rather than thirty; and in general everything was fine. The niche had become a sinecure.

This was the happiest period of Carter's life in the army. He came to like his Japanese K.P.s. He studied their language, he visited their homes, he gave them gifts of food from time to time. They worshipped him because he was kind to them and generous, because he never shouted, because his good humor bubbled over into games, and made the work in the kitchen seem pleasant. All the while he grew in confidence. He was not a big man, but his body filled out from the heavy work; he was likely to sing a great deal, he cracked jokes with the men on the chow line. The kitchen became his property, it became his domain, and since it was a warm room, filled with sunlight, he came to take pleasure in the very sight of it. Before long his good humor expanded into a series of efforts to improve the food. He began to take little pains and make little extra efforts which would have been impossible if he had been obliged to cook for more than thirty men. In the morning he would serve the men fresh eggs scrambled or fried to their desire in fresh butter. Instead of cooking sixty eggs in one large pot he cooked two eggs at a time in a frying pan, turning them to the taste of each soldier. He baked like a housewife satisfying her young husband; at lunch and dinner there was pie or cake, and often both. He went to great lengths. He taught the K.P.s how to make the toast come out right. He traded excess food for spices in Japanese stores. He rubbed paprika and garlic on the chickens. He even made pastries to cover such staples as corn beef hash and meat and vegetable stew.

It all seemed to be wasted. In the beginning the men might have noticed these improvements, but after a period

they took them for granted. It did not matter how he
worked to satisfy them; they trudged through the chow
line with their heads down, nodding coolly at him, and they
ate without comment. He would hang around the tables
after the meal, noticing how much they consumed, and
what they discarded; he would wait for compliments, but
the soldiers seemed indifferent. They seemed to eat without
tasting the food. In their faces he saw mirrored the distaste
with which he had once stared at cooks.

The honeymoon was ended. The pleasure he took in the
kitchen and himself curdled. He became aware again of
his painful desire to please people, to discharge responsibility, to be a man. When he had been a child, tears had
come into his eyes at a cross word, and he had lived in
an atmosphere where his smallest accomplishment was
warmly praised. He was the sort of young man, he often
thought bitterly, who was accustomed to the attention and
the protection of women. He would have thrown away all
he possessed—the love of his wife, the love of his mother,
the benefits of his education, the assured financial security
of entering his father's business—if he had been able just
once to dig a ditch as well as the most ignorant farmer.

Instead, he was back in the painful unprotected days of
his first entrance into the army. Once again the most casual
actions became the most painful, the events which were
most to be taken for granted grew into the most significant,
and the feeding of the men at each meal turned progressively more unbearable.

So Sanford Carter came full circle. If he had once hated
the cooks, he now hated the troops. At mealtimes his face
soured into the belligerent scowl with which he had once
believed cooks to be born. And to himself he muttered the
age-old laments of the housewife; how little they appreciated what he did.

Finally there was an explosion. He was approached one
day by Corporal Taylor, and he had come to hate Taylor,
because Taylor was the natural leader of the detachment
and kept the other men endlessly amused with his jokes.
Taylor had the ability to present himself as inefficient,
shiftless, and incapable, in such a manner as to convey
that really the opposite was true. He had the lightest touch,
he had the greatest facility, he could charm a geisha in

two minutes and obtain anything he wanted from a supply sergeant in five. Carter envied him, envied his grace, his charmed indifference; then grew to hate him.

Taylor teased Carter about the cooking, and he had the knack of knowing where to put the knife. "Hey, Carter," he would shout across the mess hall while breakfast was being served, "you turned my eggs twice, and I asked for them raw." The men would shout with laughter. Somehow Taylor had succeeded in conveying all of the situation, or so it seemed to Carter, insinuating everything, how Carter worked and how it meant nothing, how Carter labored to gain their affection and earned their contempt. Carter would scowl, Carter would answer in a rough voice, "Next time I'll crack them over your head." "You crack 'em, I'll eat 'em," Taylor would pipe back, "but just don't put your fingers in 'em." And there would be another laugh. He hated the sight of Taylor.

It was Taylor who came to him to get the salad oil. About twenty of the soldiers were going to have a fish fry at the geisha house; they had bought the fish at the local market but they could not buy oil, so Taylor was sent as the deputy to Carter. He was charming to Carter, he complimented him on the meal, he clapped him on the back, he dissolved Carter to warmth, to private delight in the attention, and the thought that he had misjudged Taylor. Then Taylor asked for the oil.

Carter was sick with anger. Twenty men out of the thirty in the detachment were going on the fish fry. It meant only that Carter was considered one of the ten undesirables. It was something he had known, but the proof of knowledge is always more painful than the acquisition of it. If he had been alone his eyes would have clouded. And he was outraged at Taylor's deception. He could imagine Taylor saying ten minutes later, "You should have seen the grease job I gave to Carter. I'm dumb, but man, he's dumber."

Carter was close enough to giving him the oil. He had a sense of what it would mean to refuse Taylor, he was on the very edge of mild acquiescence. But he also had a sense of how he would despise himself afterward.

"No," he said abruptly, his teeth gritted, "you can't have it."

"What do you mean we can't have it?"

"I won't give it to you." Carter could almost feel the rage which Taylor generated at being refused.

"You won't give away a lousy five gallons of oil to a bunch of G.I.s having a party?"

"I'm sick and tired—" Carter began.

"So am I." Taylor walked away.

Carter knew he would pay for it. He left the K.P.s and went to change his sweat-soaked work shirt, and as he passed the large dormitory in which most of the detachment slept he could hear Taylor's high-pitched voice.

Carter did not bother to take off his shirt. He returned instead to the kitchen, and listened to the sound of men going back and forth through the hall and of a man shouting with rage. That was Hobbs, a Southerner, a big man with a big bellowing voice.

There was a formal knock on the kitchen door. Taylor came in. His face was pale and his eyes showed a cold satisfaction. "Carter," he said, "the men want to see you in the big room."

Carter heard his voice answer huskily. "If they want to see me, they can come into the kitchen."

He knew he would conduct himself with more courage in his own kitchen than anywhere else. "I'll be here for a while."

Taylor closed the door, and Carter picked up a writing board to which was clamped the menu for the following day. Then he made a pretense of examining the food supplies in the pantry closet. It was his habit to check the stocks before deciding what to serve the next day, but on this night his eyes ranged thoughtlessly over the canned goods. In a corner were seven five-gallon tins of salad oil, easily enough cooking oil to last a month. Carter came out of the pantry and shut the door behind him.

He kept his head down and pretended to be writing the menu when the soldiers came in. Somehow there were even more of them than he had expected. Out of the twenty men who were going to the party, all but two or three had crowded through the door.

Carter took his time, looked up slowly. "You men want to see me?" he asked flatly.

They were angry. For the first time in his life he faced

the hostile expressions of many men. It was the most painful and anxious moment he had ever known.

"Taylor says you won't give us the oil," someone burst out.

"That's right, I won't," said Carter. He tapped his pencil against the scratchboard, tapping it slowly and, he hoped, with an appearance of calm.

"What a stink deal," said Porfirio, a little Cuban whom Carter had always considered his friend.

Hobbs, the big Southerner, stared down at Carter. "Would you mind telling the men why you've decided not to give us the oil?" he asked quietly.

"Cause I'm blowed if I'm going to cater to you men. I've catered enough," Carter said. His voice was close to cracking with the outrage he had suppressed for so long, and he knew that if he continued he might cry. "I'm the acting mess sergeant," he said as coldly as he could, "and I decide what goes out of this kitchen." He stared at each one in turn, trying to stare them down, feeling mired in the rut of his own failure. They would never have dared this approach to another mess sergeant.

"What crud," someone muttered.

"You won't give a lousy five-gallon can of oil for a G.I. party," Hobbs said more loudly.

"I won't. That's definite. You men can get out of here."

"Why, you lousy little snot," Hobbs burst out, "how many five-gallon cans of oil have you sold on the black market?"

"I've never sold any." Carter might have been slapped with the flat of a sword. He told himself bitterly, numbly, that this was the reward he received for being perhaps the single honest cook in the whole United States Army. And he even had time to wonder at the obscure prejudice which had kept him from selling food for his own profit.

"Man, I've seen you take it out," Hobbs exclaimed. "I've seen you take it to the market."

"I took food to trade for spices," Carter said hotly.

There was an ugly snicker from the men.

"I don't mind if a cook sells," Hobbs said, "every man has his own deal in this army. But a cook ought to give a little food to a G.I. if he wants it."

"Tell him," someone said.

"It's bull," Taylor screeched. "I've seen Carter take butter, eggs, every damn thing to the market."

Their faces were red, they circled him.

"I never sold a thing," Carter said doggedly.

"And I'm telling you," Hobbs said, "that you're a two-bit crook. You been raiding that kitchen, and that's why you don't give to us now."

Carter knew there was only one way he could possibly answer if he hoped to live among these men again. "That's a goddam lie," Carter said to Hobbs. He laid down the scratchboard, he flipped his pencil slowly and deliberately to one corner of the room, and with his heart aching he lunged toward Hobbs. He had no hope of beating him. He merely intended to fight until he was pounded unconscious, advancing the pain and bruises he would collect as collateral for his self-respect.

To his indescribable relief Porfirio darted between them, held them apart, with the pleased ferocity of a small man breaking up a fight. "Now, stop this! Now, stop this!" he cried out.

Carter allowed himself to be pushed back, and he knew that he had gained a point. He even glimpsed a solution with some honor.

He shrugged violently to free himself from Porfirio. He was in a rage, and yet it was a rage he could have ended at any instant. "All right, you men," he swore. "I'll give you the oil, but now that we're at it, I'm going to tell you a thing or two." His face red, his body perspiring, he was in the pantry and out again with a five-gallon tin. "Here," he said, "you better have a good fish fry, 'cause it's the last good meal you're going to have for quite a while. I'm sick of trying to please you. You think I have to work"— he was about to say, my fingers to the bone—"well, I don't. From now on, you'll see what chow in the army is supposed to be like." He was almost hysterical. "Take that oil. Have your fish fry." The fact that they wanted to cook for themselves was the greatest insult of all. "Tomorrow I'll give you real army cooking."

His voice was so intense that they backed away from him. "Get out of this kitchen," he said. "None of you has any business here."

They filed out quietly and they looked a little sheepish.

Carter felt weary, he felt ashamed of himself, he knew he had not meant what he said. But half an hour later, when he left the kitchen and passed the large dormitory, he heard shouts of raucous laughter, and he heard his name mentioned and then more laughter.

He slept badly that night, he was awake at four, he was in the kitchen by five, and he stood there white-faced and nervous, waiting for the K.P.s to arrive. Breakfast that morning landed on the men like a lead bomb. Carter rummaged in the back of the pantry and found a tin of dehydrated eggs covered with dust, memento of a time when fresh eggs were never on the ration list. The K.P.s looked at him in amazement as he stirred the lumpy powder into a pan of water. While it was still half-dissolved he put it on the fire. While it was still wet, he took it off. The coffee was cold, the toast was burned, the oatmeal stuck to the pot. The men dipped forks into their food, took cautious sips of their coffee, and spoke in whispers. Sullenness drifted like vapors through the kitchen.

At noontime Carter opened cans of meat-and-vegetable stew. He dumped them into a pan and heated them slightly. He served the stew with burned string beans and dehydrated potatoes which tasted like straw. For dessert the men had a single lukewarm canned peach and cold coffee.

So the meals continued. For three days Carter cooked slop, and suffered even more than the men. When mealtime came he left the chow line to the K.P.s and sat in his room, perspiring with shame, determined not to yield and sick with the determination.

Carter won. On the fourth day a delegation of men came to see him. They told him that indeed they had appreciated his cooking in the past, they told him that they were sorry they had hurt his feelings, they listened to his remonstrances, they listened to his grievances, and with delight Carter forgave them. That night, for supper, the detachment celebrated. There was roast chicken with stuffing, lemon meringue pie and chocolate cake. The coffee burned their lips. More than half the men made it a point to compliment Carter on the meal.

In the weeks which followed the compliments diminished, but they never stopped completely. Carter became ashamed at last. He realized the men were trying to humor him, and he wished to tell them it was no longer necessary.

Harmony settled over the kitchen. Carter even became friends with Hobbs, the big Southerner. Hobbs approached him one day, and in the manner of a farmer talked obliquely for an hour. He spoke about his father, he spoke about his girl friends, he alluded indirectly to the night they had almost fought, and finally with the courtesy of a Southerner he said to Carter, "You know, I'm sorry about shooting off my mouth. You were right to want to fight me, and if you're still mad I'll fight you to give you satisfaction, although I just as soon would not."

"No, I don't want to fight with you now," Carter said warmly. They smiled at each other. They were friends.

Carter knew he had gained Hobbs' respect. Hobbs respected him because he had been willing to fight. That made sense to a man like Hobbs. Carter liked him so much at this moment that he wished the friendship to be more intimate.

"You know," he said to Hobbs, "it's a funny thing. You know I really never did sell anything on the black market. Not that I'm proud of it, but I just didn't."

Hobbs frowned. He seemed to be saying that Carter did not have to lie. "I don't hold it against a man," Hobbs said, "if he makes a little money in something that's his own proper work. Hell, I sell gas from the motor pool. It's just I also give gas if one of the G.I.s wants to take the jeep out for a joy ride, kind of."

"No, but I never did sell anything." Carter had to explain. "If I ever had sold on the black market, I would have given the salad oil without question."

Hobbs frowned again, and Carter realized he still did not believe him. Carter did not want to lose the friendship which was forming. He thought he could save it only by some further admission. "You know," he said again, "remember when Porfirio broke up our fight? I was awful glad when I didn't have to fight you." Carter laughed, expecting Hobbs to laugh with him, but a shadow passed across Hobbs' face.

"Funny way of putting it," Hobbs said.

He was always friendly thereafter, but Carter knew that Hobbs would never consider him a friend. Carter thought about it often, and began to wonder about the things which made him different. He was no longer so worried about becoming a man; he felt that to an extent he had become one. But in his heart he wondered if he would ever learn the language of men.

1951

THE PATRON SAINT OF
MACDOUGAL ALLEY

How can one describe Pierrot? It is impossible to understand him; one may only tell stories about him. Yet with every move he makes, he creates another story, so one cannot keep up. Pierrot is an original; he is unlike anyone else on the face of the earth.

I can describe how he looks. He is now nineteen, and of average height. He has dark hair, regular features, and a very pleasant smile. There are times when he grows a moustache, and there are times when he shaves it off. During those periods when he sports a few hairs beneath his nose, he looks a year or two younger; when he strips it, he is nineteen again. I suspect he will look nineteen a decade from now; what is worse I often have the suspicion that he looked the same when he was born. Pierrot will never change. He is absolutely predictable in the most unforeseen situations.

He is the son of my friend Jacques Battigny, who is a professor of Romance languages at a university in New York, and never were a father and son more related and less alike. Jacques is a gentleman of considerable culture; as a representative French intellectual it is somewhat intolerable to him to pass through experience without comprehending it rationally. He demands order in every corner of his life. It is his cross that Pierrot is the eternal flux.

Father and son are thesis and antithesis. Put another way, Pierrot is Jacques turned inside out, the clothes-dummy of an intellectual. He has all the attributes of the French mind except its erudition; his greatest joy is to approach logically large bodies of experience about which he knows nothing. The first time I met him, Pierrot spoke to me for hours; he mentioned in passing, Marx, Freud, and Darwin; Heidegger, Kierkegaard, and Sartre; Lawrence and Henry Miller; Nietzsche and Spengler; Vico and Edmund Wilson;

Jean Genet and Simone de Beauvoir; Leon Trotsky and Max Schachtman; Wilhelm Reich, Gregory Zilboorg, and Karen Horney. There were two hundred other names of varied importance, and I do not believe he used a word which had less than four syllables. Therefore, it took some time for me to realize that Pierrot was an idiot.

In the hours between, he husked my brains. What did I think of Mr. Aldous Huxley? Pierrot would inquire, and long before I had reconstituted my recollections of Huxley's work and delivered them in some organized form, Pierrot was wondering how I evaluated Mr. Thomas Stearns Eliot. It seemed to me that I had never met an adolescent who was more intelligent: the breadth of his queries, the energy of his curiosity, and the quick reception which shone in his brown eyes, were quite impressive. Chaplin and Griffiths, Jackson Pollack and Hans Hofman, did I like Berlioz and had I heard Benjamin Britten? Pierrot was tireless. Only when the afternoon had passed and my wife felt obliged to invite him for dinner, did I begin to suspect that Pierrot did not contribute as much as I.

A few minutes later in response to a discreet inquiry or two, Pierrot confessed to me with relish that he had never seen a single one of the pictures he mentioned, nor read one of the authors we spoke about. "You understand," he said to me, "it is so depressing. I want to amass the totality of knowledge, and consequently I don't know where to begin." He sighed. "I look at the books on my father's shelf. I say to myself, 'Is it in these books that I will find the termination, or even the beginning, of my philosophical quest?' You understand? What is the meaning to life? That is what obsesses me. And will these books give the answer? I look at them. They are paper, they are cardboard. Is it possible that the essence of truth can be communicated to paper and ink?" He paused and smiled. "Reality and illusion. I think about history, and I wonder, 'Does Marxism take proper account of history?' Someone was telling me to read Engel's *Marriage and the Family*. Would you recommend it? I am very interested in the subject."

He was absolutely tireless. As dinner progressed, as the dishes were washed, the brunt of conversation shifted from my tongue to Pierrot's. He sat with my wife and me through the evening, he discussed his ambitions, his depressions, his victories, his defeats. What did I think of his parents, he wanted to know, and immediately proceeded to tell me. Pierrot's mother had died, and his father had married again. Georgette was ten years younger than Jacques, and Pierrot found this disturbing. "You understand," he said to me cheerfully, "I look for love. I search for it in the midst of my family, and I do not find it. Between Georgette and me there is an attraction, I ask myself whether it is maternal or physical? I should like to bring matters to a head, but I am a virgin, and I should detest it if I could not satisfy her. Is it true that one must serve the apprenticeship of love?" Long before I could have turned an answer, he had forgotten his question. "And then I wonder in the privacy of my thoughts if what I really seek is the conquest of Georgette, or if I am looking for her only to be my mother. I should like her to hold me close. You understand, I am masochistic. I feel so many things." He held his breast. "I am an infant and I am a lover. Which is my nature? Which do I desire to satisfy? You realize, I want to be close to my father, and yet I am repelled by him. It is like psycho-analysis. I think sometimes I wish to live *ménage à trois,* but then I decide I am destructive and desire to live in isolation. Is it man's nature to live in isolation? I feel so lonely at times. I wish to communicate. Communication is a problem which interests me. Does it you?"

At one o'clock in the morning, after numerous hints had failed, I was obliged to tell Pierrot that he must go home. He looked at me sadly, he told me that he knew he bored me, he left with an air of such dejection that my wife and I were ashamed of ourselves, and felt we had turned a waif into the streets. The next time I saw his father, I apologized for this, and was cut short.

"Apologize for nothing," Jacques shouted. "The boy is a monster. He has no conception whatsoever of time. If you had not put him out, he would have stayed for a week." Jacques held his head. "I shall certainly go mad. There is nothing to do with him but to be completely rude. Listen to what has happened."

The story Jacques told was indeed painful. Battigny the senior is a lover of books. He loves to read, he declaims on the art of reading, he loves bindings, he loves type, he loves books separately and together. It seems that Pierrot was once talking to a friend of Jacques's, a somewhat distinguished professor. The professor, taken with the boy, loaned him a copy of Florio's translation of Montaigne's essays. It was not a first edition, but it was an old one, and of some value, beautifully tooled in leather, and handsomely printed. "Do you know how long ago that was?" Jacques demanded of me. "It was two years ago. Pierrot has kept it in his brief case for two years. Has he ever read a page?" The answer was that he had not. He had merely kept it, and in the course of keeping it, the cover-board had been sheared and the spine exposed. "I screamed at him," Jacques said softly, "it was indecent. I told him it was two years he had kept it, and he told me no, it was only a short period. He cannot comprehend the passage of time. He is always about to dip into the book, to study it here and smell it there. It is shameful.

"It is intolerable," Jacques cried. "He torments me. I have talked to his English teacher at high school. He asks her if he should study *Beowulf,* and he cannot even pass the examinations. I do not care if he does not go to college, I am not a snob about it, but the boy is incapable of doing anything with his hands. He cannot even learn a trade."

I was to discover that Pierrot could not even learn to say yes or no. He was quite incapable of it, no matter to what brutal lengths I pursued him. Once in eating at my house, I asked him if he wished some bread and butter.

"I do not know," Pierrot said, "I ask myself."

"Perriot, do you want bread and butter?" I cried out.

"Why do you wish me to eat?" he asked dreamily, as if my motive were sinister. "One eats to live, which supposes that life is worth while. But I ask myself: is life worth while?"

"Pierrot! Do you want bread and butter? Answer yes or no!"

Pierrot smiled sheepishly. "Why do you ask me a yes-and-no question?"

One could say anything to him, and he enjoyed it immensely. He had been making advances to my wife for quite some time. No matter how she teased him, scolded him, or ignored him, he persisted. Yet once, when I took a walk with him, he launched into a long description of my virtues. I was handsome, I was attractive, he was stirred by me. And with that he pinched my bicep and said, "You are so strong."

"My God, Pierrot," I said in exasperation. "First you try to make love to my wife, and then you try to make love to me."

"Yes," he said morosely, "and I succeed with neither."

His father finally drove him from the house. He gave Pierrot two hundred dollars, and told him he was to find a job in the city and learn to live by his own labor. Jacques was penitent. "I am so cruel to the boy. But what is there to do? I cannot bear the sight of him. Have you ever watched him work? If he picks up a hammer, he smashes his thumb. He lays down the hammer, he sucks his finger, he loses the hammer, he forgets why he needed it in the first place, he tries to remember, he ends by falling asleep." Jacques groaned. "I dread to think of him out in the world. He is completely impractical. He will spend the two hundred dollars in a night on his bohemian friends."

Only a father could have been so wrong. Pierrot had the blood of a French peasant. The two hundred dollars lasted for six months. He lived with one friend, he lived with another; he lunched with an acquaintance and stayed for dinner. He drank beer in the Village; he was always to be found at Louis's, at Minetta's, at the San Remo, but no one remembered when he had paid for a drink. He was pretty enough to be courted, and he had frequent adventures with homosexuals. They were always finding him in a bar, they would talk to him, he would talk to them. He would tell them his troubles, he would confide, he would admit warmly that he had never discovered anyone who understood him so well. He would end by going to the other's apartment. There Pierrot would drink, he would continue to talk, he would talk even as the friend removed his shirt and apologized for the heat. It was only at the penultimate moment that Pierrot would leave. "You understand," he would say, "I want to know you. But I am so confused. Do we have a basis to find a foundation of things in common?" And out he would skip through the door.

"Why do they always approach me?" he would ask in an innocent voice.

I would make the mistake of being severe. "Because you solicit, Pierrot."

He would smile. "Ah, that is an interesting interpretation. I hope it is true. I would love to make my living in an antisocial manner. Society is so evil."

He lived with a girl who was a fair mate for him. She had a tic at one corner of her mouth, and she was a follower of Buddha. The girl was trying to start a Buddhist colony in America. It was all mixed somehow with a theory about the birth trauma which she explained to me one night at a party. The reason armies functioned in combat was because the noise of battle returned the ordinary soldier to the primal state of birth. At such a moment his officers came to represent the protecting mother, and the soldier would obey their will even if it meant death. She was proud of the theory, and snapped at Pierrot when he would attempt to discuss it with her.

"A wonderful girl," he told me once. "It is a most exciting affair. She is absolutely frigid."

It seemed that if he dropped his shoes upon the floor, she would not allow him to approach her. "There is such uncertainty. It recaptures the uncertainty of life. I think about it. People meet. Lives intersect. It is points on a plane. Would you say this is a fit topic for philosophical investigation?"

In the course of events the Buddhist threw him out. At any rate, metaphorically she threw him out. The affair ended, but since Pierrot had no place to live, he continued to stay with her while he looked for another friend to give him a bed. During this period he came to me to ask if I would put him up, but I refused. After making these requests, he would look so forlorn that I hated myself.

"I understand," he said. "One of my friends who is analyzing me by hypnosis has made me see that I exploit everyone. It is the influence of the culture, I would think. I have become very interested in the movements of political bodies. I see that previously I adopted too personal an attitude. What is your opinion of my new political approach?"

"We'll discuss it another time, Pierrot. I'm awfully sorry I can't put you up for the night."

"It is all right," he said sweetly. "I do not know where I shall sleep tonight, but it does not matter. I am an exploiter, and it is only proper that people should recognize this in me." He left with a meek forgiving look. "I shall sleep. Do not worry about me," he said as the door closed.

Five minutes later I was still trying to put the matter from my mind when the doorbell rang. Pierrot was back.

All night he had had a problem he wanted to discuss with me, but in the interest of our conversation, it had completely slipped his mind.

"What is it?" I asked coldly, annoyed at having been taken in.

He answered me in French. *"Tu sais, j'ai la chaudepisse."*

"Oh, Christ!"

He nodded. He had been to see a doctor, and it would be cleared up. There would be a wonder drug employed.

"Not by one of your friends, I hope?"

No, this was a bona-fide doctor. But he had another problem. The ailment had been provoked by the Buddhist. Of this, he was certain. At the moment, however, he was engaged in an affair with a young married woman, and he was curious to know whether he should tell her.

"You certainly should." I grasped him by the shoulder. "Pierrot, you have to tell her."

His brown eyes clouded. "You understand, it would be very difficult. It would destroy so much rapport between us. I would prefer to say nothing. Why should I speak? I am absolutely without morality," he declared with passion.

"Morality be damned," I said. "Do you realize that if you don't tell the girl, you will have to see the doctor again and again? Do you know how expensive that is?"

He sighed. This is what he had been afraid of. Like the peasant brought slowly and stubbornly to face some new and detestable reality, he agreed dourly. "In that case, I shall tell her. It is too bad."

Lately, I have hardly seen Pierrot. His two hundred dollars has run out, and he is now obliged to work. He has had eleven jobs in four months. I could not hope to describe them all. He has been let go, fired, dismissed, and has resigned. He was an office boy for two days, and on the second day, pausing to take a drink, he placed his letter basket on the lip of the water cooler. Somehow—he is convinced it is the fault of the cooler—the water ran over the papers. In attempting to wipe them, he dropped the basket, and the wet paper became dirty. Signatures ran, names became illegible, and to the fury of the officer manager, Pierrot did not attempt to excuse himself but asked instead why Americans were so compulsive about business correspondence.

He also worked in a factory. He was very depressed after the first day of work had ended, and called me up in such a mournful voice that I felt obliged to see him. He was tired, he was disgusted. "I hold a piece of metal in my hand," he said to me, "and I touch it to an abrasive agent. Slowly square corners become round. Eight hours of such work I suffer. Can this be the meaning to existence?" His voice conveyed that he expected to continue the job until the end of time. "I search for my identity. It is lost. I am merely Agent 48."

At this point I rose upon him in wrath. I told him that he had two choices. He could work in order to live, or he could die. If he wished to die, I would not attempt to discourage him. In fact, I would abet him. "If you come to me, Pierrot, and ask for a gun, I will attempt to find you a gun. Until then, stop complaining." He listened to me with an enormous smile. His eyes shone at the vigor of my language. "You are marvelous," he said with admiration.

The very last I've heard is that Pierrot is soon to be drafted. Some of my friends are very upset about this. They say that the boy will be a mental case in a few weeks. Others insist that the army will be good for him. I am at odds with both of them.

I see Pierrot in the army. He will sleep late, curled in a little ball beneath his blankets. He will be certain to miss reveille. About eight o'clock in the morning he will stumble drowsily to the mess hall, his mess gear falling from his hand, and will look stupidly at the cook.

"Oh," he will say, "oh, I am late for breakfast."

"Get out of here," the cook will say.

"Oh, I go." Pierrot will nod. "I deserve to miss a meal. I have been negligent. Of course, I will be out all day on a march, and I will be very hungry, but it is my fault. And it does not matter. What is food?" He will be so unhappy that the cook no matter how he curses will scramble him some eggs. Pierrot will suggest toast, he will induce the cook to heat the coffee, he will engage him in a philosophical discussion. At eleven o'clock, Pierrot will leave to join his training platoon, and at two in the afternoon he will find them. Hours later, at retreat parade, the inspecting officer will discover that Pierrot has lost his rifle.

That will be the beginning of the end. Pierrot will be assigned to K.P. for three days in a row. By the first morning he will so have misplaced and mis-washed the pots that the cooks will be forced to assist him, and will work harder than they have ever worked. By evening the mess sergeant will be begging the first sergeant never to put Pierrot on K.P. again.

The army cannot recover from such a blow. K.P. is its foundation, and when cooks ask to remove men from that duty, it can take only a few days before every soldier in the army will follow the trail blazed by Pierre Battigny. I see see the army collapsing two months after Pierrot enters it.

At that moment I hope to influence the course of history. Together with such responsible individuals as I may find, I will raise a subscription to send Pierrot to the Soviet Union. Once he is there, the world is saved. He will be put in the army immediately, and before his first day is over, the Russians will have him up before a firing squad. Then Pierrot will rise to his true stature.

"I ask myself," he will say to the Russian soldiers, "Am I not miserable? Is life not sad? Shoot me."

At this point the Russians will throw down their arms and begin to weep. "We do not enjoy ourselves either," they will sob. "Shoot us, too." In the grand Russian manner, the news will spread across the steppes. Soldiers everywhere will cast away their weapons. America and Russia will be disarmed in a night, and peace will come over the earth.

They will build a statue to Pierrot at the corner of Eighth Street and MacDougal. New generations will pass and spit at him. "He was Square," they will say.

1951

THE DEAD GOOK

The regiment was dispersed over an area twenty miles wide and more than ten miles deep. In the conventional sense it could hardly be called a front. Here could be found an outpost of ten men; there, one mile away, a platoon of thirty or forty men; somewhere to the rear was Hq and Hq company, somewhere to the flank another unit. Through all the foothills and mountains of this portion of the Philippines, a few thousand American soldiers in groups of ten and twenty and fifty faced approximately as many Japanese, established like themselves along the summits of advantageous heights or bedded in ambush in the tropical growth of the valleys and streams. There was almost no contact. If either army had wished to advance, and had added so much as another regiment, progress would have been rapid, but the fate of the campaign was being determined elsewhere. For a month and then another, as the mild winter ended and the tropical rains of spring began, the outposts and detachments of these isolated forces made long patrols against one another, tramped for miles over rice paddies, up small mountains, along narrow rivers, and through jungle forests—patrols which covered ten or fifteen or as many as twenty miles in a single day, and more often than not were entirely without incident. Instead of a front there was a mingling of isolated positions, with Japanese units between Americans, and Americans between Japanese. The patrols were as often to the rear as to the front, and small groups of men brushed one another with rotary manoeuvers, each detachment sweeping its own area in a circle.

It was not the worst of situations. Casualties were very few, and supply was regular. Many of the outposts had hot food brought from the rear, and some of the detachments were stationed in Filipino villages and slept beneath a roof. Still, it was not the best of situations. There were patrols almost every day for every man, and though they were invariably uneventful, they were nonetheless hard work. A squad would leave at eight in the morning; it would be fortunate to return by the end of the afternoon. The morning sun would beat upon the men, the midday rain would drench them, mud would cake upon their boots. They went nowhere, they patrolled in circles, up mountains and down cliffs, and yet each of them was obliged to carry an assortment of gear which never weighed less than twenty-five pounds. They carried their rifles, they carried two grenades hooked to the load of their cartridge belts. Over their shoulders were slung two bandoliers of ammunition, at their hips tugged the sluggish weight of water canteens, in their breast pockets chafed the cardboard corners of a food ration. None of these items was heavy in itself; taken together they were hardly to be disregarded. It was a reasonable load for a healthy man upon a hunting trip; these were unhealthy men burdened by a chronic residue of such diseases as malaria and yellow jaundice, and such discomforts as foot ulcers, diarrhea, and fungus rot.

It was dreary. There was danger, but it was remote; there was diversion, but it was rare. For the most part it was work, and work of the most distasteful character, work which was mean and long. The men, most often, did not complain. There were better things to do, but there were certainly worse, and for those who had been overseas for several years and had participated in more than this campaign, it was certainly not the most odious way in which to serve their time. They were satisfied to let events pass in the most quiet manner possible.

On a particular spring morning, the third squad of the first platoon of B Company was preparing to go out on patrol. Because of illness and a single casualty, their numbers had been reduced in the last two months from twelve men to seven, and since two men had to be left behind on the knoll of the hill where they had dug their outpost to serve as guard and answer the telephone, only five men were left to satisfy the requirements of a patrol which counted theoretically upon a strength of ten. This fact, which in a more arduous campaign would be considered a dangerous injustice, was here accepted merely as an annoyance. There was always the possibility that something could happen where their lack of numbers might be disastrous, but inasmuch as they had been operating with five men for quite some time and nothing had as yet occurred, the main source of their grievance was that they almost never received any rest. If in one of the sudden and seemingly arbitrary disposals of replacements, they had been brought up to strength, it is likely that they would have continued to patrol with five men, and gained the advantage of an alternate day of inactivity.

This morning four Filipinos were apparently joining them. They appeared in the valley which lay beneath the knoll and strolled towards the outpost. Visible from quite a distance with their loose white shirts and bright blue pants, they advanced without caution as if expecting to be recognized. Lucas, the buck sergeant in command of the squad, had been on the phone earlier in the morning, and now he said quietly, "Well, here they are. Let's get ready." He had already named the men who were to go out, and they were strapping on their equipment. In a few minutes, he and the four other men weaved down through the grass of the hill and moved towards the Filipinos in the rice paddy.

"What's up, we got the Gooks today?" Brody, a thin hard-bitten private, asked of Lucas.

"Seems like we do." Lucas was a big relaxed man who spoke slowly and thought slowly. He was not very intelligent and did not pretend to be, but perhaps for this reason he was not a bad soldier as sergeants go. Events rarely ruffled him. He had small sensitivity to distinguish between the extraordinary and the commonplace, and so he took his orders, acted upon that portion of them he understood, and was never agitated if things turned out differently than had been expected.

Private Brody was nervous, he was high-strung, he was often angry. "Well, what the hell are the Gooks here for?" he asked, pointing to the Filipinos.

"Shoot if I know," Lucas drawled. He was readjusting a grenade in his belt. "There was some kind of fuss over the telephone. The Gooks are from Panazagay, some such place. They went to headquarters this morning, and then headquarters decided to send them here."

The squad approached the Filipinos. They were small brown men with the lithe bodies of Oriental peasants, and they all smiled in unison at the soldiers.

"Sergeant Lucas, sair?" one of them inquired. By the way he stood forward from the others it was apparent that he was the only one who spoke English.

"How do," Lucas said mildly. He was courteous and bored.

The Filipino who spoke English began to talk to Lucas. He spoke at great length in a stammering mixture of what was English and of what he thought was English. The other men in the squad did not bother to listen. They squatted on their heels in the muddy turf of the rice paddy, and looked dispassionately at the Filipinos who squatted in a line, facing them, about ten yards away. From time to time one of the Filipinos would smile, and in response one of the Americans would nod. Off to one side, Lucas stood heavily, his ear inclined to catch a detail here and there in the seemingly endless story.

"Let me get this straight," he asked quietly. "The guerrillas ambushed the Japs?"

"No, sair, no don't know. Maybe Jap, maybe guerrilla, big ambush maybe. Lot of shooting. Guerrilla no come back. Now, American soldiers ambush Jap maybe."

Lucas nodded, It was obvious he knew no more than before, and as he continued to listen, it became equally obvious that he no longer bothered to distinguish the words. When the Filipino had exhausted his account, Lucas yawned.

"All right. What's your name? Miguel?"

"Yes, sair."

"Okay, Miguel, you lead us. You take us where you want. Only nice and slow, you understand? We're in no hurry, and it's a hot day."

Miguel said something to the other Filipinos in the Tagalog language, and they answered curtly. They stood up, and began to move across the paddy at a half-trot.

"That's what I meant," Lucas said to Miguel. "Tell them to slow up."

Reluctantly, he conveyed this message to the other three

Filipinos, who seemed to obey it just as reluctantly.

"Man, they're always in a hurry," Lucas drawled aloud.

The other four soldiers fell into line behind their sergeant. The Filipinos moved in a group which was bunched close together, and about thirty yards in front of the Americans, who moved in a leisurely file with some distance between them. None of the soldiers knew what the patrol was about, and they did not bother to ask. There was only so much variety to a patrol, and it had long been exhausted. There seemed no reason now to inquire. If all went well, they would find out in due time. They did not even bother to watch the direction in which they moved; they had been over these hills and paddies so often that it was almost impossible for them to get lost. They trudged along behind Lucas, their guns slung, their heads drooped forward to examine the footing before them. Not even the thought of an ambush caused them much concern. In such a large area there was small likelihood that at any given moment enemy troops might blunder into one another. To attempt to be constantly on the alert seemed a little ridiculous. Each followed the man in front of him, daydreamed a little, looked about him a little, and tried not to think too exclusively of the heat or the sores upon his legs or the familiar small distress of his chronic diarrhea.

Only Brody was an exception. Brody worried. Brody was irritable. Brody saw all kinds of possibilities. "Where are we going?" he panted as he walked behind Lucas.

"Oh, I don't know," Lucas said. "We're just following the Gooks."

Brody trotted for a few steps and caught up to the sergeant. "Well, why?"

Lucas shrugged. "I guess they sold the Old Man a bill of goods. He told me to go along with 'em."

"What did the Gooks say?" Brody persisted.

"Miguel, he said a lot, but I just can't follow that Gook talk. It's something about an ambush, and guerrillas and Japs. It's all a mess and I bet it's a false alarm. You know these Gooks, how excited they get."

"Me, I know them," Brody said with ferocity. "I hate the Gooks." He tripped in a hole the hoof of a carabao had made and jarred his ankle. "They're always laughing at us. They're dirty, you see, they're two-faced." As abruptly as he had spoken, he lapsed into a frustrated silence.

Lucas made no answer. He had pouched a cut of to-bacco in his cheek, and he moved with the long lazy pace of a big man, holding his rifle in one hand and allowing it to swing in rhythm to his steps. "Oh, there're good Gooks and bad Gooks," Lucas said after a while.

Brody cursed. "Look at them with their white shirts. They can be seen from ten miles away." His body quivered with pent emotion.

Lucas reddened. The truth was that he had not paid attention to this detail. "That don't make much difference," he muttered.

"It does to me." Lucas's dismissal of everything he had said fretted Brody. Perspiration ran into his eyes. "Hey, you," Brody shrieked at the Filipinos ahead, "hey, you Gooks, take off those shirts. You want to get us am-bushed?"

They looked at him stupidly, they smiled, they tried to understand. Blindly, Brody ran towards them, his can-teens, his ration, his bandolier and grenades jouncing with leaden metallic sounds as he trotted. He shoved the first Filipino in his path with force enough to send him almost to the ground. "Your shirt," Brody said apoplec-tically, "get it off."

They comprehended at last. They smiled again, they murmured apologies, they stripped their shirts to expose their brown chests and wrapped the white cotton about their waists like a belt.

"That's better," Brody grunted. He slowed his pace and fell into line behind Lucas who did not look at him. Lucas merely shifted the plug from one side of his mouth to the other.

Brody was in a state which all the men in the squad could recognize. It visited each of them at different times. A man's normal manner might be friendly or distant or casual, but there were periods when he seemed to consist of nothing but rage, when his outraged nerves would snap surly responses to the most insignificant questions, and everything he did expressed a generalized hatred toward the most astonishing people and objects—his best friend or a stone he might kick with his foot. Brody was ex-periencing such a period.

It started with a letter from his girl friend that told him she was to marry someone else. She had waited for four years, but she was waiting no longer. In a sense the letter hardly bothered him. His girl friend had become as remote to Brody as the moon. But the letter had nonetheless served to remind Brody of how he lived, and that was unbearable. He had seen a great deal of combat, he had gone through all the stages. He had had the excitement of the untested soldier, and the competence of the veteran; he had passed from the notion that he would never be killed to the gloomy and then indifferent acceptance of the idea that he probably would be killed. He had never come to the point where it no longer mattered particularly. Like the other men, his senses diminished, his thoughts slowed, and time was a neutral vacuum in which neutral experience was spent. Life passed in a mild and colorless depression.

The letter destroyed his armor. It reminded him of a world in which people cared enough about themselves to take such actions as getting married. It awakened in him a feeling that it might not be unpleasant to live, and that feeling made much intolerable. It made death vivid to him again, and worse than that, it made him conscious of himself. It did the worst thing which could befall a soldier in combat, it made Brody wonder who he was, and what it would mean if he would die. There was no way to find out, there was no way even to think about it connectedly. The result was that every sleeping nerve in Brody's body had become alive and asked its question. The only answer, considering conditions, was a grass-fire of hatred which smoldered within him, and rasped into flame at anything which crossed his path. On this particular day it was the Filipinos. For the moment Brody considered them as directly responsible for everything which had happened to him.

Slowly, the patrol moved on. The men crossed rice paddies and swamps, they traversed trails through bamboo groves, and climbed hills with tall grass and scattered trees. The heat increased as the sun moved towards its zenith, and gnats, mosquitoes, and flies plagued the exposed surfaces of their skin. After an hour had passed they took a break and then moved on again. It was hot and the faded green fatigues of the soldiers began to turn black with their perspiration. They were thirsty. The sun beat upon their heads.

The hills were now covered with brush. Soon the brush thickened, the ground became softer, more muddy, and the trees grew higher. Their foliage met overhead and dimmed the light of the day. It was still hot, but it was dark now, it was steamy, and the air had the stagnant expectancy of a thunderstorm. The men sweated even more profusely.

The Filipinos came to a small brook which they forded. On the other side the trail split into two forks. Miguel came back to talk to Lucas.

"Sair, is very dangerous from here, Jahpanese, many Jahpanese."

Lucas nodded. "Okay, let's watch our step." He gathered his men about him, and informed them of what Miguel had said. "Seems to me," he mumbled softly, "I was over this trail a couple of weeks ago and nothing was here. But maybe the Gooks know something. Let's keep our eyes open."

This warning from Lucas changed the character of the patrol. Now, every man was alert. It was often like this. After hours of dull marching all the men in the squad would seem to awaken at once, as if the fear or readiness of one had been communicated to all.

The trail contributed to their caution. It was very narrow, and permitted only one man to pass at a time. Moreover, it took a turn to the left or right every few yards, and each soldier had the unpleasant sensation of watching the man in front disappear around each bend. Sweat dripped from their eyes, fell from their noses, ran into their mouths. They breathed heavily, and with each step they examined the foliage on either side of them, looking for a possible sniper. Each time a man blundered over a root or made some small noise, the others winced in unison. After ten minutes of working along the trail, they were more tired than they had been at any time that day, they were hotter, they were wetter, they were more oppressed.

Lucas whistled to Miguel. "Stop your men." Miguel looked as if he wished to continue, but Lucas had sat down already. "We're taking a break. Pass it down," he whispered to the man behind him.

Quietly, each man whispered the same message to his

neighbor. They all remained standing for a moment, their damp shirts collapsed wetly upon their bodies, their mouths puffing at damp cigarettes whose paper was brown where sweat had reached it. They seated themselves cautiously, each soldier facing alternately an opposite side of the trail. Although they rested their backs against tree trunks, and draped their rifles over their knees, they were not exactly in repose. Their heads were turned upward, their eyes studied the foliage before them, and the muscles in their forearms were tense to grasp their rifles if it were necessary. Nonetheless they smoked their cigarettes.

Up ahead came a dull thumping sound. Each of the men started and then relaxed. It was the blade of a machete chopping into something—a wet branch, a mass of pulpy fruit—they did not know. A minute later the sounds ceased, and each man was rewarded with an unexpected comfort. Pieces of ripe pineapple cut from a pineapple bush by the Filipinos were passed back. They ate the fruit greedily, and watched for snipers. Their legs were tired, their eyes hurt from staring into the jungle, their throats were parched and reacted with delight to the sweet tart juices, their stomachs accepted the food with lust, and their arms trembled from the tension of holding a rifle, a piece of fruit, and a cigarette. There was both the blissful satisfaction of thirst as each mouthful was gorged from a shaking hand, and the anxious heavy knowledge that to rest on a trail like this was dangerous, in the gloom of the jungle each minute seemed more ominous, and yet the deliciousness of the feast was increased by the situation.

After some minutes, Lucas sent another message down the trail. One hoarse whisper generated the next. "Let's get going. Let's get going."

As they moved on, it became evident to Lucas that the Filipinos were heading towards a particular place. Their tension increased with every step, and they proceeded with more and more caution. Now, there were halts along the trail of a minute or more, while one Filipino would work ahead, would study the trail, and then come back to wave them forward. Half an hour passed with less ground covered every moment. The pauses increased the irritation, the fatigue, and the tension. The men would stand in the narrow trail, foliage tickling the back of their necks, insects plaguing their motionless bodies. To stand still became more onerous than to move. They were able to think of nothing but the heat, the humidity, and the smart of the sores upon their feet. They could hear sounds more intensely than when they marched. They could sense danger more acutely than if they were in motion. Altogether they felt more vulnerable and it made them cranky.

Brody fretted the most. "Tell them to get a move on, Lucas," he would whisper. Or else he would wipe his chin of its sweat. "Leave it to the Gooks," he would moan.

These protests seemed to leave Lucas quite indifferent. He stood placidly at the point, watching the Filipinos dart ahead and then work their way back, nodded solemnly each time they waved for him to come ahead, and then remained still while they reconnoitered the next few hundred feet of trail. "They're taking us into a trap," Brody hissed furiously, and Lucas shrugged. "I don't think so," his whispered back.

Travelling no more than a few hundred yards every quarter of an hour, the patrol inched forward along the trail. They crossed another brook, and while they waited several of the men quietly filled their canteens and inserted one of the pills they kept to disinfect their drinking water. A little further on, they passed the corpse of a Japanese soldier who was lying near the trail, and they took pains to keep as far away from him as possible, more from their repugnance of the feeding maggots than from the novelty of seeing a dead man.

They were soon to see another. It developed that the objective of the patrol was reached before they had even learned the objective. The trail rose for a few hundred feet, and then dipped into an empty draw. In the middle of the draw, lying behind a Japanese machine gun, lay a dead Filipino. Miguel and the three peasants stood at the top of the draw, and looked sadly upon him. One by one the soldiers reached them, until a group of nine men, five in uniform, and four in blue pants and white shirts wrapped about their middle, collected on one bank of the small ravine and stared into the quiet buzzing sunlight which glinted upon the skin of the dead guerrilla and reflected the tropical yellow-green of the grass in the draw.

"Oh, sair," Miguel said softly to Lucas, "he brave

mahn. He kill three Jahpanese last month. He come here every night."

"He came here alone every night?" Brody asked.

Miguel nodded. "Last night in village we hear shooting. Jahpanese grenade. Luiz no possess Jahpanese grenade. They kill him, we think, last night."

"What'd he want to set up for in the middle of the draw?" Lucas asked. "He's a sitting duck there."

"Oh," Miguel said, "Luiz only amateur soldier."

Lucas looked at him sharply, but Miguel's expression was impassive. Lucas yawned. "Let's scout around, men, there might still be Japs here."

The fragment of the squad divided into two men and three men. Lucas and Brody circled the draw from one side, and joined the others on the continuation of the trail. The draw seemed deserted. "Cover me," Lucas said, and darted into the open grass.

He approached the dead man cautiously to make certain no wires connected him to a booby trap. After a moment he waved to Brody to join him.

"We might as well take the gun back," he said. "That's a nice Jap machine gun." He looked at it with the professional curiosity of a hobbyist. "Man, that's a funny old gun," Lucas said.

Miguel joined them at the bottom of the draw. "Sair, we go back now?"

"I guess we found what we came for," Lucas shrugged.

"Sair. Four Filipinos. We carry back body. You come with Filipinos?"

Brody shouldered his way between them. "It's going to slow us up. Let them do it on their own."

"Sair, very dangerous without American soldiers."

Lucas was working the bolt on the Japanese weapon. "This is a real light machine gun. It's sort of like our BAR," he announced. Miguel touched him tentatively on the sleeve, and Lucas looked up. "I guess we can go along with them," he said to Brody half-apologetically.

Brody felt as if an injustice were being perpetrated. "They tricked us into coming out here," he swore. "All they wanted us for was to pick up one of their lousy men. They could have done this whole patrol themselves."

"I dunno," Lucas murmured. "I mean a man deserves

a funeral. We'll escort them, I suppose." He looked away from Brody, and patted the gun. "We ought to take this, too."

"What for?" Brody demanded. "It's heavy."

"Oh, just because." Lucas was thinking with pleasure of stripping the gun when he returned to the outpost. He intended to take it completely apart, and then put it back together again. The thought of this gave him a feeling of anticipation for the first time in months.

Brody was angrier han ever. Everything Lucas did seemed outrageous. Like a man who wishes to strike a woman and frustrates the impulse, Brody now effectively begged the woman to strike him. With passion he picked up the Japanese machine gun. "You want to take it back?" he asked rhetorically of Lucas. "Well, I'll carry the bugger."

"That's right, Brody, you carry it all the way back." Brody realized he had gone too far. "And I don't want to hear any griping," Lucas added.

The patrol started back. It was hotter than ever, it was wetter than ever, it began to rain again. The soldiers plodded forward through a gumbo muck, and the Filipinos staggered behind them, carrying the body of Luiz, the dead guerrilla, lashed to a pole. Now, it was the Americans who wanted to go fast, who wished to quit the contaminated area as quickly as possible, and it was the Filipinos mired in the labor of carrying a dead man on a heavy pole who time and again were forced to stop.

Brody stepped along in a rage. The Japanese machine gun must have weighed at least twenty pounds; added to the load of his own gear, it was a cruel increment. There seemed no way to hold the gun properly. No matter how he slung it, over a shoulder, upon his back, in front of his belly, the gun seemed all knobs, protuberances, points and edges. Either the stock, the muzzle, or the handle of the bolt was always pressing into his ribs, his arms, his shoulder blades. Worst of all the gun had a detestable odor. There was the smell of Japanese fish oil, and the smell of Luiz who had acquired the gun, a smell of Filipino peasant which to Brody meant carabao flop and Philippine dust and Filipino food, an amalgam not unlike stale soya sauce. Worst of all, there was the odor of Luiz's blood, a particularly sweet and intimate smell, fetid and suggesting to his nostrils that it was not completely dry. It was the smell of a man who had died, and it mingled with the fish oil and the soya sauce and the considerable stench of Brody's own body and Brody's own work-sweated clothes, until he thought he would gag. The odor was everywhere; it stuck to his lungs and eddied in his nostrils. As he perspired, his sweat touched the gun, seemed to dissolve from it newer, more unpleasant odors. Brody travelled on his anger. It was his luck, he thought incoherently, to have a man like Lucas for a sergeant; it was his luck to be in a squad so stupid that the stupidest of Filipinos and the most cunning could take them in, or more properly, could take them anywhere, take them on a five-mile hike, for what, for nothing, to serve as escort so they could bring one of their own men back, a man stupid enough to go out at night and get himself killed. Brody began to think it was a plot. It had all been calculated to make him carry the machine gun. The smell became Luiz to him, and he cursed the gun as he walked, talking to Luiz and telling him what a no-good Gook he thought him to be, spanking the gun away as it thudded upon his ribs and jabbed his sternum. Trust the Gooks, trust the Gooks, trust the blasted Gooks, he kept repeating to himself, saying it faster and faster like a talisman to protect him in his exasperation and growing exhaustion from bursting into tears of childish frenzy.

The walk back was exceptionally long. The Filipinos jogged and panted from their exertion, dropped the pole when the Americans would rest, and picked it up to run in their Oriental half-trot each time the Americans would start again. When they came out of the jungle, the patrol set across the fields towards the Filipino village, towards Panazagay. The sun broiled them, the rain wet them, the sun dried them again. Heat drenched their clothing with body moisture. Brody staggered, the Filipinos staggered, the others trudged, and the sun fried the bowl of earth over which they travelled. How the gun stank!

Brody would hardly have cared if they had been ambushed by Japanese. He would have flopped to the ground, and let the others worry about it. He did not bother to look ahead of him. He merely wavered along for thirty or forty steps, and then outraged his lungs by running for ten or fifteen yards to catch up with the last American. To the Filipinos behind him, he paid no attention. He was thinking of all kinds of things. Through the stupor of the march, he could not rid himself of the idea that he was carrying a dead man in his arms. A man who was completely dead. He had seen dead men whole and dead men in fractions and mutilations, but this was the first dead man who was completely dead to Brody, and it filled him with fright. He was not too far from delirium. It seemed almost possible that Luiz was carrying him, and he was the one who had died. What did it mean? He had seen so much death that death was the one thing absolutely without meaning to him. Except for now. It filled his pores. To the hot sweat of the sun he added the cold sweat of his thoughts. Brody's tortured nerves could have been relieved only by a scream.

"Pigs, the Gooks are pigs," he muttered aloud. "They live like pigs." And the gun hugged him, a dancing skeleton, jiggling its death's head in his face.

The patrol came at last to Panazagay, a village of bamboo houses upon stilts with a muddy lane between the houses, and no street at all, no stores at all. The Filipino carriers brought the body of Luiz to his home. It was a small bamboo house and stood in front of the village pump. The soldiers sprawled by the pump, bathed their heads and bodies with water, and lay around heavily, too fatigued to eat.

From the house came screams. A woman's scream, then a child's wail, then the cries of several women and children. People began to emerge from all the houses of the village, they converged upon the houses in front of the village pump, they climbed the bamboo ladder which led into the bamboo house. A concert of grief spread in volume from moment to moment. The soldiers lay on the ground and hardly heard these cries.

They were far too weary. The sounds of bereavement seemed as remote as Oriental music with its unfamiliar scale. Women wept, children wept, grief washed from the bamboo house with the regularity and monotony of surf. After a while the soldiers were rested enough to eat, and they plugged languidly at their hard cheese, their cardboard biscuits, and sipped indifferently at their antiseptic water.

When they had finished and their siesta was run, they were fresh enough to look with some curiosity at the tear-stained faces of the male and female peasants who left the bamboo house. Lucas decided it was time to return. The five men of the squad hooked up their cartridge belts, slung their bandoliers, grasped their rifles, and prepared to move out. Miguel intercepted them.

In his broken speech of English and its facsimile, he thanked the members of the patrol in the name of Luiz's widow, he expressed to them her gratitude for returning her husband, and conveyed her apologies for not inviting them to eat. Lucas accepted this like a courtier, and told Miguel to tell her that the American soldiers were happy to have been of aid. The two men shook hands and Lucas slapped the stock of his rifle to cover his embarrassment.

"Say, Miguel," he said.

"Sair?"

"What made this fellow Luiz"—he pronounced it *Louise* —"go out like that?"

"Do not know, sair, very brave mahn. His son killed by Jahpanese. Luiz go out every night for month."

Lucas whistled. "Well, what do you know."

"Yes, sair."

"Yeah, I guess he was all right," Lucas said. He waved a hand at Miguel, and strolled his men out of the village.

There was a three-mile walk back to the outpost. It ran along the ridges of bare grass-covered hills, and the men climbed up, and then down, and then around the flank of endless swells of earth. Brody walked with his head down, sucking air, his chest heaving helplessly. It was one of the longest three miles he had ever walked and he had walked some which were long indeed. When they reached the outpost, he flung himself on the ground beside the machine gun he had carried, and lay there panting. The two men who had been on guard through the day came over to examine the gun, but Brody snarled at them like an animal.

"What do you think, you own it?" one complained.

"I carried that gun, see? I get to look at it first."

While the other members of the squad were washing themselves in water which they poured from five-gallon jerricans into their helmets, or were writing letters, or were sleeping in their holes, Brody stared at the gun. He was preparing to clean it when Lucas came over to claim the prize. Brody was too tired to argue. Passively, he relinquished the gun to Lucas, and dropped into his hole to rest.

Brody fell asleep, was awakened for the evening meal which was brought up in a jeep. It consisted of hot stew in an insulated pot and heated coffee. He munched it down and fell asleep again, slumbering like a drunk drugged with his alcohol. Even when he was awakened for guard in the middle of the night, he was still tired. He sat in the machine-gun emplacement, and stared into the valley below. Illuminated by a full moon, the grass rustled in swells of silver light and shadow. There was a period of fifteen minutes when he sat with his hand on the bolt of the machine gun, convinced that he could see two men standing close to one another in the field. It turned out to be a horse which had somehow wandered there, and though Brody did not even know if the guerrilla Luiz had possessed a horse, he was nonetheless certain that the horse belonged to the dead Filipino.

Luiz had waited alone in a moonlit draw, waiting for Japanese to come so he could ambush them. Luiz had carried the machine gun in darkness down the trail where they had stopped to eat the pineapple, and he had sat alone to wait on a silver night with nothing for company but the slithering of animals and the torment of insects. It seemed impossible; it seemed . . . enormous. The force of this entered Brody's recognition like an iron spike.

For the first time Brody really heard the weeping of the Filipino women. They had all been crying for the dead Gook. In the security of his machine-gun emplacement, Brody shivered. It made him terribly uneasy. If he were killed at this moment, the men in the squad would stand around and look at him. Eventually the news would reach the few men he knew in other squads of other platoons. They would say, "Tough, wasn't it, about Brody?" or perhaps they would say no more than, "Brody, was he the guy who . . .?" Who did what? Brody had the uncomfortable sensation of wondering what in his life had he ever done?

He felt a million miles from anyone else on the face of

the earth. He had never done a thing in his life which he could consider the least bit exceptional, he could not think of anything to do. He only felt that somehow before he died he must do something. He must be remembered.

He thought of his parents. They would cry for him, but he no longer knew what they were like. He no longer believed in them. He was isolated on a little hill beneath a vast tropic night, and no one nor nothing cared for him. The family of Luiz had wept, they had wept over a dead Gook. But who would weep for Brody?

It was unfair. He was stripped of the casual monotony, the dull work, and the saving depression which had wrapped him like a bandage. He was naked, and it was one of the most terrifying experiences in his life. When his hour of guard was over, Brody lay on his back and shuddered with dread. The sky above his head was infinite and black —like death it could absorb him.

Yet somehow, in the morning, the crisis was past. His nerves had gone to sleep. Brody took up again his anonymous place in the squad. He was just another of the seven men, one who talked no more and talked no less, who wrote his letters, and played his cards, and went out laconically for the daily patrols. It was soon the turn of another to sulk, to be moody, and to spit furious answers to well-intentioned questions.

Brody, however, did not forget completely. Out of all the patrols he had made, and out of all the patrols he was to make in the months ahead, he always remembered the patrol which had found Luiz. When the campaign ended, and the regiment went into garrison to train for the coming invasion of Japan, Brody found himself thinking of the bamboo house and the village water pump at the most extraordinary times. He would remember it when he was drunk, or in the midst of a training class, and once even at the climax of a poker game when he had won a big hand. The night the war ended, he remembered the patrol in the most peculiar way of all.

He and Lucas had gone out to get drunk. They had drifted through the small Filipino city where the regiment had been garrisoned, and they had listened to the celebration of small-arms fire being shot off into the sky. They had wandered and wandered, drunk yet numb, unable to talk to one another. They each felt frozen.

At the end of town they came to a little street which had been razed in the course of the battle for the city. All the wooden and concrete homes had been destroyed, and in their place, drawn from the junkyard of war's familiar passage, were tiny shacks built from cartons and packing crates and rusted corrugated roofing. Filipinos were living in the cabins, and from several the light of a candle guttered in its holder, throwing a warm glow upon the burlap curtains which hung limply in the cool of the August evening. The shacks reminded Brody of a street of shanties at the edge of the American town where he lived, and he recalled a time when he had walked there with a girl on a warm night of summer. He kicked aside a bit of rubble, and said, "Remember the Gook with the Jap machine gun?"

"Yeah," said Lucas as if both of them had known him well, "he was a funny guy."

"Yeah."

The thaw had come. "Remember Newman, and how he got it at Aitape?" Lucas asked.

"Yeah, and Benton."

"That's right, Benton," Lucas said.

The walked, they reminisced. To Brody the two years and a fraction of harsh empty time he had spent on islands of the Pacific began to fill with the accumulation of small detail which made memory supportable. He thought it was the liquor, but he was beginning to feel very sad. He had a picture of all the men who had been killed on all the beaches, under all the coconut trees, in all the swamps and jungles and paddies of all the alien land they had traversed, and he could have wept for them if Lucas were not there. He wished that they could be present to smell the Philippine twilight on the day the war ended.

They talked, and night deepened over the rubble of a Philippine city, and they went at last to join the line of soldiers waiting to see a movie under the big tent in the tent city of the regiment. No one could sit still, and long before the movie was over, Brody and Lucas went out into the night and walked away. They bought a bottle from a Filipino dealer, and Brody drank more liquor, Brody staggered back to his cot.

As he fell asleep on the night of victory, he discovered himself weeping for Luiz, weeping as hard as the old women in the bamboo house. He wept for Luiz with all his heart because now it was no longer unbearably necessary that he find someone to weep for him.

1951

PART FIVE

Dark to Dawn, Dawn to Dark

GREAT IN THE HAY

Once there were two producers named Al and Bert. They were both short, they were both bald, they were both married, and they both produced pictures. They even had offices next to one another. Everything about them was so similar that they might have been considered twins if it were not for a difference so great that one never thought of them as being the least alike.

The difference was that the one named Al had the reputation of being great in the hay. In every other respect he was much the same as Bert, whose only reputation for want of something better was that he made a great deal of money.

This irritated Bert. He would call people in, he would talk to them, he would say: "I've known Al for twenty years. We got married within three months of each other, we make the same salary, we've had approximately the same number of big box-office grossers and box-office duds, we're the same height, we're almost the same weight, our looks are similar, and yet Al has the reputation of being great in the hay. Why should he have that reputation?"

It came to bother Bert, it came to bother him colossally. He would ask everyone, and no one would tell him the answer. He came at last to approach it as a business problem. He called in a private detective.

To the detective, he said, "I want you to find out the reason. I don't care how low-down and dirty. The man has a secret, there's a reason why Al is an expert and I'm an unknown. I want you to find that reason."

The detective went out, he scouted around, he compiled a list of names, he ended with a duplicate of the little black book which Al was keeping. To each of the addresses listed went the detective. As he obtained his answers he filed his reports, and when he was done he returned to Bert.

"Your report is wasted money," Bert cried. "You've taught me nothing. You've merely confused me. Let me read to you what they say. It's disgusting."

Bert read from the report. He read what Claudia Jane had to say, and Dianthe, and Emeline, and Fay, and Georgia, and Hortense, and all the others.

"He's the best lover I've ever used," said Claudia Jane, "because he is floppy and lets me throw him around."

"He is magnificent," murmured Dianthe, "he melts my ice. He rides over me, disdains me, leaves me convinced I am a woman."

"He is cute," wrote Emeline, "and all my own."

"A master at sexpertease," stated Hortense, "because I tell you, buster, I'm bored with less."

"Pure," dictated Fay, "and not addicted to the nasty. Love for him is a communion of purity and simplicity which intensifies my hard-won religious conversion."

"He likes to spend money," lisped Georgia, "and I think that's everything, don't you?"

Bert was enraged. "You call this a report?" he shouted at the detective. "It is nothing but a mish-mosh." He threw the sheets into the air. "You go find his secret."

The detective pounded a weary scented beat. His flat shoes trod through boudoirs while he attempted to elicit a gimmick from the mish-mosh. At last the case was closed. There came a morning when to everyone's surprise, Al left a note which read *Every year I have been getting more and more depressed,* and blew out his brains.

Bert could never understand it. When he discharged the detective, he complained with a sigh, "I still don't understand why Al was so great. It's aggravating. I've lived a full life, and I can tell you. All women are the same in the dark. I ought to know."

So the moral of this story may well be: People who live in the dark live longest of all.

1950

THE LAST NIGHT:
A Story

NOTE TO THE READER: *Obviously a movie must be based on a novel, a story, a play, or an original idea. I suppose it could even derive from a poem. "Let's do* The Wasteland," *said a character of mine named Collie Munshin. The novel may be as much as a thousand pages long, the play a hundred, the story ten, the original idea might be stated in a paragraph. Yet each in its turn must be converted into an art form (a low art form) called a treatment. The treatment usually runs anywhere from twenty to a hundred pages in length. It is a bed of Procrustes. Long stories have their limbs lopped off. Too brief tales are stretched. The idea is to present for the attention of a producer, a director, or a script reader, in readable but modest form, the line of story, the gallery of characters, the pith and gist of your tale.*

But one's duty is to do this without much attempt at style and no attempt at high style. The language must be functional, even cliché, and since one's writing prepares the ground for a movie script, too much introspection in the characters is not encouraged. "Joey was thinking for the first time that Alice was maybe in love with him" is barely acceptable. An actor on contract could probably manage to register that emotion in a closeup. Whereas,

> *. . . the little phrase, as soon as it struck his ear, had the power to liberate in him the room that was needed to contain it; the proportions of Swann's soul were altered; a margin was left for a form of enjoyment which corresponded no more than his love for Odette to any external object, and yet was not, like his enjoyment of that love, purely individual, but assumed for him an objective reality superior to that of other concrete things,*

*would bake the clay of a producer's face a little closer to
stone. A producer is interested in the meat and bone of a
story. His question as he reads a treatment is whether he
should go on to assign a writer to do a screenplay of this
story with specific dialogue and most specific situations
added, or whether he should ask for another treatment with
new characters and plot, or whether indeed he should write
off the loss and quit right now. So a treatment bears the
same relation to a finished screenplay as the model for a
wind tunnel does to the airplane. Since a treatment is
functional, any excellence must be unobtrusive. In fact, a
good director (George Stevens) once told me that good
writing in a treatment was a form of cheating because it introduced emotional effects through language which he
might not as a director be able to repeat on film.*

*So, thus modestly, I present here a treatment of a movie.
It is based on an original idea. It is a short treatment. Only
a few of the scenes are indicated. As an example of the
art of the treatment, it is not characteristic, for it is written in somewhat formal prose, but it may have the virtue of
suggesting a motion picture to your imagination.*

*Best wishes. See you in the morning after this last night.
—N.M.*

We're going to describe a movie which will take place
twenty years from now, forty years from now, or is it one
hundred years from now? One cannot locate the date to a
certainty. The world has gone on just about the way we all
expected it would go on. It has had large and dramatic con-
frontations by heads of state, cold wars galore, economic
crises resolved and unresolved, good investment, bad investment, decent management and a witch's bag full of
other complexities much too numerous ever to bring into
a movie. The result has been a catastrophe which all of
us have dreaded, all of us expected, and none of us has
been able to forestall. The world in twenty or forty years—
let us say it is thirty-six—has come to the point where
without an atomic war, without even a hard or furious
shooting war, it has given birth nonetheless to a fearful
condition. The world has succeeded in poisoning itself.
It is no longer fit to inhabit. The prevalent condition is
fallout radiation, anomalous crops, monstrous babies who

grow eyes in their navels and die screaming with hatred at the age of six weeks, plastics which emit cancerous fumes, buildings which collapse like camphor flakes, weather which is excruciatingly psychological because it is always too hot or too cold. Governments fall with the regularity of pendulums. The earth is doomed. The number of atom bombs detonated by the Americans, Russians, English, French, the Algerians, Africans, the Israelis and the Chinese, not to mention the Turks, Hindus and Yugoslavians, have so poisoned existence that even the apples on the trees turn malignant in the stomach. Life is being burned out by a bleak fire within, a plague upon the secrets of our existence which stultifies the air. People who govern the nations have come to a modest and simple conclusion. The mistakes of the past have condemned the future. There is no time left to discuss mankind's guilt. No one is innocent of the charge that all have blighted the rose. In fact, the last President to be elected in the United States has come to office precisely by making this the center of his plank: that no one is innocent. The political reactions have been exceptional. Earlier in the century the most fundamental political notion was that guilt could be laid always at the door of one nation and one nation only. Now a man had been elected to one of the two most powerful offices in the world on the premise that the profound illness of mankind was the fault of all, and this victory had prepared the world for cooperative action.

Shortly after the election of this last of the American Presidents, the cold war was finally ended. Russia and America were ready to collaborate, as were Algeria and France, China, England, Western Europe, India and Africa. The fact had finally been faced. Man had succeeded in so polluting the atmosphere that he was doomed to expire himself. Not one in fifty of the most responsible government scientists would now admit that there were more than twenty years left to life. It was calculated that three-quarters of the living population would be gone in five years from the various diseases of fallout. It was further calculated that of the one-quarter remaining women and men, another three-quarters would be dead in the two following years. What a perspective—three-quarters of the people dead in five years, another three-quarters lost in two, one in sixteen left after seven years to watch the slow extinction of the rest. In the face of this fact, led by a President who was exceptional, who was not only the last but perhaps the greatest of America's leaders, the people of the world had come together to stare into the grim alternatives of their fate. All men and women who continued to live on earth would expire. Five hundred thousand at least could survive if they were moved to Mars, perhaps even as many as one million people could be saved, together with various animals, vegetables, minerals and transportable plants. For the rocketeers had made fine advances. Their arts and sciences had developed enormously. They had managed to establish a company of astronauts on Mars. Nearly one thousand had perished earlier on the Moon, but on Mars over a hundred had managed to live; they had succeeded in building a camp out of native vegetation found on the surface. Dwellings had been fabricated from it and, in triumph, a vehicle constructed entirely from materials found on Mars had been sent back to earth, where men and women received it with extravagant hope.

No space here, or for that matter in the movie, to talk of the endless and difficult negotiations which had gone on. The movie could begin perhaps with the ratification of the most astounding piece of legislation ever to be passed in any country. In this case the piece of legislation had been passed by every nation in the world. It was a covenant which declared that every citizen in each nation was going to devote himself to sending a fleet of rocket ships to Mars. This effort would be herculean. It would demand that the heart of each nation's economy be turned over completely to building and equipping ships, selecting the people, training them, and having the moral fortitude to bid them goodbye. In a sense, this universal operation would be equivalent to the evacuation of Dunkirk but with one exception: three-quarters of the British Expeditionary Force was removed safely from the beach. In this case, the world could hope to send up to Mars no more than one million of its people, conceivably less.

It was calculated that the operation must be accomplished in eighteen months—the spread of plague dictated this haste, for half of the remaining members of mankind might be dead in this time and it was felt that to wait too long would be tantamount to populating the ships with human beings too sick, too weak, too plague-ridden to meet the rigors of life on Mars.

It was indeed a heroic piece of legislation, for the people on earth had had the vision to see that all of them were doomed, and so the majority had consented to accept a minority from within themselves to go out further across space and continue the species. Of course, those who were left would make some further effort to build new rocket ships and follow the wave of the first million pioneers, but the chances of this were unlikely. Not only would the re-sources of the world be used at an unprecedented rate to build a fleet of ten thousand rocket ships capable of carry-ing one hundred persons each out so far as Mars, but, in fact, as everyone knew, the earth would be stripped of its most exceptional people, its most brilliant technicians, artists, scientists, and executives, plus their families. Those who were left could hardly hope to form a nucleus or a new cadre brilliant enough to repeat the effort. Be-sides, it was calculated that the ravages of the plague would already be extreme by the time the fleet departed. The heroism of this legislation resided therefore in the fact that man was capable of regarding his fate and determining to do something exceptional about it.

Now the President of the United States, as indicated earlier, was an unusual man. It was a situation right for a dictator, but he was perhaps not only the most brilliant but the most democratic of American presidents. And one of the reasons the separate nations of the world had been able to agree on this legislation, and the Americans in par-ticular had voted for it, was that the President had suc-ceeded in engaging the imagination of the world's citizens with his project, much as Churchill had brought an incan-descence to the morale of the English by the famous speech where he told them he could offer them nothing but blood, sweat, toil and tears. So this President had spared no detail in bringing the citizens of America face to face with the doom of their condition. There were still one hundred million people alive in America. Of that number, one hundred thousand would voyage to Mars. One person in a thousand then could hope to go. Yet there were no riots in the streets. The reason was curious but simple. The President had promised to stay behind and make every effort to train and rally new technicians for the construction of a second fleet. This decision to remain behind had come from many motives: he had recognized the political impossibility of leaving himself—there was moreover sufficient selflessness in the man to make such a course tasteless to him—and, what was also to the point, his wife, whom he loved, was now incurably sick. It had been agreed that the first of the criteria for selection to the fleet was good physical condition, or at least some reasonable suggestion of health, since everyone on earth was now ill in varying degree.

In the first six months after the worldwide ratification of what had already become known as the Legislation For A Fleet, an atmosphere of cooperation, indeed almost of Christian sanctity and good will, came over the earth. Never before in the memory of anyone living had so many people seemed in so good a mood. There was physical suffering everywhere—as has been mentioned, nearly everyone was ill, usually of distressing internal diseases—but the pain now possessed a certain logic, for at least one-half the working force of the world was engaged directly or indirectly in the construction of the Fleet or the preparations surrounding it. Those who were to travel to Mars had a profound sense of mission, of duty and humility. Those who knew they would be left behind felt for the first time in years a sensation of moral weightlessness which was recognized finally as the absence of guilt. Man was at peace with himself. He could even feel hope, because it was, after all, not known to a certainty that those who were left behind must inevitably perish. Some still believed in the possibility of new medical discoveries which could save them. Others devoted themselves to their President's vow that the construction of the second fleet would begin upon the departure of the first. And, with it all, there was in nearly everyone a sense of personal abnegation, of cooperation, of identification with the community.

It was part of the President's political wisdom that the people who were chosen for the American Fleet had also been selected geographically. Every town of ten thousand inhabitants had ten heroes to make the trip. Not a county of five thousand people scattered over ten thousand square miles of ranches was without its five men, women, and children, all ready. And, of course, for each person chosen there were another ten ready to back them up in case the first man turned ill, or the second, or the third. Behind these ten were one hundred, directly involved in the development, training and morale of each voyager and his ten substitutes. So participation in the flight reached into all the corners of the country, and rare was the family which had nothing to do with it. Historians, writing wistfully about the end of history, had come to the conclusion that man was never so close to finding his soul as in this period when it was generally agreed he was soon to lose his body.

Now, calculate what a blow it was to morality, to courage, and the heart of mankind when it was discovered that life on Mars was not supportable, that the company of a hundred who had been camping on its surface had begun to die, and that their disease was similar to the plague which had begun to visit everyone on earth, but was more virulent in its symptoms and more rapid in its results. The scientific news was overwhelming. Fallout and radiation had poisoned not only the earth but the entire solar system. There was no escape for man to any of the planets. The first solar voyagers to have journeyed so far away as Jupiter had sent back the same tragic news. Belts of radiation incalculably fierce in their intensity now surrounded all the planets.

The President was, of course, the first to receive this news and, in coordination with agreements already arrived at, communicated it to the Premier of the Soviet Union. The two men were already firm friends. They had succeeded, two and a half years before, in forming an alliance to end the Cold War, and by thus acting in concert had encouraged the world to pass the Legislation For A Fleet. Now the Premier informed the President that he had heard the bad news himself: ten of the one hundred men on Mars were, after all, Russians. The two leaders met immediately in Paris for a conference which was brief and critical in its effect. The President was for declaring the news immediately. He had an intimation that to conceal such an apocalyptic fact might invite an unnamable disaster. The Premier of Russia begged him to wait a week at least before announcing this fact. His most cogent argument was that the scientists were entitled to a week to explore the remote possibility of some other solution.

"What other could there possibly be?" asked the President.

"How can I know?" answered the Premier. "Perhaps we shall find a way to drive a tunnel into the center of the earth in order to burn all impurities out of ourselves."

The President was adamant. The tragic condition of the world today was precisely the product, he declared, of ten thousand little abuses of power, ten thousand moments in history when the leaders had decided that the news they held was too unpleasant or too paralyzing for the masses to bear. A new era in history, a heroic if tragic era, had begun precisely because the political leaders of the world now invited the citizens into their confidence. The President and the Premier were at an impasse. The only possible compromise was to wait another twenty-four hours and invite the leaders of Europe, Asia, South America and Africa to an overnight conference which would determine the fate of the news.

The second conference affected the history of everything which was to follow, because all the nations were determined to keep the new and disastrous news a secret. The President's most trusted technical adviser, Anderson Stevens, argued that the general despair would be too great and would paralyze the best efforts of his own men to find another solution. The President and Stevens were old friends. They had come to power together. It was Stevens who had been responsible for some of the most critical scientific discoveries and advances in the rocketry of the last ten years. The Legislation For A Fleet had come, to a great extent, out of his work. He was known as the President's greatest single friend, his most trusted adviser. If he now disagreed with the President at this international conference, the President was obliged to listen to him. Anderson Stevens argued that while the solar system was now poisoned and uninhabitable, it might still be possible to travel to some other part of our galaxy and transfer human life to a more hospitable star. For several days, scientists discussed the possibilities. It was admitted that no fuel or system of booster propulsion was sufficiently powerful to take a rocket ship beyond the solar system. Not even by connecting to booster rockets already in orbit. But then it was also argued that no supreme attempt had yet been made and if the best scientific minds on earth applied themselves to this problem the intellectual results were unforseeable. In the meantime, absolute silence was to be observed. The program to construct the Martian Fleet was to continue as if nothing had happened. The President acceded to this majority decision of the other leaders, but informed them that he would hold the silence for no more than another week.

By the end of the week, Anderson Stevens returned with an exceptional suggestion: a tunnel ten miles long was to be constructed in all haste in Siberia or the American desert. Pitched at an angle, so that its entrance was on the surface and its base a mile below the earth, the tunnel would act like the muzzle of a rifle and fire the rocket as if it were a shell. Calculated properly, taking advantage of the earth's rotation about its own axis and the greater speed of its rotation about the sun, it was estimated that the rocket ship might then possess sufficient escape velocity to quit the gravitational pull of the sun and so move out to the stars. Since some of the rocket ships were already close to completion and could be adapted quickly to the new scheme, the decision was taken to fire a trial shot in three months, with a picked crew of international experts. If the ship succeeded in escaping the pull of the sun, its crew could then explore out to the nearest stars and send back the essential information necessary for the others who would follow.

Again the question of secrecy was debated. Now Stevens argued that it would be equally irresponsible to give people hope if none would later exist. So, suffering his deepest misgivings, the President consented to a period of silence for three months while the tunnel was completed. In this period, the character of his administration began to change. Hundreds and then thousands of men were keeping two great secrets: the impossibility of life on Mars, and the construction of the giant cannon which would fire an exploratory ship to the stars. So an atmosphere of secrecy and evasion began to circle about the capital, and the

mood of the nation was affected. There were rumors everywhere; few of them were accurate. People whispered that
the Russians were no longer in cooperation with us, but
engaged in a contest to see who could get first to Mars.
It was said that the climate of Mars had driven the colonists
mad, that the spaceships being built would not hold together because the parts were weakened by atomic radiation. It was then rumored—for the existence of the tunnel
could not be hidden altogether—that the government was
planning to construct an entire state beneath the surface of
the earth, in which people could live free of radiation and
fallout. For the first time in three or four years, the rates
of the sociological diseases—crime, delinquency, divorce
and addiction—began again to increase.

The day for the secret test arrived. The rocket was fired.
It left the earth's atmosphere at a rate greater than any
projectile had yet traveled, a rate so great that the first
fear of the scientists was substantiated. The metal out of
which the rocket was made, the finest, most heat-resistant
alloy yet devised by metallurgists, was still insufficient to
withstand the heat of its velocity. As it rose through the
air, with the dignitaries of fifty countries gathered to watch
its departure, it burst out of the earth, its metal skin glow-
ing with the incandescence of a welding torch, traced a
path of incredible velocity across the night sky, so fast
that it looked like a bolt of lightning reversed, leaping
lividly from the earth into the melancholy night, and
burned itself out thirty miles up in the air, burned itself
out as completely as a dead meteor. No metal existed
which could withstand the heat of the excessive friction
created by the extreme velocity necessary to blast a ship
through the atmosphere and out beyond the gravitational
attractions of the sun and its planets. On the other hand, a
rocket ship which rose slowly through the earth's atmosphere and so did not overheat could not then generate
enough power to overcome the pull of the sun. It seemed
now conclusive that man was trapped within his solar
system.

The President declared that the people must finally be
informed, and in an historic address he did so inform them
of the futility of going to Mars and of the impossibility of
escape in any other way. There was nothing left for man,

he declared, but to prepare himself for his end, to recognize that his soul might have a life beyond his death and so might communicate the best of himself to the stars. There was thus the opportunity to die well, in dignity, with grace, and the hope that the spirit might prove more miraculous and mighty than the wonders man had extracted from matter. It was a great speech. Commentators declared it was perhaps the greatest speech ever delivered by a political leader. It suffered from one irrevocable flaw: it had been delivered three months too late. The ultimate reaction was cynical. "If all that is left to us is our spirit," commented a German newspaper, "why then did the President deny us three useful months in which to begin to develop it?"

Like the leaden-green airless evening before an electrical storm, an atmosphere of depression, bitterness, wildness, violence and madness rose from the echoes of this speech. Productivity began to founder. People refused to work. Teachers taught in classrooms which were empty and left the schools themselves. Windows began to be broken everywhere, a most minor activity, but it took on accelerated proportions, as if many found a huge satisfaction in throwing rocks through windows much as though they would proclaim that this was what the city would look like when they were gone. Funerals began to take on a bizarre attraction. Since ten to twenty times as many people were dying each day as had died even five years before, funeral processions took up much of the traffic, and many of the people who were idle enjoyed marching through the streets in front of and behind the limousines. The effect was sometimes medieval, for impromptu carnivals began to set themselves up on the road to the cemetery. There were speeches in Congress to impeach the President and, as might conventionally be expected, some of the particular advisers who had counseled him to keep silence were now most forward in their condemnation of his act.

The President himself seemed to be going through an exceptional experience. That speech in which he had suggested to mankind that its best hope was to cultivate its spirit before it died seemed to have had the most profound effect upon him. His appearance had begun to alter: his hair was subtly longer, his face more gaunt, his eyes feverish. He had always been unorthodox as a President, but now his clothing was often rumpled and he would appear unexpectedly to address meetings or to say a few words on television. His resemblance to Lincoln, which had in the beginning been slight, now became more pronounced. The wits were quick to suggest that he spent hours each day with a makeup expert. In the midst of this, the President's wife died, and in great pain. They had been close for twenty years. Over the last month, he had encouraged her not to take any drugs to dull the pain. The pain was meaningful, he informed her. The choice might be one of suffering now in the present or later in eternity. In anguish she expired. On her deathbed she seared him with a cruel confession. It was that no matter how she had loved him for twenty years, she had always felt there was a part of him never to be trusted, a part which was implacable, inhuman and ruthless. "You would destroy the world for a principle," she told him as she died. "There is something diabolical about you."

On the return from her funeral, people came out to stand silently in tribute. It was the first spontaneous sign of respect paid to him in some months, and riding alone in the rear of an open limousine, he wept. Yet, before the ride was over, someone in the crowd threw a stone through the windshield. In his mind, as he rode, was the face of his wife, saying to him some months before, "I tell you, people cannot bear suffering. I know that I cannot. You will force me to destroy a part of your heart if you do not let me have the drugs."

That night the chief of America's Intelligence Service came to see the President. The Russians were engaged in a curious act. They were building a tunnel in Siberia, a tunnel even larger than the American one, and at an impossible angle; it went almost directly into the earth and then took a jog at right angles to itself. The President put through a call to Moscow to speak to the Premier. The Premier told the President that he had already made preparations to see him. There was a matter of the most extreme importance to be discussed: the Russians had found a way to get a rocket ship out of the solar system.

So, the two men met in London in a secret conference. Alone in a room, the Premier explained the new project and his peculiar position. Slowly, insidiously, he had been losing control in his country, just as the President had become progressively more powerless in America. Against the Premier's wishes, some atomic and rocket scientists had come together on a fearsome scheme which the Army was now supporting. It had been calculated that if an ordinary rocket ship, of the sort which belonged to the Martian Fleet, were fired out from the earth, it would be possible to blast it into the furthest reaches of our own galaxy, provided—and this was most important—a planet were exploded at the proper moment. It would be like the impetus a breaking wave could give to a surfboard rider. With proper timing the force released by blowing up the planet would more than counteract the gravitational pull of the sun. Moreover, the rocket ship could be a great distance away from the planet at the moment it was exploded, and so the metal of its skin would not have to undergo any excessive heat.

"But which planet could we use?" asked the President.

The two men looked at one another. The communication passed silently from one's mind to the other. It was obvious. With the techniques available to them there was only one planet: the earth.

That was what the Russian tunnel was for. A tunnel going deep into the earth, loaded with fissionable material, and exploded by a radio wave sent out from a rocket ship already one million miles away. The detonation of the earth would hurl the rocket ship like a pebble across a chasm of space.

"Well," says the President, after a long pause, "it may be possible for the Fleet to take a trip after all."

"No," the Premier assured him, "not the Fleet." For the earth would be detonated by an atomic chain reaction which would spew radioactive material across one hundred million miles of the heavens. The alloy vuranel was the only alloy which could protect a rocket ship against the electronic hurricane which would follow the explosion. There was on earth enough vuranel to create a satisfactory shield for only one ship. "Not a million men, women, and children, but a hundred, a hundred people and a few animals will take the trip to a star."

"Who will go?" asks the President.

"Some of your people," answers the Premier, "some of mine. You and me."

"I won't go," says the President.

"Of course you will," says the Premier. "Because if you don't go, I don't go, and we've been through too much already. You see, my dear friend, you're the only equal I have on earth. It would be much too depressing to move through those idiotic stars without you."

But the President is overcome by the proportions of the adventure. "You mean we will blow up the entire world in order that a hundred people have some small chance—one chance in five, one chance in ten, one chance in a hundred, or less—to reach some star and live upon it. The odds are too brutal. The cost is incalculable."

"We lose nothing but a few years," says the Premier. "We'll all be dead anyway."

"No," says the President, "it's not the same. We don't know what we destroy. It may be that after life ceases on the earth, life will generate itself again, if only we leave the earth alone. To destroy it is monstrous. We may destroy the spirit of something far larger than ourselves."

The Premier taps him on the shoulder. "Look, my friend, do you believe that God is found in a cockroach? I don't. God is found inside you, and inside me. When all of us are gone, God is also gone."

"I don't know if I believe that," answers the President.

Well, the Premier tells him, religious discussion has always fascinated him, but politics are more pressing. The question is whether they are at liberty to discuss this matter on its moral merits alone. The tunnel in Siberia had been built without his permission. It might interest the President to know that a tunnel equally secret is being constructed near the site of the old Arizona tunnel. There were Russian technicians working on that, just as American technicians had been working in Siberia. The sad political fact is that the technicians had acquired enormous political force, and if it were a question of a showdown tomorrow, it is quite likely they could seize power in the Soviet Union and in America as well.

"You, sir," says the Premier, "have been searching your soul for the last year in order to discover reasons for still governing. I have been studying Machiavelli because I have found, to my amusement, that when all else is gone, when life is gone, when the promise of future life is gone, and the meaning of power, then what remains for one is the game. I want the game to go on. I do not want to lose power in my country. I do not want you to lose it in yours. I want, if necessary, to take the game clear up into the stars. You deserve to be on that rocket ship, and I deserve to be on it. It is possible we have given as much as anyone alive to brooding over the problems of mankind in these last few years. It is your right and my right to look for a continuation of the species. Perhaps it is even our duty."

"No," says the President. "They're holding a gun to our heads. One cannot speak of the pleasures of the game or of honor or of duty when there is no choice."

He will not consent to destroying the earth unless the people of earth choose that course, with a full knowledge of the consequences. What is he going to do, asks the Premier. He is going to tell the world, says the President. There must be a general worldwide election to determine the decision.

"Your own people will arrest you first," says the Premier. He then discloses that the concept of exploding the earth to boost the power of the rocket had been Anderson Stevens' idea.

The President picks up the phone and makes a call to his press chief. He tells him to prepare the television networks for an address he will deliver that night. The press chief asks him the subject. The President tells him he will discuss it upon his return. The press chief says that the network cannot be cleared unless the President informs him now of the subject. It will be a religious address, says the President.

"The networks may not give us the time," says the press chief. "Frankly, sir, they are not certain which audiences share your spiritual fire."

The President hangs up. "You are right," he tells the Premier. "They will not let me make the speech. I have to make it here in London. Will you stand beside me?"

"No, my friend," says the Russian, "I will not. They will put you in jail for making that speech, and you will have need of me on the outside to liberate your skin."

The President makes the address in London to the

citizens of the world. He explains the alternatives, outlines his doubts, discusses the fact that there are technicians ready to seize power, determined to commit themselves to the terrestrial explosion. No one but the people of the earth, by democratic procedure, have the right to make this decision, he declares, and recommends that as a first step the people march on the tunnel sites and hold them. He concludes his address by saying he is flying immediately back to Washington and will be there within two hours.

The message has been delivered on the network devoted to international television. It reaches a modest percentage of all listeners in the world. But in America, from the President's point of view the program took place at an unfortunate time, for it was the early hours of the morning. When he lands in Washington at dawn, he is met by his Cabinet and a platoon of M.P.'s, who arrest him. Television in America is devoted that morning to the announcement that the President has had a psychotic breakdown and is at present under observation by psychiatrists.

For a week, the atmosphere is unendurable. A small percentage of the people in America have listened to the President's speech. Many more have heard him in other countries. Political tensions are acute, and increase when the Premier of the Soviet Union announces in reply to a question from a reporter that in his opinioin the President of the United States is perfectly sane. Committees of citizens form everywhere to demand an open investigation of the charges against the President. It becomes a rallying cry that the President be shown to the public. A condition close to civil war exists in America.

At this point, the President is paid a visit by Anderson Stevens, the scientist in charge of the rocket program, the man who has lately done more than any other to lead the Cabinet against the President. Now they have a conversation behind the barred windows of the hospital room where the President is imprisoned. Anderson Stevens tells the President that the first tunnel which had been built for the star shot was, from his point of view, a ruse. He had never expected that rocket ship, which was fired like a bullet, to escape from the earth's atmosphere without burning to a cinder. All of his experience had told him it would be destroyed. But he had advanced the program for that shot because he wished to test something else—the tunnel. It had been essential to discover how deeply one could dig into the crust of the earth before the heat became insupportable for an atomic bomb. In effect, the tunnel had been dug as a test to determine the feasibility of detonating the earth. And so that shot which had burned up a rocket ship had been, from Stevens' point of view, a success, because he had learned that the tunnel could be dug deep enough to enable a superior hydrogen bomb to set off a chain reaction in the fiery core of the earth. The fact that one hundred rocketeers and astronauts, men who had been his friends for decades, had died in an experiment he had known to be all but hopeless was an indication of how serious he was about the earth bomb shot. The President must not think for a moment that Stevens would hesitate to keep him in captivity, man the ship himself, and blow up the earth.

Why, then, asks the President, does Stevens bother to speak to him? Because, answers Stevens, he wants the President to command the ship. Why? Because in some way the fate of the ship might be affected by the emotions of everybody on earth at the moment the earth was exploded. This sounded like madness to some of his scientific colleagues, but to him it was feasible that if life had a spirit and all life ceased to exist at the same moment, then that spirit, at the instant of death, might have a force of liberation or deterrence which could be felt as a physical force across the heavens.

"You mean," says the President, "that even in the ruthless circuits of your heart there is terror, a moral terror, at the consequence of your act. And it is me you wish to bear the moral consequence of that act, and not you."

"You are the only man great enough, sir," says Anderson Stevens, bowing his head.

"But I think the act is wrong," says the President.

"I know it is right," says Stevens. "I spent a thousand days and a thousand nights living with the terror that I might be wrong, and still I believe I am right. There is something in me which knows that two things are true— that we have destroyed this earth not only because we were not worthy of it, but because it may have been too cruel for us. I tell you, we do not know. Man may have been mismated with earth. In some fantastic way, perhaps we voyaged here some millions of years ago and fell into a stupidity equal to the apes. That I don't know. But I do know, if I know anything at all, because my mind imprisoned in each and every one of my cells tells me so, that we must go on, that we as men are different from the earth, we are visitors upon it. We cannot suffer ourselves to sit here and be extinguished, not when the beauty which first gave speech to our tongues commands us to go out and find another world, another earth, where we may strive, where we may win, where we may find the right to live again. For that dream I will kill everyone on earth. I will kill my children. In fact I must, for they will not accompany me on the trip. And you," he says to the President, "you must accompany us. You must help to make this trip. For we as men may finally achieve greatness if we survive this, the most profound of our perils."

"I do not trust myself," said the President. "I do not know if my motive is good. Too many men go to their death with a hatred deep beyond words, wishing with their last breath that they could find the power to destroy God. I do not know—I may be one of those men."

"You have no choice," says Anderson Stevens. "There are people trying to liberate you now. I shall be here to shoot you myself before they succeed. Unless you agree to command the ship."

"Why should I agree?" says the President. "Shoot me now."

"No," says Stevens, "you will agree, because I will make one critical concession to you. I do it not from choice, but from desperation. My dreams tell me we are doomed unless you command us. So I will let you give the people their one last opportunity. I will let you speak to them. I will put my power behind you, so that they may vote."

"No," says the President, "not yet. Because if such an election were lost, if the people said, 'Let us stay here and die together, and leave the earth to mend itself, without the sound of human speech or our machines,' then you would betray me. I know it. You would betray everyone.

Some night, in some desert, a rocket ship would be fired up into the sky, and twenty hours later, deep in some secret tunnel, all of us would be awakened by the last explosion of them all. No, I will wait for the people to free me first. Of necessity, my first act then will be to imprison you."

After this interview between Stevens and the President, the ruling coalition of Cabinet officers and technicians refused, of course, to let the people see the President. The response was a virtually spontaneous trek of Americans by airplane, helicopter, automobile, by animal, by motorcycle, and on foot, toward the tunnel site the President had named. The Army was quickly deployed to prevent them, but the soldiers refused to protect the approaches to the tunnel. They also asked for the right to see the President. The Cabinet capitulated. The President was presented on television. He announced that the only justification for the star ship was a worldwide general election.

The most brilliant, anguished, closely debated election in the history of the world now took place. For two months, argument licked like flame at the problem. In a last crucial speech the night before the election, the President declared that it was the words of a man now in prison, Anderson Stevens, which convinced him how he would vote. For he, the President, had indeed come to believe that man rising out of the fiery grave of earth, out of the loss of his past, his history, and his roots, might finally achieve the greatness and the goodness expected of him precisely because he had survived this, the last and the most excruciating of his trials. "If even a few of us manage to live, our seed will be changed forever by the self-sacrifice and nobility, the courage and the loss engraved on our memory of that earth-doomed man who was our ancestor and who offered us life. Man may become human at last." The President concluded his speech by announcing that if the people considered him deserving of the honor, he would be the first to enter the ship, he would take upon himself the act of pressing that button which would blow up the earth.

The answer to this speech was a solemn vote taken in favor of destroying the world, and giving the spaceship its opportunity to reach the stars.

The beginning of the last sequence in the movie might show the President and the Premier saying goodbye. The Premier has discovered he is now hopelessly ill, and so will stay behind.

The Premier smiles as he says goodbye. "You see, I am really too fat for a brand-new game. It is you fanatics who always take the longest trips."

One hundred men and women file into the ship behind the President. The rocket is fired and rises slowly, monumentally. Soon it is out of sight. In the navigation tower within the rocket the President stares back at earth. It is seen on a color television screen, magnified enormously. The hours go by and the time is approaching for the explosion. The radio which will send out the wave of detonation is warmed up. Over it the President speaks to the people who are left behind on earth. All work has of course ceased, and people waiting through the last few hours collect, many of them, in public places, listening to the President's voice on loudspeakers. Others hear it in radios in their rooms, or sprawled on the grass in city parks. People listen in cars on country crossroads, at the beach, watching the surf break. Quietly, a few still buy tickets for their children on the pony rides. One or two old scholars sit by themselves at desks in the public library, reading books. Some drink in bars. Others sit quietly on the edge of pavements, their feet in the street. One man takes his shoes off. The mood is not too different from the mood of a big city late at night when the weather is warm. There is the same air of expectation, of quiet, brooding concentration.

"Pray for us," says the President to them, speaking into his microphone on that rocket ship one million miles away. "Pray for us. Pray that our purpose is good and not evil. Pray that we are true and not false. Pray that it is part of our mission to bring the life we know to other stars." And in his ears he hears the voice of his wife, saying through her pain, "You will end by destroying everything."

"Forgive me, all of you," says the President. "May I be an honest man and not first deluded physician to the Devil." Then he presses the button.

The earth detonates into the dark spaces. A flame leaps across the solar system. A scream of anguish, jubilation, desperation, terror, ecstasy, vaults across the heavens. The tortured heart of the earth has finally found its voice. We have a glimpse of the spaceship, a silver minnow of light, streaming into the oceans of mystery, and the darkness beyond.

1962

PART SIX

Microbes

IT

We were going through the barbed-wire when a machine gun started. I kept walking until I saw my head lying on the ground.

"My God, I'm dead," my head said.

And my body fell over.

1939

THE SHORTEST NOVEL
OF THEM ALL

At first she thought she could kill him in three days.

She did nearly. His heart proved nearly unequal to her compliments.

Then she thought it would take three weeks. But he survived.

So she revised her tables and calculated three months.

After three years, he was still alive. So they got married.

Now they've been married for thirty years. People speak warmly of them. They are known as the best marriage in town.

It's just that their children keep dying.

1963

PART SEVEN

Mutants

MINISTERS OF TASTE:
A Story

A very short story in the form of two real letters written by Norman Mailer to Robert B. Silvers, editor of The New York Review of Books, *with copies directed to the associate editors, publisher, and several interested observers.*

February 22, 1965

Dear Bob,

Your letter, January 26, invites me to an "essay" of eighteen hundred words on the new Hubert Humphrey. In the last year you have also asked me to review biographies of Johnson (Jack) and George Patton. Since it is not easy to think of three books which could attract me less, I expect I must make my position clear. Forgive me for digging in old ground.

A year and a half ago, you asked me to review *The Group*. Said you had offered the novel to seven people—all seven were afraid to review it. You appealed to my manhood, my fierce eschatological sword. St. Mary's wrath (according to you) was limned with brimfire. Would I do it, you begged, as a most special favor to you. Perhaps, you suggested, I was the only man in New York who had the guts to do it. A shrewd appeal. I did it. Two months later my book (*The Presidential Papers*) came out. You had given the copy to Midge Decter for review. Her submitted piece was, in your opinion—I quote your label—"overinflated." That is to say, it was favorable. Changes were requested. The reviewer refused to make them. The review was not printed. No review of *The Presidential Papers* appeared in *The New York Review of Books*. Only a parody. By a mystery guest. Now, we have my new book,

215

An American Dream. I hear you have picked Philip Rahv to review it, Philip Rahv whose detestation of my work has been thundering these last two years into the gravy stains of every literary table on the Eastern Seaboard.

In the name therefore of the sweet gracious Jesus, why expect me to do eight words on your subject? To the contrary, experience now suspects that a state of cordial relations with *The Review* is congruent to a lack of cordial relations with *The Review,* and marks you, Bob, on this note: negotiations with your Editorship are, by open measure, inching, tedious, and impoverished as spit. But cheer up, dear Silvers. The letter is for publication, and so should enliven the literary history of your unbloodied rag.

Yours in trust,

Norman Mailer

cc: Barbara Epstein   Samuel N. Antupit
    Elizabeth Hardwick   George Plimpton
    Eve Auchincloss   Jason Epstein
    Alexandra T. Emmet   Midge Decter
    A. Whitney Ellsworth   Malcolm Muggeridge
    Terry Ehrich

April 4, 1965

Dear Bob,

I have decided to use again our particular method of correspondence by copy. All reports say you enjoy it.

Now, your last letter informs me the *Review* has no intention of publishing my previous letter because you feel the disclosures are inappropriate. That your methods (which inspired my letter) may not be any more appropriate seems not to have entered your grasp of the issue.

In any case I want to make one more effort to change your decision. The alternative is, after all, disagreeable. I will be forced to publish the letter somewhere else: that small communication which in your pages might leaven the *Review*'s worthy academic yeastings will, printed in another place, take on a literary history larger than its merits. Furthermore, it will be out of our hands. We will both look like fools. That is disagreeable, but I have habits for playing the fool; it will bother me less, it is expected of me. Whereas—it bruises sensibility to point this out— most Americans don't know old Bob Silvers, they don't know what a marvelous and complicated fellow he is. They won't know his private reputation among his devoted friends is rich and various. No, you will be inserted most unfairly into literary history as the editor who wouldn't print an entertaining letter about himself and so gave the letter twenty times its natural publicity. That would be awful. I fear you must now face the unendurable, and make up your mind. Print or do not print my letter. Still, be of good cheer. It is these difficult decisions which make field marshals or tycoons of us all, kid.

Your devoted friend,

Norman Mailer

cc: Barbara Epstein   Samuel N. Antupit
    Elizabeth Hardwick   George Plimpton
    Eve Auchincloss   Jason Epstein
    Alexandra T. Emmet   Midge Decter
    A. Whitney Ellsworth   Malcolm Muggeridge
    Terry Ehrich

THE LOCUST CRY

On p. 293 of *The Early Masters*[1] is a short story.

The Test

It is told:

When Prince Adam Czartoryski, the friend and counselor of Czar Alexander, had been married for many years and still had no children, he went to the maggid of Koznitz and asked him to pray for him and because of his prayer the princess bore a son. At the baptism, the father told of the maggid's intercession with God. His brother who, with his young son, was among the guests, made fun of what he called the prince's superstition. "Let us go to your wonder-worker together," he said, "and I shall show you that he can't tell the difference between left and right."

Together they journeyed to Koznitz, which was close to where they lived. "I beg of you," Adam's brother said to the maggid, "to pray for my sick son."

The maggid bowed his head in silence. "Will you do this for me?" the other urged.

The maggid raised his head. "Go," he said, and Adam saw that he only managed to speak with a great effort. "Go quickly, and perhaps you will still see him alive."

"Well, what did I tell you?" Adam's brother said laughingly as they got into their carriage. Adam was silent during the ride. When they drove into the court of his house, they found the boy dead.

[1] From Martin Buber's *Tales of the Hasidim*. Published by Schocken Books. Volume I: *The Early Masters,* Volume II: *The Later Masters.*

What is suggested by the story is an underworld of real events whose connection is never absurd. Consider, in parallel, this Haiku:[2]

> So soon to die
> and no sign of it showing—
> locust cry.

The sense of stillness and approaching death is occupied by the cry of the locust. Its metallic note becomes the exact equal of an oncoming death. Much of Haiku can best be understood as a set of equations in mood. Man inserting himself into a mood extracts an answer from nature which is not only the reaction of the man upon the mood, but is a supernatural equivalent to the quality of the experience, almost as if a key is given up from the underworld to unlock the surface of reality.

Here for example is an intimation of the architecture concealed beneath:

Upsetting the Bowl [3]

It is told:

Once Rabbi Elimelekh was eating the Sabbath meal with his disciples. The servant set the soup bowl down before him. Rabbi Elimelekh raised it and upset it, so that the soup poured over the table. All at once young Mendel, later the rabbi of Rymanov, cried out: "Rabbi, what are you doing? They will put us all in jail!" The other disciples smiled at these foolish words. They would have laughed out loud, had not the presence of their teacher restrained them. He, however, did not smile. He nodded to young Mendel and said: "Do not be afraid, my son!"

Some time after this, it became known that on that day an edict directed against the Jews of the whole country had been presented to the emperor for his

[2] *An Introduction to Haiku* by Harold G. Henderson, p. 43. The poem is by Matsuo Basho, translated by Henderson.

> *Yagate shinu*
> *keshiki wa mei-zo*
> *semi-no koe*

[3] *The Early Masters*, p. 259.

signature. Time after time he took up his pen, but something always happened to interrupt him. Finally he signed the paper. Then he reached for the sand-container but took the inkwell instead and upset it on the document. Hereupon he tore it up and forbade them to put the edict before him again.

A magical action in one part of the world creates its historical action in another—we are dealing with no less than totem and taboo. Psychoanalysis intrudes itself. One of the last, may it be one of the best approaches to modern neurosis is by way of the phenomenological apparatus of anxiety. As we sink into the apethetic bog of our possible extinction, so a breath of the Satanic seems to rise from the swamp. The magic of materials lifts into consciousness, proceeds to dominate us, is even enthroned into a usurpation of consciousness. The protagonists of *Last Year at Marienbad* are not so much people as halls and chandeliers, gaming tables, cigarettes in their pyramid of 1, 3, 5, and 7. The human characters are ghosts, disembodied servants, attendants who cast their shadows on the material. It is no longer significant that a man carries a silver cigarette case; rather it is the cigarette case which is significant. The man becomes an instrument to transport the case from the breast pocket of a suit into the air; like a building crane, a hand conducts the cigarette case to an angle with the light, fingers open the catch and thus elicit a muted sound of boredom, a silver groan from the throat of the case, which now offers up a cigarette, snaps its satisfaction at being shut, and seems to guide the hand back to the breast pocket. The man, on leave until he is called again, goes through a pantomime of small empty activities—without the illumination of his case he is like all dull servants who cannot use their liberty.

That, one may suppose, is a proper portrait of Hell. It is certainly the air of the phenomenological novel. It is as well the neurotic in slavery to the material objects which make up the locks and keys of his compulsion.

But allow me a quick portrait of a neurotic. He is a sociologist, let us say, working for a progressive foundation, a disenchanted atheist ("Who knows—God may exist as some kind of thwarted benevolence"), a liberal, a social planner, a member of SANE, a logical positivist, a collector of jokes about fags and beatniks, a lover of that large suburban land between art and the documentary. He smokes two packs of cigarettes a day: he drinks—*when* he drinks—eight or ten tots of blended whiskey in a night. He does not get drunk, merely cerebral, amusing, and happy. Once when he came home thus drunk, he bowed to his door and then touched his doorknob three times. After this, he went to bed and slept like a thief.

Two years later he is in slavery to the doorknob. He must wipe it with his fingertips three times each morning before he goes out. If he forgets to do this and only remembers later at work, his day is shattered. Anxiety bursts his concentration. His psyche has the air of a bombed city. In an extreme case, he may even have to return to his home. His first question to himself is whether someone has touched the knob since he left. He makes inquiries. To his horror he discovers the servant has gone out shopping already. She has therefore touched the knob and it has lost its magical property. Stratagems are now necessary. He must devote the rest of the day to encouraging the servant to go out in such a manner that he can open the door for her, and thus remove the prior touch of her hand.

Is he mad? the man asks himself. Later he will ask his analyst the same question. But he is too aware of the absurdity of his activities. He suffers at the thought of the work he is not accomplishing, he hates himself for being attached to the doorknob, he tries to extirpate its dominance. One morning he makes an effort to move out briskly. He does not touch the brass a second and third time. But his feet come to a halt, his body turns around as if a gyroscope were revolving him, his arm turns to the knob and pats it twice. He no longer feels his psyche is to be torn in two. Consummate relief.

Of course his analysis discloses wonders. He has been an only son. His mother, his father, and himself make three. He and his wife (a naturally not very happy marriage) have one child. The value of the trinities is considered dubious by the analyst but is insisted upon by the patient. He has found that he need touch the doorknob only once if he repeats to himself, "I was born, I live, and I die." After a time he finds that he does not have to touch the knob at all, or upon occasion, can use his left hand for the purpose. There is a penalty, however. He is obliged to be con-

cerned with the number nine for the rest of the day. Nine
sips of water from a glass. A porterhouse steak consumed
in nine bites. His wife to be kissed nine times between
supper and bed. "I've kicked over an ant hill," he confesses
to his analyst. "I'm going bugs."

They work in his cause. Two testes and one penis makes
three. Two eyes and one nose; two nostrils and one mouth;
the throat, the tongue, and the teeth. His job, his family,
and himself. The door, the doorknob, and the act of opening it.

Then he has a revelation. He wakes up one morning and
does not reach for a cigarette. There is a tension in him
to wait. He suffers agonies—the brightest and most impatient of his cells seem to be expiring without nicotine—
still he has intimations of later morning bliss, he hangs on.
Like an infantryman coming up alive from a forty-eight-
hour shelling, he gets to his hat, his attaché case, and the
doorknob. As he touches it, a current flows into his hand.
"Stick with me, pal," says the message. "One and two keep
you from three."

Traveling to the office in the last half hour of the subway rush, he is happy for the first time in years. As he
holds to the baked enamel loop of the subway strap, his
fingers curl up a little higher and touch the green painted
metal above the loop. A current returns to him again.
Through his fingertips he feels a psychic topography which
has dimensions, avenues, signals, buildings. From the metal
of the subway strap through the metal of the subway car,
down along the rails, into the tunnels of the city, back to
the sewer pipes and electric cables which surround the subway station from which he left, back to his house, and up
the plumbing, up the steam pipe, up the hall, a leap through
the air, and he has come back to the doorknob again. He
pats the subway strap three times. The ship of his body
will sink no further. "Today," thinks the sociologist, "I
signed my armistice. The flag of Faust has been planted
here."

But in his office he has palpitations. He believes he will
have a heart attack. He needs air. He opens the window,
leans out from the waist. By God, he almost jumped!

The force which drew him to touch the knob now seems
to want to pull his chest through the window. Or is it a
force opposed to the force which made him touch the door-

knob? He does not know. He thinks God may be telling him to jump. That thwarted benevolent God. "You are swearing allegiance to materials," says a voice. "Come back, son. It is better to be dead."

Poor man. He is not bold enough to be Faust. He calls his analyst.

"Now, for God's sake, don't do anything," says the analyst. "This is not uncommon. Blocked material is rising to the surface. It's premature, but since we've gotten into it, repetition compulsions have to do with omnipotence fantasies which of course always involve Almighty figures and totemic Satanistic contracts. The urge to suicide is not bona fide in your case—it's merely a symbolic contraction of the anxiety."

"But I tell you I almost went through the window. I felt my feet start to leave the floor."

"Well, come by my office then. I can't see you right now—trust me on this—I've got a girl who will feel I've denied her her real chance to bear children if I cut into her hour, she's had too many abortions. You know, she's touchy"—rare is the analyst who won't gossip a *little* about his patients, it seems to calm the other patients—"but I'll leave an envelope of tranquilizers for you on the desk. They're a new formula. They're good. Take two right away. Then two more this afternoon. Forget the nausea if it comes. Just side-effect. We'll get together this evening."

"Mind if I touch your doorknob three times?"

"Great. You've got your sense of humor back. Yes, by all means, touch it."

> So soon to die
> and no sign of it is showing—
>   locust cry.

1963

PART EIGHT

Clues to Love

THE TIME OF
HER TIME

1

I was living in a room one hundred feet long and twenty-five feet wide, and it had nineteen windows staring at me from three of the walls and part of the fourth. The floor planks were worn below the level of the nails which held them down, except for the southern half of the room where I had laid a rough linoleum which gave a hint of sprinkled sand, conceivably an aid to the footwork of my pupils. For one hundred dollars I had the place whitewashed; everything: the checkerboard of tin ceiling plates one foot square with their fleur-de-lis stamped into the metal, the rotted sashes on the window frames (it took twelve hours to scrape the calcimine from the glass), even parts of the floor had white drippings (although that was scuffed into dust as time went on) and yet it was worth it. When I took the loft it stank of old machinery and the paint was a liverish brown—I had tried living with that color for a week, my old furniture which had been moved by a mover friend from the Village and me, showed the scars of being humped and dragged and flung up six flights of stairs, and the view of it sprawled over twenty-five hundred feet of living space, three beat old day beds, some dusty cushions, a broken-armed easy chair, a cigarette-scarred coffee table made from a door, a kitchen table, some peeled enamel chairs which thumped like a wooden-legged pirate when one sat in them, the bookshelves of unfinished pine butted by bricks, yes all of this, my purview, this grand vista, the New York sunlight greeting me in the morning through the double filter of the smog-yellow sky and the nineteen dirt-frosted windows, inspired me with so much content, especially those liver-brown walls, that I fled my pad like the plague, and in the first week, after a day of setting the furniture to rights, I was there for four hours of sleep a night, from five in the morning when I maneuvered in from the last closed Village bar and the last coffee-klatsch of my philosopher friends for the night to let us say nine in the morning when I awoke with a partially destroyed brain and the certainty that the sore vicious growl of my stomach was at least the onset of an ulcer and more likely the first gone cells of a thoroughgoing cancer of the duodenum. So I lived it that way for a week, and then following the advice of a bar-type who was the friend of a friend, I got myself up on the eighth morning, boiled my coffee on a hot-plate while I shivered in the October air (neither the stove nor the gas heaters had yet been bought) and then I went downstairs and out the front door of the warehouse onto Monroe Street, picking my way through the garbage-littered gutter which always made me think of the gangs on this street, the Negroes on the east end of the block, the Puerto Ricans next to them, and the Italians and Jews to the west—those gangs were going to figure a little in my life, I suspected that, I was anticipating those moments with no quiet bravery considering how hung was my head in the morning, for the worst clue to the gangs was the six-year-olds. They were the defilers of the garbage, knights of the ordure, and here, in this province of a capital Manhattan, at the southern tip of the island, with the overhead girders of the Manhattan and Brooklyn bridges the only noble structures for a mile of tenement jungle, yes here the barbarians ate their young, and any type who reached the age of six without being altogether mangled by father, mother, family or friends, was a pint of iron man, so tough, so ferocious, so sharp in the teeth that the wildest alley cat would have surrendered a freshly caught rat rather than contest the meal. They were charming, these six-year-olds, as I told my uptown friends, and they used to topple the overloaded garbage cans, strew them through the street, have summer snowball fights with orange peel, coffee grounds, soup bones, slop, they threw the discus by scaling the raw tin rounds from the tops of cans, their pillow fights were with loaded socks of scum, and a debauch was for two of them to scrub a third around the inside of a twenty-gallon pail still warm with the heat of its emptied treasures. I heard that the Olympics took place in summer when they were out of school and the streets were so thick with the gum of old detritus, alluvium and dross that the mash made by passing car tires fermented in the sun. Then the parents and the hoods and the debs and the grandmother dowagers cheered them on and promised them murder and the garbage flew all day, but I was there in fall and the scene was quiet from nine to three. So I picked my way through last night's stew of rubble on this eighth morning of my hiatus on Monroe Street, and went half down the block to a tenement on the boundary between those two bandit republics of the Negroes and the Puerto Ricans, and with a history or two of knocking on the wrong door, and with a nose full of the smells of the sick overpeppered bowels of the poor which seeped and oozed out of every leaking pipe in every communal crapper (only as one goes north does the word take on the Protestant propriety of john), I was able finally to find my man, and I was an hour ahead of him—he was still sleeping off his last night's drunk. So I spoke to his wife, a fat masculine Negress with the face and charity of a Japanese wrestler, and when she understood that I was neither a junk-peddler nor fuzz, that I sold no numbers, carried no bills, and was most certainly not a detective (though my Irish face left her dubious of that) but instead had come to offer her husband a job of work, I was admitted to the first of three dark rooms, face to face with the gray luminescent eye of the television set going its way in the dark room on a bright morning, and through the hall curtains I could hear them talking in the bedroom.

"Get up, you son of a bitch," she said to him.

He came to work for me, hating my largesse, lugging his air compressor up my six flights of stairs, and after a discussion in which his price came down from two hundred to one, and mine rose from fifty dollars to meet his, he left with one of my twenty-dollar bills, the air compressor on the floor as security, and returned in an hour with so many sacks of whitewash that I had to help him up the stairs. We worked together that day, Charlie Thompson his name was, a small lean Negro maybe forty years old, and conceivably sixty, with a scar or two on his face, one a gouge on the cheek, the other a hairline along the bridge of his nose, and we got along not too badly, working in sullen silence until the hangover was sweated out, and then starting to talk over coffee in the Negro hashhouse on the corner where the bucks bridled a little when I came in, and then ignored me. Once the atmosphere had become neutral again, Thompson was willing to talk.

"Man," he said to me, "what you want all that space for?"

"To make money."

"Out of which?"

I debated not very long. The people on the block would know my business sooner or later—the reward of living in a slum is that everyone knows everything which is within reach of the senses—and since I would be nailing a sign over my mailbox downstairs for the pupils to know which floor they would find me on, and the downstairs door would have to be open since I had no bell, the information would be just as open. But for that matter I was born to attract attention; given my height and my blond hair, the barbarians would notice me, they noticed everything, and so it was wiser to come on strong than to try to sidle in.

"Ever hear of an *Escuela de Torear?*" I asked him without a smile.

He laughed with delight at the sound of the words, not even bothering to answer.

"That's a bullfighter's school," I told him. "I teach bull-fighting."

"You know that?"

"I used to do it in Mexico."

"Man, you can get killed."

"Some do." I let the exaggeration of a cooled nuance come into my voice. It was true after all; some do get killed. But not so many as I was suggesting, maybe one in fifty of the successful, and one in five hundred of the amateurs like me who fought a few bulls, received a few wounds, and drifted away.

Charley Thompson was impressed. So were others— the conversation was being overheard after all, and I had become a cardinal piece on the chaotic chessboard of Monroe Street's sociology—I felt the clear bell-like adrenalins of clean anxiety, untainted by weakness, self-interest, neurotic habit, or the pure yellows of the liver. For I had put my poker money on the table, I was the new gun in a frontier saloon, and so I was asking for it, not today, not tomorrow, but come sooner, come later, something was likely to follow from this. The weak would leave me alone, the strong would have respect, but be it winter or summer, sunlight or dark, there would come an hour so cold or so hot that someone, somebody, some sexed-up head, very strong and very weak, would be drawn to discover a new large truth about himself and the mysteries of his own courage or the lack of it. I knew. A year before, when I had first come to New York, there was a particular cat I kept running across in the bars of the Village, an expert with a knife, or indeed to maintain the salts of accuracy, an expert with two knives. He carried them everywhere—he had been some sort of hophead instructor in the Marines on the art of fighting with the knife, and he used to demonstrate nice fluid poses, his elbows in, the knives out, the points of those blades capering free of one another—he could feint in any direction with either hand, he was an artist, he believed he was better with a knife than any man in all of New York, and night after night in bar after bar he sang the love-song of his own prowess, begging for the brave type who would take on his boast, and leave him confirmed or dead.

It is mad to take on the city of New York, there is too much talent waiting on line; this cat was calling for every hoodlum in every crack gang and clique who fancied himself with the blade, and one night, drunk and on the way home, he was greeted by another knife, a Puerto Rican cat who was defective in school and spent his afternoons and nights shadow-knifing in the cellar club-house of his clique, a real contender, long-armed for a Latin, thin as a Lehmbruck, and fast as a hungry wolf; he had practiced for two months to meet the knife of New York.

So they went into an alley, the champion drunk, a fog of vanity blanketing the point of all his artistic reflexes, and it turned out to be not too much of a fight: the Puerto Rican caught it on the knuckles, the lip, and above the knee, but they were only nicks, and the champion was left in bad shape, bleeding from the forearm, the belly, the chest, the neck, and the face: once he was down, the Puerto Rican had engraved a double oval, labium majorum and minorum on the skin of the cheek, and left him there, having the subsequent consideration or fright to make a telephone call to the bar in which our loser had been drinking. The ex-champion, a bloody cat, was carried to his pad which was not far away (a bit of belated luck) and in an hour, without undue difficulty the brother-in-law doctor of somebody or other was good enough to take care of him. There were police reports, and as our patois goes, the details were a drag, but what makes my story sad is that our ex-champion was through. He mended by sorts and shifts, and he still bragged in the Village bars, and talked of finding the Puerto Rican when he was sober and in good shape, but the truth was that he was on the alcoholic way, and the odds were that he would stay there. He had been one of those gamblers who saw his life as a single bet, and he had lost. I often thought that he had been counting on a victory to put some charge below his belt and drain his mouth of all the desperate labial libido.

Now I was following a modest parallel, and as Thompson kept asking me some reasonable if openly ignorant questions about the nature of the bullfight, I found myself shaping every answer as carefully as if I were writing dialogue, and I was speaking practically for the black-alerted senses of three Negroes who were sitting behind me, each of them big in his way (I had taken my glimpse as I came in) with a dull, almost Chinese, sullenness of face. They could have been anything. I had seen faces like theirs on boxers and ditch diggers, and I had seen such faces by threes and fours riding around in Cadillacs through the Harlem of the early-morning hours. I was warning myself to play it carefully, and yet I pushed myself a little further than I should, for I became ashamed of my caution and therefore was obliged to brag just the wrong bit. Thompson, of course, was encouraging me—he was a sly old bastard—and he knew even better than me the character of our audience.

"Man, you can take care of yourself," he said with glee.

"I don't know about that," I answered, obeying the formal minuet of the *macho*. "I don't like to mess with anybody," I told him. "But a man messes with me—well, I wouldn't want him to go away feeling better than he started."

"Oh, yeah, ain't that a fact. I hears just what you hear." He talked like an old-fashioned Negro—probably Southern. "What if four or five of them comes on and gangs you?"

We had come a distance from the art of the *corrida*. "That doesn't happen to me," I said. "I like to be careful about having some friends." And part for legitimate empha-

sis, and part to fulfill my image of the movie male lead
—that blond union of the rugged and the clean-cut (which
would after all be *their* image as well)—I added, "Good
friends, you know."

There we left it. My coffee cup was empty, and in the
slop of the saucer a fly was drowning. I was thinking idly
and with no great compassion that wherever this fly had
been born it had certainly not expected to die in a tan
syrupy ring-shaped pond, struggling for the greasy hot-
dogged air of a cheap Negro hashhouse. But Thompson
rescued it with a deft little flip of his fingers.

"I always save," he told me seriously. "I wouldn't let
nothing be killed. I'm a preacher."

"Real preacher?"

"Was one. Church and devoted congregation." He said
no more. He had the dignified sadness of a man remembering the major failure of his life.

As we got up to go, I managed to turn around and get
another look at the three spades in the next booth. Two of
them were facing me. Their eyes were flat, the whites were
yellow and flogged with red—they stared back with no
love. The anxiety came over me again, almost nice—I had
been so aware of them, and they had been so aware of me.

2

That was in October, and for no reason I could easily
discover, I found myself thinking of that day as I woke on
a spring morning more than half a year later with a strong
light coming through my nineteen windows. I had fixed
the place up since then, added a few more pieces of furniture, connected a kitchen sink and a metal stall shower
to the clean water outlets in the john, and most noticeably
I had built a wall between the bullfight studio and the half
in which I lived. That was more necessary than one might
guess—I had painted the new wall red; after Thompson's
job of whitewash I used to feel as if I were going snow-
blind; it was no easy pleasure to get up each morning in a
white space so blue with cold that the chill of a mountain
peak was in my blood. Now, and when I opened my
eyes, I could choose the blood of the wall in preference
to the ice slopes of Mt. O'Shaugnessy, where the sun was
always glinting on the glaciers of the windows.

But on this particular morning, when I turned over a little more, there was a girl propped on one elbow in the bed beside me, no great surprise, because this was the year of all the years in my life when I was scoring three and four times a week, literally combing the pussy out of my hair, which was no great feat if one knew the Village and the scientific temperament of the Greenwich Village mind. I do not want to give the false impression that I was one of the lustiest to come adventuring down the pike— I was cold, maybe by birth, certainly by environment: I grew up in a Catholic orphanage—and I had had my little kinks and cramps, difficulties enough just a few years ago, but I had passed through that, and I was going now on a kind of disinterested but developed competence; what it came down to was that I could go an hour with the average girl without destroying more of the vital substance than a good night's sleep could repair, and since that sort of stamina seems to get advertised, and I had my good looks, my blond hair, my height, build, and bullfighting school, I suppose I became one of the Village equivalents of an Eagle Scout badge for the girls. I was one of the credits needed for a diploma in the sexual humanities, I was par for a good course, and more than one of the girls and ladies would try me on an off-evening like comparison-shoppers to shop the value of their boy friend, lover, mate, or husband against the certified professionalism of Sergius O'Shaugnessy.

Now if I make this sound bloodless, I am exaggerating a bit—even an old habit is livened once in a while with color, and there were girls I worked to get and really wanted, and nights when the bull was far from dead in me. I even had two women I saw at least once a week, each of them, but what I am trying to emphasize is that when you screw too much and nothing is at stake, you begin to feel like a saint. It was a hell of a thing to be holding a nineteen-year-old girl's ass in my hands, hefting those young kneadables of future power, while all the while the laboratory technician in my brain was deciding that the experiment was a routine success—routine because her cheeks looked and felt just about the way I had thought they would while I was sitting beside her in the bar earlier in the evening, and so I still had come no closer to understanding my scientific compulsion to verify in the retort of the bed how accurately I had predicted the form, texture, rhythm and surprise of any woman who caught my eye.

Only an ex-Catholic can achieve some of the rarer amalgams of guilt, and the saint in me deserves to be recorded. I always felt an obligation—some noblesse oblige of the kindly cocksman—to send my women away with no great wounds to their esteem, feeling at best a little better than when they came in, I wanted it to be friendly (what vanity of the saint!). I was the messiah of the one-night stand, and so I rarely acted like a pig in bed, I wasn't greedy, I didn't grind all my tastes into their mouths, I even abstained from springing too good a lay when I felt the girl was really in love with her man, and was using me only to give love the benefit of new perspective. Yes, I was a good sort, I probably gave more than I got back, and the only real pains for all those months in the loft, for my bull-fighting classes, my surprisingly quiet time (it had been winter after all) on Monroe Street, my bulging portfolio of experiments—there must have been fifty girls who spent at least one night in the loft—my dull but doggedly advancing scientific data, even the cold wan joys of my saintliness demanded for their payment only one variety of the dead hour: when I woke in the morning, I could hardly wait to get the latest mouse out of my bed and out of my lair. I didn't know why, but I would awaken with the deadliest of depressions, the smell of the woman had gone very stale for me, and the armpits, the ammonias and dead sea life of old semen and old snatch, the sour fry of last night's sweat, the whore scent of overexercised perfume, became an essence of the odious, all the more remarkable because I clung to women in my sleep, I was one Don John who hated to sleep alone, I used to feel as if my pores were breathing all the maternal (because sleeping) sweets of the lady, wet or dry, firm or flaccid, plump, baggy, or lean who was handled by me while we dreamed. But on awakening, hung with my head—did I make love three times that year without being drunk?—the saint was given his hour of temptation, for I would have liked nothing more than to kick the friendly ass out of bed, and dispense with the coffee, the good form, my depression and often hers, and start the new day by lowering her in a basket out of my monk-ruined retreat six floors down to the garbage

pile (now blooming again in the freshets of spring), wave
my hand at her safe landing and get in again myself to the
blessed isolations of the man alone.

But of course that was not possible. While it is usually a
creep who generalizes about women, I think I will come on
so heavy as to say that the cordial tone of the morning after
is equally important to the gymkhana of the night before—
at least if the profit made by a nice encounter is not to be
lost. I had given my working hours of the early morning to
dissolving a few of the inhibitions, chilled reflexes and
dampened rhythms of the corpus before me, but there is
not a restraint in the world which does not have to be taken
twice—once at night on a steam-head of booze, and once
in daylight with the grace of a social tea. To open a girl
up to the point where she loves you or It or some tremor
in her sexual baggage, and then to close her in the morning is to do the disservice which the hateful side of women
loves most—you have fed their cold satisfied distrust of a
man. Therefore my saint fought his private churl, and
suffering all the detail of abusing the sympathetic nervous
system, I made with the charm in the daylight and was
more of a dear than most.

It was to be a little different this morning, however. As
I said, I turned over in my bed, and looked at the girl
propped on her elbow beside me. In her eyes there was a
flat hatred which gave no ground—she must have been
staring like this at my back for several minutes, and when
I turned, it made no difference—she continued to examine
my face with no embarrassment and no delight.

That was sufficient to roll me around again, my shoulder
blades bare to her inspection, and I pretended that the
opening of my eyes had been a false awakening. I felt
deadened then with all the diseases of the dull—making
love to her the night before had been a little too much of a
marathon. She was a Jewish girl and she was in her third
year at New York University, one of those harsh alloys of
a self-made bohemian from a middle-class home (her father
was a hardware wholesaler), and I was remembering how
her voice had irritated me each time I had seen her, an ugly
New York accent with a cultured overlay. Since she was
still far from formed, there had been all sorts of Lesbian
hysterias in her shrieking laugh and they warred with that
excess of strength, complacency and deprecation which I

found in many Jewish women—a sort of "Ech" of disgust at the romantic and mysterious All. This one was medium in size and she had dark long hair which she wore like a Village witch in two extended braids which came down over her flat breasts, and she had a long thin nose, dark eyes, and a kind of lean force, her arms and square shoulders had shown the flat thin muscles of a wiry boy. All the same, she was not bad, she had a kind of Village chic, a certain snotty elegance of superiority, and when I first came to New York I had dug girls like her—Jewesses were strange to me—and I had even gone with one for a few months. But this new chick had been a mistake—I had met her two weeks ago at a party, she was on leave from her boy friend, and we had had an argument about T. S. Eliot, a routine which for me had become the quintessence of corn, but she said that Eliot was the apotheosis of manner, he embodied the ecclesiasticism of classical and now futureless form, she adored him she said, and I was tempted to tell her how little Eliot would adore the mannerless yeasts of the Brooklyn from which she came, and how he might prefer to allow her to appreciate his poetry only in step to the transmigration of her voice from all urgent Yiddish nasalities to the few high English analities of relinquished desire. No, she would not make that other world so fast—nice society was not cutting her crumpets thus quickly because she was gone on Thomas Stearns Eeeee. Her college-girl snobbery, the pith for me of eighty-five other honey-pots of the Village aesthetic whose smell I knew all too well, so inflamed the avenger of my crotch, that I wanted to prong her then and there, right on the floor of the party, I was a primitive for a prime minute, a gorged gouge of a working-class phallus, eager to ram into all her nasty little tensions. I had the message again, I was one of the millions on the bottom who had the muscles to move the sex which kept the world alive, and I would grind it into her, the healthy hearty inches and the sweat of the cost of acquired culture when you started low and you wanted to go high. She was a woman, what! she sensed that moment, she didn't know if she could handle me, and she had the guts to decide to find out. So we left the party and we drank and (leave it to a Jewish girl to hedge the bet) she drained the best half of my desire in conversation because she was being psychoanalyzed, what a predict-

able pisser! and she was in that stage where the jargon had
the totalitarian force of all vocabularies of mechanism,
and she could only speak of her infantile relations to men,
and the fixations and resistances of unassimilated penis-
envy with all the smug gusto of a female commissar. She
was enthusiastic about her analyst, he was also Jewish (they
were working now on Jewish self-hatred), he was really
an integrated guy, Stanford Joyce, he belonged on the
same mountain as Eliot, she loved the doers and the healers
of life who built on the foundationless prevalence of the
void those islands of proud endeavor.

"You must get good marks in school," I said to her.

"Of course."

How I envied the jazzed-up brain of the Jews. I was
hot for her again, I wanted the salts of her perspiration in
my mouth. They would be acrid perhaps, but I would
digest them, and those intellectual molecules would rise
to my brain.

"I know a girl who went to your bullfighting school,"
she said to me. She gave her harsh laugh. "My friend
thought you were afraid of her. She said you were full of
narcissistic anxieties."

"Well, we'll find out," I said.

"Oh, you don't want me. I'm very inadequate as a
lover." Her dark hard New York eyes, bright with appetite, considered my head as if I were a delicious and particularly sour pickle.

I paid the check then, and we walked over to my loft. As
I had expected, she made no great fuss over the back-
and-forth of being seduced—to the contrary. Once we
were upstairs, she prowled the length of my loft twice,
looked at the hand-made bullfighting equipment I had
set up along one wall of the studio, asked me a question
or two about the killing machine, studied the swords,
asked another question about the cross-guard on the des-
cabellar, and then came back to the living-room–bedroom–
dining-room—kitchen of the other room, and made a face
at the blood-red wall. When I kissed her she answered with
a grinding insistence of her mouth upon mine, and a muscular thrust of her tongue into my throat, as direct and un-
feminine as the harsh force of her voice.

"I'd like to hang my clothes up," she said.

It was not all that matter-of-fact when we got to bed.

There was nothing very fleshy about the way she made love, no sense of the skin, nor smell, nor touch, just anger, anger at her being there, and another anger which was good for my own, that rage to achieve . . . just what, one cannot say. She made love as if she were running up an inclined wall so steep that to stop for an instant would slide her back to disaster. She hammered her rhythm at me, a hard driving rhythm, an all but monotonous drum, pound into pound against pound into pound until that moment when my anger found its way back again to that delayed and now recovered Time when I wanted to prong her at the party. I had been frustrated, had waited, had lost the anger, and so been taken by her. That finally got me—all through the talk about T. S. Eliot I had been calculating how I would lay waste to her little independence, and now she was alone, with me astride her, going through her paces, teeth biting the pillow, head turned away, using me as the dildoe of a private gallop. So my rage came back, and my rhythm no longer depended upon her drive, but found its own life, and we made love like two club fighters in an open exchange, neither giving ground, rhythm to rhythm, even to even, hypnotic, knowing neither the pain of punishment nor the pride of pleasure, and the equality of this, as hollow as the beat of the drum, seemed to carry her into some better deep of desire, and I had broken through, she was following me, her muscular body writhed all about me with an impersonal abandon, the wanton whip-thrash of a wounded snake, she was on fire and frozen at the same time, and then her mouth was kissing me with a rubbery greedy compulsion so avid to see all there was of me, that to my distant surprise, not in character for the saint to slip into the brutal, my hand came up and clipped her mean and openhanded across the face which brought a cry from her and broke the piston of her hard speed into something softer, wetter, more sly, more warm, I felt as if her belly were opening finally to receive me, and when her mouth kissed me again with a passing tender heat, warm-odored with flesh, and her body sweetened into some feminine embrace of my determination driving its way into her, well, I was gone, it was too late, I had driven right past her in that moment she turned, and I had begun to come, I was coming from all the confluences of my body toward that bud of sweetness I had plucked from her, and for a moment she was making it, she was a move back and surging to overtake me, and then it was gone, she made a mistake, her will ordered all temptings and rhythms to mobilize their march, she drove into the hard stupidities of a marching-band's step, and as I was going off in the best for many a month, she was merely going away, she had lost it again. As I ebbed into what should have been the contentments of fine after-pleasure, warm and fine, there was one little part of me remaining cold and murderous because she had deprived me, she had fled the domination which was liberty for her, and the rest of the night was bound to be hell.

Her face was ugly. "You're a bastard, do you know that?" she asked of me.

"Let it go. I feel good."

"Of course you feel good. Couldn't you have waited one minute?"

I disliked this kind of thing. My duty was reminding me of how her awakened sweets were souring now in the belly, and her nerves were sharpening into the gone electric of being just nowhere.

"I hate inept men," she said.

"Cool it." She could, at least, be a lady. Because if she didn't stop, I would give her back a word or two.

"You did that on purpose," she nagged at me, and I was struck with the intimacy of her rancor—we might as well have been married for ten years to dislike each other so much at this moment.

"Why," I said, "you talk as if this were something unusual for you."

"It is."

"Come on," I told her, "you never made it in your life."

"How little you know," she said. "This is the first time I've missed in months."

If she had chosen to get my message, I could have been preparing now for a good sleep. Instead I would have to pump myself up again—and as if some ghost of the future laid the squeak of a tickle on my back, I felt an odd dread, not for tonight so much as for some ills of the next ten years whose first life was stirring tonight. But I lay beside her, drew her body against mine, feeling her trapped and irritable heats jangle me as much as they aroused me, and while I had no fear that the avenger would remain asleep, still he stirred in pain and in protest, he had supposed his work to be done, and he would claim the wages of overtime from my reserve. That was the way I thought it would go, but Junior from New York University, with her hard body and her passion for proper poetry, gave a lewd angry old grin as her face stared boldly into mine, and with the practical bawdiness of the Jew she took one straight utilitarian finger, smiled a deceptive girlish pride, and then she jabbed, fingernail and all, into the tight defended core of my clenched buttocks. One wiggle of her knuckle and I threw her off, grunting a sound between rage and surprise, to which she laughed and lay back and waited for me.

Well, she had been right, that finger tipped the balance, and three-quarters with it, and one-quarter hung with the mysteries of sexual ambition, I worked on her like a beaver for forty-odd minutes or more, slapping my tail to build her nest, and she worked along while we made the round of the positions, her breath sobbing the exertions, her body as alive as a charged wire and as far from rest.

I gave her all the Time I had in me and more besides, I was weary of her, and the smell which rose from her had so little of the sea and so much of the armpit, that I breathed the stubborn wills of the gymnasium where the tight-muscled search for grace, and it was like that, a hard punishing session with pulley weights, stationary bicycle sprints, and ten breath-seared laps around the track. Yes, when I caught that smell, I knew she would not make it, and so I kept on just long enough to know she was exhausted in body, exhausted beyond the place where a ten-minute rest would have her jabbing that finger into me again, and hating her, hating women who could not take their exercise alone, I lunged up over the hill with my heart pounding past all pleasure, and I came, but with hatred, tight, electric, and empty, the spasms powerful but centered in my heart and not from the hip, the avenger taking its punishment even at the end, jolted clear to the seat of my semen by the succession of rhythmic blows which my heart drummed back to my feet.

For her, getting it from me, it must have been impressive, a convoluted, smashing, and protracted spasm, a hint of the death throe in the animal male which cannot but please the feminine taste for the mortal wound. "Oh, you're lucky," she whispered in my ear as I lay all collapsed beside her, alone in my athlete's absorption upon the whisperings of damage in the unlit complexities of my inner body. I was indeed an athlete, I knew my body was my future, and I had damaged it a bit tonight by most certainly doing it no good. I disliked her for it with the simple dislike we know for the stupid.

"Want a cigarette?" she asked.

I could wait, my heart would have preferred its rest, but there was something tired in her voice beyond the fatigue of what she had done. She too had lost after all. So I came out of my second rest to look at her, and her face had the sad relaxation (and serenity) of a young whore who has finished a hard night's work with the expected lack of issue for herself, content with no more than the money and the professional sense of the hard job dutifully done.

"I'm sorry you didn't make it," I said to her.

She shrugged. There was a Jewish tolerance for the expected failures of the flesh. "Oh, well, I lied to you before," she said.

"You never have been able to, have you?"

"No." She was fingering the muscles of my shoulder, as if in unconscious competition with my strength. "You're pretty good," she said grudgingly.

"Not really inept?" I asked.

"*Sans façons,*" said the poetess in an arch change of mood which irritated me. "Sandy has been illuminating those areas where my habits make for destructive impulses."

"Sandy is Doctor Joyce?" She nodded. "You make him sound like your navigator," I told her.

"Isn't it a little obvious to be hostile to psychoanalysis?"

Three minutes ago we had been belaboring each other in the nightmare of the last round, and now we were close to cozy. I put the sole of my foot on her sharp little knee.

"You know the first one we had?" she asked of me. "Well, I wanted to tell you. I came close—I guess I came as close as I ever came."

"You'll come closer. You're only nineteen."

"Yes, but this evening has been disturbing to me. You see I get more from you than I get from my lover."

Her lover was twenty-one, a senior at Columbia, also Jewish—which lessened interest, she confessed readily. Besides, Arthur was too passive—"Basically, it's very comprehensible," said the commissar, "an aggressive female and a passive male—we complement one another, and that's no good." Of course it was easy to find satisfaction with Arthur, "via the oral perversions. That's because, vaginally, I'm anaesthetized—a good phallic narcissist like you doesn't do enough for me."

In the absence of learned credentials, she was setting out to bully again. So I thought to surprise her. "Aren't you mixing your language a little?" I began. "The phallis narcissist is one of Wilhelm Reich's categories."

"Therefore?"

"Aren't you a Freudian?"

"It would be presumptuous of me to say," she said like a seminar student working for his pee-aitch-dee. "But Sandy is an eclectic. He accepts a lot of Reich—you see, he's very ambitious, he wants to arrive at his own synthesis." She exhaled some smoke in my face, and gave a nice tough little grin which turned her long serious young witch's face into something indeed less presumptuous. "Besides," she said, "you are a phallic narcissist. There's an element of the sensual which is lacking in you."

"But Arthur possesses it?"

"Yes, he does. And you . . . you're not very juicy."

"I wouldn't know what you mean."

"I mean this." With the rich cruel look of a conquistador finding a new chest of Indian gold, she bent her head and gave one fleeting satiric half-moon of a lick to the conjugation of my balls. "That's what I mean," she said, and was out of bed even as I was recognizing that she was finally not without art. "Come back," I said.

But she was putting her clothes on in a hurry. "Shut up. Just don't give me your goddamned superiority."

I knew what it was: she had been about to gamble the reserves which belonged to Arthur, and the thought of possibly wasting them on a twenty-seven-year-old connoisseur like myself was too infuriating to take the risk.

So I lay in bed and laughed at her while she dressed—I did not really want to go at things again—and besides, the more I laughed, the angrier she would be, but the anger would work to the surface, and beneath it would be resting the pain that the evening had ended on so little.

She took her leisure going to the door, and I got up in time to tell her to wait—I would walk her to the subway. The dawn had come, however, and she wanted to go alone, she had had a bellyful of me, she could tell me that.

My brain was lusting its own private futures of how interesting it would be to have this proud, aggressive, vulgar, tense, stiff and arrogant Jewess going wild on my bottom—I had turned more than one girl on, but never a one of quite this type. I suppose she had succeeded instead of me; I was ready to see her again and improve the message.

She turned down all dates, but compromised by giving me her address and the number of her telephone. And then glaring at me from the open door, she said, "I owe you a slap in the face."

"Don't go away feeling unequal."

I might have known she would have a natural punch. My jaw felt it for half an hour after she was gone and it took another thirty minutes before I could bring myself back to concluding that she was one funny kid.

All of that added up to the first night with the commissar, and I saw her two more times over this stretch, the last on the night when she finally agreed to sleep over with me, and I came awake in the morning to see her glaring at my head. So often in sex, when the second night wound itself up with nothing better in view than the memory of the first night, I was reminded of Kafka's *Castle,* that tale of the search of a man for his apocalyptic orgasm: in the easy optimism of a young man, he almost captures the castle on the first day, and is never to come so close again. Yes, that was the saga of the nervous system of a man as it was bogged into the defeats, complications, and frustrations of middle age. I still had my future before me of course—the full engagement of my will in some go-for-broke I considered worthy of myself was yet to come, but there were times in that loft when I knew the psychology of an old man, and my second night with Denise—for Denise Gondelman was indeed her name—left me racked for it amounted to so little that we could not even leave it there—the hangover would have been too great for both of us—and so we made a date for a third night. Over and over in those days I used to compare the bed to the bullfight, sometimes seeing myself as the matador and sometimes as the bull, and this second appearance, if it had taken place, in the Plaza Mexico, would have been a *fracaso* with kapok seat cushions jeering down on the ring, and a stubborn cowardly bull staying in *querencia* before the doubtful prissy overtures, the gloomy trim technique of a veteran and mediocre *torero* on the worst of days when he is forced to wonder if he has even his *pundonor* to sustain him. It was a gloomy deal. Each of us knew it was possible to be badly worked by the other, and this seemed so likely that neither of us would gamble a finger. Although we got into bed and had a perfunctory ten minutes, it was as long as an hour in a coffee shop when two friends are done with one another.

By the third night we were ready for complexities again; to see a woman three times is to call on the dialectic of an affair. If the waves we were making belonged less to the viper of passion than the worm of inquiry, still it was obvious from the beginning that we had surprises for one another. The second night we had been hoping for more, and so got less; this third night, we each came on with the notion to wind it up, and so got involved in more.

For one thing, Denise called me in the afternoon. There was studying she had to do, and she wondered if it would be all right to come to my place at eleven instead of meeting me for drinks and dinner. Since that would save me ten dollars she saw no reason why I should complain. It was a down conversation. I had been planning to lay seige to her, dispense a bit of elixir from my vast reservoirs of charm, and instead she was going to keep it *in camera*. There was a quality about her I could not locate, something independent—abruptly, right there, I knew what it was. In a year she would have no memory of me, I would not exist for her unless . . . and then it was clear . . . unless I could be the first to carry her stone of no-orgasm up the cliff, all the way, over and out into the sea. That was the kick I could find, that a year from now, five years from now, down all the seasons to the hours of her old age, I would be the one she would be forced to remember, and it would nourish me a little over the years, thinking of that grudged souvenir which could not die in her, my blond hair, my blue eyes, my small broken nose, my clean mouth and chin, my height, my boxer's body, my parts— yes, I was getting excited at the naked image of me in the young-old mind of that sour sexed-up dynamo of black-pussied frustration.

A phallic narcissist she had called me. Well, I was phallic enough, a Village stickman who could muster enough of the divine It on the head of his will to call forth more than one becoming out of the womb of feminine Time, yes a good deal more than one from my fifty new girls a year, and when I failed before various prisons of frigidity, it mattered little. Experience gave the cue that there were ladies who would not be moved an inch by a year of the best and so I looked for other things in them, but this one, this Den-of-Ease, she was ready, she was entering the time of her Time, and if not me, it would be another—I was sick in advance at the picture of some bearded Negro cat who would score where I had missed and thus cuckold me in spirit, deprive me of those telepathic waves of longing (in which I obviously believed) speeding away to me from her over the years to balm the hours when I was beat, because I had been her psychic bridegroom, had plucked her ideational diddle, had led her down the walk of her real wedding night. Since she did not like me, what a feat to pull it off.

In the hours I waited after dinner, alone, I had the sense —which I always trusted—that tonight this little victory or defeat would be full of leverage, magnified beyond its emotional matter because I had decided to bet on myself that I would win, and a defeat would bring me closer to a general depression, a fog bank of dissatisfaction with myself which I knew could last for months or more. Whereas a victory would add to the panoplies of my ego some peculiar (but for me, valid) ingestion of her arrogance, her stubbornness, and her will—those necessary ingredients of which I could not yet have enough for my own ambition.

When she came in she was wearing a sweater and dungarees which I had been expecting, but there was a surprise for me. Her braids had been clipped, and a short cropped curled Italian haircut decorated her head, moving her severe young face half across the spectrum from the austerities of a poetess to a hint of all those practical and promiscuous European girls who sold their holy hump to the Germans and had been subsequently punished by shaved heads—how attractive the new hair proved; once punished, they were now free, free to be wild, the worst had happened and they were still alive with the taste of the first victor's flesh enriching the sensual curl of the mouth.

Did I like her this way? Denise was interested to know. Well, it was a shock, I admitted, a pleasant shock. If it takes you so long to decide, you must be rigid, she let me know. Well, yes, as a matter of fact I was rigid, rigid for her with waiting.

The nun of severity passed a shade over her. She hated men who were uncool, she thought she would tell me.

"Did your analyst tell you it's bad to be uncool?"

She had taken off her coat, but now she gave me a look as if she were ready to put it on again. "No, he did not tell me that." She laughed spitefully. "But he told me a couple of revealing things about you."

"Which you won't repeat."

"Of course not."

"I'll never know," I said, and gave her the first kiss of the evening. Her mouth was heated—it was the best kiss I had received from her, and it brought me on too quickly— "My fruit is ready to be plucked," said the odors of her mouth, betraying that perfume of the ducts which, against her will no doubt, had been plumping for me. She was changed tonight. From the skin of her face and the glen of her neck came a new smell, sweet, sweaty, and tender, the smell of a body which had been used and had enjoyed its uses. It came to me nicely, one of the nicest smells in quite some time, so different from the usual exudations of her dissatisfied salts that it opened a chain of reflexes in me, and I was off in all good speed on what Denise would probably have called the vertical foreplay. I suppose I went at her like a necrophiliac let loose upon a still-warm subject, and as I gripped her, grasped her, groped her, my breath a bellows to blow her into my own flame, her body remained unmoving, only her mouth answering my call, those lips bridling hot adolescent kisses back upon my face, the smell almost carrying me away—such a fine sweet sweat.

Naturally she clipped the rhythm. As I started to slip up her sweater, she got away and said a little huskily, "I'll take my own clothes off." Once again I could have hit her.

My third eye, that athlete's inner eye which probed its
vision into all the corners, happy and distressed of my
body whole, was glumly cautioning the congestion of the
spirits in the coils of each teste. They would have to wait,
turn rancid, maybe die of delay.

Off came the sweater and the needless brassière, her
economical breasts swelled just a trifle tonight, enough to
take on the convexities of an Amazon's armor. Open came
the belt and the zipper of her dungarees, zipped from the
front which pleased her not a little. Only her ass, a small
masterpiece, and her strong thighs, justified this theatre.
She stood there naked, quite psychicly clothed, and lit a
cigarette.

If a stiff prick has no conscience, it has also no common sense. I stood there like a clown, trying to coax her
to take a ride with me on the bawdy car, she out of her
clothes, I in all of mine, a muscular little mermaid to melt
on my knee. She laughed, one harsh banker's snort—she
was giving no loans on my idiot's collateral.

"You didn't even ask me," Denise thought to say, "of
how my studying went tonight."

"What did you study?"

"I didn't. I didn't study." She gave me a lovely smile,
girlish and bright. "I just spent the last three hours with
Arthur."

"You're a dainty type," I told her.

But she gave me a bad moment. That lovely fresh-
spent smell, scent of the well used and the tender, that
avatar of the feminine my senses had accepted so greedily,
came down now to no more than the rubbings and the
sweats of what was probably a very nice guy, passive Arthur with his Jewish bonanzas of mouth-love.

The worst of it was that it quickened me more. I had
the selfish wisdom to throw such evidence upon the mercy
of my own court. For the smell of Arthur was the smell
of love, at least for me, and so from man or woman, it
did not matter—the smell of love was always feminine—
and if the man in Denise was melted by the woman in
Arthur, so Arthur might have flowered that woman in
himself from the arts of a real woman, his mother?—it did
not matter—that voiceless message which passed from
the sword of the man into the cavern of the woman was

carried along from body to body, and if it was not the woman in Denise I was going to find tonight, at least I would be warmed by the previous trace of another.

But that was a tone poem to quiet the toads of my doubt. When Denise—it took five more minutes—finally decided to expose herself on my clumped old mattress, the sight of her black pubic hair, the feel of the foreign but brotherly liquids in her unembarrassed maw, turned me into a jackrabbit of pissy tumescence, the quicks of my excitement beheaded from the resonances of my body, and I wasn't with her a half-minute before I was over, gone, and off. I rode not with the strength to reap the harem of her and her lover, but spit like a pinched little boy up into black forested hills of motherly contempt, a passing picture of the nuns of my childhood to drench my piddle spurtings with failures of gloom. She it was who proved stronger than me, she the he to my silly she.

All considered, Denise was nice about it. Her harsh laugh did not crackle over my head, her hand in passing me the after-cigarette settled for no more than a nudge of my nose, and if it were not for the contempt of her tough grin, I would have been left with no more than the alarm to the sweepers of my brain to sweep this failure away.

"Hasn't happened in years," I said to her, the confession coming out of me with the cost of the hardest cash.

"Oh, shut up. Just rest." And she began to hum a mocking little song. I lay there in a state, parts of me jangled for forty-eight hours to come, and yet not altogether lost to peace. I knew what it was. Years ago in the air force, as an enlisted man, I had reached the light-heavyweight finals on my air base. For two weeks I trained for the championship, afraid of the other man all the way because I had seen him fight and felt he was better than me; when my night came, he took me out with a left hook to the liver which had me conscious on the canvas but unable to move, and as the referee was counting, which I could hear all too clearly, I knew the same kind of peace, a swooning peace, a clue to that kind of death in which an old man slips away—nothing mattered except that my flesh was vulnerable and I had a dim revery, lying there with the yells of the air force crowd in my ears, there was some far-off vision of green fields and me lying in them, giving up all

ambition to go back instead to another, younger life of
the senses, and I remember at that moment I watered the
cup of my boxer's jock, and then I must have slipped into
something new, for as they picked me off the canvas the
floor seemed to recede from me at a great rate as if I were
climbing in an airplane.

A few minutes later, the nauseas of the blow to my
liver had me retching into my hands, and the tension of
three weeks of preparation for that fight came back. I
knew through the fading vistas of my peace, and the oncoming spasms of my nausea, that the worst was yet to
come, and it would take me weeks to unwind, and then
years, and maybe never to overcome the knowledge that I
had failed completely at a moment when I wanted very
much to win.

A ghost of this peace, trailing intimations of a new
nausea, was passing over me again, and I sat up in bed
abruptly, as if to drive these weaknesses back into me.
My groin had been simmering for hours waiting for
Denise, and it was swollen still, but the avenger was limp,
he had deserted my cause, I was in a spot if she did not
co-operate.

Co-operate she did. "My God, lie down again, will you,"
she said, "I was thinking that finally I had seen you
relax."

And then I could sense that the woman in her was about
to betray her victory. She sat over me, her little breasts
budding with their own desire, her short hair alive and
flowering, her mouth ready to taste her gentleman's defeat. I had only to raise my hand, and push her body in
the direction she wished it to go, and then her face was
rooting in me, her angry tongue and voracious mouth
going wild finally as I had wished it, and I knew the sadness of sour timing, because this was a prize I could not
enjoy as I would have on first night, and yet it was good
enough—not art, not the tease and languor of love on a
soft mouth, but therapy, therapy for her, the quick ex-
haustions of the tension in a harsh throat, the beseechment
of an ugly voice going down into the expiation which
would be its beauty. Still it was good, practically it was
good, my ego could bank the hard cash that this snotty
head was searching me, the act served its purpose, anger
traveled from her body into mine, the avenger came to

attention, cold and furious, indifferent to the trapped doomed pleasure left behind in my body on that initial and grim piddle spurt, and I was ready, not with any joy nor softness nor warmth nor care, but I was ready finally to take her tonight, I was going to beat new Time out of her if beat her I must, I was going to teach her that she was only a child, because if at last I could not take care of a nineteen-year-old, then I was gone indeed. And so I took her with a cold calculation, the rhythms of my body corresponding to no more than a metronome in my mind, tonight the driving mechanical beat would come from me, and blind to nerve-raddlings in my body, and blood pressures in my brain, I worked on her like a riveter, knowing her resistances were made of steel, I threw her a fuck the equivalent of a fifteen-round fight, I wearied her, I brought her back, I drove my fingers into her shoulders and my knees into her hips. I went, and I went, and I went, I bore her high and thumped her hard, I sprinted, I paced, I lay low, eyes all closed, under sexual water, like a submarine listening for the distant sound of her ship's motors, hoping to steal up close and trick her rhythms away.

And she was close. Oh, she was close so much of the time. Like a child on a merry-go-round the touch of the colored ring just evaded the tips of her touch, and she heaved and she hurdled, arched and cried, clawed me, kissed me, even gave of a shriek once, and then her sweats running down and her will weak, exhausted even more than me, she felt me leave and lie beside her. Yes, I did that with a tactician's cunning, I let the depression of her failure poison what was left of her will never to let me succeed, I gave her slack to mourn the lost freedoms and hate the final virginity for which she fought, I even allowed her baffled heat to take its rest and attack her nerves once more, and then, just as she was beginning to fret against me in a new and unwilling appeal, I turned her over suddenly on her belly, my avenger wild with the mania of the madman, and giving her no chance, holding her prone against the mattress with the strength of my weight, I drove into the seat of all stubbornness, tight as a vise, and I wounded her, I knew it, she thrashed beneath me like a trapped little animal, making not a sound, but fierce not to allow me this last of the liberties, and yet caught, forced to give up millimeter by millimeter the bridal ground of her symbolic and therefore real vagina. So I made it, I made it all the way—it took ten minutes and maybe more, but as the avenger rode down to his hilt and tunneled the threshold of sexual home all those inches closer into the bypass of the womb, she gave at last a little cry of farewell, and I could feel a new shudder which began as a ripple and rolled into a wave, and then it rolled over her, carrying her along, me hardly moving for fear of damping this quake from her earth, and then it was gone, but she was left alive with a larger one to follow.

So I turned her once again on her back, and moved by impulse to love's first hole. There was an odor coming up, hers at last, the smell of the sea, and none of the armpit or a dirty sock, and I took her mouth and kissed it, but she was away, following the wake of her own waves which mounted, fell back, and in new momentum mounted higher and should have gone over, and then she was about to hang again, I could feel it, that moment of hesitation between the past and the present, the habit and the adventure, and I said into her ear, "You dirty little Jew."

That whipped her over. A first wave kissed, a second spilled, and a third and a fourth and a fifth came breaking over, and finally she was away, she was loose in the water for the first time in her life, and I would have liked to go with her, but I was blood-throttled and numb, and as she had the first big moment in her life, I was nothing but a set of aching balls and a congested cock, and I rode with her wistfully, looking at the contortion of her face and listening to her sobbing sound of "Oh, Jesus, I made it, oh Jesus, I did."

"Compliments of T. S. Eliot," I whispered to myself, and my head was aching, my body was shot. She curled against me, she kissed my sweat, she nuzzled my eyes and murmured in my ear, and then she was slipping away into the nicest of weary sweet sleep.

"Was it good for you too?" she whispered half-awake, having likewise read the works of The Hemingway, and I said, "Yeah, fine," and after she was asleep, I disengaged myself carefully, and prowled the loft, accepting the hours it would take for my roiled sack to clean its fatigues and know a little sleep. But I had abused myself too far, and it took till dawn and half a fifth of whisky before I dropped into an unblessed stupor. When I awoke, in that moment before I moved to look at her, and saw her glaring at me, I was off on a sluggish masculine debate as to whether the kick of studying this Denise for another few nights— now that I had turned the key—would be worth the danger of deepening into some small real feeling. But through my hangover and the knowledge of the day and the week and the month it would take the different parts of all of me to repair, I was also knowing the taste of a reinforced will—finally, I had won. At no matter what cost, and with what luck, and with a piece of charity from her, I had won nonetheless, and since all real pay came from victory, it was more likely that I would win the next time I gambled my stake on something more appropriate for my ambition.

Then I turned, saw the hatred in her eyes, turned over again, and made believe I was asleep while a dread of the next few minutes weighed a leaden breath over the new skin of my ego.

"You're awake, aren't you?" she said.

I made no answer.

"All right, I'm going then. I'm getting dressed." She whipped out of bed, grabbed her clothes, and began to put them on with all the fury of waiting for me to get the pronouncement. "That was a lousy thing you did last night," she said by way of a start.

In truth she looked better than she ever had. The severe lady and the tough little girl of yesterday's face had put forth the first agreements on what would yet be a bold chick.

"I gave you what you could use," I made the mistake of saying.

"Just didn't you," she said, and was on her way to the door. "Well, cool it. You don't do anything to me." Then she smiled. "You're so impressed with what you think was such a marvelous notch you made in me, listen, Buster, I came here last night thinking of what Sandy Joyce told me about you, and he's right, oh man is he right." Standing in the open doorway, she started to light a cigarette, and then threw the matches to the floor. From thirty feet away I could see the look in her eyes, that unmistakable point for the kill that you find in the eyes of very few bullfighters, and then having created her pause, she came on for her moment of truth by saying, "He told me your whole life is

a lie, and you do nothing but run away from the homo-
sexual that is you."

And like a real killer, she did not look back, and was
out the door before I could rise to tell her that she was a
hero fit for me.

1958

THE MAN WHO
STUDIED YOGA

1

I would introduce myself if it were not useless. The name I
had last night will not be the same as the name I have tonight. For the moment, then, let me say that I am thinking
of Sam Slovoda. Obligatorily, I study him, Sam Slovoda,
who is neither ordinary nor extraordinary, who is not young
nor yet old, not tall nor short. He is sleeping, and it is fit
to describe him now, for like most humans he prefers sleeping to not sleeping. He is a mild pleasant-looking man who
has just turned forty. If the crown of his head reveals a
little bald spot, he has nourished in compensation the vanity
of a mustache. He has generally when he is awake an agreeable manner, at least with strangers; he appears friendly,
tolerant, and genial. The fact is that like most of us, he is
full of envy, full of spite, a gossip, a man who is pleased to
find others are as unhappy as he, and yet—this is the worst
to be said—he is a decent man. He is better than most. He
would prefer to see a more equitable world, he scorns
prejudice and privilege, he tries to hurt no one, he wishes
to be liked. I will go even further. He has one serious
virtue—he is not fond of himself, he wishes he were better.
He would like to free himself of envy, of the annoying
necessity to talk about his friends, he would like to love
people more; specifically, he would like to love his wife
more, and to love his two daughters without the tormenting
if nonetheless irremediable vexation that they closet his
life in the dusty web of domestic responsibilities and drudg-
ing for money.

How often he tells himself with contempt that he has the
cruelty of a kind weak man.

May I state that I do not dislike Sam Slovoda; it is just
that I am disappointed in him. He has tried too many
things and never with a whole heart. He has wanted to be
a serious novelist and now merely indulges the ambition;

255

he wished to be of consequence in the world, and has ended, temporarily perhaps, as an overworked writer of continuity for comic magazines; when he was young he tried to be a bohemian and instead acquired a wife and family. Of his appetite for a variety of new experience I may say that it is matched only by his fear of new people and novel situations.

I will give an instance. Yesterday, Sam was walking along the street and a bum approached him for money. Sam did not see the man until too late; lost in some inconsequential thought, he looked up only in time to see a huge wretch of a fellow with a red twisted face and an outstretched hand. Sam is like so many; each time a derelict asks for a dime, he feels a coward if he pays the money, and is ashamed of himself if he doesn't. This once, Sam happened to think, I will not be bullied, and hurried past. But the bum was not to be lost so easily. "Have a heart, Jack," he called after in a whisky voice, "I need a drink bad." Sam stopped, Sam began to laugh. "Just so it isn't for coffee, here's a quarter," he said, and he laughed, and the bum laughed. "You're a man's man," the bum said. Sam went away pleased with himself, thinking about such things as the community which existed between all people. It was cheap of Sam. He should know better. He should know he was merely relieved the situation had turned out so well. Although he thinks he is sorry for bums, Sam really hates them. Who knows what violence they can offer?

At this time, there is a powerful interest in Sam's life, but many would ridicule it. He is in the process of being psychoanalyzed. Myself, I do not jeer. It has created the most unusual situation between Sam and me. I could go into details but they are perhaps premature. It would be better to watch Sam awaken.

His wife, Eleanor, has been up for an hour, and she has shut the window and neglected to turn off the radiator. The room is stifling. Sam groans in a stupor which is neither sleep nor refreshment, opens one eye, yawns, groans again, and lies twisted, strangled and trussed in pajamas which are too large for him. How painful it is for him to rise. Last night there was a party, and this morning, Sunday morning, he is awakening with a hangover. Invariably, he is depressed in the morning, and it is no different today. He finds himself in the flat and familiar dispirit of nearly all days.

It is snowing outside. Sam finally lurches to the window, and opens it for air. With the oxygen of a winter morning clearing his brain, he looks down six stories into the giant quadrangle of the Queens housing development in which he lives, staring morosely at the inch of slush which covers the monotonous artificial park that separates his apartment building from an identical structure not two hundred feet away. The walks are black where the snow has melted, and in the children's playground, all but deserted, one swing oscillates back and forth, pushed by an irritable little boy who plays by himself among the empty benches, swaddled in galoshes, muffler, and overcoat. The snow falls sluggishly, a wet snow which probably will turn to rain. The little boy in the playground gives one last disgusted shove to the swing and trudges away gloomily, his overshoes leaving a small animal track behind him. Back of Sam, in the four-room apartment he knows like a blind man, there is only the sound of Eleanor making breakfast.

Well, thinks Sam, depression in the morning is a stage of his analysis, Dr. Sergius has said.

This is the way Sam often phrases his thoughts. It is not altogether his fault. Most of the people he knows think that way and talk that way, and Sam is not the strongest of men. His language is doomed to the fashion of the moment. I have heard him remark mildly, almost apologetically, about his daughters: "My relation with them still suffers because I haven't worked through all my feminine identifications." The saddest thing is that the sentence has meaning to Sam even if it will not have meaning to you. A great many ruminations, discoveries, and memories contribute their connotation to Sam. It has the significance of a cherished line of poetry to him.

Although Eleanor is not being analyzed, she talks in a similar way. I have heard her remark in company, "Oh, you know Sam, he not only thinks I'm his mother, he blames me for being born." Like most women, Eleanor can be depended upon to employ the idiom of her husband.

What amuses me is that Sam is critical of the way others speak. At the party last night he was talking to a Hollywood writer, a young man with a great deal of energy and enthusiasm. The young man spoke something like this: "You see, boychick, I can spike any script with yaks, but the thing I can't do is heartbreak. My wife says she's gonna give me heartbreak. The trouble is I've had a real solid-type life. I mean I've had my ups and downs like all of humanity, but there's never been a shriek in my life. I don't know how to write shrieks."

On the trip home, Sam had said to Eleanor, "It was disgraceful. A writer should have some respect for language."

Eleanor answered with a burlesque of Sam's indignation. "Listen, I'm a real artist-type. Culture is for comic-strip writers."

Generally, I find Eleanor attractive. In the ten years they have been married she has grown plump, and her dark hair which once was long is now cropped in a mannish cut of the prevailing mode. But, this is quibbling. She still possesses her best quality, a healthy exuberance which glows in her dark eyes and beams in her smile. She has beautiful teeth. She seems aware of her body and pleased with it. Sam tells himself he would do well to realize how much he needs her. Since he has been in analysis he has come to discover that he remains with Eleanor for more essential reasons than mere responsibility. Even if there were no children, he would probably cleave to her.

Unhappily, it is more complicated than that. She is always—to use their phrase—competing with him. At those times when I do not like Eleanor, I am irritated by her lack of honesty. She is too sharp-tongued, and she does not often give Sam what he needs most, a steady flow of uncritical encouragement to counteract the harshness with which he views himself. Like so many who are articulate on the subject, Eleanor will tell you that she resents being a woman. As Sam is disappointed in life, so is Eleanor. She feels Sam has cheated her from a proper development of her potentialities and talent, even as Sam feels cheated. I call her dishonest because she is not so ready as Sam to put the blame on herself.

Sam, of course, can say all this himself. It is just that he experiences it in a somewhat different way. Like most men who have been married for ten years, Eleanor is not quite real to him. Last night at the party, there were perhaps half a dozen people whom he met for the first time, and he talked animatedly with them, sensing their reactions, feeling their responses, aware of the life in them, as they were aware of the life in him. Eleanør, however, exists in his nerves. She is a rather vague embodiment, he thinks of her as "she" most of the time, someone to conceal things from. Invariably, he feels uneasy with her. It is too bad. No matter how inevitable, I am always sorry when love melts into that pomade of affection, resentment, boredom and occasional compassion which is the best we may expect of a man and woman who have lived together a long time. So often, it is worse, so often no more than hatred.

They are eating breakfast now, and Eleanor is chatting about the party. She is pretending to be jealous about a young girl in a strapless evening gown, and indeed, she does not have to pretend altogether. Sam, with liquor inside him, had been leaning over the girl; obviously he had coveted her. Yet, this morning, when Eleanor begins to talk about her, Sam tries to be puzzled.

"Which girl was it now?" he asks a second time.

"Oh, you know, the hysteric," Eleanor says, "the one who was parading her bazooms in your face." Eleanor has ways of impressing certain notions upon Sam. "She's Charlie's new girl."

"I didn't know that," Sam mutters. "He didn't seem to be near her all evening."

Eleanor spreads marmalade over her toast and takes a bite with evident enjoyment. "Apparently, they're all involved. Charles was funny about it. He said he's come to the conclusion that the great affairs of history are between hysterical women and detached men."

"Charles hates women," Sam says smugly. "If you notice, almost everything he says about them is a discharge of aggression." Sam has the best of reasons for not liking Charles. It takes more than ordinary character for a middle-aged husband to approve of a friend who moves easily from woman to woman.

"At least Charles discharges his aggression," Eleanor remarks.

"He's almost a classic example of the Don Juan complex. You notice how masochistic his women are?"

"I know a man or two who's just as masochistic."

Sam sips his coffee. "What made you say the girl was an hysteric?"

Eleanor shrugs. "She's an actress. And I could see she was a tease."

"You can't jump to conclusions," Sam lectures. "I had the impression she was a compulsive. Don't forget you've got to distinguish between the outer defenses, and the more deeply rooted conflicts."

I must confess that this conversation bores me. As a sample it is representative of the way Sam and Eleanor talk to each other. In Sam's defense I can say nothing; he has always been too partial to jargon.

I am often struck by how eager we are to reveal all sorts of supposedly ugly secrets about ourselves. We can explain the hatred we feel for our parents, we are rather pleased with the perversions to which we are prone. We seem determinedly proud to be superior to ourselves. No motive is too terrible for our inspection. Let someone hint, however, that we have bad table manners and we fly into a rage. Sam will agree to anything you may say about him, provided it is sufficiently serious—he will be the first to agree he has fantasies of murdering his wife. But tell him that he is afraid of waiters, or imply to Eleanor that she is a nag, and they will be quite annoyed.

Sam has noticed this himself. There are times when he can hear the jargon in his voice, and it offends him. Yet, he seems powerless to change his habits.

An example: He is sitting in an armchair now, brooding upon his breakfast, while Eleanor does the dishes. The two daughters are not home; they have gone to visit their grandmother for the weekend. Sam had encouraged the visit. He had looked forward to the liberty Eleanor and himself would enjoy. For the past few weeks the children had seemed to make the most impossible demands upon his attention. Yet now they are gone and he misses them, he even misses their noise. Sam, however, cannot accept the notion that many people are dissatisfied with the present, and either dream of the past or anticipate the future. Sam must call this "ambivalence over possessions." Once he even felt obliged to ask his analyst, Dr. Sergius, if ambivalence over possessions did not characterize him almost perfectly, and Sergius whom I always picture with the flat precision of a coin's head—bald skull and horn-rimmed glasses—answered in his German accent, "But, my dear Mr. Slovoda, as I have told you, it would make me happiest if you did not include in your reading, these psychoanalytical text-works."

At such rebukes, Sam can only wince. It is so right, he tells himself, he is exactly the sort of ambitious fool who uses big words when small ones would do.

2

While Sam sits in the armchair, gray winter light is entering the windows, snow falls outside. He sits alone in a modern seat, staring at the gray, green, and beige décor of their living room. Eleanor was a painter before they were married, and she has arranged this room. It is very pleasant, but like many husbands, Sam resents it, resents the reproductions of modern painters upon the wall, the slender coffee table, a free-form poised like a spider on wire legs, its feet set onto a straw rug. In the corner, most odius of all, is the playmate of his children, a hippopotamus of a television-radio-and-phonograph cabinet with the blind monstrous snout of the video tube.

Eleanor has set the Sunday paper near his hand. Soon, Sam intends to go to work. For a year, he has been giving a day once or twice a month to a bit of thought and a little writing on a novel he hopes to begin sometime. Last night, he told himself he would work today. But he has little enthusiasm now. He is tired, he is too depressed. Writing for the comic strips seems to exhaust his imagination.

Sam reads the paper as if he were peeling an enormous banana. Flap after flap of newsprint is stripped away and cast upon the straw rug until only the Magazine Section is left. Sam glances through it with restless irritability. A biography of a political figure runs its flatulent prose into the giant crossword puzzle at the back. An account of a picturesque corner of the city becomes lost in statistics and exhortations on juvenile delinquency, finally to emerge with photographs about the new style of living which desert architecture provides. Sam looks at a wall of windows in rotogravure with a yucca tree framing the pool.

There is an article about a workingman. His wife and his family are described, his apartment, his salary and his budget. Sam reads a description of what the worker has every evening for dinner, and how he spends each night of the week. The essay makes its point; the typical

American workingman must watch his pennies, but he is nonetheless secure and serene. He would not exchange his life for another.

Sam is indignant. A year ago he had written a similar article in an attempt to earn some extra money. Subtly, or so he thought, he had suggested that the average workingman was raddled with insecurity. Naturally, the article had been rejected.

Sam throws the Magazine Section away. Moments of such anger torment him frequently. Despite himself, Sam is enraged at editorial dishonesty, at the smooth strifeless world which such articles present. How angry he is—how angry and how helpless. "It is the actions of men and not their sentiments which make history," he thinks to himself, and smiles wryly. In his living room he would go out to tilt the windmills of a vast, powerful, and hypocritical society; in his week of work he labors in an editorial cubicle to create spaceships, violent death, women with golden tresses and wanton breasts, men who act with their fists and speak with patriotic slogans.

I know what Sam feels. As he sits in the armchair, the Sunday papers are strewn around him, carrying their war news, their murders, their parleys, their entertainments, mummery of a real world which no one can grasp. It is terribly frustrating. One does not know where to begin.

Today, Sam considers himself half a fool for having been a radical. There is no longer much consolation in the thought that the majority of men who succeed in a corrupt society are themselves obligatorily corrupt, and one's failure is therefore the price of one's idealism. Sam cannot recapture the pleasurable bitterness which resides in the notion that one has suffered for one's principles. Sergius is too hard on him for that.

They have done a lot of work on the subject. Sergius feels that Sam's concern with world affairs has always been spurious. For example, they have uncovered in analysis that Sam wrote his article about the worker in such a way as to make certain it would be refused. Sam, after all, hates editors; to have such a piece accepted would mean he is no better than they, that he is a mediocrity. So long as he fails he is not obliged to measure himself. Sam, therefore, is being unrealistic. He rejects the world with his intellect, and this enables him not to face the more direct realities of his present life.

Sam will argue with Sergius but it is very difficult. He will say, "Perhaps you sneer at radicals because it is more comfortable to ignore such ideas. Once you became interested it might introduce certain unpleasant changes in your life."

"Why," says Sergius, "do you feel it so necessary to assume that I am a bourgeois interested only in my comfort?"

"How can I discuss these things," says Sam, "if you insist that my opinions are the expression of neurotic needs, and your opinions are merely dispassionate medical advice?"

"You are so anxious to defeat me in an argument," Sergius will reply. "Would you admit it is painful to relinquish the sense of importance which intellectual discussion provides you?"

I believe Sergius has his effect. Sam often has thoughts these days which would have been repellent to him years ago. For instance, at the moment, Sam is thinking it might be better to live the life of a worker, a simple life, to be completely absorbed with such necessities as food and money. Then one could believe that to be happy it was necessary only to have more money, more goods, less worries. It would be nice, Sam thinks wistfully, to believe that the source of one's unhappiness comes not from oneself, but from the fault of the boss, or the world, or bad luck.

Sam has these casual daydreams frequently. He likes to think about other lives he might have led, and he envies the most astonishing variety of occupations. It is easy enough to see why he should wish for the life of an executive with the power and sense of command it may offer, but virtually from the same impulse Sam will wish himself a bohemian living in an unheated loft, his life a catch-as-catch-can from day to day. Once, after reading an article, Sam even wished himself a priest. For about ten minutes it seemed beautiful to him to surrender his life to God. Such fancies are common, I know. It is just that I, far better than Sam, know how serious he really is, how fanciful, how elaborate, his imagination can be.

The phone is ringing. Sam can hear Eleanor shouting at him to answer. He picks up the receiver with a start. It is Marvin Rossman, who is an old friend, and Marvin has an unusual request. They talk for several minutes, and Sam squirms a little in his seat. As he is about to hang up, he laughs. "Why, no, Marvin, it gives me a sense of adventure," he says.

Eleanor has come into the room toward the end of this conversation. "What is it all about?" she asks.

Sam is obviously a bit agitated. Whenever he attempts to be most casual, Eleanor can well suspect him. "It seems," he says slowly, "that Marvin has acquired a pornographic movie."

"From whom?" Eleanor asks.

"He said something about an old boy friend of Louise's."

Eleanor laughs. "I can't imagine Louise having an old boy friend with a dirty movie."

"Well, people are full of surprises," Sam says mildly.

"Look, here," says Eleanor suddenly. "Why did he call us?"

"It was about our projector."

"They want to use it?" Eleanor asks.

"That's right." Sam hesitates. "I invited them over."

"Did it ever occur to you I might want to spend my Sunday some other way?" Eleanor asks crossly.

"We're not doing anything," Sam mumbles. Like most men, he feels obliged to act quite nonchalantly about pornography. "I'll tell you, I am sort of curious about the film. I've never seen one, you know."

"Try anything once, is that it?"

"Something of the sort." Sam is trying to conceal his excitement. The truth is that in common with most of us, he is fascinated by pornography. It is a minor preoccupation, but more from lack of opportunity than anything else. Once or twice, Sam has bought the sets of nude photographs which are sold in marginal bookstores, and with guilty excitement has hidden them in the apartment.

"Oh, this is silly," Eleanor says. "You were going to work today."

"I'm just not in the mood."

"I'll have to feed them," Eleanor complains. "Do we have enough liquor?"

"We can get beer." Sam pauses. "Alan Sperber and his wife are coming too."

"Sam, you're a child."

"Look, Eleanor," says Sam, controlling his voice, "if its too much trouble, I can take the projector over there."

"I ought to make you do that."

"Am I such an idiot that I must consult you before I invite friends to the house?"

Eleanor has the intuition that Sam, if he allowed himself, could well drown in pornography. She is quite annoyed at him, but she would never dream of allowing Sam to take the projector over to Marvin Rossman's where he could view the movie without her—that seems indefinably dangerous. Besides she would like to see it, too. The mother in Eleanor is certain it cannot hurt her.

"All right, Sam," she says, "but you are a child."

More exactly, an adolescent, Sam decides. Ever since Marvin phoned, Sam has felt the nervous glee of an adolescent locking himself in the bathroom. Anal fixation, Sam thinks automatically.

While Eleanor goes down to buy beer and cold cuts in a delicatessen, Sam gets out the projector and begins to clean it. He is far from methodical in this. He knows the machine is all right, he has shown movies of Eleanor and his daughters only a few weeks ago, but from the moment Eleanor left the apartment, Sam has been consumed by an anxiety that the projection bulb is burned out. Once he has examined it, he begins to fret about the motor. He wonders if it needs oiling, he blunders through a drawer of household tools looking for an oilcan. It is ridiculous. Sam knows that what he is trying to keep out of his mind are the reactions Sergius will have. Sergius will want to "work through" all of Sam's reasons for seeing the movie. Well, Sam tells himself, he knows in advance what will be discovered: detachment, not wanting to accept Eleanor as a sexual partner, evasion of responsibility, etc. etc. The devil with Sergius. Sam has never seen a dirty movie, and he certainly wants to.

He feels obliged to laugh at himself. He could not be more nervous, he knows, if he were about to make love to a woman he had never touched before. It is really disgraceful.

When Eleanor comes back, Sam hovers about her. He is uncomfortable with her silence. "I suppose they'll be here soon," Sam says.

"Probably."

Sam does not know if he is angry at Eleanor or apprehensive that she is angry at him. Much to his surprise he catches her by the waist and hears himself saying, "You know, maybe tonight when they're gone . . . I mean, we do have the apartment to ourselves." Eleanor moves neither toward him nor away from him. "Darling, it's not because of the movie," Sam goes on, "I swear. Don't you think maybe we could . . ."

"Maybe," says Eleanor.

3

The company has arrived, and it may be well to say a word or two about them. Marvin Rossman, who has brought the film, is a dentist, although it might be more accurate to describe him as a frustrated doctor. Rossman is full of statistics and items of odd information about the malpractice of physicians, and he will tell these things in his habitually gloomy voice, a voice so slow, so sad, that it almost conceals the humor of his remarks. Or, perhaps, that is what creates his humor. In his spare time, he is a sculptor, and if Eleanor may be trusted, he is not without talent. I often picture him working in the studio loft he has rented, his tall bony frame the image of dejection. He will pat a piece of clay to the armature, he will rub it sadly with his thumb, he will shrug, he does not believe that anything of merit could come from him. When he talked to Sam over the phone, he was pessimistic about the film they were to see. "It can't be any good," he said in his melancholy voice. "I know it'll be a disappointment." Like Sam, he has a mustache, but Rossman's will droop at the corners.

Alan Sperber, who has come with Rossman, is the subject of some curiosity for the Slovodas. He is not precisely womanish; in fact, he is a large plump man, but his voice is too soft, his manners too precise. He is genial, yet he is finicky; waspish, yet bland; he is fond of telling long rather affected stories, he is always prepared with a new one, but to general conversation he contributes little. As a lawyer, he seems miscast. One cannot imagine him inspiring a client to confidence. He is the sort of heavy florid man who seems boyish at forty, and the bow ties and gray flannel suits he wears do not make him appear more mature.

Roslyn Sperber, his wife, used to be a schoolteacher, and she is a quiet nervous woman who talks a great deal when she is drunk. She is normally quite pleasant, and has only one habit which is annoying to any degree. It is a little flaw, but social life is not unlike marriage in that habit determines far more than vice or virtue. This mannerism which has become so offensive to the friends of the Sperbers is Roslyn's social pretension. Perhaps I should say intellectual pretension. She entertains people as if she were conducting a salon, and in her birdlike voice is forever forcing her guests to accept still another intellectual canapé. "You must hear Sam's view of the world market," she will say, or "Has Louise told you her statistics on divorce?" It is quite pathetic for she is so eager to please. I have seen her eyes fill with tears at a sharp word from Alan.

Marvin Rossman's wife, Louise, is a touch grim and definite in her opinions. She is a social welfare worker, and will declare herself with force whenever conversation impinges on those matters where she is expert. She is quite opposed to psychoanalysis, and will say without quarter, "It's all very well for people in the upper-middle area"—she is referring to the upper middle class—"but, it takes more than a couch to solve the problems of . . ." and she will list narcotics, juvenile delinquency, psychosis, relief distribution, slum housing, and other descriptions of our period. She recites these categories with an odd anticipation. One would guess she was ordering a meal.

Sam is fond of Marvin but he cannot abide Louise. "You'd think she discovered poverty," he will complain to Eleanor.

The Slovodas do feel superior to the Rossmans and the Sperbers. If pressed, they could not offer the most convincing explanation why. I suppose what it comes down to is that Sam and Eleanor do not think of themselves as really belonging to a class, and they feel that the Sperbers and Rossmans are petit-bourgeois. I find it hard to explain their attitude. Their company feels as much discomfort and will apologize as often as the Slovodas for the money they have, and the money they hope to earn. They are all of them equally concerned with progressive education and the methods of raising children to be well adjusted—indeed, they are discussing that now—they consider themselves relatively free of sexual taboo, or put more properly, Sam and Eleanor are no less possessive than the others. The Slovodas' culture is not more profound; I should be hard put to say that Sam is more widely read, more seriously informed, than Marvin or Alan, or for that matter, Louise. Probably, it comes to this: Sam, in his heart, thinks himself a rebel, and there are few rebels who do not claim an original mind. Eleanor has been a bohemian and considers herself more sophisticated than her friends who merely went to college and got married. Louise Rossman could express it most soundly. "Artists, writers, and people of the creative layer have in their occupational idealogy the belief that they are classless."

One thing I might remark about the company. They are all being the most unconscionable hypocrites. They have rushed across half the city of New York to see a pornographic film, and they are not at all interested in each other at the moment. The women are giggling like tickled children at remarks which cannot possibly be so funny. Yet, they are all determined to talk for a respectable period of time. No less, it must be serious talk. Roslyn has said once, "I feel so funny at the thought of seeing such a movie," and the others have passed her statement by.

At the moment, Sam is talking about value. I might note that Sam loves conversation and thrives when he can expound an idea.

"What are our values today?" he asks. "It's really fantastic when you stop to think of it. Take any bright talented kid who's getting out of college now."

"My kid brother, for example," Marvin interposes morosely. He passes his bony hand over his sad mustache, and somehow the remark has become amusing, much as if Marvin had said, "Oh, yes, you have reminded me of the trials, the worries, and the cares which my fabulous younger brother heaps upon me."

"All right, take him," Sam says. "What does he want to be?"

"He doesn't want to be anything," says Marvin.

"That's my point," Sam says excitedly. "Rather than

work at certain occupations, the best of these kids would rather do nothing at all."

"Alan has a cousin," Roslyn says, "who swears he'll wash dishes before he becomes a businessman."

"I wish that were true," Eleanor interrupts. "It seems to me everybody is conforming more and more these days."

They argue about this. Sam and Eleanor claim the country is suffering from hysteria; Alan Sperber disagrees and says it's merely a reflection of the headlines; Louise says no adequate criteria exist to measure hysteria; Marvin says he doesn't know anything at all.

"More solid liberal gains are being made in this period," says Alan, "than you would believe. Consider the Negro—"

"Is the Negro any less maladjusted?" Eleanor shouts with passion.

Sam maneuvers the conversation back to his thesis. "The values of the young today, and by the young, I mean the cream of the kids, the ones with ideas, are a reaction of indifference to the culture crisis. It really is despair. All they know is what they don't want to do."

"That is easier," Alan says genially.

"It's not altogether unhealthy," Sam says. "It's a corrective for smugness and the false value of the past, but it has created new false value." He thinks it worth emphasizing. "False value seems always to beget further false value."

"Define your terms," says Louise, the scientist.

"No, look," Sam says, "there's no revolt, there's no acceptance. Kids today don't want to get married, and—"

Eleanor interrupts. "Why should a girl rush to get married? She loses all chance for developing herself."

Sam shrugs. They are all talking at once. "Kids don't want to get married," he repeats, "and they don't want not to get married. They merely drift."

"It's a problem we'll all have to face with our own kids in ten years," Alan says, "although I think you make too much of it, Sam."

"My daughter," Marvin states. "She's embarrassed I'm a dentist. Even more embarrassed than I am." They laugh.

Sam tells a story about his youngest, Carol Ann. It seems he had a fight with her, and she went to her room. Sam followed, he called through the door.

"No answer," Sam says. "I called her again, 'Carol Ann.'

I was a little worried you understand, because she seemed so upset, so I said to her, 'Carol Ann, you know I love you.' What do you think she answered?"

"What?" asks Roslyn.

"She said, 'Daddy, why are you so anxious?'"

They all laugh again. There are murmurs about what a clever thing it was to say. In the silence which follows, Roslyn leans forward and says quickly in her high voice, "You must get Alan to tell you his wonderful story about the man who studied yogi."

"Yoga," Alan corrects. "It's too long to tell."

The company prevails on him.

"Well," says Alan, in his genial courtroom voice, "it concerns a friend of mine named Cassius O'Shaugnessy."

"You don't mean Jerry O'Shaugnessy, do you?" asks Sam.

Alan does not know Jerry O'Shaugnessy. "No, no, this is Cassius O'Shaugnessy," he says. "He's really quite an extraordinary fellow." Alan sits plumply in his chair, fingering his bow tie. They are all used to his stories, which are told in a formal style and exhibit the attempt to recapture a certain note of urbanity, wit, and *élan* which Alan has probably copied from someone else. Sam and Eleanor respect his ability to tell these stories, but they resent the fact that he talks *at* them.

"You'd think we were a jury of his inferiors," Eleanor has said. "I hate being talked down to." What she resents is Alan's quiet implication that his antecedents, his social position, in total his life outside the room is superior to the life within. Eleanor now takes the promise from Alan's story by remarking, "Yes, and let's see the movie when Alan has finished."

"Sssh," Roslyn says.

"Cassius was at college a good while before me," says Alan, "but I knew him while I was an undergraduate. He would drop in and visit from time to time. An absolutely extraordinary fellow. The most amazing career. You see, he's done about everything."

"I love the way Alan tells it," Roslyn pipes nervously.

"Cassius was in France with Dos Passos and Cummings, he was even arrested with e.e. After the war, he was one of the founders of the Dadaist school, and for a while I understand he was Fitzgerald's guide to the gold of the

Côte d'Azur. He knew everybody, he did everything. Do you realize that before the twenties had ended, Cassius had managed his father's business and then entered a monastery? It is said he influenced T. S. Eliot."

"Today, we'd call Cassius a psychopath," Marvin observes.

"Cassius called himself a great dilettante," Alan answers, "although perhaps the nineteenth-century Russian conception of the great sinner would be more appropriate. What do you say if I tell you this was only the beginning of his career?"

"What's the point?" Louise asks.

"Not yet," says Alan, holding up a hand. His manner seems to say that if his audience cannot appreciate the story, he does not feel obliged to continue. "Cassius studied Marx in the monastery. He broke his vows, quit the Church, and became a Communist. All through the thirties he was a figure in the Party, going to Moscow, involved in all the Party struggles. He left only during the Moscow trials."

Alan's manner while he relates such stories is somewhat effeminate. He talks with little caresses of his hand, he mentions names and places with a lingering ease as if to suggest that his audience and he are aware, above all, of nuance. The story as Alan tells it is drawn overlong. Suffice it that the man about whom he is talking, Cassius O'Shaughnessy, becomes a Trotskyist, becomes an anarchist, is a pacifist during the second World War, and suffers it from a prison cell.

"I may say," Alan goes on, "that I worked for his defense, and was successful in getting him acquitted. Imagine my dolor when I learned that he had turned his back on his anarchist friends and was living with gangsters."

"This is weird," Eleanor says.

"Weird, it is," Alan agrees. "Cassius got into some scrape, and disappeared. What could you do with him? I learned only recently that he had gone to India and was studying yoga. In fact, I learned it from Cassius himself. I asked him of his experiences at Brahnaputh-thar, and he told me the following story."

Now Alan's voice alters, he assumes the part of Cassius and speaks in a tone weary of experience, wise and sad in its knowledge. " 'I was sitting on my haunches contemplating my navel,' Cassius said to me, 'when of a sudden I discovered my navel under a different aspect. It seemed to me that if I were to give a counterclockwise twist, my navel would unscrew.' "

Alan looks up, he surveys his audience which is now rapt and uneasy, not certain as yet whether a joke is to come. Alan's thumb and forefinger pluck at the middle of his ample belly, his feet are crossed upon the carpet in symbolic suggestion of Cassius upon his haunches.

" 'Taking a deep breath, I turned, and the abysses of Vishtarni loomed beneath. My navel had begun to unscrew. I knew I was about to accept the reward of three years of contemplation. So,' said Cassius, 'I turned again, and my navel unscrewed a little more. I turned and I turned,' " Alan's fingers now revolving upon his belly, " 'and after a period I knew that with one more turn my navel would unscrew itself forever. At the edge of revelation, I took one sweet breath, and turned my navel free.' "

Alan looks up at his audience.

" 'Damn,' said Cassius, 'if my ass didn't fall off.' "

4

The story has left the audience in an exasperated mood. It has been a most untypical story for Alan to tell, a little out of place, not offensive exactly, but irritating and inconsequential. Sam is the only one to laugh with more than bewildered courtesy, and his mirth seems excessive to everyone but Alan, and of course, Roslyn, who feels as if she has been the producer. I suppose what it reduces to, is a lack of taste. Perhaps that is why Alan is not the lawyer one would expect. He does not have that appreciation—as necessary in his trade as for an actor—of what is desired at any moment, of that which will encourage as opposed to that which does not encourage a stimulating but smooth progression of logic and sentiment. Only a fool would tell so long a story when everyone is awaiting the movie.

Now, they are preparing. The men shift armchairs to correspond with the couch, the projector is set up, the screen is unfolded. Sam attempts to talk while he is threading the film, but no one listens. They seem to realize suddenly that a frightful demand has been placed upon them. One does not study pornography in a living room with a beer glass in one's hand, and friends at the elbow. It is the most unsatisfactory of compromises; one can draw neither the benefits of solitary contemplation nor of social exchange. There is, at bottom, the same exasperated fright which one experiences in turning the shower tap and receiving cold water when the flesh has been prepared for heat. Perhaps that is why they are laughing so much now that the movie is begun.

A title, *The Evil Act,* twitches on the screen, shot with scars, holes, and the dust lines of age. A man and woman are sitting on a couch, they are having coffee. They chat. What they say is conveyed by printed words upon an ornately flowered card, interjected between glimpses of their casual gestures, a cup to the mouth, a smile, a cigarette being lit. The man's name, it seems, is Frankie Idell; he is talking to his wife, Magnolia. Frank is dark, he is sinister, he confides in Magnolia, his dark counterpart, with a grimace of his brows, black from make-up pencil.

This is what the title read:

FRANKIE: She will be here soon.
MAGNOLIA: This time the little vixen will not escape.
FRANKIE: No, my dear, this time we are prepared.
(He looks at his watch.)
FRANKIE: Listen, she knocks!

There is a shot of a tall blond woman knocking on the door. She is probably over thirty, but by her short dress and ribboned hat it is suggested that she is a girl of fifteen.

FRANKIE: Come in, Eleanor.

As may be expected, the audience laughs hysterically at this. It is so wonderful a coincidence. "How I remember Frankie," says Eleanor Slovoda, and Roslyn Sperber is the only one not amused. In the midst of the others' laughter, she says in a worried tone, obviously adrift upon her own concerns, "Do you think we'll have to stop the film in the middle to let the bulb cool off?" The others hoot, they giggle, they are weak from the combination of their own remarks and the action of the plot.

Frankie and Magnolia have sat down on either side of the heroine, Eleanor. A moment passes. Suddenly, stiffly, they attack. Magnolia from her side kisses Eleanor, and Frankie commits an indecent caress.

ELEANOR: How dare you? Stop!
MAGNOLIA: Scream, my little one. It will do you no good. The walls are soundproofed.
FRANKIE: We've fixed a way to make you come across.
ELEANOR: This is hideous. I am hitherto undefiled. Do not touch me!

The captions fade away. A new title takes their place. It says, *But There Is No Escape From The Determined Pair*. On the fade-in, we discover Eleanor in the most distressing situation. Her hands are tied to loops running from the ceiling, and she can only writhe in helpless perturbation before the deliberate and progressive advances of Frankie and Magnolia. Slowly they humiliate her, with relish they probe her.

The audience laughs no longer. A hush has come upon them. Eyes unblinking they devour the images upon Sam Slovoda's screen.

Eleanor is without clothing. As the last piece is pulled away, Frankie and Magnolia circle about her in a grotesque of pantomime, a leering of lips, limbs in a distortion of desire. Eleanor faints. Adroitly, Magnolia cuts her bonds. We see Frankie carrying her inert body.

Now, Eleanor is trussed to a bed, and the husband and wife are tormenting her with feathers. Bodies curl upon the bed in postures so complicated, in combinations so advanced, that the audience leans forward, Sperbers, Rossmans, and Slovodas, as if tempted to embrace the moving images. The hands trace abstract circles upon the screen, passes and recoveries upon a white background so illumined that hollows and swells, limb to belly and mouth to undescribables, tip of a nipple, orb of a navel, swim in giant magnification, flow and slide in a lurching yawing fall, blotting out the camera eye.

A little murmur, all unconscious, passes from their lips. The audience sways, each now finally lost in himself, communing hungrily with shadows, violated or violating, fantasy triumphant.

At picture's end, Eleanor the virgin whore is released from the bed. She kisses Frankie, she kisses Magnolia. "You dears," she says, "let's do it again." The projector lamp burns empty light, the machine keeps turning, the tag of film goes *slap-tap, slap-tap, slap-tap, slap-tap, slap-tap, slap-tap.*

"Sam, turn it off," says Eleanor.

But when the room lights are on, they cannot look at one another. "Can we see it again?" someone mutters. So, again, Eleanor knocks on the door, is tied, defiled, ravished, and made rapturous. They watch it soberly now, the room hot with the heat of their bodies, the darkness a balm for orgiastic vision. To the Deer Park, Sam is thinking, to the Deer Park of Louis XV were brought the most beautiful maidens of France, and there they stayed, dressed in fabulous silks, perfumed and wigged, the mole drawn upon their cheek, ladies of pleasure awaiting the pleasure of the king. So Louis had stripped an empire, bankrupt a treasury, prepared a deluge, while in his garden on summer evenings the maidens performed their pageants, eighteenth-century tableau of the evil act, beauteous instruments of one man's desire, lewd translation of a king's power. That century men sought wealth so they might use its fruits; this epoch men lusted for power in order to amass more power, a compounding of power into pyramids of abstraction whose yield are cannon and wire enclosure, pillars of statistics to the men who are the kings of this century and do no more in power's leisure time than go to church, claim to love their wives, and eat vegetables.

Is it possible, Sam wonders, that each of them here, two Rossmans, two Sperbers, two Slovodas, will cast off their clothes when the movie is done and perform the orgy which tickles at the heart of their desire? They will not, he knows, they will make jokes when the projector is put away, they will gorge the plate of delicatessen Eleanor provides, and swallow more beer, he among them. He will be the first to make jokes.

Sam is right. The movie has made him extraordinarily

alive to the limits of them all. While they sit with red faces, eyes bugged, glutting sandwiches of ham, salami, and tongue, he begins the teasing.

"Roslyn," he calls out, "is the bulb cooled off yet?"

She cannot answer him. She chokes on beer, her face glazes, she is helpless with self-protecting laughter.

"Why are you so anxious, Daddie?" Eleanor says quickly.

They begin to discuss the film. As intelligent people they must dominate it. Someone wonders about the actors in the piece, and discussion begins afresh. "I fail to see," says Louise, "why they should be hard to classify. Pornography is a job to the criminal and prostitute element."

"No, you won't find an ordinary prostitute doing this," Sam insists. "It requires a particular kind of personality."

"They have to be exhibitionists," says Eleanor.

"It's all economic," Louise maintains.

"I wonder what those girls felt?" Roslyn asks. "I feel sorry for them."

"I'd like to be the cameraman," says Alan.

"I'd like to be Frankie," says Marvin sadly.

There is a limit to how long such a conversation may continue. The jokes lapse into silence. They are all busy eating. When they begin to talk again, it is of other things. Each dollop of food sops the agitation which the movie has spilled. They gossip about the party the night before, they discuss which single men were interested in which women, who got drunk, who got sick, who said the wrong thing, who went home with someone else's date. When this is exhausted, one of them mentions a play the others have not seen. Soon they are talking about books, a concert, a one-man show by an artist who is a friend. Dependably, conversation will voyage its orbit. While the men talk of politics, the women are discussing fashions, progressive schools, and recipes they have attempted. Sam is uncomfortable with the division; he knows Eleanor will resent it, he knows she will complain later of the insularity of men and the basic contempt they feel for women's intelligence.

"But you collaborated," Sam will argue. "No one forced you to be with the women."

"Was I to leave them alone?" Eleanor will answer.

"Well, why do the women always have to go off by themselves?"

"Because the men aren't interested in what we have to say."

Sam sighs. He has been talking with interest, but really he is bored. These are nice pleasant people, he thinks, but they are ordinary people, exactly the sort he has spent so many years with, making little jokes, little gossip, living little everyday events, a close circle where everyone mothers the other by his presence. The womb of middle-class life, Sam decides heavily. He is in a bad mood indeed. Everything is laden with dissatisfaction.

Alan has joined the women. He delights in preparing odd dishes when friends visit the Sperbers, and he is describing to Eleanor how he makes blueberry pancakes. Marvin draws closer to Sam.

"I wanted to tell you," he says, "Alan's story reminded me. I saw Jerry O'Shaugnessy the other day."

"Where was he?"

Marvin is hesitant. "It was a shock, Sam. He's on the Bowery. I guess he's become a wino."

"He always drank a lot," says Sam.

"Yeah." Marvin cracks his bony knuckles. "What a stinking time this is, Sam."

"It's probably like the years after 1905 in Russia," Sam says.

"No revolutionary party will come out of this."

"No," Sam says, "nothing will come."

He is thinking of Jerry O'Shaugnessy. What did he look like? what did he say? Sam asks Marvin, and clucks his tongue at the dispiriting answer. It is a shock to him. He draws closer to Marvin, he feels a bond. They have, after all, been through some years together. In the thirties they have been in the Communist Party, they have quit together, they are both weary of politics today, still radicals out of habit, but without enthusiasm and without a cause. "Jerry was a hero to me," Sam says.

"To all of us," says Marvin.

The fabulous Jerry O'Shaugnessy, thinks Sam. In the old days, in the Party, they had made a legend of him. All of them with their middle-class origins and their desire to know a worker-hero.

I may say that I was never as fond of Jerry O'Shaugnessy as was Sam. I thought him a showman and too pleased with himself. Sam, however, with his timidity, his desire to travel, to have adventure and know many women, was obliged to adore O'Shaugnessy. At least he was enraptured with his career.

Poor Jerry who ends as a bum. He has been everything else. He has been a trapper in Alaska, a chauffeur for gangsters, an officer in the Foreign Legion, a labor organizer. His nose was broken, there were scars on his chin. When he would talk about his years at sea or his experiences in Spain, the stenographers and garment workers, the radio writers and unemployed actors would listen to his speeches as if he were the prophet of new romance, and their blood would be charged with the magic of revolutionary vision. A man with tremendous charm. In those days it had been easy to confuse his love for himself with his love for all underprivileged workingmen.

"I thought he was still in the Party," Sam says.

"No," says Marvin, "I remember they kicked him out a couple of years ago. He was supposed to have piddled some funds, that's what they say."

"I wish he'd taken the treasury," Sam remarks bitterly. "The Party used him for years."

Marvin shrugs. "They used each other." His mustache droops. "Let me tell you about Sonderson. You know he's still in the Party. The most progressive dentist in New York." They laugh.

While Marvin tells the story, Sam is thinking of other things. Since he has quit Party work, he has studied a great deal. He can tell you about prison camps and the secret police, political murders, the Moscow trials, the exploitation of Soviet labor, the privileges of the bureaucracy; it is all painful to him. He is straddled between the loss of a country he has never seen, and his repudiation of the country in which he lives. "Doesn't the Party seem a horror now?" he bursts out.

Marvin nods. They are trying to comprehend the distance between Party members they have known, people by turn pathetic, likable, or annoying—people not unlike themselves—and in contrast the immensity of historic logic which deploys along statistics of the dead.

"It's all schizoid," Sam says. "Modern life is schizoid."

Marvin agrees. They have agreed on this many times,

bored with the petulance of their small voices, yet needing the comfort of such complaints. Marvin asks Sam if he has given up his novel, and Sam says, "Temporarily." He cannot find a form, he explains. He does not want to write a realistic novel, because reality is no longer realistic. "I don't know what it is," says Sam. "To tell you the truth, I think I'm kidding myself. I'll never finish this book. I just like to entertain the idea I'll do something good some day." They sit there in friendly depression. Conversation has cooled. Alan and the women are no longer talking.

"Marvin," asks Louise, "what time is it?"

They are ready to go. Sam must say directly what he had hoped to approach by suggestion. "I was wondering," he whispers to Rossman, "would you mind if I held onto the film for a day or two?"

Marvin looks at him. "Oh, why of course, Sam," he says in his morose voice. "I know how it is." He pats Sam on the shoulder as if, symbolically, to convey the exchange of ownership. They are fellow conspirators.

"If you ever want to borrow the projector," Sam suggests.

"Nah," says Marvin, "I don't know that it would make much difference."

5

It has been, when all is said, a most annoying day. As Sam and Eleanor tidy the apartment, emptying ash trays and washing the few dishes, they are fond neither of themselves nor each other. "What a waste today has been," Eleanor remarks, and Sam can only agree. He has done no writing, he has not been outdoors, and still it is late in the evening, and he has talked too much, eaten too much, is nervous from the movie they have seen. He knows that he will catch it again with Eleanor before they go to sleep; she has given her assent to that. But as is so often the case with Sam these days, he cannot await their embrace with any sure anticipation. Eleanor may be in the mood or Eleanor may not; there is no way he can control the issue. It is depressing; Sam knows that he circles about Eleanor at such times with the guilty maneuvers of a sad hound. Resent her as he must, be furious with himself as he will, there is not very much he can do about it. Often, after they have made love, they will lie beside each other in silence, each offended, each certain the other is to blame. At such times, memory tickles them with a cruel feather. Not always has it been like this. When they were first married, and indeed for the six months they lived together before marriage, everything was quite different. Their affair was very exciting to them; each told the other with some hyperbole but no real mistruth that no one in the past had ever been comparable as lover.

I suppose I am a romantic. I always feel that this is the best time in people's lives. There is, after all, so little we accomplish, and that short period when we are beloved and triumph as lovers is sweet with power. Rarely are we concerned then with our lack of importance; we are too important. In Sam's case, disillusion means even more. Like so many young men, he entertained the secret conceit that he was an extraordinary lover. One cannot really believe this without supporting at the same time the equally secret conviction that one is fundamentally inept. It is— no matter what Serigus would say—a more dramatic and therefore more attractive view of oneself than the sober notion which Sam now accepts with grudging wisdom, that the man as lover is dependent upon the bounty of the woman. As I say, he accepts the notion, it is one of the lineaments of maturity, but there is a part of him which, no matter how harried by analysis, cannot relinquish the antagonism he feels that Eleanor has respected his private talent so poorly, and has not allowed him to confer its benefits upon more women. I mock Sam, but he would mock himself on this. It hardly matters; mockery cannot accomplish everything, and Sam seethes with that most private and tender pain: even worse than being unattractive to the world is to be unattractive to one's mate; or, what is the same and describes Sam's case more accurately, never to know in advance when he shall be undesirable to Eleanor.

I make perhaps too much of the subject, but that is only because it is so important to Sam. Relations between Eleanor and him are not really that bad—I know other couples who have much less or nothing at all. But comparisons are poor comfort to Sam; his standards are so high. So are Eleanor's. I am convinced the most unfortunate people are those who would make an art of love. It sours other effort. Of all artists, they are certainly the most wretched.

Shall I furnish a model? Sam and Eleanor are on the couch and the projector, adjusted to its slowest speed, is retracing the elaborate pantomime of the three principles. If one could allow these shadows a life . . . but indeed such life has been given them. Sam and Eleanor are no more than an itch, a smart, a threshold of satisfaction; the important share of themselves has steeped itself in Frankie-, Magnolia-, and Eleanor-of-the-film. Indeed the variations are beyond telling. It is the most outrageous orgy performed by five ghosts.

Self-critical Sam! He makes love in front of a movie, and one cannot say that it is unsatisfactory any more than one can say it is pleasant. It is dirty, downright porno dirty, it is a lewd slop-brush slapped through the middle of domestic exasperations and breakfast eggs. It is so dirty that only half of Sam—he is quite divisible into fractions —can be exercised at all. The part that is his brain worries along like a cuckolded burgher. He is taking the pulse of his anxiety. Will he last long enough to satisfy Eleanor? Will the children come back tonight? He cannot help it. In the midst of the circus, he is suddenly convinced the children will walk through the door. "Why are you so anxious, Daddie?"

So it goes. Sam the lover is conscious of exertion. One moment he is Frankie Idell, destroyer of virgins—take that! you whore!—the next, body moving, hands caressing, he is no more than some lines from a psychoanalytical text. He is thinking about the sensitivity of his scrotum. He has read that this is a portent of femininity in a male. How strong is his latent homosexuality worries Sam, thrusting stiffly, warm sweat running cold. Does he identify with Eleanor-of-the-film?

Technically, the climax is satisfacory. They lie together in the dark, the film ended, the projector humming its lonely revolutions in the quiet room. Sam gets up to turn it off; he comes back and kisses Eleanor upon the mouth. Apparently, she has enjoyed herself more than he; she is tender and fondles the tip of his nose.

"You know, Sam," she says from her space beside him, "I think I saw this picture before."

"When?"

"Oh, you know when. That time."

Sam thinks dully that women are always most loving when they can reminisce about infidelity.

"That time!" he repeats.

"I think so."

Racing forward from memory like the approaching star which begins as a point on the mind and swells to explode the eyeball with its odious image, Sam remembers, and is weak in the dark. It is ten years, eleven perhaps, before they were married, yet after they were lovers. Eleanor has told him, but she has always been vague about details. There had been two men it seemed, and another girl, and all had been drunk. They had seen movie after movie. With reluctant fascination, Sam can conceive the rest. How it had pained him, how excited him. It is years now since he has remembered, but he remembers. In the darkness he wonders at the unreasonableness of jealous pain. That night was impossible to imagine any longer—therefore it is more real; Eleanor his plump wife who presses a pigeon's shape against her housecoat, forgotten heroine of black orgies. It had been meaningless, Eleanor claimed; it was Sam she loved, and the other had been no more than a fancy of which she wished to rid herself. Would it be the same today, thinks Sam, or had Eleanor been loved by Frankie, by Frankie of the other movies, by Frankie of the two men she never saw again on that night so long ago?

The pleasure I get from this pain, Sam thinks furiously.

It is not altogether perverse. If Eleanor causes him pain, it means after all that she is alive for him. I have often observed that the reality of a person depends upon his ability to hurt us; Eleanor as the vague accusing embodiment of the wife is different, altogether different, from Eleanor who lies warmly in Sam's bed, an attractive Eleanor who may wound his flesh. Thus, brother to the pleasure of pain, is the sweeter pleasure which follows pain. Sam, tired, lies in Eleanor's arms, and they talk with the cozy trade words of old professionals, agreeing that they will not make love again before a movie, that it was exciting but also not without detachment, that all in all it has been good but not quite right, that she had loved this action he had done, and was uncertain about another. It is their old familiar critique, a sign that they are intimate and well disposed. They do not talk about the act when it has failed to fire; then they go silently to sleep. But now, Eleanor's enjoyment having mollified Sam's sense of no enjoyment, they talk with the apologetics and encomiums of familiar mates. Eleanor falls asleep, and Sam falls almost asleep, curling next to her warm body, his hand over her round belly with the satisfaction of a sculptor. He is drowsy, and he thinks drowsily that these few moments of creature-pleasure, this brief compassion he can feel for the body that trusts itself to sleep beside him, his comfort in its warmth, is perhaps all the meaning he may ask for his life. That out of disappointment, frustration, and the passage of dreary years come these few moments when he is close to her, and their years together possess a connotation more rewarding than the sum of all which has gone into them.

But then he thinks of the novel he wants to write, and he is wide-awake again. Like the sleeping pill which fails to work and leaves one warped in an exaggeration of the ills which sought the drug, Sam passes through the promise of sex-emptied sleep, and is left with nervous loins, swollen jealousy of an act ten years dead, and sweating irritable resentment of the woman's body which hinders his limbs. He has wasted the day, he tells himself, he has wasted the day as he has wasted so many days of his life, and tomorrow in the office he will be no more than his ten fingers typing plot and words for Bramba the Venusian and Lee-Lee Deeds, Hollywood Star, while that huge work with which he has cheated himself, holding it before him as a covenant of his worth, that enormous novel which would lift him at a bound from the impasse in which he stifles, whose dozens of characters would develop a vision of life in bountiful complexity, lies foundered, rotting on a beach of purposeless effort. Notes here, pages there, it sprawls through a formless wreck of incidental ideas and half-episodes, utterly without shape. He is not even a hero for it.

One could not have a hero today, Sam thinks, a man of action and contemplation, capable of sin, large enough for good, a man immense. There is only a modern hero damned by no more than the ugliness of wishes whose satisfaction he will never know. One needs a man who could walk the stage, someone who—no matter who, not himself. Someone, Sam thinks, who reasonably could not exist.

The novelist, thinks Sam, perspiring beneath blankets, must live in paranoia and seek to be one with the world; he must be terrified of experience and hungry for it; he must think himself nothing and believe he is superior to all. The feminine in his nature cries for proof he is a man; he dreams of power and is without capacity to gain it; he loves himself above all and therefore despises all that he is.

He is that, thinks Sam, he is part of the perfect prescription, and yet he is not a novelist. He lacks energy and belief. It is left for him to write an article some day about the temperament of the ideal novelist.

In the darkness, memories rise, yeast-swells of apprehension. Out of bohemian days so long ago, comes the friend of Eleanor, a girl who had been sick and was committed to an institution. They visited her, Sam and Eleanor, they took the suburban train and sat on the lawn of the asylum grounds while patients circled about intoning a private litany, or shuddering in boob-blundering fright from an insect that crossed their skin. The friend had been silent. She had smiled, she had answered their questions with the fewest words, and had turned again to her study of sunlight and blue sky. As they were about to leave, the girl had taken Sam aside. "They violate me," she said in a whisper. "Every night when the doors are locked, they come to my room and they make the movie. I am the heroine and am subjected to all variety of sexual viciousness. Tell them to leave me alone so I may enter the convent." And while she talked, in a horror of her body, one arm scrubbed the other. Poor tortured friend. They had seen her again, and she babbled, her face had coarsened into an idiot leer.

Sam sweats. There is so little he knows, and so much to know. Youth of the depression with its economic terms, what can he know of madness or religion? They are both so alien to him. He is the mongrel, Sam thinks, brought up without religion from a mother half Protestant and half Catholic, and a father half Catholic and half Jew. He is the quarter-Jew, and yet he is a Jew, or so he feels himself, knowing nothing of Gospel, tabernacle, or Mass, the Jew through accident, through state of mind. What . . .

whatever did he know of penance? self-sacrifice? mortification of the flesh? the love of his fellow man? Am I concerned with my relation to God? ponders Sam, and smiles sourly in the darkness. No, that has never concerned him, he thinks, not for better nor for worse. "They are making the movie," says the girl into the ear of memory, "and so I cannot enter the convent."

How hideous was the mental hospital. A concentration camp, decides Sam. Perhaps it would be the world some day, or was that only his projection of feelings of hopelessness? "Do not try to solve the problems of the world," he hears from Serigus, and pounds a lumpy pillow.

However could he organize his novel? What form to give it? It is so complex. Too loose, thinks Sam, too scattered. Will he ever fall asleep? Wearily, limbs tense, his stomach too keen, he plays again the game of putting himself to sleep. "I do not feel my toes," Sam says to himself, "my toes are dead, my calves are asleep, my calves are sleeping . . ."

In the middle from wakefulness to slumber, in the torpor which floats beneath blankets, I give an idea to Sam. "Destroy time, and chaos may be ordered," I say to him.

"Destroy time, and chaos may be ordered," he repeats after me, and in desperation to seek his coma, mutters back, "I do not feel my nose, my nose is numb, my eyes are heavy, my eyes are heavy."

So Sam enters the universe of sleep, a man who seeks to live in such a way as to avoid pain, and succeeds merely in avoiding pleasure. What a dreary compromise is our life!

1952

Have you read these paperbacks from

CATCH-22 Joseph Heller 75c

THE MAGIC BARREL Bernard Malamud 75c

IDIOTS FIRST Bernard Malamud 75c

A NEW LIFE Bernard Malamud 60c

THE NATURAL Bernard Malamud 75c

THE DEVIL'S ADVOCATE Morris L. West 60c

THE SHOES OF THE FISHERMAN Morris L. West 75c

THE GUNS OF AUGUST Barbara Tuchman 95c

THE ZIMMERMANN TELEGRAM Barbara Tuchman 60c

THE FEMININE MYSTIQUE Betty Friedan 75c

THE CAINE MUTINY Herman Wouk 95c

THE CITY BOY Herman Wouk 60c

PORTRAIT IN BROWNSTONE Louis Auchincloss 75c

THE HOUSE OF FIVE TALENTS Louis Auchincloss 75c

SEVEN PILLARS OF WISDOM T. E. Lawrence 95c

THE LEANING TOWER and Other Stories Katherine Anne Porter 50c

BRIDESHEAD REVISITED Evelyn Waugh 75c

THE LOVED ONE Evelyn Waugh 50c

MOSQUITOES William Faulkner 60c

GO TELL IT ON THE MOUNTAIN James Baldwin 60c

THE FIRE NEXT TIME James Baldwin 50c

CAT'S CRADLE Kurt Vonnegut, Jr. 60c

THE WHITE NILE Alan Moorehead 75c

THE BLUE NILE Alan Moorehead 60c

If you cannot obtain copies of these titles at your local bookseller's, just send the price (plus 10c per copy for handling and postage) to Dell Books, Box 2291, Grand Central Post Office, New York, N.Y. 10017. No postage or handling charge is required on any order of five or more books.

Dell Laurel Editions

THE AMERICAN DRAMA·SERIES

FAMOUS AMERICAN PLAYS OF THE 1920s
Selected and introduced by Kenneth Macgowan. Eugene
O'Neill: *The Moon of the Caribbees;* Maxwell Anderson
and Laurence Stallings: *What Price Glory?;* Sidney How-
ard: *They Knew What They Wanted;* DuBose and Doro-
thy Heyward: *Porgy;* Elmer Rice: *Street Scene;* Philip
Barry: *Holiday.* 75c

FAMOUS AMERICAN PLAYS OF THE 1930s
Selected and introduced by Harold Clurman. Clifford
Odets: *Awake and Sing;* S. N. Behrman: *End of Summer;*
Robert E. Sherwood: *Idiot's Delight;* John Steinbeck: *Of
Mice and Men;* William Saroyan: *The Time of Your Life.*
75c

FAMOUS AMERICAN PLAYS OF THE 1940s
Selected and introduced by Henry Hewes. Thornton
Wilder: *The Skin of Our Teeth;* Arthur Laurents: *Home
of the Brave;* Arthur Miller: *All My Sons;* Maxwell Anderson and Kurt Weill: *Lost in the Stars;* Carson McCul-
lers: *The Member of the Wedding.* 75c

FAMOUS AMERICAN PLAYS OF THE 1950s
Selected and introduced by Lee Strasberg. Tennessee Wil-
liams: *Camino Real;* Lillian Hellman: *The Autumn
Garden;* Robert Anderson: *Tea and Sympathy;* Edward
Albee: *The Zoo Story;* Michael Gazzo: *A Hatful of Rain.*
75c

Don't Miss These
Bestsellers From Dell

THE BILLION DOLLAR BRAIN Len Deighton 75c

THE DIRTY DOZEN E. M. Nathanson 95c

THE MAGUS John Fowles 95c

IN THE SPRING THE WAR ENDED Steven Linakis 75c

THE EMBEZZLER Louis Auchincloss 75c

FUNERAL IN BERLIN Len Deighton 75c

STORIES NOT FOR THE NERVOUS
Alfred Hitchcock, ed. 50c

80 MILLION EYES Ed McBain 50c

THE PALACE OF MONEY William H. Manville 75c

THAT SUMMER Allen Drury 75c
